The Lion Rampant

ROBERT LOW

HarperCollins*Publishers*

HarperCollins*Publishers*
77–85 Fulham Palace Road,
Hammersmith, London W6 8JB

www.harpercollins.co.uk

Published by HarperCollins*Publishers* 2013
1

ISBN: 978-0-00-748163-7

This novel is entirely a work of fiction.
The names, characters and incidents portrayed in it,
while in some cases based on historical figures, are
the work of the author's imagination.

Set in Sabon by Palimpsest Book Production Limited,
Falkirk, Stirlingshire

Printed and bound in Great Britain by
Clays Ltd, St Ives plc

MIX
Paper from
responsible sources
FSC **FSC™ C007454**
www.fsc.org

FSC™ is a non-profit international organisation established to promote
the responsible management of the world's forests. Products carrying the
FSC label are independently certified to assure consumers that they come
from forests that are managed to meet the social, economic and
ecological needs of present and future generations,
and other controlled sources.

Find out more about HarperCollins and the environment at
www.harpercollins.co.uk/green

To all Scots, everywhere

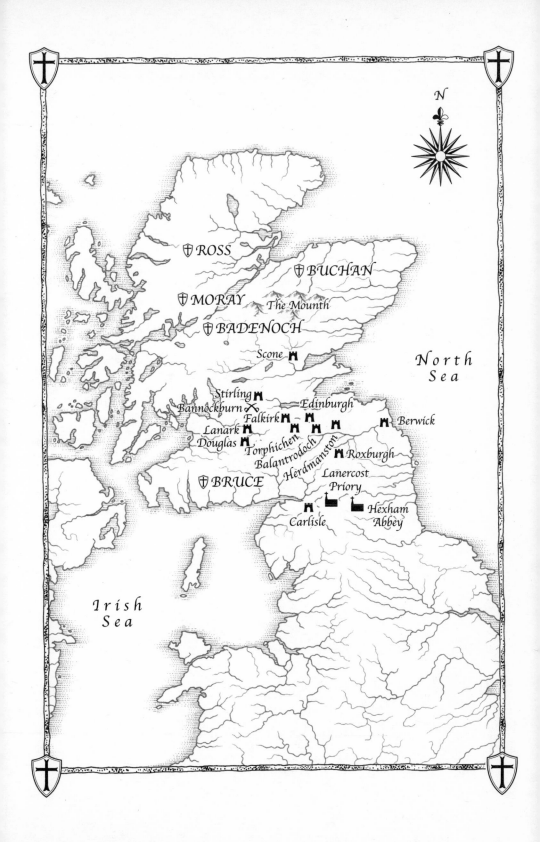

Being a chronicle of the Kingdom in the Years of Trouble, written at Greyfriars Priory on the octave of Septuagesima, in the year of Our Lord one thousand three hundred and twenty-nine, 23rd year of the reign of King Robert I, God save and keep him.

In the year of Our Lord one thousand three hundred and fourteen, the King had reigned for eight hard years, driving his enemies with fire and sword so that the Balliol and Comyn were crushed out of the realm and those still alive fled to the south. The aged Earl of Buchan, wasted by the harrying of his people and lands, died there, pleading with the English King Edward for help while ensuring that his former wife, Isabel, languished in a cage on the walls of Berwick for daring to support the Bruce cause. Buchan's henchman, the cruel Malise Bellejambe, was left as her keeper, a task he pursued assiduously.

But this second King Edward was not his father. He had abandoned all attempts to exert his power in Scotland, preferring to squabble with his own barons, who sought to remove his favourite, Piers Gaveston, and impose restrictions – Ordinances – on his rule.

Thusly, with a free hand, good King Robert chased the

occupying English and their Scots allies from the realm. At the start of this year of Our Lord, in all the Kingdom there remained but three great fortresses of major note still held by the English: Roxburgh, Stirling and Edinburgh.

It was now that our king chose to bring the Kingdom to freedom and determined to remove these last bastions from the enemy, so he came and closed off all of these great castles all around. But, without proper weapons of sieging war, it did not look as if the Scots would prevail and the English took heart from this.

Then Sir James Douglas came to Roxburgh . . .

ISABEL

Heaven is dark and God is ugly. Yet may He do ye hurt. Liar. Fornicator. Torturer. Murderer. May He send ye toads beneath your serk, ants in your beard and up your nethers and flies into your eyes, auld wickedness. Please God in Your mercy let me become the wildfire abune the marsh and let me lead him into the sucking pit. Praise God for ever and ever, let me be the white hart that leads huntsmen to the wolves of the forest that I may lure him to their fangs. Blessings of Heaven, make me the wasp that might fly about his head and never give him peace. God in Your Mercy let me bury him so deep he will never find his way up to Judgement Day, so deep even worms cannot find him. Or give me leave to die, Lord, rather than suffer longer in this Berwick cage from the vile of Malise Bellejambe.

CHAPTER ONE

Roxburgh,
Shrove Tuesday, 1314

Frixco de Fiennes scurried across the cobbles into the shelter of the gatehouse in a drizzling dusk as miserable as wet ash. It matched his mood, especially when he saw the dark shape lurking under the cullis, bouncing slightly and swaying left to right: Aggie, nursing her bairn.

He sighed and went to them, peeling off his hat and beating the drops from it.

'Aggie,' he said wearily. 'You should not have met me here.'

'None can hear. The guards are in their wee cubbyhole,' she retorted tartly. 'Asleep.'

Frixco cursed silently and made a note to rout them out when this business was done; somewhere behind him came a burst of laughter from the main hall, where they were already deep into celebrating the Shrove feast, stuffing their faces on the eve of Lent.

'Aye, you need not worry,' Aggie added bitterly. 'You will not be long with me – the same time it took to make this wee mite.'

Frixco managed a weak smile and wished the woman a hundred miles away and the child with her.

'I can spare a few silvers only,' he wheedled and saw that she knew it for the lie it was. Desperation made her lips a thin line and she merely nodded, holding out one free hand for the bag of coin.

Even this was passed over reluctantly and, not for the first time, Frixco cursed the castle cook's daughter even as he prayed she would keep her mouth closed on who the father of the child was. The image of Sander and his meat cleaver made him close his eyes briefly and then offer a last weak smile.

He had back scorn for it, started for the main hall, remembered the sleeping guards, turned and shuffled past her; Aggie heard him vent his wrath on the luckless pair as she drew up her shawl to cover herself and the babe before stepping out of the shelter of the gatehouse into the mirr.

She did not go back to her cookhouse bed, all the same, to the scowls and the demands her father made to name the man who had filled her belly with bastard. Even now she found it hard to believe that she had let Frixco have his way – but she knew the why of it, in the end. He was brother to the seneschal, with power of a sort, had coin when he could be parted from it and seemed, for one bright summer, her escape from Roxburgh.

Climbing up to the rain-smeared night of the gatehouse battlement she recalled the Prisoner, the one she had brought food to every day for as long as she could safely carry the bowl, spoon and cup without spilling any – seven years at least. He and I are the same, she thought, held in this stone gaol, stitched in on three sides by water. She was fifteen and her life was over.

She went up, above the gate and close to the brazier, sizzling coals spitting as the drizzle landed on them. The wind swept in, blowing the loop of wool off the baby and she covered him up quickly.

'Away, lass,' said a voice and she turned into the helmeted

smile of Leckie. 'Ye should tak' the mite down to the warm and away from this wind. Ye'll catch yer death of chill and so will the bairn.'

Aggie liked Leckie, if only because he never looked at her askance, or asked what everyone asked about her baby. He was kind, too, and frequently shared his bread and cheese when she came up here, to feel the wind and smell the promise in it, the taste of somewhere else.

Now she nodded and smiled and moved away, anxious now to be in warmth and shelter, pausing for one last look out beyond the raised bridge and the rutted track that led to it – and led away from it, to that fabled Somewhere Else.

'Nae rebels on a night like this,' Leckie declared firmly, thinking she was fretting about the dark beyond the fortress, and she smiled again. Rebels preoccupied everyone's thoughts now. Roxburgh was one of the last big fortresses held against them in this realm; everywhere else had fallen to the usurper king, Robert Bruce, and now panic was rife.

But nothing moved in the deep pewter dim save for a grazing scatter of black cattle, shadows in the mirk. She moved off, crooning to the babe.

'Hush ye, hush ye, the Black Douglas will no' get ye the night.'

At the foot of the gatehouse rock, half a dozen black kine milled slowly, as if searching out the lusher grass that grew around the jakes fall. When one put an elbow in something wet and noxious, his curses were immediately hissed to silence by the others.

Sim Craw, fumbling furiously, threw off his black cloak in a fury of frustration and fought the coiled ladder off his back.

'Aye,' said James Douglas, merciless and bitter. 'Ring a bell, Sim. Let them hear where we are.'

'The hooks were stabbin' me,' Sim muttered back. 'And I have crawled in shite besides.'

'Whisht, the pair of you, or we are undone.'

The other two turned at the sight of the wet, scowling face thrust at them. A wee wet mirror of the Black Jamie Douglas, Sim noted. The only folk who have not noted that Jamie and Dog Boy are kin are the pair themselves. James the Black because he is lord of Douglas and will not admit that the Dog Boy, a mere cottar of no account, is a byblow of his father. Dog Boy because, even if he suspects it, will not want to shame his boyhood friend and now liege lord with it.

Sim, as ever, never voiced any of it, but simply scowled back at the pair of them.

'I hope you have the spear, Dog Boy,' he whispered harshly and had back an exasperated grunt.

'I have, shoved through the grass as I crawled. And it is Aleysandir, not Dog Boy. I have said this afore.'

'Aye, aye,' muttered Sim, untangling the confection of rope and wood and iron. Dog Boy had never been the same after finding out that he had a real name. Sim recalled how and when that had been uncovered: from the houndsman rolls at Douglas Castle when Jamie and Dog Boy had raided it. Christ betimes, a fistful of years ago now.

That was when Sir James had found his own new name – the Black Douglas – for what he had done to the English garrison in his own dispossessed keep. He had taken it from the occupying English by as clever a ruse as the one they now planned, but knew he could never hold the place – so he had wrecked it.

He and his men had soiled everything spoilable, from fodder to well, stacked the cellar with loot, pissed on it, and then lopped the heads off the surrendered English – and their Scots lackeys – before roasting the lot in a fire. The Douglas Larder, they called it with grisly humour and the memory of it was as black as the stones they left. Blacker still was the scowl of Jamie, but only because he had had to do this to his boyhood home and his rightful inheritance.

There was no scowl on him now, all the same, only the mad gleeful grin that always made Sim's flesh ruched as goose-skin.

'Ah, you are a cunning man, Sim Craw,' James Douglas enthused in a hissed whisper, clapping the man on his sodden shoulder. 'This will take the shine off Randolph.'

Sim eyed the dark, wild-haired lord sourly. As if this is for the glory of Douglas over Randolph, the latter sitting at Edinburgh and wondering how to take its castle, us sitting at Roxburgh and pondering the same. Now the lord of Douglas is out to scoop Roxburgh in a single blow and it is mainly to put Randolph's nose askew . . . not for the first time, Sim marvelled at how the diffident, lisping lord of Douglas could turn, in an eyeblink, into a red-handed killer with a heart the same shade as the Earl of Hell's own cloak.

Using my cunning to further himself, he added moodily to himself as the ladder finally unveiled its grapple-hooked top, with the slot for a spearshaft. Twenty feet of it was coiled up, the rope steps bolstered with wool-padded wood to keep them just far enough from the wall for a foot to fit – his da and other well-diggers had taken the idea from the miners at Leadhouse and Sim had recalled it from his boyhood, and then adapted it for this one purpose.

Now he moved to the crag of rock on which the blocky gatehouse was built and looked up, shaking mirr from his eyelashes. He nodded to Dog Boy, who put his back to the rock and cupped his hands, while Sim took the long pike-spear and shafted it into the slot on the ladder, handing it to James Douglas.

Then he stepped into Dog Boy's hands, heard him grunt and curse.

'You are getting fat, Sim.'

Fat and auld, Sim agreed, stepping on to the Dog Boy's shoulders, then up to a toehold on the rock, then higher still on the treacherous wet until he could climb no more. He reached out one hand and felt the slap of the spearshaft in it, and raised it, waving it as high as he could, balanced precariously with the sibilant mirr making tears on his face. Teetering, he lifted it higher still with two hands, straining until he felt the ladder on top of it slide over the crenellation; he heard the grate of it catching.

He tugged the cord and the ladder unravelled with a soft pattering, as if a cat ran down the stones. Sim felt a touch on his boot, looked down and saw the Black himself staring anxiously up.

'Are you certes you want to be first?'

Sim did not answer. He knew the reason for the Black's concern: too old for this sort of work. But it is my ladder, Sim thought to himself. Mine. So he said nothing at all, tugged hard to make sure it had settled, and then started to climb.

Frixco, mollified by shouting at the gate guards, hurried back through the wet to the main hall, aware of the glares at his back – more so than ever before, he knew. It was the way of things, as arranged by custom and so by God, that those he had power over would resent it and scowl when they were sure they would not be seen.

But Frixco, for all the time he had been here – Christ's Bones, eighteen years at least – had always been seen by the English as a Gascon and by the Scots as an interloper, no matter his stripe. Gascons had been preferred under the old Edward and under the new – especially under the new, for Gaveston, the King's favourite, had been a Gascon.

But Gaveston was dead and the lords who had murdered him circled and scowled and barked at the King and his loyal barons, two dog packs with bristling hackles. Now every Gascon serving King Edward was under suspicion from all those not of the King's mind: a warden had been appointed to Roxburgh town, forced on the King by his Ordinancer barons to ensure the loyalty of the castle's Gascon garrison commander, Sir William de Fiennes, Frixco's brother.

Inside the hall, the blast of heat and noise drowned Frixco in delight for a moment, so that he took his time shaking out his wet cloak and chaffering with those feasters nearest him, but he had one task left before he could join in and hurried after it, out of the hall and up the steps to the private chapel.

The Prisoner knelt, a humble supplicant, before the carved wooden panels brought out specially for this day: the fourteen Stations of the Cross. The Prisoner, permitted this worship for the Holy Day, knelt at the ninth, the third Falling of Christ, and Frixco hoped the man was not about to argue for lengthy prayers at all fourteen; he had come to return him to his prison and then get to the food and the drink.

'It is time,' he said and had no response, so he repeated it, more loudly.

Hal did not hear him, lost in the carving, which was very beautifully rendered, every agony transcribed lovingly. Christ prone, held up by one hand, the other gripping the crushing weight of his Cross. He remembered all the other times he had attended Confession at the wee stone chapel in Herdmanston, waiting in the queue, Lord Hal or no, while others shuffled in. There had hardly been time to babble out a sin because there was only Father Thomas issuing pardons.

Father, I have stolen. Father, I have sworn. I ate meat at Lent. I beat my wife. I drink. Most folk knew already what others would murmur in supposed secret and those who took longer went on the end of knowing nudges and looks from those waiting impatiently. Must have done red murder, or robbed a bishop at least, they would offer with irritated scowls.

Were any prayers ever answered? Were God and His saints asleep? Was the Lord still a refuge? *Non accedet ad te malum* – there shall no evil befall thee.

Seven years. For her, too . . . He wondered if Isabel's prayers had been answered and hoped, at least, that she was no longer in a cage. Yet he thought that unlikely. The treacherous Isabel MacDuff had been hung on the walls of Berwick by old King

11

Edward, with the tacit agreement of her husband, the Earl of Buchan. Longshanks had done it because she had dared to place the crown on the head of Robert Bruce and Buchan had agreed to it as a warning to cuckolding wives everywhere. He would have killed the cuckolder, Hal, if he had been able.

Hal's attempt at seeking her out in a dashing rescue had ended with his own capture and, for a time, it looked as if Buchan would have his final triumph – but then the old King Edward had died. A miracle, Hal thought, which left him held at the new king's pleasure, inviolate until he was remembered and dealt with.

The new Edward had had more to occupy his mind and now Hal had been here in Roxburgh, forgotten, for seven years. The stumbled Christ looked back at him with blank wooden eyes and Hal admitted that the Lord might well still be a refuge – for certes, Hal no longer feared anything, though he was relieved, every day, to discover that this was not because he no longer desired anything.

Freedom. Isabel. The words rang him like a bell and the carved Christ seemed to shift, though it was the light from wind-wafted candles. He remembered, as he did every day, the promise he and Isabel had made to each other never to be parted. You should be wary of swearing oaths to God, for the Devil is always listening.

Yet God was always watching, Hal thought, staring at the blank wooden eyes of Christ. You Yourself refused to be carried by the angels and wounded Your feet on the stones of the way. For this You came into the world in a stable on a winter's night. You love my lost Isabel, too, and I hope You keep her safer than I did . . .

The blow on the back of his head blasted him back to the moment and he half fell, recovered and turned into the scowl of Frixco, who had cuffed him.

'Hear me now?' the man demanded and Hal nodded dumbly.

'Time to go,' Frixco growled, weary of it all. Seven years they had tended this one, waiting for some word from someone – anyone – as to his fate. None had come and even Frixco had almost forgotten what the lord of Herdmanston – wherever that was – had done.

Murder, Frixco recalled vaguely. And a Scots rebel. He would hang one day or the next and it could not come soon enough for Frixco de Fiennes, set the task of caring for him. Down below he heard shouts and bellows and scowled even more deeply – he was missing the best of the night's feast.

Leckie heard the peculiar pink-pink sound, could not place it, cocked his head and strained. Silly wee sound, he thought. Like a wee moose dancin' in clackety shoes. Or a faerie redcap, whetting his steel claws. He crept, following the noise past the brazier, away to the dark corner of the gatehouse battlements, where he caught the gleam of metal where none should be.

His heart skipped and he moved to it, saw the hooks and blinked, stunned, barely comprehending. A wee powrie's steel-clawed fingers, right enough, he thought, hanging off my wall. He looked at the far side, to where Aggie crooned to her bairn, wanted to call out to her to get away, and then looked back at the steel talons, heard the pink-pink as they grated, shifting slightly from side to side.

Because something – someone – was climbing up the ladder they were attached to. The realization was a dash of ice down Leckie's back. He should have made for the alarm iron. He should have bawled his lungs raw. Instead, he went forward and peered over the edge – and came face to face with a grey-haired man with an ugly grin.

'Boo,' said Sim, shot out a hand, grabbed Leckie by the front of his tunic and hauled him over and away before as much as a squeak had passed the man's lips.

A little way below and climbing steadily, Jamie and the Dog

Boy saw the blurring rush, heard the dull crunch. There was a muffled curse as the men waiting to climb dealt with the shock of a man cracking his brains and bones at their feet.

'Christ betimes,' Jamie hissed. 'What was that?'

'Sim at work,' Dog Boy answered grimly and they climbed on.

Up on the battlements, Aggie had had enough of crooning and hoping. She turned to go, paused to wave farewell to Leckie, but saw only the vague shape in the far shadows, so she shrugged and turned away heading for the stairhead; the babe wailed a little as the rain hit his wee face.

'Hush you, hush you,' she sang, folding him into the safe warmth of a cloak corner. 'The Black Douglas will no' get ye the night, wee lamb.'

'In truth, wee lamb,' said a voice in her ear, even as a horned, calloused hand closed off her screams, 'your ma is almost completely mistook in that regard.'

Frixco, following Hal to the top of the wind of stair that led to the hall, paused uncertainly. Screams had never been part of a Shrove feast before. Nor the clash of steel and shouts – perhaps a fight had broken out? Frixco was anxious not to miss it and turned to scowl and urge Hal on, saw the Prisoner's face and whirled to look behind him.

Horror shrieked up the steps at him, one eye dangling from a bloody cord, his face a mass of gore and his mouth wide, every tooth outlined in red.

'Back,' his brother screamed. 'Back. Up the stairs and bar the door. The Black is here . . .'

Frixco, stunned as a slaughter-ox, stood open-mouthed at the bloodied vision of his brother and the men spilling after him, turning fearfully to guard his back with drawn knives. William de Fiennes, his face a raw agony, half-blind and wholly afraid, slapped his brother's gawp from him in a fury of panic.

14

Behind him, Hal saw Jamie Douglas, a flash as if scrawled against the dark by a bolt of lightning and as sure to him as if seven years had not passed at all: wild black hair flying, a sword in one hand, a dirk in the other. And at his back, as strange as a two-headed calf, was another Jamie Douglas, standing fierce guard on a shivering girl with a swaddled wean in her arms.

It was only after, shoved and kicked into the chapel, with men piling up what little furniture there was against the door – all fourteen carved Stations included – that Hal realized that it had been Dog Boy he had seen.

Sim saw the men on the stairs, falling back with shields up to protect their lord; he was hurt bad was Sir William de Fiennes, for Sim had done it with a backlashed blow from a dirk and panted that out to Jamie Douglas as they crashed into the hall.

'Poked oot his eye,' he declared and Jamie nodded thoughtfully; both men agreed that such a wound might colour a man's decision to resist.

They did not debate it long, for a sudden rush of new foes spilled on them and Sim crashed through a scatter of benches towards them, his breath harsh in his ears. There were men running away from him, to the back of the hall where there was no way out. On the table to his left, Red Rowan kicked through a slurry of sauce and meat and gruel, kicking trenchers like a boy jumping in puddles; he turned to grin at Sim and then seemed to be hauled backwards, though Sim knew fine well it was the force of the quarrel hitting him with a deep shunk of sound.

Sim leaped towards the man with the latchbow, who gave up feverishly attempting to span it, tried to swing it like a club, shrieking out his fear and anger. Sim's sword blurred in the hazed candle-reek and cut into the man's neck, so that his shouting was choked off in a gurgle; Sim kicked the body away with his boot, scooping up half a round of cheese on the way, so that it flew into the air.

15

'Aaahh!'

Sim spun, blocking the snake-like blow with a frantic movement, though the stun of it almost lifted the sword out of his hand. The man who had rushed at him, yelling, was elderly, with a white beard and rheumy eyes; he jumped back and waved his weapon threateningly.

A fire iron, Sim saw. He is attacking me with a fire iron. A retired soldier, said the thought flickering through his mind as he chopped hard at the man's knee. The man dodged; Sim felt his foot skid on a soggy trencher and then was on his arse, legs and arms flailing.

The old man screamed, wet-mouthed, and raised the fire iron high – but the point of a sword erupted out and upwards from his chest so hard and fierce that it went on into the underside of his jaw. He wailed, high and thin, falling away to reveal the grinning face of Jamie Douglas, staggering as the man's weight dragged the sword down; he struggled to work his blade free.

'Christ betimes, that was almost too good to waste: a brace of auld yins at it like Rolands. You will have little better entertainment at this feast.'

Sim's mask of disgust was ignored and, grinning broadly, Jamie hauled him to his feet, put his boot against the old man's dead neck, using the leverage to drag his sword free; the blood crept sluggishly out in a viscous tarn, lapping at the apples and plums, the buttered capons, the Shrove griddle cakes and bread spilled from the tables.

Another bloody larder for the Black, Sim thought bitterly as he heard more shouting and turned to it, aware of his weariness. He saw Dog Boy and raised his bloody blade in salute.

Dog Boy had been charged with the woman and her bairn, though he did not know why the Black set such store by it. For all that, he kept her close and grinned as friendly as he could every time he caught her eye; it did not seem to help the tremble in her.

16

He lost the grin in the hall, with everyone running and shouting and clashing steel. He saw a party break away and head for the stairs and a measure of safety. He saw Sim and Jamie cut down a brace of fighters and thought it was all over until a last knot of men ran at him, wailing desperately. They were led by a big man with a bald head like a flesh fencepost, so that the knob of his original chin alone showed where there had once been a neck. He had a meat cleaver and a deal of trapped-rat courage.

Dog Boy thrust the woman behind him and leaped at this fat giant, hacking overhand with his sword to make the man block with his cleaver, the dirk curving round in his other hand and sinking into the fat man's belly. He thought he heard a scream from behind him and fought the urge to look and see if the woman and her bairn were under attack.

The fat man reeled away, clutching his belly and looking alternately at Dog Boy and the blood on his palm, a bemused disbelief in his whipped-dog eyes. Another man surged in, Dog Boy struck out and had the blow parried with a small shield – it was only later that Dog Boy saw it was a pot lid – the man grunting as it took the blow. Then he stabbed out with a vicious carving knife.

They are servants, Dog Boy realized suddenly, getting his sword in the way and managing to turn the blow. At his side, Patrick slapped down the knife, smashed his studded leather shoulder into the man's pot-lid shield and sent him staggering back; a bench caught him just behind the knee and he went over with a despairing cry.

Patrick, snarling like a mad hound, lunged after him, his elbow flailing like a fiddler at a dance, the longsword rising and falling, spraying gleet and blood.

Dog Boy turned and saw the woman, clutching her wailing brat to her and staring, open-mouthed with horror. Aye weel, he thought, hearing the wet, ugly sounds of Patrick making sure his opponent was truly dead, such sights would give you pause.

'Dinna fash,' he panted, leaning on his sword, knowing the

worst of the matter was done with. 'The Black ordered you safe and safe you shall be.'

Patrick appeared, his bluff face speckled with blood, and offered her a grin of his own as he cleaned gore and bits of brain from his blade with the hat of the man he had killed.

'Hot work,' he offered, but the woman merely buried her face in her swaddled bairn and wept, so he shrugged.

'Ach – weemin,' he said. 'Have you told the quine she is safe?'

'I have,' Dog Boy answered firmly, but frowned and added loudly: 'So it is a puzzle why she is weepin' so.'

The woman surfaced, tear-tracks streaking through the grime of her face and pointed a shaking hand at the quivering giant, who had dropped his meat cleaver, sunk like a stricken ox and bled to death through the fingers clutching desperately at the hole Dog Boy had put in his belly.

'That was my da.'

Hal marvelled on that vision of the two Jamies all the rest of that night, strangely detached from the fetid sweat of fear in the chapel, where men crouched like panting beasts listening to the thud and crash on their battened door.

Sir William roared curses back at them and wheedled courage into his own before he collapsed, breathing like a mating bull; one of his men-at-arms mercifully severed the last shreds of his eyestalk and then tried to hand it to Frixco, who shied away in horror.

By morning, it was clear to everyone that Sir William was dying and that Frixco was no leader, so Hal was unsurprised when a man – the same who had physicked the eye off Sir William's cheek – came and knelt beside him in the stale dim, where the tallow candles gasped. He announced himself as Tam Shaws, a good Scot, and said as much with an air of challenge. Hal said nothing, though he had his own ideas on what made a good Scot.

'Is he set on red murder, or will the Black spare us?' Shaws demanded, which was flat-out as a sword on a bench.

Hal shrugged. Truth was, he did not know. He had heard, as had everyone, of Jamie Douglas and his savagery and could only vaguely equate it with the youth he had known. But Dog Boy was with him and, for the life of him, Hal could not see Dog Boy indulging in such tales as were told, with wide-eyed, breathless horror, under every roof in the Kingdom. He said as much and saw the man-at-arm's eyebrow lift laconically.

'It is not your life,' he answered dryly, which was only the truth. Hal rose up, stiff after sitting so long.

'Is it your wish to surrender provided no harm comes?' he asked and, after a pause and some exchanged glances – one of them with the whimpering Frixco – Shaws nodded.

'Unbar the door,' Hal ordered.

It came as a shock to Jamie Douglas when the clatter of moving furniture heralded something imminent, for he had not thought the defenders had that much courage in them. Still, he thought savagely, better this way – I need this place taken and swiftly.

'Ready, lads,' he called out, and the black-cloaked men on the stair behind and trailing into the bloody ruin of the hall, still picking wolfishly at the wreck of the feast, flexed chapped knuckles on their weapons.

Dog Boy, standing guard over the crouched woman – Christ betimes, hardly more than a girl in the pewter dawn light of the hall – saw her tremble and touched her shoulder reassuringly; she had wept most of the night and hugged her bairn to her, so that the episode of killing her da had fretted Dog Boy more than a little and he felt she should know other folk cared yet for her.

'The Black has placed you under his cloak, yourself and bairn both,' he reminded her and saw the wan smile.

The door above creaked open and everyone tensed, waiting for the last mad leap of the desperate. Instead, a man stepped through, nondescript in hodden, with a matted tangle of iron hair and beard. Folk squinted, not knowing who he was.

'Young Jamie,' the man said quietly. 'They will surrender if you spare them. It would be sensible to consider it.'

Only Sim knew, as soon as he heard the voice, and looked up.

'Sir Hal,' he yelled and Jamie Douglas jerked like a stung beast. Recovering, he grinned and shook his head in awe at this, a hero sprung like a tooth sown by Cadmus – a man, he was forced to admit, whose presence in Roxburgh he had shamefully overlooked.

'Sir Hal of Herdmanston. Here you were, a prisoner we came to free,' he called out for the others to hear, for it did no harm to stamp your mark on the moment, 'and here you are, having taken this wee fortalice of your ain accord.'

ISABEL

The nuns are here, the one called Sister Constance and the other, Alise. What kind of name is Alise for a nun? One for a nun who thinks herself boldinit and more mighty than the Almighty, that's what kind. Wee Constance is kind enough in her way, though she believes what she is told, of this hoor of Babylon kept in a cage on the walls of Berwick until Hell calls her for a seat at her personal bad fire. The convent they come from is the same one where I was held for ransom by Malenfaunt long years since, but all his charges have been scourged from it – I wonder what became of the little oblate, Clothilde? She and all the rest have been replaced, Constance told me primly, by decent, Christian women. Well – all but Alise, who is a goad in the hands of one of Satan's lesser imps. From woman sprang original sin, she tells me often, and all evil and all suffering and all impurity – with a sly little smile that tells me she does not include herself as any kin of Eve in it. Who is without sin? Even an Order Knight would need to live in a desert to obey God's Law in this kingdom. I said as much to her at first and saw the little cat's-arse purse she made of her lips at having been so spoken to, though she could do nothing then. Afterwards, the number of folk allowed into the bailey to gawp seemed to increase for a time, and had been encouraged to jeer until they were stopped by, of all folk, Malise, who does not like his authority

over me challenged, never mind by a mere nun. Sister Alise hates being one of those given the task of sleeping across my door each night on a straw pallet, to make sure nothing ungodly happens and no visitor takes advantage. Not unless it is Malise Bellejambe, of course. What does she know of me, this Alise? What do any of them know, slobbering and laughing below me like I am some babery beast? I am Isabel MacDuff and I am loved. My Hal lives yet – I would know if he did not – and he will come. Miserere nostri. Dies irae, dies illa, solvet saeclum in favilla. *Pity us. Dreaded day when the universe will be reduced to ashes.*

Amen.

CHAPTER TWO

Edinburgh Castle,
Feast of St Fergna of Iona, March 1314

They came up to the glowering rock and the black fortress on it through a haar-haze hung thick as linen, with Hal sore and tired from unaccustomed riding. They passed a huge cart tipped back and weighted so that the trace pole could support the carcass of a hog; the gory butchers paused to look and wave and call out good-natured greetings to Jamie as he passed.

'The Good Sir James,' Sim said, nudging his mount easily alongside Hal so that he could speak soft. 'Darling of the host, is the Black Lord of Douglas. A derfly, ramstampit man o' main.'

Hal met Sim's eye, saw the mock in it and managed a smile. He saw, too, the white of Sim Craw – he had got used to it now, though it had come as a shock, all that snow on his lintel. It had come to him, when the Dog Boy suggested he brighten himself for the arrival of the Earl of Carrick, that he himself was old – each pewter curl that fell from his clipped head, courtesy of the spared girl, Aggie, told of that. And Sim was older by only a handful and a half of years.

Since no one had had much care for the style of a prisoner, wee poor noble or not, Hal had not realized how he'd looked

23

until sat in front of the water-waver of a bad mirror and witnessed this apparition with a greasy tangle of grey hair matting its way into a madness of bushed beard.

Only the eyes, grey-blue and blank, could be seen and when Hal looked in them he was dizzied, for it felt as if there was someone else looking back at him, as if his body had been rented like an abandoned house. When his beard vanished, the gaunt lantern-jawed man who appeared was no more familiar.

Aggie, rocking her bairn in a shawl looped across her back while she clipped, tongue between her teeth, eventually announced that she could do no more. The result, Dog Boy announced critically, was suitable and Hal, seven years removed from the gawky youth who had cared only for dogs, was astonished by this new Dog Boy, a muscled, skilled warrior and the shadow of the Black himself. He was even called Aleysandir now, a fine set-up man with a name and the style and wit to know how a wee lord from Lothian should be seen by an earl. Yet he was still Dog Boy to those who knew him well.

Hal had heard some matters of the outside world in his prison, enough to know that he had missed even more, but the arrival of the Earl of Carrick had confused him. He had been expecting the Bruce, but it was the brother who came and Hal cursed himself for a fool.

Had he not been there when the Earl of Carrick became king? Now brother Edward was Earl of Carrick – and the last of the brothers, too. The memory of the others, dead and gone in the furtherance of Robert Bruce to the throne, had soured the fête of Edward Bruce's arrival at Roxburgh, a day after Hal's release.

He and Hal had met once the mummery had been done with: the greetings and fine speeches, the official surrender and promises made. Sir William Fiennes, barely clinging to life, left in a litter with Frixco, uncaring little bachle, trailing after and hugging close to the bier as if the dying brother was a sealed surety for his own safety. Dog Boy saw Aggie hawk and spit pointedly and scornfully as he went; she was clearly bright with the wonderful possibility of being allowed to go where she would and with a sum of money to keep her and the bairn for a time.

Edward had been all delight and grins, his face flushed, fleshy and even broader than it had been, though there were harsh lines at the corner of eye and mouth which spoke of the hardships of the seven years since Hal had last seen him.

'Aye, times have changed and for the better,' he had growled, handing the fresh-shorn Hal a horn cup of wine. 'The King wants Edinburgh, Stirling and Roxburgh in his grip by summer. It is an ambitious swoop – but, by God, the Black has opened the account well.'

'As well he chose this yin first,' Hal had answered, 'else I would be in prison still.'

'Isn't it, though?'

Edward had walked to the tent entrance and stood for a moment, shaking a sad head.

'A pity,' he had said in French. 'It is a pretty place, Roxburgh, and shame on us for having to tear it down.'

Hal knew why: they could not garrison it sufficiently to keep the English out if they came back and Roxburgh, like Edinburgh and Stirling, was a bastion for the English in the Kingdom, a fount of supply and centre of domination. Still, there were others.

'Even if they all fall, the English will still have Berwick and Bothwell,' he'd said and Edward nodded.

'Aye, and Dunbar, but none are as brawlie as the great fortalices of Stirling, Edinburgh and here. Besides, taking them throws most of the last garrisons of English out of the Kingdom and sends a sign to English Edward's enemies that, once again, he is the weak son. Not a Longshanks, for all his length of leg.'

He'd paused, swilled wine in the goblet, frowning at it as if some clegg had flown in.

'I know why you speak of Berwick,' he'd said suddenly and Hal jerked with the gaff of his words. They stared at each other for a moment.

25

'She is there still?'

The question hunched itself like a crookback beggar with a hand out and was not answered for a long time. Then, however, Edward had shifted slightly.

'Isabel MacDuff is there still. In a cage hung from the inside wall. The King ordered us to try Berwick's castle two years since. Got one of Sim of Leadhouse's fancy ladders up and disturbed a dog on the same battlement. It set up a din of howling and barking, so that the guard came to kick its arse and found us.'

He'd stopped, shaking his head at the memory of the mad scrambling retreat.

'You left her because of a wee dug,' Hal had said and it was not a question; it had enough bleak censure in it for Edward's eyes to blaze and his head to snap up.

'My sister Mary was in a similar cage – Christ's Bones, if ye had looked up at any time ye would have seen her hanging on Roxburgh's battlements. My other sister Christina is held in a convent. My niece is held in yet another and the Queen's whereabouts is not even known. D'ye think we do not care, Lord Henry?'

Hal saw he had gone too far and with no justice in it, so he'd nodded grudgingly.

'For the first year they kept me close and mainly in the dark,' he'd told Edward blankly, and for all the light his tone made of it his eyes were as smoked as the locked dim he'd had to endure for so long.

'They hourly expected word from English Edward,' Hal had gone on, hearing his voice as if it belonged to someone else, conscious of his pathetic attempt to be wry and matter-of-fact, 'but he was busy dying, so it never came and the son became too busy with his catamite and his annoyed barons. In the end, they brought me out and treated me better – but Princess Mary was gone by that time.'

Mollified, Edward Bruce had subsided a little, finishing his wine and pouring more.

'Aye. Beyond our reach – so you know the taking of Roxburgh was not on her account,' he had growled.

Nor on mine, Hal had thought grimly to himself, for all Jamie Douglas gave out that it was. When he'd said it aloud, Edward had agreed with a curt nod.

'So also with Berwick,' Edward had added pointedly, 'which will be taken in the end and the doing of it will be less about Isabel MacDuff and more to deny it to the English.'

He'd then thrown himself into a curule chair, draping one leg over the arm.

'Yet we care about our womenfolk, Lord Hal. I would not be so free and easy with the King as regards these matters. He is not the man you knew, being fresh to the kingship then.'

He'd stared moodily, glassily, into the wine and had spoken almost to himself.

'Now he is fixed on securing matters, on ensuring that everyone kens he is king. Nothing else matters but that and you step soft round him these days.'

'I have read the Declaration of the Clergy,' Hal had told him and had back a surprised look.

'Have you indeed? They were solicitous of your welfare in the end, to fit you with a copy of that in your cell. Shame we had to poke out Sir William's best eye, then, for it seems he did not deserve it – what did you think of that document?'

Hal remembered what that question had raised in him. Aggie, the girl who had served him meals, had brought it and she had plucked it from the kirk door, one of the many expensive and laboriously made copies nailed there. She had wanted to know what was in it but could not read, nor dared take it to anyone in Roxburgh who might.

What was in it? At first, the joyous honey of a candle, the first Hal had seen up close in an age and even the blur of tears it brought to his squinting eyes was a joy. The second was the smell: the musk of the parchment, the sharpness of the oak-gall ink – the breath of Outside. That, in the end, was worth more than the Declaration of the Clergy itself, a pompous piece of huff and puff to make Robert Bruce seem the very figure of a king and his sitting on the throne far removed from any hint of murderous usurping.

'Smoke and shiny watter,' Hal had told Edward eventually. 'Bigod, though, they almost convinced me that the Bruce is descended from Aeneas o' Troy himself. A Joshua and white as new milk on a lamb's lip.'

Edward had laughed then, sharp and harsh, spilling wine on his knuckles and sucking it off. It came to Hal that the Earl of Carrick was mightily drunk and that it was no strange thing for him.

'Ah, Christ's Wounds, we have missed you, Lord Hal – but it is as well you were safe locked up, for plain speaking is not the mood of now, certes. I would not share your view of the bishops' fine work with my brother. If you even get to see him.'

He'd paused moodily.

'I mind you were close to him, mark you. You and Kirkpatrick. Like a brace of clever wee dugs working sheep for their master.'

There was old envy and bitterness there, which Hal had decided was best to ignore.

'How is Kirkpatrick?' he'd asked, suddenly ashamed that he had not thought of the man since he had been released.

'Auld,' Edward had replied shortly. 'You may not see the King at all,' he then said. 'And if you do, it will not be a straight march in to where the Great Man sits, taking your ease in the next seat. Naw, naw. There are steps, neat as a jig: walk forward and stop. Kneel. Never look at him. Never speak to him unless invited.'

This kingdom is not large enough for the pair, Hal had thought, hearing the savage bile in his voice. Then Edward had recovered himself and smiled, drained the goblet and risen.

'Well, good journey to you. I am away to kick the stones out of Roxburgh. Pity – it is a pretty place.'

Prettier than here, Hal thought now, looking up at the rotting-tooth rock of Edinburgh Castle, while they wound a way through the siege lines.

They passed tents, a black Benedictine who was crouched like a dog to hear confessions, a sway-hipped gaud of shrill, laughing women who stared brazen invites at the newly arrived heroes of Roxburgh. Somewhere behind them a pair coupled noisily while the camp dogs circled, looking to steal anything vaguely edible.

Hal felt the heat of forges, tasted the sweat and stale stink of a thousand unwashed, the savour of cook and smith fire as they picked their way through the tangle and snarl of a siege camp. He was fretted and ruffled by the place even as it seemed to him that he moved in a dream, too slowly and somehow detached from it all.

Too much, too quick after seven years of being a prison hermit, he thought, yet the sights and sounds flared his nostrils with old memories.

The world passed him like a tapestry in a long room: a ragged priest singing psalms; squires rolling a barrel of sand through the mud to flay the maille in it of rust; a hodden-clad haughty with his lord's hawk on one wrist; two men, armoured head to toe but without barrel-helms, running light sticks at each other in practice tourney, pausing to raise greeting hands to Jamie. Only their eyes could be seen in the face-veiled coifs of maille.

Out beyond them, close under the great rock and walls, was a line of hurdles, pavise protection for the crossbows and archers. Beyond that, close under the looming hunch of Edinburgh's rock, a cloak of murderous crows picked mournfully through the faint stench of rot and the festering corpses of men who were too far under the enemy bows to be recovered for decent burial.

Men moved in blocks, drilling under the bawls of vintenars; Hal saw that some had only long sticks, as if the spearheads had been removed from their shafts, and that too many were unarmoured, with not even as much as an iron hat.

'Thrust – thrust. Push.'

29

The sweating men clustered in a block, hardly knowing right from left, half of them unable to speak the other half's tongue and none of them having met before; they staggered and stumbled and cursed.

The ones who had done this before, the better-armed burghers and armoured *nobiles* of the realm, moved smoothly through the drills, but they did not laugh at the rabble; they would all depend on each other when push came to thrust.

Hal moved through this misty, half-remembered world of noise and stink and death, made more grotesque by the shattering bright of banners and tents and surcotes dotting it like blooms.

Brightest of all was the Earl of Moray's flag, big as a bedsheet, fluttering in the dank breeze. It did not show the arms Hal remembered, but the old lessons dinned into him by his father surfaced like leaping salmon: *or, three cushions within a double tressure flory counterflory gules*. It was the arms of Randolph, right enough, but new-wrapped in the red and gold royal trappings of Scotland.

He saw Jamie Douglas jerk at his reins, black-browed, but then order his own banner dipped; Sim Craw, knee to knee with Hal, gave a quiet coughing bark of laughter and touched Hal's arm as the entrance of the rich yellow panoply parted to reveal Randolph himself.

'The paint is scarce dry on his new earl's arms,' Sim whispered hoarsely. 'Jamie resents having to hand Randolph his due as Earl o' Moray, him being a mere lord of Douglas. Resents, too, the royal mark in that shield that reminds folk Randolph claims the King's kinship.'

'Good Sir James,' Randolph called in French, sweet as milk so that the grue in it was almost masked. 'I hear you have triumphed at Roxburgh. Bigod, you are a byword for trickery, certes.'

Hal expected wildness and ranting, but Jamie lost his black brow almost at once and threw back his head; the mock of laughter he flung out was more stinging than any curse.

'Bigod, Thomas, are you still sittin' here?' he lisped back. 'Would you like some ideas on taking fortresses?'

Flushing, Randolph managed a twist of smile.

'His Grace the King, of course, demands to see the Good Sir James – and the rescued Sir Henry of Herdmanston. Welcome, my lord. Seven years gone from us and now plucked forth like a plum from a pie.'

Hal, taken aback by the sudden focus on himself, managed only a weak nod, but Randolph had never been part of the circle round Bruce seven years ago, so neither man knew the other save by repute – and Hal's had moss on it.

The moment was broken by a distant thud and all the heads swivelled and craned skywards.

'There.'

Hal saw the shaped stone arc downwards, scurf up a huge wad of mud and bounce harmlessly almost to the foot of the hurdles; a protesting smoke of crows rose up off their old feasts.

'They are trying lighter stones out of the fortress,' Sim muttered. 'You will note what is absent on our side of the siege.'

Engines. Not a trebuchet nor a mangonel – not so much as a springald. No towers or rams. Nothing.

Jamie Douglas inclined his head in a curt, mocking bow to Randolph.

'You have sat here since last winter, my lord earl,' he noted with mock sadness. 'Shame there does not seem to be a balk of timber that can be laid one on the other, or any trickery to supplant it. Still, I have it that you will persevere, certes, though it is my fervent hope that your lordship manages it before a big stone rolls over your curly pow. It is no good look for an earl, that. God be praised, my lord.'

He went off, laughing and chattering either side to the adoring, trailing everyone after him and leaving the thunder-cloud of Randolph in his wake. They quit the dripping sour of the camp, cavalcading down from under the black rock along the sullen mile of cramped houses and wynds that led to the peace and dry of Holyrood Abbey, where the King demanded to see the darling captor of Roxburgh.

The way of matters, Sim explained on the way, is not as it was. Randolph and Douglas and the last brother, Edward Bruce, were mighty captains, seasoned in the wars with the Buchan and Comyn which had finally exterminated all Bruce's enemies.

'A sore slaughter that,' Sim declared, grimed with the memory of it and shaking his head in sorrow. 'The Comyn are harrowed and ploughed under; the Earl of Buchan himself fled south and turned his face to the wall years since, poor auld man that he was – killed of a broken heart, they say.'

He looked sideways at Hal, but saw only a blank stone stare back at him, though Hal had his own thoughts on the poor auld man who had died of a broken heart. If the Earl of Buchan ever had one, Hal wanted to say, you could not have smashed it with hammer and anvil – but he did not have to voice it and was aware that Sim was still able to read him even after seven years.

Buchan, Isabel's husband and the nemesis of their loving for a decade and more, was gone like smoke. As if he had never been. Hal wondered if Isabel knew. It was as likely that someone would tell her for spite as they would keep her from the comfort of knowing, in marriage at least, she was free at last.

There was more, spilled out from Sim while Jamie Douglas climbed into his finery in order to come formally into the presence of the court. Hal, it seemed, had been forgotten already, though that suited him well enough, as did the corner of canvas and stick that Sim shared as part of the Douglas retinue. Sim, of course, was more outraged than Hal.

'You are the lord o' Herdmanston,' he fumed. 'Christ betimes, we rescued wee Jamie from the grip of the English when he was a snot-nose, carted him to safety and his da.'

'Aye. You cuffed his ears if I remembrance it right,' Hal said with a twist of grin. 'Has he forgave you yet?'

Sim glowered.

'He barely had fluff on his balls then, but I should cuff his lug again for this, which is no little insult to a lord of Sientclers. Ignored by the King ye served fine well and stuck in a corner of the Douglas panoply like lumber? It is not proper. And where is your kin of Roslin in this, eh?'

'That was then, Sim Craw. This is now. Now I am lord of nothing at all, for Herdmanston is still a ruin, you tell me. Roslin's Sientclers have done enough in keeping the wardship of the place alive at all. Besides, even a corner of this is better and lighter than the stone room I have lived in until recently.'

Sim had no answer to that. He sat with his head bowed, bleared by the memory of the last time he had seen Herdmanston, still black with the seven-year-old stain of fires, the floors fallen in and the weeds sprouting from the rotting-tooth of it. All the Herdmanston folk had gone to Sir Henry Sientcler of Roslin, yet their own field strips were at Herdmanston and too valuable to let lie, so some were back at the plough and the harvest, living in cruck houses under the ruins of the old tower.

'It would not take much to return it,' he added after telling Hal this, but then fell silent. None of the old riders remained, the ones who had once followed Hal, sure of that lord's ability to pluck gold out of a cesspit; they had died at Stirling's brig and Callendar's woods and on every herschip since. Those who had survived had long since grown too old for the business after – Christ's Wounds – fifteen years of fighting.

'Nearer twenty,' Hal corrected when Sim hoiked this up and Sim grew even more morosely silent at the truth of it. Out of all that time, Hal thought bleakly, Isabel and I have had no more than a year and a day in total together, tallied in months here, a week there.

Yet he would give as much for the same again.

'The new lord of Badenoch keeps her fastened,' Sim said suddenly, as if reading Hal's mind. Hal looked up and saw the grim gimlet of Sim's eyes, pouched and rheumy, but hard enough still.

The new lord, Hal thought, and almost laughed aloud. The youth Kirkpatrick had almost killed in Greyfriars, until Hal had prevented it, thinking enough blood had been spilled on a holy altar with the death of the father, the Red Comyn.

'Aye,' Sim agreed, seeing that chase itself across Hal's face. 'The stripling is grown to man and come into his lordship of Badenoch and all the attainments thereof. Mind you, the most of it he can actually lay his hands on without an army at his back consists of Malise Bellejambe and Badenoch has confirmed that man in the duty once given him by the Earl of Buchan: keep her in her cage.'

Bellejambe. Sim saw Hal's eyes turn to haar on grey water.

'I had hoped Malise Bellejambe was gone down the brae,' Hal said flatly. 'Then hoped the opposite, for I want to end his life myself.'

'He lives yet,' Sim said, and then laughed dryly. 'Greyer, as we all are these days, but his heart is as black as ever, I hear.'

Bellejambe, who was guilty of murder by knife and poison, who had snaked his way after Isabel on behalf of her husband until, finally, he had coiled round his capture. Hal did not want to think of what he had done to her, was almost rushed off the bench he sat on with the mad, frantic urge to charge down to Berwick.

It washed over him like fire, sank and ebbed, leaving him trembling and bitter with the reality. Seven years detached from swordplay or even wearing maille or riding a horse. Nothing left of his Herdmanston lands but the title. No men at his back and no future at his front. Some gallant rescuing knight, he thought, who has even been forgotten by the King I helped put on the throne.

But not by Isabel. He was sure of that and it nagged him like a knife in the ribs, the knowledge that she had squatted in her cage for seven years, willing him to her rescue. It was a scorching force that, every now and then, drove him to his feet as if to rush there alone and beat the walls down. The effort of staying shook him like ague and it had been this way for all of the seven years; the old weals on his knuckles told of the blood he had spilled hammering uselessly on stone and door.

An hour later, the world changed again when a squire came up and declared that the King requested Sir Hal of Herdmanston's presence in his chambers. The boy said it politely enough, for he was court-skilled enough to realize that there might be more to this old man than poor clothes and a bad haircut, since the King was not only seeing him in private, but had requested it.

'Come as you are,' the servant added, seeing Hal hesitate and look down at his tunic. Sim laid a hand on Hal's wrist as he started to move after the servant.

'Dinna fash when you see him,' he hissed, his Lenten fish-breath close to Hal's ear.

Which was not a comfort to a man anxious about meeting a king he had not seen for so long. Eight years ago, the Bruce had been freshly crowned, awkward under it and hag-haunted by what he had done to the Red Comyn in Greyfriars.

Even behind Roxburgh's walls, Hal had heard the argument, the monks of Bishops Wishart and Lamberton piercing the stones with their shouted debates, that it had not been red murder because there was no 'forethocht' in it. Rather, according to the carefully primed monks, it was a *chaude-melle*, a 'suddenty of temper' brought on by the lord of Badenoch's provocations. Besides, Hal thought as he clacked into the great nave on his thick-soled shoes, the new Joshua of Scotland could not be so base as to have deliberately sought the murder of a rival.

But he remembered the stricken Bruce, seemingly struck numb and appalled at his act of temper. Seemingly. Even now, Hal was hagged by the possibility of mummery, for the speed of Bruce's recovery, the smoothness with which Kirkpatrick and himself had been sent to make sure the Red Comyn was indeed dead, all left an iced sliver of doubt.

The bloody altar and the high, metal stink rolled out of

Hal's old thoughts, so that he paused and stood, mired in memory. The way Badenoch's heels, those vain, inch-lifted heels on his fancy boots, had rattled like a mad drummer as he kicked his way out of the world, splashing his own puddled gore up even as Kirkpatrick made sure . . .

'Sir Henry.'

The familiar voice wrenched him back and he stood in front of a clean altar under the great bloom of stone and glass that formed the nave window of the abbey. A figure, silhouetted against the stain of light, walked forward and the servant boy stepped back, bowing.

'Hal. God be praised.'

'For ever and ever,' Hal repeated by rote and then, remembering too late, bobbed his head and added: 'Your Grace.'

He was aware of figures and the servant, dismissed with a wave, sliding off into the shadows, then he looked up from the floor, blinking, as Bruce swung round into plain view.

The height and the body were the same, tall and hardened, unthickened by age – he must be in his fortieth year, Hal thought wildly, yet his hair is still mostly dark.

But the face. Hail Mary, the face . . .

It had coarsened, the lines of age in it deepened to grooves, the skin lesioned and greyish, so that he looked older than his years – Christ's Wounds, Hal thought, he looks older than Sim. The right cheek – that old wound, Hal remembered, given to him by Malenfaunt in a tourney *à l'outrance* – was a thick weal of cicatrice. As if in balance there was the slash taken in the fighting round Methven, a gully of old scar tissue that began above the left brow, broke over the eye and continued down the inside of his cheek almost to the edge of his mouth. Two such dire wounds would have been bad enough, but there was more in that face than hard usage, Hal realized with a sudden shock. There was now clear reason for the whispers of sickness – or even the famed Curse of Malachy.

Yet the eyes were clear and quizzical, the smile a wry

36

lopsided twist as he saw Hal's shock. He should look at himself, Bruce thought, and was not as sure as he had been when Kirkpatrick convinced him that Hal was the very man for the task he had in mind.

Seven years had not been kind to the lord of Herdmanston; he was too lean, too stooped, too grey – Christ in Heaven, too old. And had not handled weapons for all that time, so that the rawest squire could probably beat him.

He had pointed this out to Kirkpatrick, who had waved it away with a dismissive 'tschk'.

'He will muscle up and recover his skills as we go,' he had argued, then put the only argument likely to win the moment. 'Who else can you trust for a task like this, my lord king, but the auld dugs?'

So Bruce took Hal's hands in his own and smiled into the recovering eyes.

'Welcome,' he said. 'Your king is pleased to see you back in the world and back in his service.'

It was the ritual jig of kingship, played for long enough now that Bruce had forgotten any other way and the next words were an old part of it.

'What reward can your king bestow on his faithful subject?'

The answer should have been a low bow and something about how new freedom was the only reward required, with a profuse bouquet of thanks for it.

'The Countess of Buchan.'

There was a sharp suck of breath that turned Hal's head to the prelate who made it, standing with his eyes shock-wide in his smooth, bland face. The one next to him was older, more seamed, less shocked; he even seemed to be smiling.

The silence stretched as Bruce blinked. No one had spoken like this for some time and his mind was whirled back to the times when he and Hal's Lothian men had shared fires in the damp mirk. The one who now served Jamie Douglas – Dog Boy – had been one of them and they had all been plain

37

speakers; he had taken delight in that then and the memory of it warmed him now.

'I should have expected no less from you,' he answered with a slight bark of laugh. Then he indicated the two prelates.

'This is my chaplain, Thomas Daltoun, and Bernard of Kilwinning, former abbot of that place and now my chancellor. Sirs, this is the bold Sir Hal, proving that seven years' captivity has not dulled him any.'

The prelates nodded and then, sensing the mood, made their obeisances to the King and left, whispering away across the flags with an armful of seal-dangled scrolls. Bruce watched them go – waiting until they were out of earshot, Hal saw.

'The Countess of Buchan', he said, turning the full weight of his blunt-weapon face on Hal, 'is married to Henry de Beaumont.'

He waited, viciously long enough to see Hal's stricken bewilderment, and then laughed again, a sound like shattering glass.

'Alice Comyn inherited the title when the Earl died, for he repudiated Isabel at the last. The lands are actually held by me, as king, of course. Henry de Beaumont married Alice and now claims to be Earl of Buchan, a vellum title only. He does not care for me much and not only over his Buchan lands – he was twice handed Mann by the Plantagenet and twice had it removed by the Ordainers. Since I took it last year, he has precious slim chance of ever getting that isle back and less of claiming the lands of Buchan.'

He paused, his face now looking like a bad clay mask.

'Isabel MacDuff is now no more than a lady from Fife,' he went on. 'Though I am sure the title was never the attraction between you and her.'

Bruce did not add – did not need to – that he once had an interest there himself when he was younger and Hal, who had known it then and come to terms with it well enough since, simply nodded.

He wondered, though, if kingship had driven all obligation for Isabel's sacrifice out of him.

'A lady of Fife in a cage,' he dared, aware that this exchange was Bruce's revenge for his bluntness and fighting the anger it brought, at the easy way Bruce assumed he was 'back in service', with no questions asked of seven years' captivity. More galling yet was the realization that it was true, since there was little else for him and no other way to set about freeing Isabel.

'Indeed,' Bruce answered smoothly. 'As was my sister until recently. And she and my wife and daughter are all held captive – but we shall soon have release for them all.'

He lost the frost in his voice, fuelled it with a smile.

'I have not forgotten Isabel's bravery in defying husband and Comyn entire to be a hereditary MacDuff Crowner,' he added gently, and then drew himself up a little, shaking the soft from him like a dog coming out of a stream.

'Events are moving,' he said portentously. 'I have issued an ultimatum to those Scots lords still serving King Edward, so that they have until November of this year to swear fealty to me or be dispossessed of their Scots lands.'

Hal thought about it, but could only see that this would bring the English down on their heads, which was no help to taking Berwick or freeing Isabel, and said so. Bruce's smile widened; the cheek stretched and seemed almost to be parting.

'Just so. King Edward will have no choice. He must muster an army and come at us. And I shall take his last fortresses from him, so they cannot be used in the furtherance of his rampage.'

Hal saw it then, acknowledging it with grudging admiration. The English would plooter north in the old style, achieve nothing and, because they had no firm bases or supply, would suffer even more quickly than usual and retire, because Bruce would not face them in the field.

'Indeed,' Bruce confirmed, touching two fingers to the cheek, as if to reassure himself that it was not split and leaking. It was an old habit, Hal saw, ingrained over the years.

'When Edward Plantagenet fails again, it may be that his own disaffected will round on him,' the King went on. 'The

Scots lords who follow him will see sense and abandon him. The Kingdom will be secured.'

Your crown will sit steadier, certes, Hal thought; he wondered if he had said it aloud and was flustered enough to say the next thing that came into his head. 'A decent enough plan. If they ask a truce, then the release of captives will be part of it.'

Bruce, eyebrows raised, offered him a slight mocking bow, so that Hal flushed with his own presumption.

'I need your service, Lord Hal,' Bruce went on but Hal was not sure what use he could be and said as much, adding – again forgetting he addressed a king – that he was equally unsure if he had the belly for the work now.

Bruce nodded, as if he had considered the matter, which was true. He also knew that he had already captured the man, yet the triumph of bending Hal to the royal will was not as savage a joy as with others he had snared; it seemed like calming a fine stallion you must geld.

'If it will provide belly, let me tell you that the reward will be our utmost effort to free Isabel and her safe delivery into your care,' he answered. 'If events work out as planned, Berwick will fall to us. At worst, we will negotiate the freedom of all captives.'

He saw the gaff of that go in.

'As for your abilities,' he went on, 'they are well remembered.' He paused and smiled, lopsided so as not to strain the cheek. 'Betimes, someone vouches for you.'

He raised one hand into the red and gold stain of light from the nave window. There was a pause, and then a figure stepped forward from the shadows, limping a little, moving slow and silent across the flagged floor.

An auld chiel, Hal thought. Another wee monk?

Then the light poured through the nave on to the iron-grey head, turning it to blood and honey and a shock of the familiar.

'Ah, Hal,' said Kirkpatrick, almost sadly. 'You were ever a man for good sense, save ower that wummin.'

ISABEL

He came to me in the night. He does not do it often these days – so little that, may God forgive me, I was almost glad to see him in my loneliness, for he has long since ceased to pain me with his foulness, which is harder for him to achieve each time. He blames me and beats me for it, but even that strength is going from him. You gave me Malise Bellejambe, Lord, an image of Man in my world, for there is no other here save those I can remember. Is it my own sins that make You even more cruel than he is? I do not understand, O God, for what he does to me is surely cruelty to Yourself. May it be that this is a mirror to make me understand that nothing can protect me, O God, unless it is the shield on which there is no device, but all the heavens and the sun displayed. The only pure thing I have to offer You is my mind. Take it, Lord, and offer me that shield.

CHAPTER THREE

Palais du Roi, Paris
Feast of St Joseph of Arimathea, March 1314

The stink of it swamped from the Île des Juifs, pervasive and acrid, wrapping round them like snake coils so that the Queen of England had to raise a scented hand to her nose. It was an irony that the fire which had burned Isabella's hands and arms so badly the year before should now be of a help; the wounds had festered and she wore scented gloves to hide the glassy weals.

Out on the Seine, the daring were collecting the ashes of her godfather, Jacques de Molay, Grand Master of the Temple, burned the day before alongside Geoffroi de Charney, Master of Normandy. They had recanted their confessions publicly and her father had ordered the pyre built and the two Templars roasted slowly on it. Too slowly, as it turned out, for de Molay had uttered a long and pungent curse prophesying that his tormentors would be in Hell within the year.

Isabella thought her godfather's name would live a long time in memory, as a martyr to the Order and not least because of the Curse he had brought down on the Pope and her father. She said it aloud, which made Beaumont, Badlesmere and the young Earl of Gloucester shift a little at the daring in it. They were well used to this slip of a queen having the cunning of a fox and more backbone than her husband, but they kept those thoughts to themselves.

As they did their views on the Templars – but publicly at least, the Order had been condemned at Vienne two years since and England's king had followed the Pope's instructions on it. Now the Knights of St John were taking over the Templar holdings and, for all he might gnaw his nails, Edward could do nothing about it without annoying the Holy Father, whom he needed.

'Will my father see us?' Isabella asked and the envoy, bland face setting itself like a moulded pudding into regret and sadness, began to expound on why King Philip of France would not. The curt wave of the scented glove cut him off in mid-flow and no one marvelled at the 18-year-old girl's poise and command.

Well, there it was. Her father, it seemed, was in mourning for what he had had to do and she wondered if it was genuine contrition, or because he had been cursed. If she knew her father at all, he would be gnawing his knuckles with concern, as much about the macula on his glory as on his soul. Both agonies, she thought, will last long after the smell and the ashes have blown away.

This was the Philip the Fair she remembered, the handsome, cunning, treacherous, vain father and king she had known. The one who could commit the vilest acts, yet agonize over the stain on his relationship with God – but even that man seemed strangely diminished by what had happened, as if this last act of spite had sucked all the juice from him. That and the six-year search for the Templar treasure which Isabella knew had spawned this plot in the first place, a search which had uncovered . . . nothing.

She had no doubt that the news of the latest outrage on the last Grand Master of the Order of Poor Knights would be speeding to all the hidden ears; she wondered what they would do with their hidden treasure, these last angered Templars of the Order.

Not hand it over to her desperate husband for his wars, certes, so he would have to rely on Isabella, who had to persuade her ailing father to permit King Edward of England to mortgage the ducal dues of Gascony to the Pope, since Philip of France was Edward's liege lord for those lands. In return, the Pope would loan Edward the money to help finance his latest enterprise, a war against the Scotch.

It was a complex dance that Isabella knew well, the intricate gilded steps that took in the wool-eager mercantile houses of Pessagno in Genoa, the Bardi and Peruzzi of Naples. None of them bothered in the slightest that their biggest rival, the Florentine Frescobaldi, had ruined themselves with similar speculative loans to Edward I.

It was simply the work of mercantiling, where a mistake would plunge you to the depths and a success make you richer than God. It was, as Isabella had long realized, the true sinew of war: gold into a muscle to fight with.

So it would be no fault of hers if the entire intricate cat's cradle of it failed and her husband never got the money for his new invasion. So sad. A great pity that he would then have to suffer the bit and bridle on his powers by his own barons. Not her fault . . .

Yet, even as she flirted with the indecent treachery of it, she knew that her husband's curbing and the fall of his latest detested favourite would need to be better planned. In the end, she would get him what he needed – God send her a sign – but let him fret a little first, as he fretted her with so many small humiliations . . .

'Isabella.'

The voice turned her into the smiling face of Blanche, her brother's wife. She smiled in return, embraced her, admired her prettiness and her dress and all the time wondered if the rumours about her adultery were true – and how God seemed so speedily to answer her.

Both Blanche and Marguerite, her brothers' wives, were

vapid creatures, bored and beautiful. She would find out the truth of the rumours, she determined, and they would tell her, for she was young and could play bored and smile and nod, clap her hands at the thought of diversion and pretty young men. Perhaps what she discovered would further keep her father from discussing loans from the Pope a little longer and that would suit her. So sad. Not her fault . . .

Beaumont watched the exchange, the fox-sharp smiles of his queen, the eager Blanche, anxious to ingratiate and to be diverted by something new.

Beware, little chick, he thought, my king's wife is a snake who will swallow you whole.

The tang of burned flesh trailed through the window, bringing back the sorry mess of the Templar burnings and de Beaumont wished he also had a scented glove. He wondered what rich secrets de Molay had taken into the flames rather than hand over to Philip of France, the accursed king.

Where had all the wealth of the Poor Knights gone?

Edinburgh
Octave of St Benedict of Montecassino, March 1314

The air thrummed and cracked with the roars from hundreds of throats, enough to filter through the slit window and raise Bruce's head a little, so that he smiled; Jamie Douglas was drilling his block. Again.

'He is keen,' Abbot Bernard commented wryly when Bruce voiced this and did not betray anything on his bland face when fixed with a challenging, quizzical stare. Instead, he merely moved the document a little closer and hinted that the wax was cooling.

'He is furious,' Bruce went on, studying the scroll. 'Randolph has taken Edinburgh's fortress and by as rare a stratagem as the Black himself concocted at Roxburgh. If he does not vent his spleen, young Jamie will explode.'

He looked up at his Chancellor, who was searching out a bar of wax.

'When I seal this, the Brothers who cannot be called by name will have the fortress at Glaissery. Much good may it do them.'

'It may do you much good,' Bernard replied portentously and Bruce levered himself up from the table; his bones ached more and more.

'Besides,' Bernard continued smoothly, 'they are known only as the Benedictine Brothers in Christ these days.'

'So you and others of your like have convinced me – but you are Abbot of Arbroath and must make it clear to your brothers in Christ that they may call themselves whatever they choose provided there is no mention of the Poor Knights of the Temple in it. This is not a commanderie, nor will there be a new Templar Order with me as Grand Master.'

He stared at the charter and shook his head.

'No one will be fooled by these supposed Benedictines, who wear a sword underneath their scapular – unless folk can be persuaded that the penance of Hail Mary has been replaced by something harsher and more sharp.'

The Chancellor laughed dutifully but Bruce was serious.

'The Templars believe that because this kingdom is under interdict I can defy the Pope and give them succour. Remind them that I am not under interdict by choice, Abbot Bernard; sooner, rather than later, I will be reconciled to Mother Church and will not make it harder by giving comfort to every condemned heretic in the world.'

'They know this, my lord,' the Chancellor replied softly and with a taint of bitter steel in the tone, not missed by Bruce. 'That is why they offer what they offer. There is no Order of Poor Knights in Scotland, as anyone will confess, only some mendicant Benedictines in the wilds of the north.

With a deal of coin to lend and the whereabouts of an armoury to purchase with it.'

'Whisht on that,' Bruce declared, breaking from French in his alarm. 'No mention here of siller or arms.'

'Even between us alone?'

'Voices travel, Chancellor,' Bruce muttered, hearing the distant cries. And God is listening, he added morosely to himself. Worse still, Malachy is listening and that wee saint hates me.

His curse on the Kingdom was the unsteadiness of the crown on my head, he brooded, which makes all the folk who should be trading with us less than eager to commit. For certes, it was not possible to find one wee cunning merchant willing to loan the rebel King of Scots any sum, on any promise.

So I am fallen back on heretics and fables of Templar treasures, he thought, pushing away from the table and walking to the slit window, hands behind his back and twisting this way and that. And two auld dugs . . .

Far out on the green beyond the castle rock, horsemen galloped back and forth – four hundred at least, lances glittering. It was an illusion, all the same – and one Bruce had used to his advantage more than once – for these were no knights, nor even armoured serjeants. They were mounted infantry in padded coats with long, wicked spears, who finally came together like a flock of sparrows, hurling from their shaggy garrons to form up in a thick block bristling with twelve-foot pikes while the horse-holders led away fistfuls of excited, plunging mounts.

There was confusion, a few fell here and there and even from this distance, Bruce fancied he could hear the poisonous roars of their vintenars, each one determined that their twenty-man command would not be a disgrace.

He craned to see better, but could not distinguish anyone and certainly not Jamie Douglas, who was simply one man in the crowd of them. Closest to the pennant, certes, Bruce thought. At least his block has proper arms and not merely long poles – he wondered if Kirkpatrick and Hal of Herdmanston would succeed and vowed more candles to St Malachy to ensure that they did.

There was a flurry behind him and he heard mutter, turning to see his chaplain Thomas Daltoun scurrying up. Come to give the King confession? It was not on any list Bruce remembered and he frowned.

'Your brother is here, my lord,' the chaplain declared and Bruce's frown started to become painful over his eyes. Edward here? He had been sent to Stirling to prosecute the siege – had demanded the command, in fact, and Bruce had relented, for he knew that he had a trinity of troublesome commanders on his hands, not just Randolph and Douglas vying for glory.

He had thought Edward wanted to devise some equally cunning and glorious way to take Stirling and, if he dared admit it, had manufactured that ploy as surely as he had pitted Randolph against Douglas for the same reason.

But Edward was here in Edinburgh – surely he could not have taken Stirling by storm?

He came in, big and bluff and broad. He nodded to the exiting Chancellor but his usual beaming grin seemed forced and Bruce grew apprehensive.

'Brother,' he said, ignoring – as he always did – the lack of protocol Edward used. 'You have news of Stirling – Mowbray is in chains, the fortress is ours and your glory outshines all others.'

'It is your glory I am polishing,' Edward declared grimly, and then glanced pointedly at Daltoun. Bruce said nothing and, eventually, Edward took the hint, though he scowled at the favour shown the chaplain. He took a deep breath, as if about to plunge into freezing water – and now Bruce was frankly afraid.

'Mowbray is on his way south to English Edward,' his

brother said quickly, as if anxious to spit the words from him before his mouth was stopped up. 'He carries news of the truce we made, him and I, that Stirling will be surrendered if not relieved by an English army by the Feast of the Nativity of St John.'

The words hung like black smoke, slowly dissipating. Bruce blinked and his head reeled with it, could only gape at his brother and, gradually, felt the thunder in his temples as his brother's cool, challenging stare would not be broken.

Daltoun shrank as the moment stretched and seemed to thrum like a taut rope.

'What were you thinking, brother?' Bruce asked eventually, his voice trembling. 'Were you thinking?'

Edward flushed a little and the arrowed furrow between his eyes deepened – but he held his temper, which amazed Daltoun and confused his brother.

'I was thinking that something had to be done,' he answered slowly and Bruce gave a strangled gasp.

'Something was done,' he roared, before catching himself and standing, breathing heavily, his face a strange mask of red flush and unhealthy pallor; Daltoun, fascinated, saw the cicatrice bead with clear drops.

'You issued an ultimatum to the Scots still with the Plantagenet,' Edward declared truculently and Bruce exploded.

'I did,' he bellowed. 'I did, brother. I tied the Plantagenet to a time. Now you have shackled me to a place. Have you gone mad, brother? Do you think YOU are king here?'

The French was spat out so that Daltoun swore he saw the words form in the air, though it might, he concluded afterwards, simply have been spit. But the last statement lurched out like a sick dog and sat there festering while the air twisted and coiled between the two.

It was what he wanted, Bruce thought bitterly, wildly. He is not content with Carrick, my last brother . . .

Edward Bruce leaned forward on the balls of his feet and,

for a wild moment, Daltoun thought he was about to do the unthinkable and assault his brother. Assault the King . . .

'The opposite, brother,' Edward replied, sinking back a little, his voice sibilant-soft. 'I thought to secure you the throne.'

Bruce, stunned, could only gawp and open his mouth like a landed fish. Edward forced a lopsided wry smile.

'You want the Scots lords on your side? Win them,' he went on, suddenly pacing to and fro. 'This Plantagenet is not his father. This one is idle and apathetic and took himself to the brink of warring with his own barons over his catamite. Now he seeks revenge for the catamite's death.'

He paused and turned.

'This is the man you will not fight, brother? This is the man you taunt and then run from? How will that sit with the lords whose fealty you want – or even with those whom you already have?'

Bruce said nothing, could only stare while his head rang like a bell with the words 'Curse of Malachy'.

'You usurped the throne,' Edward said flatly and Daltoun heard himself suck in his breath. 'Took it by force and there is no shame in that – but if you want to keep it, brother, you will have to fight for it. Running away may be the German Method, as you have pointed out many times – but it will not keep this prize in the end.'

Daltoun knew that the German Method was a way of tourney fighting which involved avoiding the charge of your enemy, moving nimbly to one side and then attacking. Bruce had used it to advantage many times, in and out of tourney, but it was frowned on by all those chivalrous knights who believed the French Method – a fierce charge to tumble horse and rider in the dust – was the only honourable way of fighting.

Daltoun had time to dredge this up from the depths of his memory as the silence spread, viscous as old blood and broken

51

only by the brothers' heavy breathing, like galloped stallions. Then Bruce shifted slightly.

'Get you gone, Edward,' he said wearily and, when his brother made no move, looked up sharply at him. 'Get out of my sight,' he roared and Daltoun, seeing the storm clouds gather on Edward's brow, forced his legs to move at last and cleared his throat so that both heads turned to him, as if seeing him for the first time.

The tension snapped; Edward scowled at his brother, spun and strode away; the heavy door banged. Daltoun followed him, almost colliding with the returning Chancellor, who had heard everything even beyond the thick door.

'Christ betimes,' Bruce spat. He turned and said it again, this time slamming his fist on the table so that the papers and wax jumped.

Typical of Edward. There is the enemy, set your lance, lift your shield – charge. No matter the odds or the sense in it, one good charge might win all . . .

Yet he was the last of them, his brothers. All gone to his regal desires; ambition, he thought, is the Devil.

Rash, he thought. Rash brother Edward – and with his own Devil, too. This kingdom is too small for both of us, when one is a king and the other desperately wants to be . . .

His brother's words were a scourge, all the same, a rasping cilice on common sense. Edward was right, of course – he had a crown but not a kingdom, and until he faced the Invader he never would. Too soon, he thought. We are not ready – not enough trained men, not enough arms or armour . . .

Yet there never would be, not if he lived his three-score and ten – and he would not make that, he was sure. Not without losing some vital bits along the way, he thought with chill wryness.

I am forty, he thought to himself. If not now, then when?

Bernard, who did not like the flush on the face of the King, saw that the cheek scar was leaking fat, slow, yellow drops.

He dropped a fresh blob of wax on to the parchment, his hand shaking, and pushed it towards Bruce.

The King blinked, touched his cheek, inspected the tips of his fingers and, for a moment, looked weary and afraid. Then he shoved his fist and the royal seal stamped his authority on the parchment giving Glaissery Castle, lately ripped from the MacDougalls of Loch Awe, to the heretic remnants of the Order of Poor Knights, whatever they called themselves now.

Now it was done, he thought bleakly and, thanks to my brother, suddenly I need the secret Templars and what they can provide.

Above all, I need Kirkpatrick and Hal, those old dogs, to succeed more than ever, else I will be facing the might of England with sticks and poor hope.

Irish Sea
At the same moment

It was a scawmy water, a stained-iron bleakness of shattered gulls, heaving in slow, deep swells, sluggish as old skin; Hal hated it but that was less to do with the heaving deck than with his inability to cope with it, despite the patience of Gerald de Villers.

'Again,' he said and the robed figure, black scapular removed, merely inclined his head graciously and came at him once more, the great broadsword arcing left, right, feinting, coming in again. Sweating, unsteady and wheezing, Hal blocked, parried, and then stumbled from weariness; he felt the sharp kissing wind of de Villers's blade whick past his cheek.

'Better,' said the monkish figure, splitting his spade beard with a grin. 'You are growing stronger each day.'

Sourly, Hal allowed himself to be hauled up, wrist to wrist, and the man's sword vanished into the sheath strapped round his white kirtle with its discreet red cross over the heart. In turn, that all vanished under the plain black robes – yet, no matter the lack of markings, Hal thought, no one could mistake these men for mere monks.

Kirkpatrick watched the grey-faced Hal peel off the maille coif and then bend at the waist to shake himself like a dog until the hauberk slithered off and pooled at his feet. It took the tunic with it, so that Hal sluiced water from a bucket on his naked top half.

Ill-used, Kirkpatrick thought, seeing the glassy weals. And too lean, so that the muscle is wasted. He felt ashamed, as he always did when he remembered that last night, the night Hal was taken; it was hard to speak of it to anyone, let alone Hal himself, though they had done it in the quiet of dark, talking as if their words were halt and lame, remembering the murder and betrayal that had taken them into and then out of Closeburn Castle. Almost to safety . . .

What happened, Kirkpatrick had asked, after you sat me on the horse and sent it off? Hal had heard the depths of shame and bitterness in his voice and was surprised at it; to him it had been no more than sense: Kirkpatrick had secrets best not tested with the Question, there was one horse that would not carry them both and, besides, Kirkpatrick was wounded. Of course, there was the sick in it, the callous way Kirkpatrick had used him for his own ends by pretending that they were rescuing Isabel rather than red-murdering another target of the Bruce.

Even so, there had not been a conscious tallying of all that, merely a matter of seconds to leg the bleeding Kirkpatrick on the beast and slap it into a gallop, and turn to face the men and dogs coming for them.

He had killed the snarling dogs, losing the sword in the last of them, so that all the men who came up rushed him and forced him to the ground. When he told this, in fits and starts, Kirkpatrick nodded.

'It must have been sore,' he said simply and Hal wanted to tell him the truth of it. Kicked and punched and smacked with sword hilts, with John Fitzwalter bellowing out to take him alive, by God. Smashed by the studded gauntlet of the Hospitaller Oristin del Ard, while young Ross of Wark screamed at him to get up. Get up – why? So you can knock me down again?

A boot into his cheek and nose, so that his head rang; that's for the killing of the Master of Closeburn. Not me, Hal thought. Kirkpatrick did that. To his own kin, no less.

A flurry of kicks in the ribs and half of his face; that's for the Jew prisoner. Not a Jew, Hal thought, a wee Languedoc Cathar, physicker to Bruce and holder of some secret that could not be allowed out, the true nature and condition of the Bruce's sickness. The Master, his own kin, Kirkpatrick did for pleasure, Hal had wanted to shout, but he was sent to do the physicker down to Hell, dragging me in his wake with his lies. All the same, Hal only yelped and groaned as he took the painful price for Kirkpatrick's killings: a vicious flurry of stamps that broke fingers and an elbow.

A further series of savage whacks with something heavy – a spearshaft or the flat of a sword – which drove the air from him and agony in, so that he threshed and gasped, thinking, Jesu, they have done for me now. For Dixon, someone yelled. Poor auld Dixon.

The gaoler, clanking his keys, Hal thought. Kirkpatrick did that. Or perhaps it was the servant who had lain across the door to the Master's solar and was killed in his sleep – Kirkpatrick did that as well. Or one of the guards on the postern gate – I confess it, I killed the pair of them, though Kirkpatrick helped.

Blood on blood, a trail of it and most left by Black Roger Kirkpatrick. I should not even have been there, Hal had wanted to tell them, save that Kirkpatrick led me to believe I was rescuing Isabel, who was long gone.

To a cage in Berwick.

Hal had thought of that every day he woke in Roxburgh, nursing his injuries and his anger, trying to stare through the dark, imagining a similar cage mere feet of stone away, where Bruce's sister languished. By the time they had allowed him to hobble up to the battlements for air and exercise, Bruce's sister was gone. Just like that, cage and all, and it had taken a deal of wheedling persuasion to discover that she was not dead, merely so sick that she had been removed to the care of nuns to recover.

Hal had wondered if Isabel had sickened; for a long time he did not even know if she still lived and had only been sure of it when the King had spoken of her. King Robert . . . the title was still strange to Hal.

He wondered, having recently seen the King's face as everyone else must have seen it, if the murder to cover up whether Bruce had lepry or not had been worth seven years behind Roxburgh's stones. He wondered it aloud now, sitting on the tarred deck under the flapping belly of the sail, staring into Kirkpatrick's face.

There was silence for a moment, smeared with the creak of rigging and rope, the slap of wave on the cog's hull and the dull flap of the huge square sail, puffing with weak breath, like a man dying.

'Well,' answered Kirkpatrick at length, 'it seemed so at the time, with our backs to the wall and the ram at the gates. Later, when the King fell ill – near to death, in fact – the rumours grew stronger than ever. Worth it? Not for you, I am thinking, but you will have a warmer welcome at Closeburn these days.'

Hal had heard how Bruce had handed the liberated Closeburn lands to his faithful dog, Roger Kirkpatrick, so that he was now Lord Roger Kirkpatrick. Same name as the kin he had killed on that night and there was the Devil's hand in that contrivance.

56

'All I need is a knight's dubbing, promised this very year, and I am achieved of all,' Kirkpatrick went on proudly. 'Nigh on twenty years' service to the Bruce, mark you.'

'Aye,' Hal answered slowly. 'You have been raised.'

Kirkpatrick fell silent, realizing how far Hal of Herdmanston had fallen and ashamed and angry at himself for letting his pride get in the way of appeasement. He smiled, trying to recover a little.

'I will change my device,' he said, attempting to make amends. 'Those fat sacks on a shield are too arrogant and mercantile for my taste.'

'Arrogant and mercantile,' Hal repeated and found himself smiling at this new-found knightly fire from Kirkpatrick, who had the decency to flush a little and make a wry smile of his own.

'I hear you are eyeing up a wife as well,' Hal added and Kirkpatrick nodded, trying to make light of it, though the lady in question was an heiress with a good few acres.

'What happened to the wummin whose man stabbed you for yer dalliance?'

The question was, as usual from Hal, a bolt that took away Kirkpatrick's breath, though he reeled away from it and recovered quickly, the memories fleeing through him like panicked deer. He had used an old love as cover for their task and shamelessly taken advantage of her former regard. He remembered Annie and himself in the cellar before they gained entrance to Closeburn's castle. Nicholl, her man, coming out of the dark later, weeping angry at Kirkpatrick's ruining of his nice life and taking revenge.

He was supposed to have horses for their escape, but delivered a dagger instead; Kirkpatrick felt the burning memory of where it had gone in his back and all but crippled him. It had taken a long time to recover and he never fully had – but it had given him time to plan vengeance.

'Fled,' he answered thickly, though it was only half the

57

truth and he had spent a deal of time and silver tracking them both down. 'He could scarce remain in Closeburn with me as lord and master.'

'And the wummin – what was her name? Annie?' Hal queried and saw the flat stare of Kirkpatrick, so that he knew the truth of it; Annie's man, Nicholl, had not survived Kirkpatrick's wrath. It was the mark of the man that Hal could not be sure that Annie had, childhood sweetheart or no. Blood and blood, Hal thought, a trail of it, thick and viscous as a snail track, leading always back to Kirkpatrick.

'For your new device,' he said harshly, 'you should consider a hand with a bloody dagger in it. Fitting.'

Kirkpatrick did not even blink.

'You must take better care of that maille,' said a voice in French, splitting the moment like a wedge in a tree; they both turned into the spade-bearded face of Rossal de Bissot.

'The sea air will rust it unless you do,' he went on blandly, 'though it is good that you wear it constantly, to get used to the weight again.'

Hal, in the act of heaving it up and slithering back into its cold embrace, was less smiling about the affair, but de Bissot's approval was genuine and his enthusiasm uplifting.

'By the time we reach Crunia,' he beamed, clapping Hal on his metalled shoulder, 'you will be as before – fit to be a Poor Knight of the Order.'

'Slight chance of that these days,' Hal replied shortly and Rossal nodded.

'God wills,' he answered, and then smiled again, thinly. 'There was a time when you were considered for such an honour,' he went on, to Hal's astonishment. 'Your kinsman, Sir William, approached your father on the matter.'

'Sir William? The Auld Templar?'

De Bissot frowned at the term, but nodded.

'Yes, so you called him. It was shortly after the loss of your wife and child. Sir William asked to approach you and was refused, since you were sole heir to Herdmanston and your father did not want to lose you as well.'

Hal was astounded. Sir William Sientcler of Roslin, the Auld Templar, had never mentioned it, nor had his father. It could easily have been done, too, for Hal's grief at losing his wife and young son had been great enough to have driven him to the monkish life of a Templar, while Sir William, as Gonfanonier – banner-bearer – of the Order, had the clout to arrange it.

De Bissot saw his look and his smile broadened the grey-streaked spade beard.

'Yes. You might have been standing here with us,' he said and Kirkpatrick shifted a little at that.

'Kneeling,' Kirkpatrick corrected and de Bissot turned to see de Villers and Sir William de Grafton at prayer.

'Terce,' Rossal said, still smiling. 'Time is given by God and should not be wasted. I will join them.'

'They spend a deal o' time on their knees,' Kirkpatrick noted sourly, watching de Bissot join his fellow knights. 'If they had climbed up off them long enough they might still be in the Holy Land.'

'They fight well enough when they are on two feet,' Hal noted, remembering. 'Callendar Woods.'

Kirkpatrick let the words drift like acrid smoke. Callendar Woods, where Wallace's army had been helped to shattered ruin by Templars, a Christian Order fighting Christians; Kirkpatrick had not been there, but knew that the odious taint of it had stained the Order and added to its final ruin.

Yet here they were, sailing with disbanded heretics of the Templars, carrying Templar treasure to a former Templar stronghold in Spain to fetch stored Templar weapons.

It was a deal brokered on behalf of the King of Scots with the Order of Alcántara, the Spanish who had taken over the former Templar fortress; in return, Hal knew, de Bissot and the others had been given a rickle of land and a castle somewhere in the north that they might call their own, provided no mention was made of Poor Knights.

It was, to say the least, the strangest quest he had been on with Kirkpatrick and he had been on a few. A royal request, of course, which is to say only slightly less of a command than from God.

Desperate, too, Hal had realized. Bruce sends out his two faithful auld hounds because he can trust no one else to exert their utmost, in ingenuity, strength and, above all, loyalty; he felt his grin twist wryness into his face.

Loyalty. Kirkpatrick will do it for a dubbing, a blade on the shoulder that ranks him with the other *nobiles* of the Kingdom. I would give mine back, if it were possible, he thought, to not be here at all.

Only for Isabel. Only for her.

He and Kirkpatrick sat in silence for a while as the ship wallowed on, the crew trying to make themselves look busy so that Pegy Balgownie would not give them something worse to do in his scowling temper at the lack of wind.

'Matins to Compline and during the night as well,' Kirkpatrick muttered, watching the kneeling men and reluctant to let go of his Templar bone.

'"O Lord, You will open my lips and my mouth shall declare Your praise,"' Hal intoned with mock piety. 'The Order Knights have a deal of questions to ask of God, who seems to have abandoned them. Unlike the King.'

Kirkpatrick shook his head.

'The King will not openly support the Order of Poor Knights, which no longer exists, according to the Pope. But he will not cast aside folk he owes – nor will I.'

The last was said with quiet vehemence and Hal knew why. De Bissot had once plucked Kirkpatrick from certain death and had been quietly instrumental in garnering support and information for the beleaguered Bruce, even before Hal's capture.

And now, Hal thought, he brings even more. He met Kirkpatrick's eyes and was sure they shared the same golden thought; snugged up in the depths of the *Bon Accord*'s foul swill of ballast was a nest of stout, bound boxes as full of riches as any eggs. Templar riches, plucked from the ruin of their collapse.

A stir on deck made them turn to see the other richness that nestled in the cog's belly: a fragrant drift of periwinkle-blue dress, a lush curve of lip, two large eyes, dark as olives in a fine, breath-stopping beauty of a face. Her black hair was caught up in a net of pearls and she moved sinuously, aware that every eye was on her.

Yet Hal thought the Doña Beatriz Ruiz de Castro y Pimental's beautiful face had a sharp look, like a razored heart. She was the one sent by the Order of Alcántara to finalize the details of this secret deal and if ever anything marked the difference between the two religious commands, it was Doña Beatriz, walking like a gliding dream, shadowed by her Moor, Piculph. The Templars did not care for Moors – and for women even less.

Kirkpatrick's soft chuckle turned Hal's head to where the man gazed: the supposed Benedictines, rising hastily and moving away, as politely as they could, but pointedly nevertheless.

'If nothing else betrayed them,' Kirkpatrick said, 'then their Order's disdain for weemin is as clear as a Judas kiss.'

They watched as Rossal de Bissot, braced stiffly, walked to the lady and inclined his head in a curt bow, and had it in return. Piculph, after a short pause, moved away – out of earshot, Hal thought – and the lady began to walk quietly along the deck, with Rossal falling in beside her, his every celibate step as if he walked barefoot on nails.

Hal saw that the other black-robed knights watched Piculph, while the rest of the crew moved from their path, throwing surreptitious looks at Doña Beatriz which left little to anyone's imagination. They were a rag-bag collection of ill-favoured lumpen pirates, Hal thought, but Pegy Balgownie keeps them in line and he, according to Kirkpatrick, is to be trusted.

He had an idea what Rossal and the lady discussed, but he only knew that Doña Beatriz had come to Rossal from Villasirga in Castile, a Templar hold now handed to the new Order of Alcántara; the lady's brother, Guillermo, was high in it, close to the Grand Master.

There was little brotherly love or fellow Christian charity here, Hal thought moodily. The Order of Alcántara needed money and was prepared to sell the former Templars their own weapons and the unlikely pairing now strolling the deck were brokering the deal.

'"The company of women is a dangerous thing,"' Kirkpatrick muttered, quoting from the Rules of the Order.

'Aye,' said a savage growl of voice, 'the pair o' you would know that best, for sure.'

They turned into the tinged face of Sim Craw, clutching a huge bundle to him and looking liverish. If there is one who hates the sea more than me, Hal thought, it is Sim.

'You have ceased feeding the fish,' Kirkpatrick responded viciously and Sim nodded, though there was no certainty in it.

'I am fine when matters are moving,' he answered, 'but wallowing here is shifting my innards.'

Hal looked at the sail, filling weakly and sinking again; down at the tillers, a muscled red-head teased the cog into what wind there was while the barrel-shaped Pegy Balgownie scowled at the fog bank, swirling ahead as proof there was no wind.

'You should set that bairn on deck,' Kirkpatrick mocked Sim, 'afore you lose it ower the side when you are boaking.'

'Would make little difference,' Sim mourned back, glancing sadly at the swaddled bundle of his arbalest. 'Soaked or safe, the dreich will rust it.'

He paused, looked Hal up and down meaningfully.

'And your maille, lord . . .' he began, but paused, blinked a little and headed feverishly for the side of the cog, clapping a hand over his mouth.

Pegy was scarcely aware of the retching and the good-natured jeers, too busy with fretting over the lack of wind. Next to him, Somhairl bunched the muscles needed to shift the heavy tiller and grumbled, in his lilting Islesman English, about wetting the sail.

He had the right of it, for sure, Pegy thought. A good man, Somhairl, who learned his craft crewing and leading *birlinn* galleys for Angus Og of the Isles. Somhairl was a raiding man every bit as skilled as any old Viking and called Scáth Dearg – the Red Shadow – by those who feared to see him oaring up swift and silent, with his red hair streaming like flame.

No chance o' that here, Pegy mourned. Scarce enough wind to shift as much as the man's brow braids and even soaking the sail would not gain them much; they were moving, but slowly. Now would be the time, he thought bitterly, when the Red Rover would appear out of yon fog, with myself close behind, to pluck some becalmed chick.

But the pirate scourge de Longueville, better known as the Red Rover, had long since thrown in his lot and was now married into the *nobiles* of Scotland and calling himself Charteris. While his auld captains, Pegy thought bitterly, were left scrambling for the favour of kings. I liked life better when I was a wee raider – though he crossed himself piously for the heresy of such thinking.

As if in answer, a sepulchral voice boomed out from above. 'Sail ho, babord quarter.'

It was not God, it was Niall Silkie high in the nest, but even as Pegy sprang for the sterncastle for a better look, he knew that the De'il's hand was in this.

ISABEL

My God, You have chastised me by this man's hand and I have learned submission, I swear it on Your mother's life. I have suffered and learned about the power of the body over us and how, by way of it, the soul is branded. Grant me, O Lord, that I have learned, that I may not have to bring this branded body to You broken also, as this Malise would wish, given away by him as waste goods. Your will has compassed me round, O Lord, and closed all other ways to me.

CHAPTER FOUR

Irish Sea
Octave of St Benedict of Montecassino, March 1314

A white flag with a red cross, that was what Niall Silkie, squinting furiously, declared he could see. On his mother's eyes he swore it. Fluttering – limply – from the topmost mast of another cog. The pegy mast, ironically, which was what John of Balgownie was ekenamed after.

'A Templar flag?' Kirkpatrick demanded, and the black-robed figures looked at one another and chewed their drooping moustaches. The English flew three golden pards on red, so it was not them.

Finally, de Grafton stared meaningfully at Rossal de Bissot.

'We sent out decoy ships, Brother, did we not?'

Rossal, stroking his close-cropped chin, nodded uneasily.

'Two from Leith and another, the *Maryculter*, two days before we sailed ourselves,' he replied thoughtfully. 'It could be the *Maryculter*.' He looked at Pegy Balgownie. 'Can you tell from here?'

'A cog is a cog,' Pegy said, after a pause. 'Twenty-five guid Scots ells long, six wide, with fighting castles and a sail – they look much similar, yin to another. Nor do we fly any flag . . .

but the captain of the *Maryculter* is Glymyne Ledow, as smart a sailor as ever tarred his palms on a rope. He might ken me and my *Bon Accord*.'

Hal did not see how, since the one that approached them was the same as the one he was on: an ugly, deep oval bowl with a pointed bow and a squared stern and two fighting castles of wood rearing at both ends. The prospect of a fight on it did not fill him with confidence.

'Mind ye, he would ken it as the *Agnes*,' Pegy went on, peering furiously up at ropes and sails, as if to spring something to life, 'though it is presently named *Bon Accord*.'

He paused and beamed at Kirkpatrick.

'After the watchword on the night our goodly king took Aberdeen.'

'Very apt and loyal,' growled Kirkpatrick dryly, 'but of little help.'

'I named it *Agnes*,' Pegy went on, almost to himself, 'after my wife.'

He paused again, before bellowing a long string of instructions which sent men scurrying. Then he hammered a meaty fist on the sterncastle.

'She was also a wallowing sow who could not be made to move her useless fat arse,' he roared at the top of his voice. Someone snickered.

Rossal's quiet, calm voice cracked in like a slap on a plank.

'Mantlets to the babord,' he said and the black-robed figures sprang to life. Rossal smiled, almost sadly, at Hal.

'Assume that this is not the *Maryculter* and not friendly,' he said in French. 'Brother Widikind, please to escort the lady to the safety of below and guard her well.'

The big German Templar blinked, paused uncertainly, and nodded, the forked ends of his black beard trembling with indignation. Doña Beatriz, with a slight smile, swayed to the companionway that led below, the dark Piculph at her back.

'That's a tangle of "nots" ye have there, Brother,' Sim said, unwrapping his swaddled bundle and bringing the bairn – a great steel-bowed arbalest – into the daylight. 'I hope you are mistook.'

Unlikely, Hal thought. If Pegy Balgownie could not tell the *Maryculter* from any other cog, then the reverse held true – yet no ship would flaunt that Beauseant banner of the heretic Templars unless it knew at whom it was waving.

'And if it is not the *Maryculter*,' Kirkpatrick finished, after Hal had hoiked this up for everyone to consider, 'then it is flying a false flag in order to gull us anyway.'

'Which means it expected us and was lying in wait,' Hal added and the rest was unspoken: we have a traitor, who might even be aboard. He met the eyes of Kirkpatrick and Rossal, saw the acknowledgement in them – saw, too, a lack of surprise that thrilled anger into him; this pair have knowledge kept from me, he thought bitterly. As if this old dog was not capable of learning the new trick of them, or did not matter in the scheme of it.

Kirkpatrick, oblivious to Hal's bile, sucked a whistle through his teeth and grinned at Sim.

'Bigod, man, that is a fearsome weapon you have. Sma' wonder the Pope has banned it.'

'Holy Faithers has scorned this, our king, the Kingdom an' these Templars,' Sim growled back. 'Seems to me like every wee priest who sticks on yon fancy hat wants to put a mock on something.'

'Lord bless and keep ye,' Kirkpatrick answered, signing the cross over Sim, but it was hard to tell whether it was in chastisement or admiration, while his wry smile did not help.

'God be praised,' Sim answered, checking that the winding mechanism of his fearsome beast was oiled and smooth.

'For ever and ever.'

The rote reply went almost unnoticed, while Sim worked methodically.

'Are you fit for this?' Hal asked and felt a fool when Sim

looked at him and frowned, all trace of sickness burned away by the fire of imminent action. He said nothing, but his look hurled the same question back and Hal was not so sure he could answer it truthfully.

'Aye til the fore,' Sim said suddenly, grinning at him, and Hal felt the rush of years, like a whirl of leaves in a high wind. Still alive – the greeting that they had given one another as they staggered, amazed at the miracle of it, out of other lethal affairs.

Aye til the fore. The names of all the others who had fought reared up in his head and he wondered where they were – those he had last seen alive, at least. Sore Davey and Mouse; Chirnside Rowan and Jeannie's Tam and a handful of others. Auld men, he thought, like me. If they lived yet.

Then he thought of Dog Boy and wondered where he was and if he was safe.

Herdmanston, Lothian
At the same moment . . .

Dog Boy could not help glancing behind him every other minute, for the sick lure of the Herdmanston remains would not stop itching a spot between his shoulderblades.

There, high in that arched folly of a gaping window, was where he had shinned down in the dark and sneaked off to find help when the tower was besieged by the Earl of Buchan and Patrick, the son of the March Earl. Now that same Patrick had taken the title and Dog Boy wondered if the ruin of his face, scalded by boiling water during the assault, was still as sorry a sight as the tower, gawping at the rain, draped with misery and withered grass.

There was where he had sneaked through Herdmanston's garth, stumbling over the bodies of his slaughtered deer-hounds, but then he'd had to scale the barmkin wall and now it was more gap than drystane.

The wee chapel was sound enough and had managed to take some of Jamie Douglas's riders in shelter from the rain, though they had crept in, crossing themselves piously and apologetically to the blind-eyed Magdalene and the recumbent weathered stone tombs in which mouldered Hal's parents. Beyond the chapel stood the solid haloed cross that marked where Hal's wife and son lay buried; it was there, Dog Boy recalled, that the besiegers had assembled their springald, whose bolts had burst in the yett . . .

'See anything?'

Dog Boy started guiltily at the voice, turning to see Jamie Douglas approach with his lithe, purposeful stride. He shook his head automatically.

'Be a better view on the tower,' he said and Jamie nodded, grinning.

'I heard that you srauchled down it once. You would be hard put to shin back up now, though, despite the handholds nature has provided.'

He peeled off his bascinet and shoved the maille coif back off his head like a hood, peering into the dying mirk of a wet day.

'They are there,' he growled. 'I can feel them and smell them, like dung on my shoes.'

Dog Boy had no doubt that the Black was right, for the man could spy English in a mile round and only his hate was greater than his uncanny ability. Besides, they had seen a scatter of mounted men an hour before and only natural caution on both sides had kept them apart.

'*Gules semy of crosses paty and a chevron argent,*' Jamie intoned darkly and Dog Boy, though he spoke no French, knew that Jamie was reeling off the fancy words for the banner they had spotted: red, covered with wee white crosses and with a big white chevron.

Sir Hal had the same skill, but he would have known whom the banner belonged to; wisely, Dog Boy did not voice this to the scowl of Jamie Douglas.

'It is not the Earl of March,' Jamie said, almost to himself. 'His device is a rare conceit involving a lion rampant to remind everyone that Patrick of Dunbar thinks himself regal enough to be considered for the throne, like his da before him.'

He scrubbed his dark hair with confusion.

'So who is it?'

'No matter,' Dog Boy answered. 'They are unlikely to be friendly to us this close to Dunbar, for if Edward the Plantagenet stops of a sudden, wee Earl Patrick will be sticking his biled face up the royal arse.'

Jamie gave a harsh chuckle and clapped Dog Boy on the shoulder.

'Little room up there,' he answered. 'Despensers an' Gascon relations of Gaveston are elbowing for space.'

There was a long pause while the curlews wheeped in a rain-sodden sky. Dog Boy saw the ruin of fields round him, ones he remembered thick with oats and barley, studded with sheep. Sir Hal would be sore hurt to see his demesne in such a state, he thought.

Not that the rest of the land was better; Dog Boy had seen nothing but fields of rot all spring, for the early harvest had been ruined by rain and now folk were slaughtering livestock they could not feed. When all that was gone, starvation would set in and the rising leprous heat was now withering late-planted crops and forage. Coupled with the war that was clearly coming, it would be a harsh year for the Kingdom, where folk would eat grass.

It did not help that he was part of their bad luck – Jamie Douglas was raiding, with fast wee pack ponies and a couple of lumbering carts to load cut fodder and grain bags, his men all mounted to herd kine and sheep; the army slinking round Stirling like wolves on a kill needed a lot of feeding.

They had torn and scorched furrows back and forth across the Lothians, concentrating on the holdings of those they knew still supported the enemy. Then they had been chased by mounted men, whom they presumed came from Dirleton or Dunbar and had been running now for three days; Jamie Douglas did not like to run, Dog Boy thought, even when it was prudent.

'I would like to ken them better,' Jamie Douglas said and Dog Boy jerked out of his revery to look at him, and then followed the Black's steady, meaningful stare. The top of Herdmanston tower.

'Can you do it?' Jamie demanded and Dog Boy grinned at him, sharp-toothed as any wolf.

'Bigod, does a wee hound go three-legged at a tree? I came down it once, so I can get up it as well.'

Nor far away, Addaf took a knee and rubbed his grizzled chin. He knew there were riders somewhere ahead of him, but he could not be sure what they were – the Scots put everyone they could on tough, half-wild ponies, so it was more than likely just a band of ragged-arsed raiders, for he was sure he had seen scrubby little black cattle with them.

Yet the thought that they might be men with maille and lances made him uneasy and he did not like the feeling, not least because he was called Addaf Hen these days, which meant both old and respected for the cunning and knowledge it brought. *Henaint ni ddaw ei hunan* – old age does not come by itself, he thought, which is a comfort every time I climb up off my aching knees.

He looked round at his own men, a long hundred of whey-faced and grey-grim Welsh archers. Well they might look like corpses, he thought moodily, which was no more than they deserved for drinking the soured wine given to them to wash the heads of their own horses.

Mixed with water and applied carefully, it repelled the vicious flies and soothed their bites – Addaf's own little mare had a forehead of fat lumps from them – but drink, no matter how foul, was never to be wasted by a good Welshman on sluicing a horse.

So they had swallowed it down and now groaned and shat noxiously down their legs and over their horses, for Addaf, viciously, would not let them rest. Scout the area, he had been told, and so that is what he forced them to do, even though the task was tedious. The point of it was to deter the Scotch from scouring it clean of anything that might help the King's army when it arrived.

Small good the drink had done them. Now they had soiled the good coloured tabards issued by Sir Thomas Berkeley, complete with his badge on the breast; they would wipe their arses with the banner, too, Addaf was sure, if they got the chance. Sir Thomas would not like that – but Sir Thomas was not within a hundred miles of this hot, damp, flyblown, God-cursed place.

Hwyel came to his elbow, silent and narrow-eyed, taking a knee with a grunt that let Addaf know his innards stabbed him. He spared the man a glance, taking in the dark, close-cropped beard and the filth-grimed lines; he remembered the man when he had been young and colt-eager, full of irrepressible humour. It had been a long time since he had heard Hwyel laugh and the men now called him Hwyel Cuchiog – the Frowning.

'*Dduw bod 'n foliannus*,' he grunted – God be praised. Addaf stared unpityingly into his jaundiced eyes and gave him the rote response.

'*In ois oisou*.' For ever and ever.

'Now that we know that enemies of Christ do not inhabit us,' Addaf went on wryly in a fluid cough of Welsh, 'save for the devils in your belly, have you any thoughts on who might be ahead of us and, more to the point, where?'

'None,' Hwyel growled back. 'Does it matter? If we go to them, there they will be and we can shoot them to ruin, same as ever, Mydr ap Mydvydd, for we are better than they.'

Mydr ap Mydvydd. Aim the Aimer was another of Addaf's hard-earned names, though the truth of that these days was less than honest, since Addaf's eyes were not what they had once been and he was sure folk knew it but stayed quiet, out of deference.

He half turned, glancing at the sour sky and then at the men waiting patiently beside their horses; he heard one retch and saw Lowarch suddenly thrust the reins to his neighbour and dart off, half squatting and moaning even as he moved.

Then Y Crach moved to him like a scowl, his roseate face flaring in the leprous heat.

'Ye needs must punish these,' he said in his singsong way and now Addaf matched him for frowns. Y Crach – Scab – was thin and wiry, a good archer but with no great muscle on him. Some said he had been a priest, licked by a sickness known to be a killer, yet he had survived untouched but for his plaguey face and was convinced the Hand of God was in it. Now he was hot for the Lord and hotter still to do His work against the heathen Scotch, but it made him careless of hierarchy.

'*Bedd a wna bawb yn gydradd,*' Addaf answered, pointedly dismissive – the grave makes everyone equal. Y Crach bristled and Hwyel laughed, but then winced as another fierce reminder of his transgression rippled his bowels.

'Well, are we after fighting, or can we go home?' he asked and Addaf cursed him for cutting to the core of matters. Of course they could not go home, even if they had one, without having done what they had been told to do. They were now in the retinue of the Berkeleys and, even if Sir Thomas was not here, his son Maurice was, fretting about his sick wife back in England and unlikely to be consoled by failure.

Addaf looked pointedly at Y Crach until the man took the hint and went away. Then he levered himself up.

Hwyel rose up with Addaf, taking in the silver and iron look of the man, the hump of muscle on one shoulder that made him look like a crookback. Hwyel had been with Addaf for seven years of hard life and killing and knew it had infected his leader with a disease which had driven out joy.

He wondered what Addaf had once been like, in the part

long burned away by war. For a moment, he remembered his own younger self and grinned as Addaf turned to him.

'We will make them dance, we will make them kick,' he said, 'with a clothyard shaft and a crooked stick.'

The echo of the boy he had been fell like dull pewter between them; Addaf's gaze was sour.

'*Teg edrych tuag adref*,' he answered – it is good to think of home. Which was a lie for him, who had not thought of his little patch, two brothers and mam in many a long year.

Mam will be dead and gone, he thought with a sudden, vicious wrench of all that he had abandoned. Brothers, too, likely . . . and if they live yet it will no longer be my patch, but will belong to them now and the *babanod* they have made who grew up into it after them. No one there would know me if I walked into the centre of the place.

He shook it all off like a dog from water and went rolling away on bad knees.

Hwyel watched Addaf's lumpen back as he hirpled away towards the others, barking orders; he wondered how long it would take and what he must endure to become as black-avowed as him.

An hour later, he found out.

Irish Sea
At the same moment . . .

Niall Silkie skinned down from the mast-nest on a tarred rope, swinging on to the sterncastle like some long-armed babery. He landed lightly, almost on the toes of the scowling Pegy Balgownie.

'It is my sure opeenion', he said, 'that yon weirman weltering astern is afire.'

Pegy blinked and Hal saw the bewilderment in Rossal's eyes.

'He says the warship astern of us is burning.'

'There's after being a wheen o' smoke,' Niall Silkie persisted and Pegy stroked his beard, scowling at Rossal.

'Perhaps it really is the other ship, this *Maryculter*,' de Grafton offered in French, his spade-bearded face heavy with concern. 'In which case, we must help, surely, if only to discover why it is afire and who attacked it.'

'A ruse,' Kirkpatrick countered, tension thickening his Braid Scots. 'Designed to play on the chivalry of your graces . . . aw, it is creishie wi' cunning, for they must ken that we have proper Knights of the Order here, who once wore the white mantle rather than the grey of lesser lights. They will rely on your nobility and honour blinding you, sirs, whether you are disbanded or no'.'

Rossal's brow lashed itself with frowns and Pegy, sensing the balance, glanced at the filling sail, then at the fog bank.

'The wind is up a notch. Two nicks on the steerin' oar to farans and we can be in the haar and vanished like wraiths, my lord.'

Somhairl, looking up through the castle planks at the booted feet and able to hear every word, leaned expectantly on the starboard-quarter tiller, bunching his muscles to turn the ship at Pegy's order. Men waited with coiled rope to lend their muscle to haul the unwieldy vessel quickly on to a new course; the moment clung and sucked the breath away.

Then Rossal shifted.

'Bring in your sail, captain,' he said firmly. 'We will await the arrival of this burning vessel.'

Kirkpatrick made a disgusted growl in the back of his throat and Pegy, after a short pause, nodded and bawled out the orders; men sprang to obey and the *Bon Accord* balked and then started to roll and pitch. Sim gagged and stumbled to the thwarts.

'Leave a gap in the mantlets,' de Villers called out, almost joyously, 'so our comrade can lose his belly over the side in peace.'

Below, Widikind heard the laughter and began to take his leave of Doña Beatriz, offering her a stiff little bow from the neck.

'Are you afraid?'

He heard her voice, light and musical, the French tinged with a delicious accent; his eyebrows went up at the question.

'If there is to be a fight, the Lord will hold His Hand over me – or He will lift me up and I will be gathered into His Grace. What is to fear?'

Her laugh was a trill and she unloosed the net of pearls, signalling Piculph to help; Widikind found the sight of the Moor-dark man running his fingers through her hair to tease the net free disturbing and uncomfortable.

'I meant of me,' she replied and he blinked, then recovered himself.

'We believe it is a dangerous thing for any religious to look too much upon the face of a woman.' He recited from memory the old catechism. 'The Knighthood of Jesus Christ should avoid, at all costs, the company of women, by which men have perished many times.'

'The Rule of Benedict,' she answered, which astonished him; she saw it and smiled sweetly. 'Though I remember the Rule as being that the Knighthood of Jesus Christ avoid, at all costs, the *embraces* of women rather than simply the company.'

Widikind felt himself prickle with an awkward heat and could not speak.

'My brother is of the Order of Alcántara, whose knights have taken over your holdings in Castile,' she went on. 'He is, as are they all, Cistercian in his rulings and he says that all Templar Knights follow the Benedictine belief, which is altogether too harsh. He says you – when you were not a heretic, pardon me, Brother – slept in shoes, shirt and hose in order to avoid the sin of being catamites to each other. Do you still hold to that, Brother, even though your Order is dissolved?'

Widikind's mouth opened and closed and he was aware of

how stupid he must look, while his French grew thick with his Cologne accent, so that it sounded crow-harsh to his own ears.

'Not seemly,' he managed at last. 'This talk. I must join my brethren. Battle.'

She waved a languid hand and slapped Piculph's wrist as he tugged too hard.

'La, sir, this is the slowest pursuit since Aesop's Tortoise. There will be no fighting for an hour or more and none at all unless we are foolish enough to allow it. Which is worse?'

The last question sent Widikind reeling and he gaped, flustered and feeling his face flame.

'Worse?'

'Lying with men or with women? Which is worse for your Order . . . former Order?'

Widikind was staggering now, unable to think clearly or protest further. He wanted to turn and go, he wanted to spit out that all monastic life was a war against passions which women were ill equipped to resist. But he was rooted and saw, with the last edge of his eyes not locked like a stoat-fixed rabbit on the lady's face, the slight mocking sneer on the lips of the Moor.

'Men,' he managed to gasp and Doña Beatriz snapped her fingers, a sharp sound that seemed to cut the strings that fixed Widikind to her face; he half fell, and then righted himself and, appalled, straightened. He felt the sweat roll down his back and forehead.

'So,' she said, softly vicious. 'You avoid speaking or having contact with my sex, sir, because the Rule of Benedict considers the embrace of women to be . . . dangerous.'

She leaned forward, her beauty like a blade.

'Yet the embrace of men is worse,' she concluded, light as the kiss of a razor on a cheek, 'and you are happy to consort with them freely. I do not understand this. Perhaps you can enlighten me, since I am a mere woman?'

Widikind blinked and grew suddenly cold. This was the Eden serpent, for sure, and an added coil was the sly, sneering Moor at her back. But Widikind von Esbeck was of the Order, his grandfather had been Master in Germany and, even interdicted and abandoned by the Holy Father, he would not be afraid of evil . . .

'As you say, lady, you are a mere woman. Filling you with such enlightenment would be like pouring fine wine into a filthy cup. A pointless waste.'

He nodded briefly, turned on the spot and fumbled his way up the steps and on to the deck, feeling the sudden breeze like balm; behind, he heard the soft chuckle of the Moor.

Doña Beatriz waited until his shadow was gone.

'Typical,' she murmured, 'and revealing. There is steel in these Knights of Christ, but a waft of perfume and a girlish laugh unmans them easily enough.'

She turned to smile at Piculph.

'He imagines I am Satan's own daughter, with a Moorish imp as a servant – did you see how he stared at you? If you had brought out a forked tail he would not have been surprised.'

Piculph, who was a good French Christian and a serjeant in the Order of Alcántara, nodded, though his smile was a bland cabinet that hid his own secrets.

'This Widikind and his so-called brethren were once Templar Knights, the wearers of white. You should be wary of thinking them the same as those grey-clad lay dogs you saw scampering away from Villasirga, señora.'

'When the time comes,' Doña Beatriz replied, 'wile will win over weapon, Piculph.'

She heard the drumming of feet on the deck above, felt the lurch and sow-wallow of the ship and frowned.

'We are slowing. Surely these fools are not about to fight. They do not even know how many enemies lie in wait on that boat.'

Piculph's eyes narrowed and he folded the net of pearls neatly.

'That is what I mean, señora. Fighting is what they do and they do not consider odds.'

Herdmanston
An hour later . . .

The odds, as Y Crach had declared, loudly and with relish, were perfect. . . . four carts, a scatter of sumpter ponies, a milling herd of long-horned black cattle and a handful of men, half-crouched with spears waving, clustered with desperate courage in front of the wagons.

Hwyel – the traitor, Addaf thought blackly – had agreed.

'We will make them dance,' he bawled out and Addaf saw the men who agreed, grinning and nodding between sick belches. Too many sick belches and more so than last time.

Reluctantly, Addaf signalled for his men to dismount, the younger ones grabbing handfuls of reins and dragging the horses away as the old hands slid easily into familiar ranks and heeled their bows, running the string up to the nock in a smooth movement.

Addaf looked at his own bowstave, the ribbon on the tip fluttering softly so that he knew the wind speed and direction. Twenty men oppose us, he thought, no more. Twenty and a handful of dogs for driving the kine – five to one he outnumbered them and one single volley would pin them to the turf.

So why was he so fretted? Because Y Crach seemed to have taken charge of this? He eyed the black ruin of the tower, the weathered cross and the battered chapel and did not like the omen of this place at all; his men, bows smarted and drooped to the ground, waited for the command that would lift the arrow points up, draw back the braided horsehair and silk string to the ear and release an iron sleet on the enemy.

There was a flurry from the spearmen then and heads turned

81

from watching Addaf to anxiously scan the enemy, for everyone knew that the only hope for the rebel Scotch was to run at the archers instead of standing like a set mill. They did not want these shrieking caterans closing on them, with their rat-desperate bravery and sharpened edges.

But there was no frantic, screaming rush. Instead, bewilderingly, the front rank seemed to have melted away, scurrying for cover behind the carts, leaving the others to face the arrows. One of them, dunted by a hurrying shoulder, tilted and fell over, the spear falling. Another leaned slowly sideways as if drunk.

False. Addaf saw it the same time as everyone else. A front rank of men, now under cover, had hidden the truth of hastily made dummies of lashed crosspoles and twisted grass, capped with a helmet, draped with a tunic.

False.

Even as it rang in him like a bell, he heard the savage shrieking yell, that blood-chiller the archers knew so well.

Then, behind them, the ground drummed with the mad gallop of garrons, every one with a nightmare of wet-mouthed savagery wielding that wicked Jeddart staff, with blade and spear and dragging hook.

And in front, wild dags of black hair flying, bearded face twisted in a snarl of anger and utter hate, a rider swung a hooked axe in one fist, split the skull of young Daiwyn and scarcely seemed to notice.

Addaf did not know who it was, only what it was. It was time to be somewhere else and in a running hurry.

Irish Sea
At the same moment . . .

It is, Niall Silkie declared in a shrill yell from the nest, showing a deal of smoke from the sterncastle. And it has lost its flag for another, a red horsehoe.

The cog was so close that Hal and everyone else could see that for themselves, peering out from behind the hastily lashed mantlets that provided cover from arrows. A thread of smoke and a red flag with a downward curve, like a droop of moustache.

Pegy went red-faced and furious then, bawling and screaming orders that sent men lurching at ropes; the sail banged down and filled, heaving the *Bon Accord* ponderously forward. Others of the crew fetched out long knives and two near-identical brothers, copper-haired and wiry, sprang up to the sterncastle, one with a bow, the other with arrows.

'Not a horseshoe,' Pegy growled at the grim assembly beside him. 'A crab.'

He managed a mirthless smile at the anxious faces round him.

'A wee jest on his name. Jack Crabbe was yin o' Red Rover's better captains afore the Rover embraced the Kingdom's cause. Now Jack Crabbe's ship, the *Marrot,* is a skulking moudiewart in the service of any who will pay – or more likely his own self.'

'Hardly his own, I fancy,' Rossal answered in steady, unaffected French. 'He is not here by happenchance, flying a banner of the Order.'

He was not, Hal thought, and the thread of smoke nagged at him while the brothers, Angus and Donald, argued about who should shoot first.

'The range is too great,' Angus declared. 'Give it to me – I have the muscle for the work.'

'You? Ye couldna hit a bull's erse if ye clung to its tail.'

'In the name o' Christ an' all His bliddy saints – God forgive me – will yin o' ye shoot.'

Pegy's exasperated bellow made everyone wince, but Donald drew back until the bow creaked protest, then almost flung the arrow from him. It splashed a score of feet short.

'Ye see? Ye bummlin fruster – wait until she closes.'

83

The brothers scowled at each other, but Hal had finally worked out what the smoke was and the chill of it tumbled the words from him like frost.

'They will not close, nor have need to. They will fire off that engine they have up the sharp end and drop carcasses on us until we burn.'

'Christ's Blood.'

The words were out of Rossal's mouth before he could stop them and he crossed himself at once and fervently offered penance for his sin at the first opportunity. Kirkpatrick grunted out a laugh at Hal's elbow.

'I hope you have the chance,' he added and then glanced at the sail and the fog bank; he noted wryly that the more wind there was shoving the ship, the more the fog bank receded in front of them. It was a grim humour folk had come to expect from Kirkpatrick, but the rasp of it was a grate on the nerves for all that.

There was a dull thud of release, a deeper burst of smoke and a brief flowering of red. Then a tailed star shot up, trailing an arc across to them; it hit the water with a gout of sizzle and splash.

'In the name of Christ,' muttered Angus. 'Yon's a bad sight – but I am pleasured to see that they can shoot no better than you, brother.'

'A warning,' de Villers declared, adjusting the fold of his maille coif so that it covered all of the lower part of his face. 'This Crabbe does not want us burned to the waterline. He knows what we carry.'

Yet again unspoken words hung above them like a corpse from a gibbet: they had a traitor.

Painfully, the pursuing ship overhauled them, for all Pegy's bawling and the frantic bucket chain soaking the sail to garner more wind, for all Somhairl's muscled skill at tillering the bulky cog to suck up the last puff.

Another star trailed smoke out and this time the gout of

steam and the splash were far closer. Hal saw Sim climb to the forecastle, stick a foot in the stirrup of the arbalest and begin to wind it; he wanted to call out for the auld fool to watch his white pow, but smiled at himself, standing half-naked and ill-armed and almost as ancient.

'They want us to heave to,' Niall bawled from his mast-nest.

'Signal them to eat shite,' Pegy howled back and men laughed, though it was mirthless and tied with tension like a harsh twist of cord. Angus did his best to obey, baring his buttocks and pretending to eat the contents, so that the men laughed, harder and more shrill.

Hal could now see small figures on the other ship, using iron rods to carefully lift the burning ball of oil-soaked withies; it was so like the ribs of some beast that men called it a carcass. Drop it, he wished wildly; if you roll yon on your own deck there may be a chance for us this day.

He looked at the sail and then over his shoulder; the fog bank was a cable length away and he groaned – he knew that the pursuers could not risk them escaping in the haar and that this shot would be for a hit. They were close enough that they might actually manage it, too.

Rossal and the others knew it; knew also that the target would be the huddle of black-robed men on the sterncastle, so clearly the ones who mattered that they might as well have waved their own Beauseant banner.

'Away,' Rossal said gently. 'If you value your lives.'

At the same time, Pegy hammered his feet on the deck in a mad dance to signal Somhairl, bellowing at him to heel over hard to farans, to put the enemy off their aim.

Somhairl was leaning hard on the tiller, obediently turning the heavy ship to starboard, when the world whirled from behind him and blasted him to blackness. Uncontrolled, the tiller waved and the cog floundered.

Pegy felt it, yelled out furiously and men turned from their tasks to see, amid the sudden flutter of men spilling from the sterncastle, the slumped form of the Red Shadow; at once Donald and Angus sprang to the tiller and strained, cursing.

'Dunted,' Kirkpatrick said, kneeling by the slumped form of the big Islesman. 'There, ahint the ear. Bigod, it is as well his braid took the brunt, else he would be standing before his Maker.'

A blow, Hal thought, designed to kill, not just to lay the man out for a while. He and Kirkpatrick exchanged glances, each knowing the thoughts of the other at once, from long association; the traitor was here, on board. Hal's eyes flitted from sailor to black-clad knight; de Villers met his stare and then turned away, while de Grafton laid his shoulder to the tiller and helped the straining brothers. It could have been anyone in the shadows under the sterncastle, Hal thought bitterly.

'Brace,' bawled Pegy and the threat of the carcass scorched back on them.

Up on the forecastle, Sim had loaded and rested the arbalest on the merlon, squinting at his target. Bigod, age is a terrible thing, he thought, for I can scarce see more than a blur.

But a blur was fine, provided he could tell man from mast. He shot and the deep whung of the release brought heads round.

Up on the forecastle of the *Marrot*, Jack Crabbe's expensively hired *ingéniateur* studied the roll of the wave, waiting for the second just before it started on the rise. He was a Gascon expert, was Ferenc Lop, even if shooting a mangonel from a moving ship was a new experience and he had, he was pleased to see, mastered it as he had mastered everything else to do with engines.

His hand was up and men watched for the cutting swathe of it, the signal to release. The bird-wing whirr of the crossbow bolt took them by surprise and they recoiled from it, the one with the release rope among them. The latch clicked, the mangonel arm flung forward – just as Ferenc slammed back into it, pinned through the chest.

The power of the muscular mangonel ripped him forward and sent him over the side in a bloody whirl of arms and legs. The carcass, balked out of the spoon, shot sideways, ploughed a burning furrow through the nearest men, spun off the castle and hissed into the sail, where it clung for a moment, before dropping to the deck and rolling a trail of sputtering fire, ponderous as a blazing snail. Flames and smoke shot up, broiled with screams.

Over on the *Bon Accord*, men stared in awe as the *Marrot* veered, the smoke obscuring her and the flames clearly leaping up the sail. They turned to where Sim was winding the arbalest, elbows working like two mad fiddlers, and broke into howls of delight. Sim affected nonchalance, shot one more bolt into the smoke, and slithered down to the deck as the first witch-fingers of comforting haar enveloped him.

'Christ betimes,' Kirkpatrick declared, beaming, 'as fine a shot as any by a man half your age.'

'Aye, aye,' Sim acknowledged easily, pulling out a rag to clean the steel-bowed arbalest as the crew crowded in to admire it and him. It was only later and only to Hal that he admitted he had been aiming at what he thought was Jack Crabbe – a span of hands to the left of the man he hit.

Doña Beatriz stood, apart from the delight and shadowed by Piculph, watching Pegy and the two stupid brothers attending to the giant Islesman. She was frowning at what she had seen done to him and about the man who had done it, wondering how best to use the knowledge to her advantage.

Herdmanston
Two hours later . . .

They came up, fox wary and stepping in crouched, swinging half-circles, arrows nocked on smarted bows, heedless of the rain and what that would do to strings.

Addaf knew the Scotch would be gone and his lungs burned from the long run, a frantic hare-leap of panic amid the scattering of their own horses. Now, on foot, they padded back like slinking hounds, for Addaf had lost forty-five men, all the horses and a deal of dignity, which trailed in shreds behind him with the mutters of his men.

They had recovered four horses so far and found all their missing men, though it did them little good: most were dead and at least nine had their right hand or more missing and had died of the blood loss or the horror of it happening. Taken alive, everyone saw, and badly handled.

Five were alive, but none of them would see day's end. They had used their one good hand and teeth and any thonging or laces they could find to tie off the raw stumps so that the blood did not pump out of them. But they had lost too much and Addaf ordered the bindings cut, to let them slip into the mercy of a long sleep as they lay in sluggish red tarns.

He was aware of Y Crach as a feverish heat at one side of him, but the man – wisely for once – kept silent round him; yet, when Addaf looked, he was head to head with others, who were nodding and scowling.

Addaf had not time for it. He knelt at Hywel's side, seeing the grey face and the blued lips, the slantwise horror of his severed forearm.

'No time, the man said,' Hywel echoed in a soft, twisted wheeze, 'for niceties. Like taking off our thumbs. The other one, the one called Dog Boy, said his leader would be hard. Hates archers above all his enemies, he said. Hates Welsh more than he hates English, for the Welsh should know better than to serve English Edward.'

Hywel gripped Addaf's arm hard with the last bloody-fingered hand he had, so that the cloth bunched between his knuckles.

'Dog Boy, he said he was. Said if any of us lived we should tell the others, all the Welsh, that they are on the wrong side.'

'The right side is the one that wins,' Addaf replied, looking into the misting eyes.

'The other one lashed our right hands with ropes, had a man hold us and another haul our arms out. Then he went down the line of us with his axe. Like he was coppicing . . .'

'Who? Who did this? This Dog Boy?'

Hywel was more out than in this world, Addaf realized, but his eyelids flickered and his voice was a last breath.

'Douglas,' he said, so slight that Addaf had to put his ear to the lips. 'The Black himself.'

Then, suddenly, in a clear, strong voice with laughing in it, he said: 'We will make them dance, we will make them kick . . .'

Addaf closed the eyes.

'*Bedd a wna bawb yn gydradd*,' he said grimly. The grave makes everyone equal.

ISABEL

O God, whose charity is more painful than Your harshness. In all the years since his father's death in Greyfriars, the new lord of Badenoch has never visited, simply paid Malise his stipend for guarding me – as his Comyn father did before – on behalf of his kin, my long-dead husband. Yet, Lord, You brought Badenoch to the Hog Tower this year, accompanied by a simpering Malise, anxious for his quarterlies to be continued. A little mirror of his murdered father, this new Badenoch, freckled, red-haired and bantam. He looked round at my straw-strewn stone niche, the window that is a door and the cage beyond it. Then he looked me up and down and slowly wondered at my state and age, not having realized it before. Not quite the Hoor o' Babylon, wee Johnnie, I told him and watched how prettily he pinked. He ordered my whim for pots and paints and women's essentials 'in remembrance of the man who spared me' – but confirmed Malise in the constant caring of me. The man who spared wee Badenoch was Hal, on that day in Greyfriars when this frowning little lord was a lad, brought to say last farewells to his murdered da to find the killers returned to make sure of it. Kirkpatrick would have done for him, save for my Hal; Malise fled and young Badenoch clearly remembered it, for his look flushed Bellejambe to the roots of his pewter hair. Later, Malise took his revenge with me and, as always, lost

91

more than he gave. I suffered his grunting, futile foulness and learned that Badenoch did not come only to see me, but to put Berwick in order; the English are coming in midsummer, to put an end to Bruce. You may dream of it, I told Malise, and, for once, he had no strength left to punish me. So a victory for endurance – let us hope, O Lord, that this is not a beguilement of empty hope for the Kingdom.

CHAPTER FIVE

Westminster
Feast of St George, April 1314

The Pope was dead and the shiver of it added to the cold ache in the bones. Drip and ache, that was Easter, thought Edward, every miserable cunny-rotted day of it, when the damp crept up your back and no amount of stoked fire could keep the wind from looping in and up your bowels until you coughed and shat hedgepigs.

Like Father. He threw that thought from him, as he always did when it crept in like a mangy dog seeking shelter. Shitting his life down his leg; for all his strength and longevity brought low by a foul humour up the arse, king or no.

Death did not care for rank. The Pope had found that, just as Jacques de Molay had promised from his pyre. Edward, even as the delicious chill of it goosed his flesh, could not help the hug of glee that he was not his father-in-law, the King of France, who had also been cursed in the same breath.

Still, there was room enough for Edward to wonder if his own treatment of the Order of Poor Knights had inherited a waft of that smoke-black shriek from de Molay. He had been light on the Templars, but followed the Pope's edict and handed their forfeited holdings – well, most of them – to the Hospitallers. Much good may it do them, he thought, though it does me very little for I cannot see the Order of St John coming to my army. The Templars made that mistake by joining my father's army and the lesson in it is plain enough for a blind man to see.

He wished someone would come to his army, all the same.

'Who has not responded?' he demanded and de Valence made a show of consulting the roll, squinting at it in the bright glow of wax candle which haloed the small group in the dim room. No one was fooled; everyone there, the King included, knew he could recite it from memory.

Lancaster, Arundel, Warwick, Oxford, Surrey: the greatest earls of his realm. Plus Sir Henry Percy, bastion of the north.

'We issued summons to all earls and some eighty magnates of the realm to prepare for war with the Scots,' de Valence pointed out, as if to say that these six were nothing at all. Edward shifted in his seat, scowling and aching.

Summons to eighty magnates and every earl – even his 13-year-old half-brother, Thomas, Earl of Norfolk – not to mention Ulster and personal, royal-sealed letters to twenty-five rag-arsed Irish chieftains. But the realm's five most powerful and the north's shining star, Percy, had all refused and the gall of it scourged him almost out of his seat.

'When we defeat Bruce, my liege, all matters will be resolved,' de Valence went on, hastily, as if he sensed the withering hope of the King. 'We will have twenty thousand men, including three thousand Welsh, at Berwick by this time next month, even without these foresworn lords.'

With smiths and carpenters, miners and *ingéniateurs*, ships to transport five siege engines and the means to construct an entire windmill sufficient to grind corn for the army. Plus horses – a great mass of horses.

Edward thought sourly of the man who had just left, elegantly dressed, with a plump face that had yet to settle into anything resembling features. But Antonio di Pessagno, the Genoese

94

mercantiler who was as seeming bland as a fresh-laid egg, held the realm of England in his fat, ringed hand, for it was his negotiated loans which were paying for the Invasion.

Edward did not like Pessagno, but the Ordainers – Lancaster, Warwick and the other barons who tried to force him into their way – had banished his old favourites, the Frescobaldi, so he had no choice but to turn to the Genoese. The same earls who ignored him now, Edward brooded, feeling the long, slow burn of anger at that. The same who had contrived in the death of my Gaveston . . .

'They claim', he rasped suddenly, 'what reasons for refusing my summons to defend the realm?'

'That they did not sanction the campaign.'

The answer was a smooth knife-edge that cut de Valence off before he could speak. Hugh Despenser, Earl of Winchester, leaned a little into the honeyed light.

'They say you are in breach of the Ordinances,' he added with a feral smile.

No one spoke, or had to. They all knew the King had deliberately manipulated the affair so that he breached the imposed Ordinances by declaring a campaign against the Scots without the approval of the opposing barons. Honour dictated they should defend the realm, no matter what – but if they agreed, then they supported the King's right to make war on his own, undermining everything they had worked for. Their refusal, however, implied that they were prepared to let the Scots mauraud unchecked over the realm and that did no good to their Ordinance cause.

They were damned if they did and condemned if they didn't, so the King won either way, though he would have preferred to have them give in and send their levies. Still, it was a win all the same and, since Despenser had suggested the idea, he basked in the approval of the tall, droop-eyed Edward while the likes of de Valence and others could only scowl at the favour.

Yet Edward was no fool; Despenser was not a war leader and de Valence, Earl of Pembroke, most assuredly was. Better yet, the Earl hated Lancaster for having seized Gaveston from his custody and executing him out of hand and Edward trusted the loyalty of revenge.

Edward leaned back, well satisfied. All he had to do was march north, to where this upstart Bruce had finally bound himself to a siege at Stirling and could not refuse battle without losing face with his own barons.

'Bring the usurper to battle, defeat him and we win all – roll the main, *nobiles*. Roll the main.'

Roll the main, de Valence thought as the approving murmurs wavered the candle flame in a soft patting like mouse paws massaging the royal ego. But the other side of that dice game was to throw out and lose.

That is why they call it Hazard, he thought.

Crunia, Kingdom of Castile
Feast of St James the Less, May 1314

The port was white and pink and grey, hugged by brown land studded with dusty green pines and cypress – and everywhere the sea, deep green and leaden grey, scarred with thin white crests and forested with swaying masts. Light flitted over it like a bird.

Crunia was the port of pilgrims, those who had wearily travelled from Canterbury down through France and English Gascony into Aragon and Castile and could not face the journey back the same way. The rich, or fortunate beggars, would take ship back to Gascony, or even all the way to England – the same ships which brought the lazy or infirm to walk the last little way to the shrine at Compostella and still claim a shell badge.

Hal stared with bewilderment at them, the halt and twisted, the fat and self-important, shrill beldames and sailors, those who thought they could fool God and those footsore and shining with the fervour of true penitents. He had never seen a foreign land and it made his head swim with a strange fear that Kirkpatrick noted with his sardonic twist of smile.

'Can suck the air from you, can it not,' he said gently and laid a steady hand on the tremble of one shoulder. Hal looked at him, remembering what he had learned of Kirkpatrick's past in the land of Oc, fighting Cathars in a holy crusade. Oc was not so far from here, he thought, though he had trouble with the map of it in his head – trouble, too, with the realization that Kirkpatrick was the closest to a friend he had left other than Sim, who came rolling up the quayside as if summoned.

'No' very holy,' Sim growled, staring at the huddled houses before kneeling and laying a hand flat on the cobbles. 'Mark you, any land is fine after yon ship. Bigod, I can hardly walk straight on the dry.'

No one walked straight on the dry, but Hal tried not to turn and gawp as they helped unload the heavy, precious cargo into the carts they had hired, making it seem as anonymous as dust.

Everyone, pilgrim and prostitute, seemed moulded from another clay entirely, while the stalls were a Merlin's cave of jeweller's work and carpets, tableware worked in silver, glass and crystal, ironwork made like lace.

There were Moors, too, swarthy and robed, turbanned and flashing with teeth and earrings; Hal would not have been surprised to meet a dog-headed man, or a winged gryphon on a leash.

'Are we stayin' the night?' demanded Sim. 'I had a fancy to some comfort and a meat pie.'

'Little comfort in this unholy town,' Kirkpatrick answered grimly, 'and you would boak at the content of such a pie, so it is best we shake this place off our shoes. We will be escorted by the Knights of Alcántara, no less, to a safe wee commanderie some way on the road to Villasirga.'

Hal had seen the Knights arrive, a score of finely mounted men sporting a strange, embellished green cross on their white robes – *argent, a cross fleury vert*, he translated, smiling, as he always did, at the memory of his father who had dinned heraldry into him.

The new Knights were all in maille from head to foot, with little round iron caps and sun-smacked faces that made them almost as dark as the trading Moors, at whom they scowled in an insult that would have had them skewered in Scotland.

'They frown at everyone,' Kirkpatrick answered, when Hal pointed this out, 'save Doña Beatriz.'

It was true enough – the leader of the Knights bowed and fawned on the elegant, cool and sparkling lady, and then was presented to everyone who mattered as 'el caballero Don Saluador', followed by a long string of meaningless sounds which Kirkpatrick said was the man's lineage. Don Saluador looked at everyone as if he had had Sim's old hose shoved under his nose.

'But they hate those ones even more than they hate the Moors,' Kirkpatrick added, nodding towards a group of men shouldering arrogantly through the crowds. Dressed richly, they had faces as blank and haughty as the statues of saints and wore billowing white blazoned with a red cross which looked like a downward pointing dagger.

'*Fitchy*,' Hal said, still dizzy with the sights and smells of it all.

'Just so,' Kirkpatrick confirmed. 'The *cross fitchy* of the Order of Santiago – the wee saint's very own warriors. The Order of Alcántara is so new it squeaks and yon knights never let them forget it.'

'You have it wrangwise,' Sim answered, wiping the sweat from his face, and Kirkpatrick, scowling, turned to him.

'There are others they hate even harder,' Sim went on and nodded to where the black-robed former Templars walked, stiff-legged and ruffed as dogs, refusing to be anonymous or duck under the scorch of stares from all sides. For all that they sported no device, everyone knew them by their very look, though none dared call them out as heretics.

Christ betimes, Hal thought, the world is stuffed with God's warrior monks, and it seems the only fighting they do is against each other.

By the time the carts were loaded and ready, the sun was brassed and high, the road crowded with pilgrims fresh from Mass and still in the mood to sing psalms along the dusty road, as if their piety increased with the level of noise they made.

The locals knew better and sneered, both at the singing of these lazy penitents and their foreigner stupidity at walking out in the midday heat. They did not sneer at the Knights of Alcántara, Hal noted, who were riding out in the midday heat with four carts and a motley of strange foreigners.

Rossal and the others took their leave of de Grafton, who had volunteered to stay with the *Bon Accord*, as if only he was capable of defending it; they needed the ship victualled and ready if they were to succeed, so it seemed sensible – but Hal saw Kirkpatrick frowning thoughtfully over it and wondered at that.

Beyond the port, the air was so clear that it seemed you could see every tree on the foothills that led to the dust-blue horizon etched against the gilding sky. The pilgrims rapidly ran out of enthusiasm for psalms and the column began to shed them like old skin, each one tottering into some panting shade and groaning.

'Fine idea,' Sim declared, mopping his streaming face. 'If I was not perched on a cart, I would be seeking that same shade.'

'You would not,' Kirkpatrick answered grimly and jerked his chin to one side, where distant figures squatted, patient as stones.

'Trailbaston and cut-throats,' he said with a lopsided grin. 'Waiting for dark and the passing of the fighting men to come down and snap up the tired and weary, like owls on mice.'

'Christ betimes, they are robbing pilgrims,' Sim said, outraged.

'So they are – almost. The wee saint's warriors are busy protecting the proper pilgrim route, the Way of St James. Since there are two roads to Santiago, it takes them all their time – though the northern route is used less these days, now that the Moors have been expelled from the road from Aragon to Castile.'

'This is what happens when you try and cheat God,' Hal added with a grin.

He had lost the humour in it by the time the day died in a blood and gold splendour, wiped from his lips by too much heat and dust, the ten different languages that made the psalms a babble, the quarrels that broke out on every halt, the stink that hung with them in the dust.

Hal was sharply aware that this was but a lick of what Crusaders had experienced here and that it was worse by far further south and east, in the Holy Land itself; his estimation of his father went up when he thought of him enduring this in the name of God. By the time they turned off the road and into a tree-shaded avenue, Hal was heartily sick of the Kingdom of Castile and the commanderie of St Felix was a blessed limewashed relief.

Stiff-legged, he climbed off the palfrey he had been given and had it removed by a silent figure, blank and shadowed as the dark which closed on them. Led by flickering torches, Hal and the others were escorted into a large room with a stout door to the right and a curtained archway to the left; there were tables and benches, fresh herbs and straw.

'It is not much,' said a smooth voice, the French accented heavily, 'but it is what we use as bed and board.'

They turned to see a tall man with the Alcántara cross on a white *camilis* that accentuated the dark of his face and the neatly trimmed black beard; his smile was as dazzling as his robe and Doña Beatriz hung off his arm with a familiarity intended to raise the hackles of the black-robed Templars, even if it was only his sister.

'I am Don Guillermo,' he announced, raking them with his

100

grin. 'I assure you, this is really how we live – you see, we can be as austere as Benedictines. Up to a point.'

Rossal, unsmiling, bowed from the neck; the others followed and Hal saw the scowl scarring the face of the German.

'Our thanks for your hospitality and escort. I will see to my charge before prayers.'

'Of course,' Guillermo answered smoothly. 'Be assured, our best men guard those carts.'

'I have no doubt of it,' Rossal answered. He turned to look briefly at Kirkpatrick and then went out, trailed by de Villers. Sim stretched noisily and farted.

'Not a bad lodging, mark you,' he declared, glancing at the wall whose bare, rough whiteness was broken by a trellis of poles supporting a short walkway reached by an arched doorway. It was the height of two tall men from the floor.

'A gallery for minstrels,' he said and grinned. 'Some entertainment later, eh, lads?'

In a commanderie of a religious Order? Hal looked at Kirkpatrick, who held the gaze for a moment, and then moved to the nearest door, which was beneath the gallery. It was clearly locked. The curtained archway on the other side of the room led to some steps and Kirkpatrick was sure they reached up to a belltower he had seen on the way in.

'As neat a prison as any you will see,' he offered to the returned Rossal, who nodded grimly, and then turned to the door he had been escorted through; the rattle of the locking bar was clear to everyone and he frowned.

'Where is Brother Widikind?'

The Lothians
At the same time

They roared through the March, looting and burning and with no care now that they had rid themselves of the Welsh.

Using fire, using blade, using lies and deceit, they harried the wee rickle of fields and cruck houses in Byres, Heriot, Ratho and Ladyset. They felled ramparts and broke wooden walls, ravaged the Pinkney stronghold at Ballencrieff and showed their faces to the frightened burghers of Haddington.

Fell and bloody were the riders of Black James Douglas, who gorged on fire and sword and pain and never seemed to have enough of it to drive out the hatred he felt for all that had been taken from him.

Then they came down on the weekly market at Seton, because that lord was firmly in the English camp and Black Jamie wanted him scorched for it. They rampaged through the screamers, scattering them with half-mocking snarls and a waved blade. There was little of fodder anywhere, Dog Boy noted, and Jamie nodded, pointing to the church.

'You can rely on God to make sure of his tithe,' he said, and bellowed at the others to be quick and to take only the peas and barley, the live chooks and the dead coneys.

They were good, too, careful when loading the stolen eggs and ignoring trinkets – well, in the main. Everyone took a little something, as a keepsake or a token for a woman some-where, while a bolt of new cloth was blanket and cloak both on a bad night.

Jamie and Dog Boy rode up to the stout-walled tithe barn and Dog Boy skipped off the garron and kicked open the double doors; it was an echoing hall, bare even of mice, and Jamie's eyebrows went up at that. At the nearby church, the door of it clearly barred from the inside, the priest stood outside, defiant chin raised.

'The silver is buried,' he said bitterly, 'and you are ower late to this feast – others have beaten you.'

Jamie, leaning forward on the pommel, calm as you please, offered the man a smile and a lisping greeting in good Latin.

'Father Peter,' the priest replied, clearly unable to speak the tongue, which Dog Boy knew was common enough among parish priests, who understood only the rote of services and would not know Barabbas from Barnabas.

'Your wealth is safe enough – silver-gilt chalice, is it?' Jamie replied easily. 'A pyx, of course – silver or ivory? A silver-gilt chrismatory, a thurible, three cruets and an osculatorium.'

Dog Boy turned to stare in wonder at Jamie, but the priest was unimpressed.

'One cruet, for we are not rich here. And a pewter ciborium, which you forgot – but since this is the minimum furnishing for a house of God, as any learned man knows, I do not consider you to have the power of Seeing.'

'God forbid,' Dog Boy offered and everyone crossed themselves.

'These others who came', Jamie went on lightly, 'were equally restrained, it appears, and only took fodder – unless you have also hidden the contents of your tithe barn.'

'I wish it were so. They sought food only, as you do,' the priest replied coldly. 'Came out of Berwick, but were no skilled raiders, only poor folk starving in that place.'

'Berwick . . .'

Dog Boy knew why Jamie was so thoughtful. Berwick was a long way off and if the residents were scourging the country from that distance, then they were starving right enough. Which was news enough for Black Sir James to smile, wish the priest well – and his women and weans, too, which brought a scowl, but no denial.

It was all friendly enough, but Dog Boy threw the first torch that fired every house in the vill, so that they rode away from it leaving flames and weeping and sullen stares in the smoke. I am filled to the brim with shrieks and embers, Dog Boy thought, and wondered if there would ever be an end.

He was called Brother Amicus, though there was nothing friendly about him.

'You should repent and confess your sins, Brother,' he spat. 'If you go unshriven, you go to Hell, to be broken on the wheel by foul demons, smashed over and over for the sin of pride. You will be thrown into freezing water until you scream for your arrogance. You will be dismembered alive by gibbering imps armed with dull knives for your impiety, thrown into a boiling pit of molten gold for your pride, forced to eat rats, toads and snakes in remembrance of your greed.'

He paused, breathing heavily and frothing at the corners of his mouth.

Widikind laughed through his burst lips, the words coming slowly because his arms were twisted up behind him and fastened by chains, which suspended his whole weight and constricted his breathing. He was naked and streaked with his own and other people's foulness.

His voice came in spurts for he found it hard to get air into his flattened lungs – but he had breath enough for this.

'You may dream of it, torturer. I have suffered all that and more in the service of God and the Temple, even to the eating of toads and snakes. However, I am sure you can verify your visions – I will be seeing you in Hell, certes.'

The Inquisitor scowled and turned away, leaving Widikind in his pain. The start of it had been the blow, sharp and sudden, which had whirled stars into him as he went to check the carts. Even as he went down, he knew what it was, even if he did not quite know who.

He learned that soon enough, knew it even when he could not raise his head to look – her perfume, spiced and insidious as a snake's coils, left him in no doubt as he hung in the shadow-flickering room.

'You would do well to speak, Templar,' Doña Beatriz said softly. 'My brother needs what you know and he will not be kind.'

Widikind was more ashamed of his nakedness than concerned for future agonies, but he knew now that his soul was safe and he only laughed; he knew, by the stiffness in her body, that she was irritated, felt the grip in his beard as his head was raised. The Moor, her servant, held Widikind's stained beard in one fist so that he could see both their faces; his was unsmiling as a stone, but hers was a blaze of fury.

'You will speak,' she said, her voice a razor, and smiled like a sweet sin as she waved another man into Widikind's eyeline. This one was lean, grizzled and seemed nothing – until you looked in his eyes. There was nothing in them at all, save a bland, studied interest and Widikind knew what he was at once.

'This is Rafiq,' Doña Beatriz said. '*Buscador de demonios*.'

She turned away and left. For a moment, Piculph hesitated, flicking his eyes sideways to the blank-eyed Rafiq, and then he relinquished his grip, so that Widikind's head fell forward and he lost sight of them all.

But he was aware of Piculph's going, more aware still of the one they called 'seeker of devils' stepping close; Widikind heard him crooning, soft and melodious as a monk at plainchant, wondered if it was a psalm against evil, or a spell.

He would have been surprised to discover that it was a lullaby. He was not surprised to discover that Rafiq was an expert and that his skill was in pain. He hoped that he had been missed, though he expected no rescue, for the others would now have their fears confirmed.

He would have been gratified to hear them discuss his absence.

'It seems your fears may be justified,' Rossal admitted grudgingly to Kirkpatrick. 'In which case, we should take some precautions.'

'What is happening?' demanded Sim, an eyeblink before Hal did. Rossal issued crisp orders and the other two began turning tables up on their ends.

'I was of the opinion', Kirkpatrick answered slowly, 'that this Guillermo and his lady sister would make some move against us.'

'The gold . . .'

'Aye, just so.'

There was no urgency in the man, nor in Rossal now that the tables had been upended like a siege pavise, and Hal could not understand why this Guillermo and his sister should wish to attack them – and why everyone seemed acceptingly calm about it. He said so and Rossal clapped him on the shoulder.

'In a moment, we will know whether this Guillermo is to be trusted.'

'Look to your weapons, mark you, in case he cannot,' Kirkpatrick added, 'but keep behind our defences – I am sure he has used that wee minstrel gallery before this.'

Minstrel gallery, Hal thought. And pigs have wings.

'If they mean to red-murder us and steal the gold,' Sim blustered, confused and angry at the feeling of it, 'then we should not be sittin' here like a set mill.'

'Doucelike, Sim Craw,' Kirkpatrick said, laying a hand on the man's big shoulder and smiling into the bristle of his beard. 'I may have it wrangwise. We might be locked in for our own safety.'

'Pigs have wings,' Hal muttered.

The Seeker of Demons was Satan's own creation, Widikind was sure of it. He caressed with blades, peeling back skin until the pain was so burning intense that the German felt the rawness like ice. He worked through the long hours, while Widikind hung and dripped sweat, blood and vomit.

At some point – Widikind did not know day from night

– the Seeker of Demons broke off to eat bread and cheese and refresh himself with wine, and began on the hot irons.

The smell of his own flesh roasting nauseated Widikind, but he swallowed it rather than give the torturer the satisfaction of knowing it. But this time the pain was enough to make him call to God, to the Virgin, and he found himself babbling in German. But he knew what he said and it was nothing they wanted or could use.

He slipped into a grey veiled world, was aware of figures moving in it and recognized the perfume of the lady. The man with her, his voice clearly used to command, snapped at another, his voice sharp and grating with annoyance, and the man's soothing assurances confirmed him as Brother Amicus, who called the one he spoke to 'Don Guillermo'.

He heard Guillermo speak again, softer this time and in French, rather than the elegant Castilian of the court.

'This de Grafton – is he to be trusted?'

'No, darling brother, but he can be relied on to serve our interests as long as he is serving his own.'

Doña Beatriz's voice was a sneer and Widikind heard her brother laugh.

'Go to Crunia. Search the ship – the treasure must be there. Send word in a hurry.'

'What of the crew?'

There was silence, which was answer enough.

Afterwards – it might have been a minute, an hour or a week – the Seeker of Demons took Widikind's eye with a white-hot iron, a lancing shriek of agony that had him bucking and twisting as he dangled in chains, feeling his flesh bubble and dissolve in the heat, pouring down his cheek, sizzling like meat on a skewer.

He surfaced from the cool dark of oblivion into the agony of life.

'Where is the Templar treasure?'

It was the first thing the Seeker of Demons had asked, the

107

first time he had spoken and the only sound he had made other than the crooning gentleness of song.

Widikind, who wondered what he had babbled while his mind cowered elsewhere, grinned a bloody grin, for he knew by the question that he had said nothing of value. He remembered the feeling of his own flesh melting on his cheek like gold and what Brother Amicus had promised. For his pride. He was proud of resisting, yet aware that such arrogance was unfit for a Templar, proscribed or no.

Yet he could not resist it.

'Found any demons?' he mushed and laughed his way back to the coverlet of dark.

The sluice of cold water slashed him into the light again, into the world of pain the torturer had made with vicious beatings. He could feel his arms and realized he had been lowered a little and refastened so that his hands were now bound with rope rather than chain and the suspension on his dangling arms could be alleviated if he raised himself on the balls of his feet.

Whose toes had been broken, so that doing so seared agony through him like a knife.

He raised his wobbling head and stared with his one good eye into the face of the torturer and saw no pleasure in the other's witnessing of his realization. Which was, he thought, worse than a leering grin; Widikind let his head loll, though he could see the man's face through the spider-legs of his remaining lashes.

The Seeker of Demons, his face still blank, touched the white-hot iron to Widikind's abdomen and, for the first time, showed emotion: surprise at the lack of response.

He wonders if he has gone too far, Widikind thought.

'Where is the Templar treasure?'

Widikind heard the querulous note in his voice and knew it was time. He wanted him near, wanted him close with his hot iron. He felt fingers at his neck, checking pulse, felt the length of forearm on his chest, so he knew where the Seeker of Demons stood. He was a Knight of the Temple and had the power of God still with him . . .

He swept his legs up and locked them round the man's waist, crossing his ankles until his broken feet flared howls from him; he welcomed the pain, for there was more triumph and anger in it now and the agony fuelled his strength like fire in his veins. God give me strength . . .

The man was strong but Widikind had trained every day for years in every facet of horsemanship; his feet were broken, but the thighs and calves on him were crippling and the Seeker of Demons arched and shrieked, unable to break free. He tried to beat Widikind with his one free hand, the one with the hot iron in it, but each time he began, Widikind crushed him further until something snapped. The man twisted and screamed.

'That was a rib breaking,' Widikind told him, so close that the blood from his cracking lips spotted the Seeker of Demons's cheek. 'There will be more if you do not do as I say. If you resist me further, I will break your back and you will never stand unaided again.'

'Let . . . me. . .'

'No.'

They strained, panting like dogs.

'Raise the iron,' Widikind hoarsed at him, panting close to the man's ear, feeling the rank fear-sweat of him cinched tight and obscene as a lover. 'Raise it slowly and touch it to the ropes on my wrist. If you do anything else, I will crack all feeling from your back, so that you will drag yourself around with padded rags on your hands the rest of your short and miserable life.'

The torturer was hovering at the edge of fainting, so the cooling red tip of the iron wavered back and forth, searing Widikind's flesh as it charred through the rope. The parting brought them crashing down, but Widikind was ready for it, sprang free, grabbed the iron and smashed it on the Seeker of Demons's head.

He did it twice more before the pain in his feet seemed to drive up into the core of him and he fell over into emptiness. When he woke, he stared up into a sweat-gleamed familiar face, whose wild eyes looked at the splintered gourd that was the head of the torturer, then into Widkind's melted ruin of a face.

Piculph, the German thought and almost sobbed with how close he had come to escape. The Moor licked his lips, stuck out a hand and hauled Widikind to his agony of broken feet.

'Move,' he said in good French, 'if you want to live.'

There was a thump and a crash which brought heads up. Then came the unmistakable sound of the bar being lifted from the far side of the door and, even as they crouched and lifted their weapons, the door flung open and a body fell in.

For a moment, no one moved – and then everyone did. De Bissot and Kirkpatrick sprang to the body, Hal and de Villers moved to the open door, beyond which lay the guard, his head cracked and leaking over the flagstones; Sim covered the gallery, just in case. But the hissed, broken, bubbling voice stopped them all.

'Stay,' Widikind managed. 'Piculph says there is no way we can escape this way, so he brought me here. Listen closely – I have much to tell and no time left to tell it.'

He spoke, hoarse and swift and laid out what he knew. When his voice trailed off, de Bissot straightened and looked at Kirkpatrick.

'You were right.'

'Bar the door,' Hal advised and they fell to it, moving the heavy trestles. Then they shifted the lolling Widikind, his naked, streaked body trailing fluids like a bad winesack; Kirkpatrick did not say it, but he thought the man was not long for this world. Unless they could find a way out of this place, at once prison and fortress, none of them were.

'This Guillermo will come to talk soon,' Kirkpatrick informed everyone with certainty. 'He will threaten and cajole. After that will come the hard part.'

Hal was on the point of demanding to know the whole of it, annoyed at being kept so in the dark, but Kirkpatrick's prophecy was proved true with the innocuous twitch of the hanging over the gallery entrance. Sim, watching carefully, called the warning.

'Cover,' he snapped and Hal, glancing backwards as he scurried behind a table, saw the figures move smoothly out on to the gallery, latchbows ready. Behind them came the tall, saturnine figure of Guillermo, a scowl on his handsome face.

'Ach,' Sim declared with disgust, cranking the arbalest like a madman. 'There are times when I wish you were no' as sharp in your thinkin', Kirkpatrick, but I prig the blissin' o' the blue heaven on you for it.'

'God be praised,' Kirkpatrick answered piously.

'For ever and ever.'

Guillermo stared down at them and silence fell, broken only by the harsh of breathing and the clank of Sim resting his arbalest on a steadying edge. That slight sound seemed to break the moment.

'You would be wise not to trigger that monster,' Guillermo warned. 'Those tables will not stand against the quarrels from my own bows at this range.'

'You dare not kill us,' Rossal said quietly and stepped from behind cover. Hal moved as if to drag him back and felt Kirkpatrick's hand on his forearm; when he looked, he was given a quiet smile and a shake of the head, which only left him more bewildered than ever.

'You do not know which of us holds the secret of the treasure you seek,' Rossal went on, 'now that you have discovered the truth.'

Hal's gaze was wide-eyed, matched only by Sim, but

Kirkpatrick merely flashed them a smile and put his fingers to his lips.

'Sand,' Guillermo declared with disgust. 'Boxes of sand. And some lead for the weight. Clever. Now you will tell us where you have hidden the treasure. You will do this or suffer.'

'You should not', Rossal flung back, 'have left the likes of us our arms, for you cannot inflict suffering without a fight and we will neither step back nor surrender, so you will have to kill us. You cannot do that, my lord, if you want the secret you seek. So your threats are an empty mistake. And not nearly as bad as the one which led you to this betrayal. You are a serpent in Eden, my lord, whose own bite will be fatal for you.'

'Three Poor Knights,' Guillermo sneered, 'one half-dead already. And three old men. A jester with a bladder on a stick could overpower you.'

'Bigod!' Sim bellowed. 'I will send a bolt to rip away his liver and lights.' He was held back only by the combined efforts of Kirkpatrick and Hal and eventually forced silent.

'You have one hour to consider matters,' Guillermo declared, unfolding his arms and sweeping back through the archway, the two archers filtering warily after him.

The breath came out of them sudden and together, so that it sounded like a small wind; Kirkpatrick and Hal let go of Sim, who shook himself angrily, like a bristling dog.

'You had better explain this,' Hal said wearily to Kirkpatrick, 'for it seems to me everyone kens the meat of it save myself and Sim. I am sick of your close mouth, Kirkpatrick, particularly when you drag me and those I care for by your side.'

'Guillermo is an ambitious wee scrauchle,' Kirkpatrick answered blandly, ignoring Hal's scowls, 'winsome, but with a wanthrifty soul, whose sister is as black-avowed as he is. Guillermo wants to be Grand Master of his Order and the one who occupies that space is no capering fool – his name is Ruy Vaz and he had his suspicions.'

'He might well be behind it,' Hal pointed out and Rossal shook his head, a quiet, sad smile lifting the black beard.

'Ruy Vaz is the one who sent warning to us and a solution. The warning came by one of his agents, one close to the sister.'

'Piculph,' Sim declared, remembering the hissed revelations of Widikind; all heads turned to where the German, bundled in a cloak, lay trembling and rolling-eyed. Dying, Hal thought dully.

'So it appears, though we were not told of it,' Kirkpatrick went on. 'But we devised this cheatry about the gold. Even sent out decoy ships as if it was real.'

'It is fake?' Sim demanded truculently. 'We came all this way – I boaked up my guts for a ruse?'

'The fish send their thanks,' de Villers declared, grinning as he arranged the trestles round the door leading to the belltower.

'The treasure is here,' Rossal answered before Sim bubbled up, 'and we must get it to Ruy Vaz to exchange for the weapons we have promised King Robert.'

'It is not in the carts,' Kirkpatrick explained, seeing Hal's bewilderment, 'nor is it on the ship, which Guillermo suspects and will have confirmed. Widikind—'

'Brother Widikind has said nothing,' Rossal interrupted sharply. 'Else Guillermo would know the truth of matters. He is no fool, all the same, and will work to the meat of it in the end. Even without Brother Widikind.'

Hal heard the bitter sadness in his voice and realized that de Bissot already considered Widikind as dead. Worse occurred to him as he recalled the German's halting last words.

'The others have been taken,' he said. 'We have no ship, then, and if we have a treasure as you say I cannot see how it is to be got to this Ruy Vaz, nor the weapons all the way back to King Robert.'

He stopped, seeing Rossal and de Villers scramble out of

their black priests's robes, so that they stood in white under-shirts, each with a small red cross on the breast. Rossal hauled out a leather pouch and handed it to Kirkpatrick.

'The treasure,' he declared solemnly, and leaned closer, so that his next words were low and hissed.

'*Ordo ex chao*,' he said and Kirkpatrick took the pouch, nodded and stuffed it inside his own tunic.

'It is my task to get to Ruy Vaz,' he said lightly, grinning at Hal and Sim. 'It is yours to get back to the coast and find out what has happened to the *Bon Accord*. De Grafton is the traitor who nearly did for Somhairl.'

He broke off and shook his head in genuine sorrow.

'He has fallen a long way from grace. He may well now have thrown in his lot with Guillermo and his sister. Whether de Grafton has shackled himself to her or not, he is an agent of the English, I am sure of it.'

'Christ betimes, how are we to achieve any of this?' roared Sim, scrubbing his head with confusion. 'You have contrived to fasten us up in a prison, Kirkpatrick.'

'Mind yer station, ye moudiewart,' Kirkpatrick replied, his wry smile balming the sting of it. 'I hope you are as clever at getting down a long drop as you are at scaling one, Sim Craw. I will need your belts and those black robes, for we do not have one of your cunning ladders.'

De Villers returned, grim and spade-bearded, to tell them he had muffled the bell with his own small clothes, cut the long bell rope and refastened it securely.

'It is short,' he replied tersely and Hal knew what they were about to do, for he had seen the commanderie, perched on the edge of a ravine: the belltower rope would lead to the base of the rock it was built on and then there would be another drop, a good ten ells, to the bottom of the brush-choked ravine. A man could break every limb in such a fall. A man could break his head.

'The belts and cloth strips should make the difference,'

Kirkpatrick said cheerily and Hal looked at him; they were three men past their prime for hand-over-hand descents down makeshift ropes and his look said it all.

Almost all. Sim, as ever, had his own thoughts on the drop and the dark.

'God be praised,' he declared piously and crossed himself.

'For ever and ever.'

Rossal came to Hal, looming sudden as a wraith.

'Brother de Grafton', he said, his French soft and sibilant, 'was released into the care of Sir Henry Percy after the Order was proscribed in England and all Templars arrested. It is possible that he has renounced his vows to God in favour of King Edward, but probably works only for Percy. De Grafton was the only one of us who did not know the truth of the Templar treasure. Like this Guillermo and his sister, he believed that the wealth was boxed and in our carts.'

Hal nodded, frowning and trying hard to keep pace with it all. Guillermo, if he had any sense at all, would wonder where the boxed treasure had vanished. If not here, or on the ship, it could only have been spirited away on a rest halt and that under the eyes of the escorting knights.

Rossal nodded at this, his smile a sardonic twist in the dim.

'De Grafton will know by now, for he is of the Order. He may even tell Guillermo the truth of it, though I am sure he will look for his own advantage first. If he does not tell, Guillermo will be left wondering. We are the Templars, after all, who worship Baphomet and have strange powers. Who is to say what spells such magi could cast on the eyes and minds of men? Or even on gold.'

'If you have one to make us fly, now is the time to conjure it up,' Sim Craw growled. 'Better still, turn us invisible.'

'God be praised,' Rossal answered, cross-signing Sim's blasphemy away.

'For ever and ever,' Hal intoned frostily, glaring at the unrepentant Sim. Then he looked at Rossal. 'Mark you, he

115

has a point – Guillermo is not so much of a fool that he will have forgot to have the tower surrounded.'

'Not down in that ravine,' Kirkpatrick answered, bustling up. 'Mak' haste – we have little time.'

'They will expect us to try an escape,' Hal persisted and Rossal laid a hand on his arm.

'With the greatest of respect,' he said, 'they consider you three old men of little worth. It is the Templars they want and myself in particular. As long as they see us here, that is what they will fix on.'

The sick lurch of it reeled Hal sideways; he had not considered what the Order knights would do and realized it now, all in a rush.

'We are the last Templars,' Rossal declared simply. Nearby, faint as a moth's breath, came the sound of de Villers praying. *Non nobis, non nobis, Domine, sed nomini tuo da gloriam . . .* not to us, not to us, O Lord, but to Your Name give glory.

Rossal rolled his shoulders a little.

'We will fight them in the narrow door and up the steps to the tower. It will take them a long time to overcome us and they must try and take at least one of us alive, in order to question.'

He nodded to each of them.

'You will have the night, perhaps more if God is with us. Then they will come after you.'

Stunned, they watched him move away to kneel with the others. Kirkpatrick cleared his throat and exchanged glances with Hal.

'Defending the treasure and the honour of his Order to the end,' he growled. 'No better way to end it.'

Hal heard the gruffness tremble all the same and remembered that Kirkpatrick owed his life twice to the intervention of Rossal de Bissot. He followed the man up the steps, with Sim grunting behind him. At the top, panting, Sim rounded on Kirkpatrick.

'Whaur's the treasure?'

Sim's truculent demand was a blot in the mirror of the moment.

'Seems to me,' he went on sullenly, 'you are placing a deal of trust in this Ruy Vaz.'

'The Grand Master of Alcántara has flushed out his traitor,' Kirkpatrick declared, 'who thinks Templar treasure can be lifted and weighed in boxes. Ruy Vaz kens the truth of matters.'

'I wish I did,' Sim muttered. 'Are you payin' for good King Robert's armoury with the blessings of God?'

'No,' Hal said, remembering the pouch and the whisper: *Ordo ex chao*. Order out of chaos. A fitting password to go with the Templar jetton. He explained it to Sim, who also remembered it from the time they had ransomed Isabel using one – more years ago now than either of them cared to recall.

A tally note for sums deposited elsewhere, it could be presented, together with the secret word known only to the deliverer and the recipient, in exchange for all or part of the sum. There was no gold in boxes or anywhere else, only a slip of scribbled parchment and a few spoken words.

'There is a fearsome sum on this wee *jetton* tally note, stamped by the Templar seal and the Schiarizzi mercantilers of the Italies,' Kirkpatrick declared, patting his tunic where the pouch was hidden. 'One of those merchants waits in Villasirga with Ruy Vaz and when he gets this wee scrap o' paper and the secret word, he will nod and Ruy Vaz will know his money is assured.'

Sim worried it in his head, licked his lips and nodded uncertainly. Once he would have crossed himself and spat over his shoulder at this, as clear an indication of unholy magic as there could be – how else could the Templars transfer a man's coin from one place to another, unseen and unheard?

'You must get to the port and see to the crew and the ship,' Kirkpatrick went on, grim as old rock. 'When I bring this to Ruy Vaz, he will scourge Guillermo and his supporters and we are assured of weapons and armour – but we still need to bring them safe to King Robert.'

Kirkpatrick's eyes and sweat-sheened face seemed to gleam in the dark and the snake-hiss slither of the rope going over the side was loud. For a moment, Hal saw de Bissot and Kirkpatrick lock eyes with one another, saw the jaw muscles work Kirkpatrick's beard. Then Kirkpatrick nodded once and turned away; he and Hal clasped wrist to wrist, brief and wordless, and Kirkpatrick, grunting with effort, levered himself over the belltower lip, hung for a moment and was gone.

Blinking sweat from his eyes and rubbing his palms, Hal remembered when he, Isabel and Sim had watched Dog Boy perform the same feat out of the window of a besieged Herdmanston. The three of them had had to lie together on the great box bed to stop it being dragged across the floor by the makeshift rope Dog Boy hung from; Isabel, smiling bright, had sworn them all to secrecy about her lying abed with the pair of them, easing the strain on the moment if not the rope.

Hal blinked back to the present, helped Sim grunt and pech his way over the lip and was not sure the big man had the strength of arm and leg to get him all the way down. Still, he heard no wild cry and thump so thought it went fine enough.

He wondered if he had that strength himself and was taking up the rope when a soft voice stopped him; he turned to see Rossal de Bissot, a shadow at the top of the belltower stairs.

'Take this,' the Templar said, holding out his sword, 'and give me your own. I would not see this fall into the hands of Guillermo and can think of no one better to wield it with honour. You are a Sientcler, after all.'

Numbed and dumb, Hal took the sword and handed over his own; the new one felt heavier, though it slid into his sheath easily enough – all but a fingerwidth of blade below the hilt.

'Hubris,' Rossal declared with a smile like a sickle moon in the dark. 'That sword is longer, heavier and has more decoration on it than was ever proper for a Poor Knight.'

'I am honoured to wield it – though you put a deal of faith in the Sientcler name,' Hal growled, dry-mouthed with the moment and aware, yet again, of that peculiar Sientcler connection with the Order, so that every member of that family seemed to have drunk from the Grail itself. And all because a female ancestor had once been married to Hugues de Payens, the founder.

'You will not disgrace the blade,' Rossal answered and Hal was not sure whether it was a statement or a command. Below, he heard de Villers chanting: *Vade retro Satana, nunquam suade mihi vana* – begone Satan, never suggest to me thy vanities.

He knew the Knight was facing his own fear and desire for life, rejecting any possibility of salvation. Preparing to die.

Hal glanced at de Bissot and saw nothing of fear or regret, only a slight sadness when the man revealed that Widikind had already died. The Templar raised his hand in a final salute and was gone like a wraith.

Hal stood for a moment, and then crossed to the stone lip, wriggled his hips to the balance point and, with a final fervent prayer for his own salvation, slithered over the edge.

Vade retro Satana, he heard as he scrabbled in a blind sweat for footholds. *Ipse venena bibas*. Begone Satan. Drink thou thine own poison.

Hal, his hands straining, the sweat in his eyes, wondered how in the name of all Hell had Dog Boy ever managed this.

ISABEL

Now am I ripe in the understanding of what the love of God means. You sent me the little nun, the one called Constance, who whispered to me briefly, so briefly I hardly believed I had heard it all. He is free, she said to me. Roxburgh is taken and Hal is free. Blessed is the Lord.

CHAPTER SIX

Chapel of St Mary and the Holy Cross, Lothian
Feast of the Invention of the Cross, May 1314

Dog Boy wondered how he had done it. He had never killed a woman before and felt strange about the fact of it, even though it had not been deliberate.

They had caught the raiders off guard; those who didn't have their thumbs up their hurdies were howkin' lumps of fresh meat out of a boiling pot with their stolen livestock lowing and cropping grass nearby – the lucky beasts that were not jointed and bloody under sacking in the carts.

Hunger was the reason the men had raided out so far and it had been their ruin, for they should just have taken their scourings and run for it, not stopped to boil beef. But there were no skilled fighting men here, only shoemakers and fishmongers, tanners and labourers from Berwick, out on a desperate herschip for supplies because none were coming up from the south and bread was ten times the usual price.

The fact that they raided into the lands of the Earl of Dunbar, who was on their side, did not matter to them when their bellies were notched to their backbones. The fact that they were eating the badly boiled kine of the lord of Seton, another ally, did not count one whit.

Dog Boy was of the opinion that they should have left the raiders alone, since they were doing Black Jamie's band a service with their ravaging and, besides, most were Lothian men themselves. Some of them, it was clear, knew one end of a spear from the other and probably served in the Berwick town garrison. They might have kin standing with the army sieging Stirling for the Bruce. Some might even have kin among the men here.

The Black considered Dog Boy when he had voiced this in the growing dark, frowning to show he was giving it serious thought, because that last part had made his men think. No one was fooled as to what he would decide in the end, all the same.

After a long moment of considered mummery, he had shrugged and met the knowing, feral grins of the others with one of his own.

'As you ken, I hate the Welsh worse than the English and God will stand witness that I truly hate the English.'

He paused for the effect of it.

'But I hate yon Plantagenet Scots worse than either.'

'Is there any your lordship likes?' asked a voice, daring in the dim. Patrick, Dog Boy thought. It will be Patrick and the mouth that will get him hanged this day or the next.

'I am not overfond of you,' Jamie Douglas answered, soft and sibilant. 'But if you fasten your lip and follow where I lead, you will earn my liking by and by.'

The laughter was quiet and knowing, from men willing to follow the Black anywhere so that those left holding the horses were sullen at being left out of it. The others filtered a little closer to the red flowers of enemy flame, creeping like foxes on a coop; the Black shrilled out a piercing whistle and they rushed down on ragged men, blowing on barely cooked lumps of meat to cool them enough to cram down their throats.

No finesse, no spearwork in the tight formations they had been drilling in for weeks, just a slavering, howling madness of long knives and little axes, a growling rush that came up between tethered horses, Jamie bawling to 'look out for rope'.

Dog Boy was so busy watching for the thin sliver of dark that would betray the horse tether, belly height and as good as a gate, that he did not realize these men had staked their horses to their own reins until he tripped on one of the pegs and fell, sprawling like a new-born calf to roll almost to the feet of an astonished man.

Gaping, the half-raw beef falling slowly from his open mouth, the man was so stunned that Dog Boy was able to spring to his feet, slashing with the little axe; that woke the man up and he fell back, screaming a spittled cream of pink froth, scrabbling away from this horror.

Dog Boy followed, battering him with the axe, hearing the flung-up forearm crack, the shriek of the man as the blade chopped lumps off his hands, flailing like desperate bird wings to ward off the swings to his head.

A blow finally cracked his skull and he rolled away, moaning; Dog Boy saw a flicker among the mad, dancing shadows and screams around him and half turned into the snarl of a new opponent, a rusted sword up and falling on him.

He jigged sideways, fell into the man and heard the long puffed roar of the air being driven out. Staggering, he had time to recover and backhand a swipe with the axe, for the man was on his knees and trying to suck in breath from lungs that were not working. The blow slipped the top of his head off, neat as tapping out a boiled egg, but Dog Boy had no time to admire the work of it; another snarler was coming from his left.

He flung the axe, watched it whirl, saw the man jerk his head sideways so that the weapon whined past his ear and struck the woman behind him in the chest, a dull thump Dog Boy could hear above the rest of the howling din.

He had time to see the woman fold round the blow like a half-empty bag – and then the man he had missed was on him, slashing right and left with a long knife as notched as a broken dyke.

Dog Boy only had the estoc left. That and the axe were the preferred weapons of men who stood in tight spear ranks, for when you dropped the spear and went for the fallen men-at-arms, you wanted a blade to bash in a face unprotected by a fancy bucket helm, or a thin flat needle to shove through the eyeslit of one that was.

The man Dog Boy faced was not a fancy man-at-arms, with maille and a bucket helm, though he dreamed of it, Dog Boy was sure. Instead, he was a garrison man in hodden grey, whose metal-flaked leather jack lay somewhere nearby with his iron hat and who had snatched out the knife because he had nothing else to hand.

He would be good at standing gate guard, or raiding the defenceless, Dog Boy thought, crabbing round in a half-circle, but he is no match for a good knifer in a deadly wee jig such as this. He said so and the man already knew it, licked his dry lips and kept his eyes fixed on Dog Boy's blade as if the winking light fascinated him.

Should be watching my eyes, as I watch his, Dog Boy thought. Yet it was Dog Boy who made the mistake; he heard the woman gasp and cry out, the one who had taken his axe in the chest with a noise like a stone dropped on a slack drum, and he half turned his head. The man sprang forward and Dog Boy saw it at the last, knew it to be the last – but then the man careered sideways, stood for a moment and shook his head.

'Warra?' he demanded and Dog Boy saw Patrick stare at the back of the man's head where he had thrust his own estoc; then he gazed at the bloody length of thin blade he had shoved into the base of the man's neck and finally, bewildered as to why the man had not gone down like a felled ox, looked at Dog Boy.

'Gurrurr,' the man said, the side of his face gone slack. One eye had drooped almost shut, but he grasped his knife and rushed at Dog Boy. Away sideways, like a mad crab, straight through the fire where he fell over and lay, slobbering softly and smouldering up smoke as his limbs moved pointlessly, still running and not even aware that he lay on his side, burning.

'Nivver seen that afore,' Patrick declared, grinning madly, moving to finish the man. 'Must have cut somethin' loose in his head.'

Dog Boy was only vaguely aware of it, for he was with the woman. She was already dead, blood all over her mouth and her chest cracked inside, for sure. Not old nor young, once pretty and now nothing at all, as if she had never been.

He sat now and looked at where she had lain before the other women – captives, it was clear – came and took her away to be decently buried in the dark. He watched them filter back to the fires while his fingers turned and turned the axe that had killed her. He wondered if she had been kin to the other women, or even known to them.

They were wary, these women, but had nowhere else to go, as they said to Patrick and the others round the fire.

'These yins you slew took us from our hearths,' one declared, a big beldame with arms she could barely fold over her bosoms. 'They were too hungered to bother us much – but it is timely, your arrival.'

'You may not think so,' Leckie's Tam leered loudly, 'for we have already eaten.'

'You daur approach myself an' I will clap yer lugs, you muckhoon',' countered another, equally formidable woman, jutting her chin out defiantly. 'I had thought better of you, with our own menfolk off to the aid of King Robert.'

It could have been true, Dog Boy thought. The ragged-arse folk had never been needed for wars before, since armies were gathered up from tenants and burghers who could afford at least an iron hat and a stout spear. Not now, though. Now there were bare-footed chiels arriving in the siege litter round Stirling at the behest of their lieges, stripping vills and farms bare and looking to be fed and armed and trained, for the call had gone out that

127

the Invader was coming with the biggest host ever seen and their king needed them. That and the ruin war had made of their lives made most of them bring their families, following their own stolen fodder and cattle in the hope of leaching a little of it back.

'Aye, weel, we are braw, brave fighters for the King,' Rowty Adam declared to the women, 'so what you give to us, as it were, is no loss to your menfolk and a service to His Grace, King Robert.'

'There will be no harm done to you,' said a firm voice and Jamie stepped in to be blooded by firelight, his black dags of hair down round his cheeks. He put one foot up on a log bench and neck-bowed politely to the big beldame with the bosoms. 'You have the word of Sir James Douglas on it.'

You could see men's crests fall at the sound of that, but no one as much as whispered against it, while the big beldame grew red in the face and the other women simpered. Dog Boy was sure any one of them, gripped by an arm and led into the dark by the Black Douglas, would have gone eagerly, swaying her hips and with no thought of her missing man.

'Weel,' Leckie's Tam said bitterly when Jamie had gone, 'since the Black has put the reins on us, it seems we will have need of entertaining ourselves – a tale it is and your turn to tell it, Parcy Dodd.'

Dog Boy sat and twirled the axe as Parcy Dodd began his tale, thinking on how he had once sat with Bruce himself, before he was king and a wheen of years since. They had discussed the merits of knightly vows and Bruce had been drunk. 'Nivver violet a lady,' Dog Boy had said then, for he had been younger and more stupid; well, younger, at least.

He glanced to where the dead woman had lain, the stain on the grass merely one more shadow in the shadows. He had 'violeted' a lady now and though it was more than stupid to dwell on it, he thought he could feel the stain on him, as if he had foresworn some knightly vows.

'So,' Parcy Dodd was saying, 'I am stravaigin' with Ill-Made Jock, when—'

'Ill-Made?'

They all turned to Dog Boy and Parcy, flustered and left threadless in his tale, blinked once or twice.

'Aye – him who was with Bangtail Hob when he was murdered by the Wallace . . .'

He tailed off, aware of the frantic, silent eyes like head-shakes; he sat with the air of a man who had plootered into a sucking bog and could neither go forward nor back.

'That was me that was with Hob,' Dog Boy said, bitter with the awareness that Parcy did not, in fact, know Ill-Made and had probably never met him. 'Ill-Made died at Herdmanston, during the siege of it. Button your lip on folk ye never knew.'

'Aye, aye,' Parcy answered suddenly and Leckie's Tam hauled him free of the morass with a joke and the conversation flowed shakily back.

'You are ower harsh,' said a voice and Dog Boy turned into Jamie Douglas's half-amused stare. 'He only gilded his tale a wee bit, with some name he thought the others would recall.'

'Ill-Made?' Dog Boy answered, bewildered, and Jamie chuckled and clapped him on the shoulder.

'Ill-Made Jock, Bangtail Hob, Sir Hal Sientcler,' Jamie recited. 'All famous men who fought with the Wallace and some now with the King.'

Then, seeing the bemused stare persist, he leaned a little closer.

'Yourself, Aleysandir of Herdmanston,' he declared with a wry grin. 'A legend, with a name folk huddle closer to, as if they can take some heat and comfort out of it, like a good fire.'

Stunned, Dog Boy could only sit and think about Ill-Made Jock, who had died coughing in his own blood while folk hammered axes on the door of Herdmanston. He had not looked anything like a hero all the long, sore time he took doing it.

Now he is a hero warrior of the Kingdom. Like Aleysandir of Herdmanston.

I am not, neither one nor the other. I am Dog Boy, worn to a nub by war and who has just 'violeted' a lady. It will not be the last vow broken, he thought, for this struggle has grown mean.

Crunia, Kingdom of Castile
Feast of the Siete Varones Apostólicos, May 1314

Sun-ripened, breathing air heady as peaches, they came down to the mottled, dun-coloured roofs of the port amid the bang and clatter of the Seven Apostolic Men, a perfume of incense clinging to every sill of the unshuttered windows brocading the street.

Anonymous as dirt, Hal and Sim blessed the foresight that had paid two Compostella-sated pilgrims for their ragged filth of robes, they happy with the knowledge that not only had they extirpated their sins but they now had the silver to go home by ship – blessed be the Name of God.

Now those robes blended in with the rest of the throng as Hal and Sim came down to the chanting town, a sound at first muted as sea-surf, rising and falling like a distant marker bell on wrack, barely a disturbance to the birdsong and the smell of warm green and myrrh.

By the time Hal and Sim had traded ruts and dust for rough cobbles, heading for the last clear sight of the ships crowding the harbour, they were plunged into a sweaty noise and a swirl of perfumed smoke.

Torquatus, his painted nose already dented, wavered uncertainly, rising and falling in a sea of eager hands; Ctesiphon ploughed grimly through the throng, with Sts Hesychius and Secundius seemingly battling each other for some undetermined precedent. The rest of the Seven Apostolic Men were lost in the chants and the shouts.

'Christ betimes,' Sim bawled out, 'how are we to achieve anythin' in this conflummix?'

'Keep moving,' Hal said, shoving and jostling. Find the *Bon Accord* first – down to the harbour. In the end he had to bellow and point. Sim elbowed his way through, cursing folk roundly until they reached the fringes of the crush and popped out like pips from a squeezed apple.

'Bloody lumes,' Sim fumed. 'Moudiewarts – look at my cloots.'

He pulled the filthy ragged robes out indignantly and Hal eyed him back with a raised brow until even Sim had to laugh ruefully; if there was a new stain or tear on his robe there was no way of telling.

Hal looked at the haven they had found, discovered the stone faces of men with brown arms folded across their chests and knives prominently displayed.

'It looks like a tavern or an inn,' he said and then realized why the men stared; paid to keep out the riffraff, they were plainly considering which way Hal and Sim should leave: upright or horizontal, with balance favouring the latter. Sim scowled back at them, which was no help and only served to have the men look one to the other and, as if on some unseen signal, start to move.

Hal, swift as winking, hauled out his purse, held it up like the dangle of a fresh-neutered sheep bollock and jingled it; as if spellbound the two men stopped, faces broadened into brown grins and they stood aside like two opening doors.

Beyond, the yard was as much a mayhem as the street outside, though the worship was different; here, men bellowed and waved fistfuls of deniers and silver pennies, *tournois* and *grossi* while a Savoyard with a black cloth over one eye grabbed them, matched them and, in some way neither Hal nor Sim could fathom, accepted the bet and the odds.

Beyond this quarrelling shriek was a cleared square where two men half crouched, the docked birds churring and baiting in their hands, one gold and green, the other red and white,

131

their shaved necks stretching and straining like serpents.

'Cockfight, bigod,' Sim declared with delight, just as the men let go and fell back. Released, the birds sprang forward like tourney knights, their gilded spurs glittering, dashing towards each other with a clash, beak to beak. There was a pause, a strange sound like a sheet in a mad wind and then they fell on each other, wings flailing, beaks snapping, leaping and twirling in a mad dance as they struck out with their deadly feet.

A man screeched as the white drew blood with a strike, flinging up his arms, knocking his neighbour's hat off and elbowing Sim in the ear; Sim swore and elbowed him back, hard enough to make the man grunt and double up, but Sim's heart was not in it, for he was roaring for the white and red.

Hal spared the winded man a glance, no more, just to make sure he was not about to take revenge when he got his breath back – and then he saw Piculph moving through the crowd, oblivious to their presence. Hal almost cried out, but buckled it in his mouth. Widikind had said Piculph was on their side, a spy for Ruy Vaz, but Hal was no longer sure whom to trust.

There was a great roar and a surge forward; the gold had sunk one spur into the neck of the white and red and the fight was all but done. When Hal looked back, Piculph was gone; he caught Sim's arm and dragged him close enough to shout what he'd seen in the man's ear. Sim swivelled madly left and right while, out on the mud-bloody sand, the white cock staggered.

'Do not look round.'

The voice was pitched low, no louder than normal and almost in Hal's ear, so the first thing he did was start to turn until a knuckle drove into his kidneys.

'Do not look, I said.'

It was Piculph. Hal caught himself, stared to the front, where the white cock reeled, a splash of blood forming a red cross on its breast, the spurs glittering and flashing still in the dust and the roars. Like a Templar, Hal thought. Like Rossal and the others, dying in their own final pit.

'I thought you were all dead.'

The voice was tense and harsh, close enough so that Hal could smell the man's wine breath and feel the hot flicker of it on his lobe; any minute now, Hal thought, Sim will turn and see this, ruining any further subterfuge in it. He spoke quickly.

'Kirkpatrick and myself and Sim escaped. Kirkpatrick is gone to your Grand Master, who will now have proof of Guillermo's treachery.'

He hoped this was true, though he had last seen Kirkpatrick as a wraith in the dim, vanishing in the opposite direction from the one he and Sim took from the base of the tower.

'Then my master has won and there is hope,' answered Piculph. 'I am watched and suspected – in truth, I was abandoning this enterprise when I saw you as you saw me. De Grafton has worked out that the treasure, if not in the carts, was some Order magic I do not understand. He now knows that your king was warned long beforehand. That trail leads to me.'

'De Grafton has told of this?' Hal asked and felt the nod behind him.

'To Doña Beatriz. He wishes the Templar called Rossal brought to him here, but the lady does not entirely trust him.'

A snake-knot of plots, Hal thought. Out on the sand, the white's beak fell open, gasping, and the tongue trembled like a snake; one wing trailed and the gold and green battered it with a frenzy of wingbeats and slashes.

'Doña Beatriz saw him fell the big steersman with a blow behind the ear,' Piculph declared, 'and so forced him to join her. He is sent by the enemies of your king to make sure no weapons arrive for your army but he has long fallen from the Grace of God and his Order; I am sure he sees profit in this now for himself.'

'The crew?'

'Held in the lady's house,' the voice replied. 'The big white one to the west of the harbour on the hill above it. They were led by the Judas goat of de Grafton, told they were to be feasted and fêted – drink, whores and all. Instead, they found themselves locked in the emptied wine cellars. Your ship is guarded by Guillermo's men of the Alcántara, and the plan was to use them to kill your crew – but they will abandon Doña Beatriz if they find this plot is unveiled and Guillermo exposed.'

'Someone should let them know,' Hal replied, seeing Sim turn in his direction. The white raised its stained head, twitching and shivering and, in a single moment, a miracle of energy and courage and anger, hurled itself into the fray for the last time, the whirl of spurs scything round to strike its enemy's golden, red-crowned head.

'It is dangerous—' Piculph began.

'Anything you do now is dangerous,' Hal pointed out, just as the light of recognition went on in Sim's head and the scowl came down on his brows.

'Here,' he began and then a great bellowing roar went up, jerking him back to the fighting birds.

'There is still de Grafton and Doña Beatriz,' Piculph said uncertainly, his voice drowning in the clamour, but still loud enough for Hal to hear the fear in it. 'I do not want go there.'

For terror of the Knight or the lady? Hal could not work it out, but told Piculph he must; Sim swung back, his face sheened with sweat and excitement.

'Blinded, bigod. The white has blinded the gold . . . where is yon moudiewart?'

'Whisht,' Hal said and fingered his lips to strengthen it, He half turned. Piculph had vanished.

On the sand, the gold spun and reeled in its terror of sudden darkness while the white gathered the last of itself and slashed and slashed the green plumage to bloody ruin. Then, one wing dragging a bloody line in the sand, it half crawled on to the barely moving body and wavered out a crowing triumph while the crowd went mad.

They love to fight, Hal had heard folk say. Bred in the bone of them, an instinct. Like a parfait, gentle knight. Like a Templar.

As I am supposed to be.

The siege lines at Stirling
At the same moment

It was already warm and fly-plagued, Thweng saw. In a week, perhaps less, there would be real sickness here, as always when too many folk gathered with no sense of where to safely shit. It was not, he noted, what King Robert would want the likes of him to see, but exactly what Aymer de Valence and the others would want to hear.

Clustered round the slabbed fortress on its great raised scab of rock, the mushroom sprout of shelters and tents brought back a shiver of memory to Sir Marmaduke Thweng; the last time he had been at Stirling was the disaster at the brig, when Cressingham had died and de Warenne fled from Wallace. Then Sir Marmaduke Thweng had taken charge of the defence of the castle – and had had to surrender it and himself in the end.

Mowbray saw his look and thought Thweng was studying and worrying on the besieged castle.

'We will hold, my lord,' he said, reassuringly cheerful, 'until Midsummer's Day.'

He had back a look as mournful as a bull seal on a wet rock.

'So I thought myself, once,' Thweng replied. With a jolt, he realized that he had been ransomed after Stirling fell in return for one of this Mowbray's kin. Comyn connections, he recalled, which accounts for their change of cote.

Seventeen years since; the thought made his bones ache and he wondered, yet again, at the wisdom of dragging his three-score plus years all the way from the peace of Kilton to another round of Scottish wars.

135

At least this duty was simple if onerous: escort the commander of Stirling's fortress under safe writ through the Scots siege lines and back to his castle where he would await, as per his agreement with Edward Bruce, the outcome of events.

'Take careful note as you go,' de Valence, Earl of Pembroke had said to him. 'Ascertain if Bruce will stand and fight.'

Stand and fight, Sir Marmaduke thought. Pembroke and Beaumont think it is all a matter of bringing the army north and forcing the Scotch rebels to battle. The King himself, a copy of his father in everything but wit and wisdom, scarcely cares what happens after, only that a victory here will settle matters with Lancaster, Warwick and all the other disaffected. The King's worst fear is that the Scots will run back to the hills.

He and Mowbray had come up Dere Strete, as much on a scout as ambassadors charged with the official chivalry of the upcoming affair round Stirling. They had taken the straight road to the castle, as the army would when it arrived, with the great loom of Coxet Hill on their left, heading to meet Bruce and the other lords at St Ninian's little chapel.

Mowbray, his face sharp and ferret-eager with watchfulness, pointed out the pots dug at the crossings of the Bannock stream, each hole's flimsy covering hiding the sharp stake within; beyond, to the north, a line of men sweated and dug.

'Dangerous for horse,' he pointed out, as if Thweng was some squire in need of instruction. 'Trenches and pots, my lord: it means the Scotch will stand and fight as the King wishes.'

After what he had seen, the drilling men and the numbers of them, the grim hatred and the entire families they had brought – which you did not do if you thought of defeat – Sir Marmaduke felt a small needle of doubt lancing into the surety of an English success.

And yet . . . he knew Bruce of old, from the stripling days when he had been a tourney fighter of note and the pair of them had clattered round the circuit in a welter of expensive saddlery, horses and gear. They had shared bruises, victory, drink and jests – he was Sir M, Bruce was Sir R, which sounded like 'sirrah' and was the laugh in the piece.

The tourney-fighting Bruce he knew had not liked a straight pitched battle then, the French Method of fighting where you trained horse and rider to bowl a man over. His was the German Method, mounted on a lighter horse and avoiding the mad rushes to circle round and strike from behind.

His tactic was to grab knights round the waist and drag them bodily from the saddle, so that the Kipper – the man on foot with a great persuading club – could invite the lord to surrender himself to ransom. He and Bruce had played Kipper for each other, time and about for one profitable, glorious season, and Thweng recalled it with a dreamy mist of remembrance.

He has waged war the same way, Thweng thought as they rode up through the litter of men and shelters, avoiding anything that looked like a full commitment of all his force. He did it in '10 and long before that. He'd had Wallace as teacher for it – why would he contemplate changing it now?

They passed Bannock vill, a rude huddle of cruck houses and drunken fences, where men leaned on spears and watched them; one spat pointedly. Nearby, hung from the shaft of a tipped-up and weighted two-wheeled cart, a festering corpse turned and swung, smoked with flies.

A black reminder about pillage, Thweng thought; the wee households in this hamlet had not fled, though they risked kitchen gardens and chooks, because armed men and Bruce's bright writ ensured no looting.

That was order and organization and Thweng felt a slim sliver of cold slide around his backbone; when you see your enemies in discord, fill your cup and take your ease. When they are grim and resolved and of one mind, gather your harness and set your shield . . .

They dismounted outside the small stone chapel, garlanded with a splendid panoply of bright tents and banners. They had been brought the last little way by Sir James Douglas, though Sir Marmaduke found it hard to equate the lisping cheerfulness of dark youth with the man he had heard was a scowling scar on the lip of the world and whose very name, the Black, set men and women and bairns howling.

The small *mesnie* of English men-at-arms remained by their horses, nervous as levrets in a snakepit, while Mowbray and Sir Marmaduke clacked along the stones to the door of St Ninian's and ducked under the Douglas smile into the musty dim of the chapel.

'You will wait to be called, *gentilhommes*,' said a voice from a shadow. 'Then you will step forward and bow. You will not parley unless asked a question. Understood?'

'Understood, my lord Randolph,' Thweng answered, recognizing the voice and forcing the man into better light, where his unsmiling face could be clearly seen. 'My lord earl, I should say. You have risen in the world since you betrayed one king for another, it appears.'

Randolph flushed.

'I am loyal to the King,' he blustered, but Thweng had made his point and waved, at once apologetic, insouciant and dismissive, which deepened Randolph's flush – but their names were called and the Earl had no chance to reply.

Bruce was standing behind a table littered with papers, half-rolled, unfolded and pinned – the corner of one by a dagger. Beside him was his brother Edward, a coarse copy hewn of rougher stone, and behind was a coterie of shadows, waiting and watching.

'My lords,' Edward declared. 'Present your writ.'

Mowbray passed across the rolled vellum, had it taken, examined and placed to one side.

'You may proceed to the castle. Take no detours. Once inside, you will be considered quit-claimed from this writ. Is that understood?'

Edward was matter-of-fact and harsh, much changed from the smiling, eager man who had negotiated the midsummer

138

surrender of Stirling, Mowbray thought and almost smiled at what must have passed between the brothers at the news of it. Instead, he merely inclined his head and hovered uncertainly until he realized he had been dismissed; he shot Sir Marmaduke a stiff look and vanished. There was a silence, thick as gruel.

'You have seen enough to satisfy the Plantagenet?'

The voice was rough and rheumed and the face, when it was presented to the filtered light inside the still, close tent, was a stone to the temple; Sir Marmaduke jerked a little and blinked before he recovered his wit.

'A deal of men,' he answered, staring at the lesioned skin and the wounds. A scar down the left eye – Methven for that, he recalled – and the ruin of his right cheek. A tourney wound, he remembered, though that had been long since and if it had never healed there was something festering wrong; there had been rumours of sickness and reports that the usurper King of Scots was taken to his bed, feverish and practically dead, but Sir Marmaduke had always dismissed them as wishes. Now he was not so sure and he fought for more sense to his words.

'A deal of men,' he repeated, 'in rough wool and drilling with sticks.'

'For all that,' Bruce said, stiff as old rock, 'Plantagenet will find us here when he finds the courage to seek us out. And we will have sharp on the sticks.'

'So I understand, sirrah,' Thweng answered and heard the court of shadows suck in their breath at this breach of protocol. But the King smiled a little at the old joke only the pair of them knew, stretching the cheek – bigod, Sir Marmaduke thought, there is discolour on it all the way back to the ear . . .

'I have a gift,' Bruce declared suddenly. He turned to take an armful of folded cloth from one of the shadows behind him and then shook it out.

'Return this to my lord Berkeley – he lost it recently in my domains.'

The bloodied, torn Berkeley banner taken by Jamie Douglas

seemed to glow balefully as Thweng reached out and gathered the rough brocade, folding it into a loop over his arm, and all the time could not take his eyes from the face of the man he had known from youth.

God blind me, he thought, the changes in him. The fierce ambition had always been there, though Thweng had not realized what the young, chivalrous knight that had been Robert Bruce had had to sacrifice for it. It was as if the stains on his soul had manifested themselves, for all to see, on his face.

Thweng shook the idea from him as a bayed stag does a hound; he had his own stained liege and enough personal sins not to want to burden himself with others. And he had his own tasks. He steeled himself, couched his lance and dug in his spurs.

'A gift for a gift,' he replied, 'and a counterweight to the knowledge I have garnered: Strathbogie has fallen from your chaplet.'

It was a strike, sure as point on shield. There was a long silence, followed by a moth-wing murmur from the unseen shadows as the news went round. David of Strathbogie, Earl of Atholl, had been a recent convert to the Bruce cause, despite being married to the daughter of the murdered John Comyn of Badenoch. His defection back to the English would send a shiver through the other titled lords who supported Bruce; they were few enough and he depended on them for the best of his army.

'It seems', Sir Marmaduke went on, driving home the spike of it, 'he did not care much for your brother's shift of dalliances to the daughter of the Earl of Ross. I am told wee Izzie Strathbogie is blinded with snot and red-eyed with weeping.'

Edward growled a little and leaned forward, flexing his knuckled hands on the table, for it was his seductions that had brought this about; Bruce cleared his throat and Edward, black scowling, straightened a little.

'Fair exchange,' Bruce said flatly. 'And your observations on the reasons for it are cogent – you would know, of course, of the problems women can cause. How is Lady Lucy?'

140

Sir Marmaduke fought down his own hackles, admiring Bruce's smooth parry even as he did so; Lucy Thweng's wayward, single-minded progress through lovers, husbands and even abductions was a scandal to the Thwengs in general and himself, her uncle, in particular. Yet he fought the flicker of a wry smile on to his walrus-moustached face.

'A splendid animal,' he answered, which was how his own king had described her, grinning knowingly and nudging Despenser as he did so, for the rumours that old Sir Marmaduke had also plucked his niece's fruit was rife. It had clearly reached here, too, for someone tittered in the dark behind Bruce and muffled it swiftly.

There was silence after that and Sir Marmaduke realized he had probably been dismissed, was turning to clack his way across the stones when the Bruce voice harshed out again.

'You have seen our sticks, sir. Tell Plantagenet we will defend this realm with the longest one we have.'

And Thweng, nodding a lower bow, heard the last whispered phrase as he found his way back to sunlight.

'Farewell, Sir M.'

Bruce watched him go with a dull ache of another lost friend settling stonelike in his belly. An old friend – he had been surprised at the sunk cheek, the white wisp of hair, yet now wondered why he had been so shocked; Sir M had to have sixty years lying on his shoulders – at least. He had seemed old when he and Bruce had tourneyed together – bigod, he must have been the age I am now.

A long time of friendship, now smoked away as if it had never been. Small wonder folk spoke of being raised to the throne – it was a place as high and lonely as any eyrie.

'Did he see, d'ye think?'

Edward's voice was harsh with eagerness, his great broad face shining, but his brother's eye was jaundiced when it turned on him, blood-filled with Edward's misdemeanours.

'Sir M misses nothing,' he answered shortly and Edward,

141

sensing the mood, wisely tightened his lips, aware that the Strathbogie business was too raw; he could feel the accusing eyes of all the other *nobiles* searing his back.

'He saw the work, Your Grace,' Jamie confirmed, and then frowned. 'Though I cannot see why you had men digging pretend holes as well as true.'

'I want the Plantagenet blocked from coming up Dere Strete,' Bruce answered patiently. 'When he moves round to the north, as he then must if he wishes to officially relieve the siege on Stirling, I want him to believe I have trenched to our front there, too. That way he will think I wish to stand and fight.'

'But you must,' blurted Jamie and Edward's sharp bark of laughter drowned the disapproving murmurs at this breach of etiquette.

'If I fight at all,' Bruce answered, slow and cold as a glacier and as much to them all as the flustered Jamie, 'I will not be standing, my lords. This will not be Falkirk.'

The air was heavy with the sudden tense interest of all the others, who hung on whether the King would stand and fight. And Jamie understood it, sudden as a flaring light: if the area between the armies was trenched it would be as much a barrier to the spear blocks they had been drilling in and they needed to stay tight and together as they moved. That was why the holes were pretend: Bruce would not wait for the English; he would attack them, as Wallace did at the brig.

He almost exclaimed it out loud, but then recovered himself and bowed like a bobbing hen.

'If Your Grace stands to fight,' he added.

Bruce favoured him with a twist of smile.

'Just so. If that is the case, you will attend in my own Battle on the day, with your *mesnie*. Until then, I want your men mounted and riding.'

'We are not horse, Your Grace,' Jamie argued lightly in French. 'You have Sir Robert Keith's men for that.'

'The Earl Marischal's horse are few and needed,' Bruce

answered. 'Your men are good riders and I want them broken in two – yon Dog Boy will command the other half – and riding about the Lothians making a deal of noise and fire and smoke.'

'Aleysandir? He is not stationed enough for command.'

'Stationed or not, he is vital,' Bruce replied. 'I will tell you why, good Sir James, since I am your liege lord and king and can do so where others tremble – he is your double. The twig does not fall far from the tree and whether your difference in stations admits that you are sired by the same loins, the truth is palpable each time you stand side by side.'

He saw Jamie Douglas stiffen and frowned.

'Loose your hackles, lad – I need the country in turmoil. I need every handful of horsemen as heralds of the terrible Sir James. If the Black can be in two places at once, all the better.'

Jamie Douglas saw it and his flattered anger subsided slowly. He glared round the other lords, daring them to comment on this shame on his father's name – though the truth was that all of them could name some wee common woman tupped by a noble relative.

'I need herschip, but of a particular sort,' Bruce went on. 'Fetch back all the iron you can carry from Northumberland's smiths and forges. Strip it from the Church if needs be – we will need as much as we can, to beat ploughshares into swords.'

Nor will there be enough, he thought to himself, if the weapons fail to arrive from Spain.

'Above all,' Bruce added, 'you watch. Put eyes on the road from Berwick and do not remove them until you can ride and tell me proud Edward is coming over the Tweed with his host, by which route and how many.'

He watched Jamie Douglas stride off and heard Randolph clear his throat.

'The Earl of Atholl is a sore loss.'

Indeed. As if I had not realized that – Bruce almost spat it back, but swallowed it and offered an insouciant shrug instead.

'If the great and good cannot be persuaded to fight for

their king, then the sma' folk can be persuaded to fight for their kingdom instead, my lord,' he replied in English, and then turned to the shadows, picking one out from the others; Sir Henry Sientcler of Roslin bowed.

It was unkind and Bruce knew it as he spoke, but fear made him careless of the Roslin lord's feelings.

'And if your Herdmanston kinsman and namesake falters, my lord,' he declared to the stricken lord of Roslin, 'we will, in truth, be defending this realm with nothing better than long sticks.'

Crunia, Kingdom of Castile
That night . . .

They made a plan, of sorts; Sim levered himself up and flung himself into the turmoil of the streets like a man plunging into surf, while Hal stayed with a flask of watered wine in the maelstrom of cockfighters, waiting to see if Piculph returned.

The day slid to a groaning end, the sun a raw, bloodied egg trembling on the horizon. The cockfights filtered to an exhausted finish and the victors fed and watered their weary, wounded champions, before cosseting them carefully in the dark comfort of linen bags, which they hung high on posts to thwart the vermin. The losers made more pragmatic arrangements and chicken stew was cheap on the tavern bill of fare.

Sim ate his with considerable gusto, but Hal neither liked the taste nor the idea that the white and red might be mixed in with the green and gold – though the truth was that the dying light brought out hordes of fluttering insects, mad for the sconces and, in the dim, Hal could not tell what had started out in his stew and what had landed since, drunk with light.

Sim, presented with this, paused, shrugged and spooned on, observing only that the folk of Compostella could take perfectly good food and make it 'as heated as the Earl of

Hell's hearth'. Yet he ate Hal's bowl as well and, at the end, slid it away from him, belched and sighed.

'They ken how to bliss saints, mark me well,' he observed, swallowing watered wine and grimacing at the water. 'The seven holy men have been duly worshipped, I can tell you. The wee saints they name Segundo and Tesifonte had a good stushie at the entrance to a street, though I think it had more to do wi' the fact that tanners carried one and cobblers the other. And Cecilio cowped off his bier and crushed a wee nun, so she and God are not on speaking terms.'

'God be praised,' Hal said, to protect Sim from his own blasphemy.

'For ever and ever – did yon Piculph come back?'

'He did not,' Hal answered. 'Did ye spy out the ship?'

'I did,' Sim said, slurping; he paused and belched again. 'Yon fightin' chooks is fightin' back . . . It is a good swim out in the bay,' he went on, 'unless we can find a wee boatie.'

They mulled this in silence, for neither of them swam well; none of the crew of the *Bon Accord* did, apart from Niall, who was called Silkie – half-man, half-seal – because he could dog paddle a bit.

'There is not a sign of any of yon fancy Order Knights with the green crosses, either on board the *Bon Accord*, or anywhere in the town,' Sim offered as a ribbon of hope. 'Nor at yon Doña's house on the hill.'

'You went there? That was reckless.'

'Not close,' Sim soothed. 'But we need to ken where it lies.'

Which was true enough, though Hal's feathers were not smoothed by the lack of presence of the Alcántara men; it could be that they had slithered out of maille and marking surcotes, the better to spy out the pair they sought. Sim, frowning, considered this and reluctantly admitted, between belches, that it might be true, though he had thought any in the Holy Orders considered it a sin to be out of their garb as well as their cloistered commanderie.

The Order of Alcántara, Hal pointed out, was not like the Poor Knights and Sim had also to admit the truth of that.

'Still,' he added. 'We can hardly bide here like a millstone. The crew are in that house, according to Piculph, and needs be freed.'

'I would prefer to know more of what is also in that house. Piculph would answer it – if we knew where he was,' Hal said.

'Fled,' Sim declared. 'You said he was doing so when we stumbled on him.'

Their mood matching the gloom, they sat until darkness fell and slid away from the tavern into the drunken streets, moving carefully until the crowds thinned and straggled to an end and the streets grew steep and broad. Then Sim's hand halted Hal.

'That's the place.'

It was a walled edifice, menacingly dark, which could mean that it was empty or a trap. Hal heaved in a deep breath and brought the hidden sword out from under his ragged robes. Sim, frowning at the gurgle in his belly, shouldered the bulk of the wrapped arbalest and brought out his knife, which was much better for close work.

They looked at each other, sweat-gleamed faces tense and ghostly in the dark.

'Aye til the fore,' Sim muttered with a grim tightening of lips and Hal shouldered into the shadows under the gate.

They moved into the hot closet of a walled garden, thick with scent and singing with night insects, both strange to Hal's senses. Stranger still was the low gurgle, like a rain-washed drain in an Edinburgh wynd – and a groan which whirled him round in alarm, squinting into the silvered moonlight shadows.

'Sim?'

There was another low groan and the rustle of cloth.

'Are ye hurt, man?'

He pitched his second question more urgently than the first whispered hiss, and moved towards the groans, in time to hear an ugly wet sound; the rushing gush of stink made him reel.

'Christ and His saints,' Sim moaned. 'The flux . . .'

Greed and two bowls of spiced chicken stew, Hal thought, and had to grit his teeth to keep from bellowing it. There were more sounds and Hal moved upwind a little.

'Ah, bigod . . .'

'Whisht,' Hal hissed, but Sim, a squatting shadow in the dim with a face pale as moonlight, waved a hand.

'If this has not brought a dozen guards then the place is empty,' he grunted, which made enough sense for Hal to relax a little.

'Go on,' Sim added. 'I'll follow in a breath or two.'

Hal hestitated, but only briefly, for he needed a breath or two that did not have Sim's innards in it. He moved through the neat undergrowth; no useful plants here, only decorative ones, which was a waste of growing land as far as Hal was concerned. The whirr and flap of wings made him pause, half-crouched in the bulked shadow of a building dominated by a tall, circular tower.

The double doors of the place were open, the inside dark as the Earl of Hell's yett hall; Hal, sweating and icy, crept in, rolling his feet and wincing at every careless clack of booted sole on tiled floor.

The only light came from the moon and the faintest of pale glows ahead, but Hal's eyes were dark-adapted now and made out the shape of arch and doorway. Cellar, he thought. That was where Piculph had said the crew of the *Bon Accord* were kept, so he looked for a way that led downward.

He scouted the edge of the room, slow and cat-wary, avoiding candlestand and statue, chair and bench, until he came to stairs leading down. Four steps and he was at a door, which yielded a fingerlength before the key-lock rattled it to a halt; a voice froze the blood in Hal.

'Fit's that thaur?'

Pegy's northern Braid, faint and muffled through the thick

timber of the door, permitted Hal to breathe again. He told Pegy who he was and heard the excited rush of murmurs from the others, but found that the door was thick, stout and locked. According to Pegy, Doña Beatriz had the key. Fretting and sweating, he promised them he would return and slid back into the shadows.

No guards; no sign of life. Perhaps, Hal thought, Piculph has done his work after all – there was a whirring sound and he ducked instinctively, throwing himself flat on the tiles. After a moment, when nothing else happened, he climbed back to a low crouch, heard a soft fluting call and perched, bewildered.

Light flared like a blast of icy breath and bobbed through the open door, a torch held in Sim's big hand, so that Hal, blinking blindly into it, knew he was caught in a half-crouch, sword ready.

'Whit why are ye hunkered there?' Sim boomed and Hal sprang up.

'Whisht, you – I heard something.'

Sim peered round, raising the sconce torch higher.

'There is nobody . . .' he began, then the whirr and the soft call came again, making Hal cry out.

'Cooshie doos,' Sim exclaimed with a bark of laughter. 'Ye are hiding from the attentions o' some cooshie doos.'

Hal realized Sim was right and that the high-roofed place had doves in it, though the next thought that struck him was where had they come from? He was too embarrassed to mention that as he straightened up and gave Sim a vicious glance.

'Yer arse back in order?' he demanded and Sim scowled, angry and ashamed.

'For the minute,' he admitted, 'though I am black-affronted.'

'Black-behinded as well, I am sure.'

Sim's reply was interrupted by a dove which fluttered down, tame as a lap dog, and strutted into the torchlight in a hopeful search for food.

'Cooshie doo,' he declared with a triumphant grin. Hal

scowled back. Doves did not fly in the dark normally, which he mentioned. Nor did they spontaneously bleed, which brought Sim's head round to study the bird more carefully; it hopped and flapped up but there was time enough to see the pink staining on one wingtip.

Then, in the lip of light expanded by Sim holding up the torch at arm's length, they both saw the limp white hand beyond.

Doña Beatriz had died quickly, struck from behind by a single blow from a blade that had sliced upwards off her shoulderblades and cracked open her skull; her hair lay like dead wet snakes in the spreading darkness of blood.

'Backhand stroke wi' a broadsword,' Sim growled, waving away the flies greedy for gleet. 'She was running, which spoiled the aim – planned to swipe her head off her neck but missed.'

'Piculph?' Hal suggested, bemused, but Sim had run out of knowledge and merely shrugged, winced and massaged his belly, trying not to look as Hal, swallowing his own spit hard, fumbled in the stiff, bloody ruin of the woman's body.

'No key,' he declared finally, smearing the back of his clean hand across his sweat-moist lips.

They moved towards the faint pale glow, unnerved enough now for Sim to stub out the torch on the tiles, pressing his boots on the embers, swift and silent, as a prudent man would who had known only rush floors and wood surrounds; the acrid stink of the smoke trailed them towards the light.

There was a door, open just enough to let out the faintest of glows, an alarmed dove which flew off in a rattle of wings – and a faint, regular heartbeat of sound which paused them both and brought their heads together.

'A wee fountain,' Sim hissed, his breath foul in Hal's face.

'A horologe,' Hal replied, having seen the ticking wonder of gears and cogs that had been mounted in Canterbury. Sim, who had only heard of such a thing, looked sceptical as they slid, fast and quiet, into the room.

The light came from the moon, which was almost straight

above and shining through a roof tight-slatted with wooden beams, but otherwise open – Hal realized they were inside the tower he had seen from the outside and that this view of it was as strange.

The floor was earth and blue-tiled meandering paths, spattered with white splashes where it was not thick with exotic plants. A pool dominated the centre and the walls, all around, top to bottom, were pocked with regular square niches, as tall and wide as two fists one on top of the other; even as he stood and gaped, Hal heard the flute-note call that was now familiar.

It was the sprung stones, girdling the entire thing at waist height like a belt, that finally clicked it into place for the pair of them.

'A doocot,' Sim marvelled. It was exactly that: the sprung stones to keep the rats from climbing up to the eggs and squabs; the slatted roof to keep the hawks from the same, while allowing the doves in and out. Yet something had killed a couple of birds, their bodies splayed like orchids veined with blood. The ticking was louder.

'Water,' Sim declared, pushing through the veil of blossoms to the pool.

It was almost all blood, the pool, drained from the gently swinging nakedness of Piculph, hanging from the sorrowful bend of a willow-tree bough.

He had been hard used so that death had come as a mercy to him, but not before he had suffered the shrieking terror of being whipped to a flayed ruin. Nor had he been dead long enough for all the life to have drained away; it fell, viscous and soft as cat's paws, drop by ticking drop from the dangle of his arms and head.

The slamming door whirled them round and Sim gave a sharp cry as something whirred like a dove wing through the air, curved round his neck and jerked him off his feet; he flew forward and was dragged, choking.

150

Hal, with reflexes even he did not know he possessed, slashed out with the sword and the black, thin snake that seemed to have leaped out and grabbed Sim round the neck whipped away; there was a curse and Hal sprang to Sim's side as the man rolled over, coughing and choking.

He had time to see that it was no snake but the remains of a leather thong – a whip, he realized, remembering Piculph's ruined body – and then a voice cut the air.

'Quick, for an old man. You have spoiled my surprise – and I had spent a deal of time perfecting that lash; I did not know how many would come and needed an advantage.'

De Grafton stepped into the moonlight like a verse in black and silver, the limp dangle of the whip in one hand, the flash of steel in the other. He wore black Templar robes and it seemed as if the dark had eaten him.

'Two only? Then Piculph told it true.'

He shrugged ruefully.

'Pity. I did not believe him. I thought this Ruy Vaz would send his host at least – two old men is not a little insulting.'

'Enough for you,' Sim managed, but his voice was hoarse and the throat burn in it palpable.

'Ruy Vaz and his men are on their way,' Hal added, hoping it was true.

De Grafton moved, sudden as an adder, the tongue of ruined whip flicked and a dove veered off and flew away, calling alarms. De Grafton frowned.

'You have severed enough to ruin my aim,' he said and tossed the whip away with disgust. It was that, more than anything so far, which drove a cold steel blade of determined hate into Hal, suddenly revolted by a man who had spent the long, hot afternoon practising his whip on an innocence of doves while his human victims marbled in the heat.

'Wee birds and women,' Hal answered, finding his voice at last. 'This seems your strength, de Grafton.'

He moved as he spoke, between the fronds of a palm,

151

crushing the jade-pale stems and heads of some flowers, so that a cloying perfume rose up.

'The lady? She believed this Piculph, thought to go with him and throw herself on the mercy of Ruy Vaz.'

De Grafton's lip curled with revulsion.

'Thought to use her women's ways', he said, 'to slither out from punishment and leave me to bear the brunt of wrath. I killed her as you would the snake in Eden and then found out what was needed from Piculph.'

'Who was no great fighter,' Hal answered, sidling closer.

'A Serjeant of the Order of Alcántara,' de Grafton sneered. 'If they are all like that, the Moors will be in this port within the year.'

'You will never ken,' roared Sim, bulling up from the floor, even as Hal shouted at him to stay.

De Grafton slid to one side, the sword flicked, fast as the whip, and there was a dull clang and a splash which curdled Hal's blood; he sprang forward, but recoiled to a halt as the sword flicked out at him. From where he stood he could see Sim sprawled on the far side of the pool where the blow had flung him, half in and half out, covered in blood and not moving; Piculph's disturbed body swung and turned while doves mourned in the moonlight.

'You have a key I need,' Hal said, trying not to look at Sim, while de Grafton cocked his head to one side like a curious bird.

'I am charged with delaying you – preventing you entire if I can,' he replied, almost sadly. 'I gave my oath to my lord Percy and his English king, as a Poor Knight.'

'The Poor Knights are no more and your oath is as worthless as your honour – you are long fallen from any grace,' Hal replied, moving a bough of fragrant blossoms from in front of his face. 'Piculph did not die because you wanted to know how many were coming here – he died because you wanted to know if Rossal was. Himself and the Templar writ

152

he carries. Which you would take from his whipped body after he had revealed the secret word.'

There was silence, broken only by the gory drip and the flutter of terrified doves.

'Did you work out that you alone had not been party to the knowledge? They did not trust you, de Grafton, even though they could prove nothing. Yet Rossal knew – perhaps God told him.'

He shifted slightly for advantage, poised and ready for a strike.

'You can deny your oaths and cheat the Order enough to gull foolish men and silly women,' he went on. 'But God is watching, my lord.'

There was a pause, and then the doves erupted in fragile terror as de Grafton launched into a snarling frenzy, seeing all his plans shredded at the last.

He was fast and trained with all the honed skills of a Templar, so that Hal reeled away, a shock jolting through him at how slow he was, how far removed from his own old skills. Yet the same reflex that had cut the whip from Sim sprang the bough of blossoms from his hand and slapped its fragrance into de Grafton's face, making him turn his head to avoid it; the scything blow hissed over Hal's ducking shoulder like a bar of light.

Then the clouds drifted over the moon and everything was sunk into darkness.

There was silence, broken only by the frantic bird-sounds, which clouded Hal's ears. There was nothing but scent and space and blackness – but it was the same for de Grafton, he thought, and fought to control the ragged rasp of his treacherous breathing.

A flurry of thrashing came from his left – a bird had blundered into de Grafton and he had struck out, so Hal moved as swiftly as he dared and slashed left and right, then retreated without, it seemed, hitting anything.

Birds whirred and slapped through the dark, flute-wailing their distress. Something splashed in the fountain and Hal wondered if de Grafton was there; the idea that he was finishing off a wounded Sim almost sprang him recklessly forward, but he fought the urge.

Sweat trickled down him and he found himself in a half-crouch, as if the ground would open up a safe hole and let him crawl in; the scent of flowers and old blood drifted on the night breeze.

The clouds slid off the moon; a silver and black shadow flitted across from his left and the blow almost tore the sword from Hal's grip, forcing him to dance backwards. He parried once, twice, managed to block a low cut to the knee, and then was alone as de Grafton whirled away like a wraith.

In a moment he was back; the swords clashed and sparks flew, the blades slid together to the hilt and, for an eyeblink, Hal was breath to fetid breath with de Grafton, feeling the sweat heat of him, seeing the mad eyes and the white grin; but then the Templar's head bobbed like a fighting cock and Hal reeled back from the blow on his forehead. Something seemed to snag his arm and he knew he had been cut.

De Grafton laughed softly.

'Do you have the writ, I wonder? Or the secret word? Or both? I will cut you a little, then we will find out the truth.'

The pain crept through and Hal felt blood slide, felt the grip of his hand on the hilt grow slack and reinforced it with the left. A bird called throatily and de Grafton was suddenly close, his blade beating down Hal's own.

'We will find out,' he repeated and Hal knew the next strike would be to render him helpless, for de Grafton to truss up and question.

'It will do you no good,' Hal panted through the red swirls of pain. 'The writ and the word are both gone to Ruy Vaz.'

There was a pause and Hal cursed himself. Clever, he thought, gritting through the pain of his arm – give him no excuse to spare you. Yet he could only kneel like a drooping bullock at the slaughter and wait for it.

There was a whirring thump – De Grafton screamed and arched, and then bowed at the waist with the agony of the steel arbalest prong driven like a pickaxe into the join of neck and shoulder; behind, the bloody apparition that was Sim bellowed like a rutting stag, his face sliding with gore.

'Kill me, would ye? Ye bliddy wee limmer, I will maul the sod wi' ye.'

De Grafton, reeling and shrieking, gave up trying to reach the prong and started to swing round on the unarmed Sim – Hal's desperate, lunging two-handed stroke tore his own sword from his weakened grasp, but not before it had cut the Templar from his wounded shoulder almost to his hip. He fell in two directions and his heels drummed.

The birds whirled and called and the heels danced to still-ness. Sim wiped the mess on his face into a horror mask of streaks and heaved in a breath; his teeth were bright in the moonlit scarlet of his cheeks.

'Aye til the fore,' he panted and Hal blinked from his numbness.

'I thought he had killed you,' he said and Sim scowled.

'The blow hit the arbalest – look, his cut has ruined it entire.'

He prised the weapon from the ruin of De Grafton and flourished it with disgust.

'He has severed the string and put a bliddy great gash in the stem. I will never find another.'

'Ye are all bloody,' Hal managed to say and Sim wiped his gory face again.

'From the pool – Piculph's blood. Apart from a dunt on my back, I am unhurt – more than can be said for yerself.'

Hal allowed himself to be led away from the corpses and the stink of blood and exotic blooms. Sim struck up a light, which made them blink, and presented Hal with his sword, worked free from de Grafton's corpse. Then he examined the arm with a critical eye.

155

'Nasty and deep, but the lacings in yer arm are intact, so ye will get the use of it back.'

Hal tried not to let the pain wash him, concentrated on staring at the sword and wondering at the keen edge which had slashed de Grafton to ruin. Too fancy, Rossal had admitted when he had handed the sword over and now Hal saw the extent of it: the Templar cross in the pommel and letters etched down the blade and now outlined clearly in de Grafton's blood: C+S+S+M+L. Across the hilt was N+D+S+M+L and Hal wondered if there was a Templar left who could tell him what they meant.

Sim searched de Grafton for the key and vanished with it; not long afterwards the place was suddenly filled with the *Bon Accord* sailors. Hal let Pegy have his head, listened dully to him sending Somhairl and some men to check on the ship while he sat, fired with the agony of his arm and trying not to move at all.

The big Islesman was back all too soon; the ship was foundered and half-sunk at its moorings, the steering whipstaff cut.

'Baistit,' Pegy swore and kicked the bloody ruin of de Grafton so that the head lolled sickeningly. 'He knew he had won afore ye arrived, Sir Hal.'

Hal, crushed with the black dog of it, fell back to studying the sword, half-numbed, watching the gleet and blood crust into the grooves of the letters in a haar of weariness, until light and voices burst over him, driving him up and out of it, as if breaching from a dark pool.

'Christ betimes,' said a familiar voice, 'what a charnel hoose.'

It was an effort to raise his head and stare into the wide grin.

'Kirkpatrick,' Hal slurred like a drunk. 'You are late.'

ISABEL

Thou deckest Thyself with light as if it were a garment and spreadest out the Heavens like a curtain. A sign, Lord, to silence my weeping and I thank You for it. I saw him, through the smoke, through the crowds howling at the shrieks of the burning woman, a dark and strange angel, hooded and careful but the only one not looking at the poor soul writhing on the pyre, but up at me. He knows I saw him, too. O Lord. Joy of joys – a sign. Matters are changing; winds are shifting.
   Dog Boy.

CHAPTER SEVEN

Berwick Town, Berwick
Ember Day, Feast of the Visitation, May 1314

He should not have been there, in the thronged Marygate.
He could hear Jamie say it even as he walked into the crowd
of the place. You are not meant to be strolling inside Berwick
town, Aleysandir. You are supposed to be observing the folk
in it, their movements and their bought truce. You are
supposed to be me, Aleysandir – so says the King – and I am
too kent a face for you to be waving its like at the English
in Berwick.

I am supposed to be kin, Dog Boy answered himself, grimly
exultant with the daring of it, though he would never say it
to Jamie's face. My blood is your blood, Jamie Douglas – and
your blood would bring you here if you were in my boots.

His boots were clotted with filth of alleys and wynds choked
with 'English sojers', though the truth of matters was that
they were not English at all, but the *mesnies* of those Scots
lords still loyal to the Plantagenet and fearing for the loss of
their lands in the north. Unable now to go home, they were
lost men, all of their old lives torn from them and only
soldiering left. Swaggering and roaring, they lurched through

the streets in search of drink and whores and, above all, food.

That was part of what had brought Dog Boy into the town, mingling easily with the other travel-stained, just one more well-worn fighting man with an iron hat, a gambeson that had seen better days and a festoon of hand weapons dangling from belt and back.

He and Jamie knew the place was starving already, with ale a sight cheaper than bread, yet those Scottish *nobiles* bound to King Edward were clearly mustering – and food was arriving, grain and meat and ale, in carts guarded by English wearing the badge of Aymer de Valence, Earl of Pembroke.

The presence of his own *mesnie* meant the Earl was here, but with just enough numbers to garrison the castle and keep all the food and drink safe. Not for the town, nor even for the garrison, nor the Scots lords, but for others – supplies, stockpiling here for the bulk of the army because the fortresses they usually relied on for invasion were all gone. That meant the English were due here in force soon – but where were they now?

Dog Boy had heard that labour on the Berwick town-wall defences had stopped because the workers were too weak and he saw for himself the ditch and rampart, half-finished and no more than a dyke. You could take the town, he thought to himself, with a jester's bladder on a stick – though the castle was still formidable.

He had heard, too, that Isabel MacDuff was the sight to see, dangling from the Hog's Tower in her cage, but in the time it took to battle for a leather jack of warm ale at Tavish's Tavern, Dog Boy learned that her charms had been overcome by a new entertainment.

They were burning a witch under the walls of the castle.

The mob gathered in the moody dim of a day gone to haar off the sea, expectant and lusting with the desperation of those who need bread but will take blood if it is offered.

Dog Boy filtered along with them, the Napiers and Harpers and Butlers from Edinburgh and the Lothian March roistering alongside the sullen MacDougalls and McNabs from beyond the Mounth, who patently wished they were not here at all, in a soft southern place where no one spoke the True Tongue.

Dog Boy was elbowed and shouldered, growling so that folk knew he was no easy mark, with his dagger and old sword, an axe and a rimmed iron hat dangling from his belt. He searched the battlements, squinting in the growing fog and premature pewter dim and not expecting to see her at all, having heard she could only be viewed if you stood in the bailey, which was a step too far for him. Surprise stiffened him, then, when he saw her.

Cage-freed, she stood high on the battlemented wall beside Malise – grey-haired now that one, Dog Boy saw – with a loop of cloak over her own head, which still seemed fox-russet bright. They stood like lord and lady above the crowds and anyone who did not know the truth would have been fooled by it.

Dog Boy dragged at her with his eyes, willing her to look – and then she did. He was sure of it, saw the jerk in her like a hooked fish, was certain she had seen and recognized him – but the arrival of the witch threw up a surge and a roaring bellow that snapped the lock between them.

The woman moved in the midst of a coterie of censer-swinging priests and an intoning canonical. She stumbled forward draped in a clinging shift and a hagging terror between spear-armed, grim-faced guards lent by the castle; her face was a cliff, grey with the numb of fear.

Dog Boy knew her. Knew her and her accuser, the wee pinch-faced man who walked with his chin triumphant and defiant, basking in having caused all this. Frixco de Fiennes looked right and left and never behind at the woman he had condemned. Dog Boy wondered dully where Aggie's bairn was.

It was easy to read the truth between the long, rambling pronouncement, half-drowned in the shrieks and howls of the baying mob. Frixco had declared Aggie the traitor who had let the Scots into Roxburgh, using foul Satanic spells to hide them from view. The fact that the Church was promoting the woman's death and not the seneschal of Berwick showed that the Common Law considered the evidence flimsy at best. The Church needed no other evidence than the woman's confession and her bloody fingers and bruised face showed how that had been achieved.

Now she was a witch. Not a woman, for each inquiring priest would have to look himself in the mirror glass of his soul after what had been done to a woman, but *you shall not suffer a witch to live* so the broken, split-lipped, weeping ruin they fixed to the stake was a witch, spawn of Satan and not any human thing at all.

Fastened with chains, Dog Boy noted dully, since ropes would burn through and roll her messily to the feet of her accusers and the gaping, howling mob. If Christ Himself walked among them, they would deceive Him, he thought.

The priests smeared her soles and jellied legs with pitch, daubed it on the shift and made it cling more provocatively; a red-faced soldier, all drink-broken veins and bad teeth, clutched his groin and bellowed out that this was her last chance for a decent fuck outside of Hell.

'Ye brosy-faced hoorslip,' Dog Boy growled and elbowed him hard enough to double the man over, gasping and boaking cheap ale over all the shoes nearest him.

Nivver violet a lady. Never was a lady more violated than Aggie, finding the harsh truth of what lay beyond the confines of Roxburgh. Not adventure and freedom, but turning slowly to a shrieking horror of black, with a sweet stink so like pork as to make you retch at the saliva it brought to starving mouths. The priests solemn and canting, invited the last blister of Aggie to repent her sins; it was, Dog Boy realized with a sour curl to the lip of him, an Ember Day.

Through the haze of smoke and witch-hair tendrils of haar, Dog Boy found Isabel's eyes again – or thought he did – before he turned away and slouched through the crowd, heading back down to Scotch Gate and the bridge, hunched and moody and careless.

Frixco de Fiennes was more than a little drunk, on wine and fame both. He had watched his brother die of the festering wound he had taken at Roxburgh and discovered that, without him, he was that worst of creatures, a noble so low and Gascon he might just as well have been dung.

He had taken work – welcome to a man with scarce two coins to rub against each other – with the harassed officials still trying to carry out King Edward's writs in a land where he had no power. It had taught him, in short order, that the years of juggling accounts in Roxburgh had honed a talent for tallying, where a merk was two thirds of a pound, a shilling of twelve silver pennies one-twentieth of a pound and the penny the only actual coin in all of it.

It had taught him, too, that there was a new-fangled way of tallying, using some foul heathen Moorish numbering system which made it all easier, according to the young, thrusting clerks who promoted it. Frixco saw the tallying up for his own talents and the bleak future of it soured him.

It was Aggie's misfortune to stumble on him at that moment, pleading for help for 'his bairn'. Turning her in had been desperation – but it had also netted him a reward, which he had spent on clothes and wine. Now he was staggering from the burning stink and wondering where he could make more such coin.

He collided with the man, the pair of them as much at fault as the other. Frixco, alarmed at having annoyed one of the hundreds of rough, armed men slouching and reeling about the streets, stammered out an apology – and then saw the face.

He blinked, puzzled, for he knew the face but could not place it . . . the knowledge crashed on him like the apple in Eden flung at his forehead; he saw the black, dagged hair and the bearded face, saw it as he had at Roxburgh, the scowl arched over a fistful of steel.

Dog Boy and Frixco stared at one another for a long moment and Dog Boy knew he had been recognized, knew it was all up with him in Berwick and felt a sudden, savage exultation.

'Nivver violet a lady,' he growled and slammed a horny-handed fist into Frixco's face, wishing he had a dagger in it. He leaped over the mud-spattered sprawl of the man and was off down the street like a new lamb. He ran no more than a few paces, fell into a swift walk and filtered on down through the throng lurching away from the remains of the pyre.

He was a hundred ells away before he heard the distant shouts, but they floated clear and eldritch through the encroaching sea-haar.

'The Black is in Berwick. Ware. The Black Douglas is in Berwick.'

The sea, off Colonsay
At the same time

The *Señor Glorioso* was like a ship, Pegy declared, in that it floated and had sails. Other than that it might well have been an ox cart to him and, despite the alleged generosity of Grand Master Ruy Vaz in presenting it in exchange for the half-sunk *Bon Accord*, Pegy was sullen and convinced that they had had the worst of the deal.

He said it loud and often, all the struggling way back towards Scotland, and Hal, drifting in and out of wound fever, knew it was because the new beast was a long-runner more suited to the Middle Sea, whose ropes and spars and sails were as strange as a six-legged foal to the cog-men of the old *Bon Accord*. They knew it as a carib, the best way they could pronounce the Moorish word for it: *qaríb*.

The lateen rig, with its huge, unwieldy yardarms, defeated the best efforts of Niall Silkie, Angus and Donald, while the single big rudder confused Somhairl. Pegy, unable to judge the speed of 'the ugly baist', was barely able to work out where they were never mind where they were going; he knew the cargo was overloaded, too, and prayed for good weather.

Somewhere, the Devil laughed.

A wind rose and freshened as they came up round the shoulder of Colonsay – Pegy was fairly sure it was Colonsay – and the sailors brought in as much sail as they thought might work, only to find the *Señor Glorioso* blundering and pitching like a mad, blind stot.

Then, whirling away the sea-haar and the sunshine, the gale backed up with a witch's shriek, backed up full south and west and hurled them like a driven stag towards the coast.

Berwick town
Some hours later

His back hurt from crouching, so that he swore he heard it crack when he finally straightened and began to move into the dark and the fog, out of the stinking alley he had been hiding in since God forged the world, it seemed.

Surely, Dog Boy thought, they would have given up by now. It had been hours since the alarm was raised, was now dark and the sea-haar had witch-fingered in and grown thicker and stronger. He had heard the soldiers calling for *couvre-feu* at least an hour ago, so the streets were dark, wet and should have been empty.

Save that they were not. Torches, lambent in the swirling mist, showed the bobbing presence of men in packs, still searching, relentless as an avalanche; the Black Douglas was trapped in Berwick and, sooner or later, would be found. Dog Boy cursed his likeness to Jamie. Then, for the first time, he cursed his own stupidity.

Not long after that he was found.

He came creeping out of the shadow of the Holy Trinity and practically ran into a barrel of a man with a sputtering flambeau and a face which had the pucker of an old scar running from the patch of his left eye down through cheek and jawbone.

'The Bla—' he yelled before Dog Boy's wild lashing smashed the hilt of his sword into the man's forehead, felling him like an ox. But it was enough; the cries went up, the marsh-light flames trailed towards him and he ran.

Flitting into the wynds, night-black as Auld Nick's serk, up steps, skidding on cobbles, over courtyards and through deep wynds like writhing tunnels, Dog Boy wraithed like a running fox.

He turned and twisted away from every pale light which appeared, trying, always, to work his way to the bulk of stone that had once belonged to the Friars of the Sack, for next to it was the Briggate, portal to the ford and freedom.

He swooped like a mad crow from space to space, leaped up wynd stairs and paused once to tip a waterbutt down on too-close pursuers. Later he paused again, long enough to unsneck the door of a sty to let out a charge of swine, and then left them, laughing.

Balked by a blind alley, he sprang sideways to a lintel, then a balcony, along it with a leap into a new courtyard, bombarding his pursuers with mad curses and laughter, pots and, once, a pie dish set out to soak in the rain. Doors and shutters banged, children and women shrieked, dogs barked and howled.

He skipped and skidded along steep-pitched roofs, tore off slates and flung them, swung down past the leering, open-throated faces on the fine guttering and, once, swung into a carelessly unshuttered window.

The women inside shrieked like harpies and he stopped only long enough to offer them a mocking bow and a grin from a sweat-sheened face before scooping up the night-bucket and emptying it out of the window. He heard the gratifying curse and sizzle as he headed for the door, the stairs and the way out to the back court.

Finally, somewhere in Silver Street, he sprang for a lintel, swung up to a folly of a balcony, then up the newel post of that to the slated roof, where he sat, astraddle the steep pitch as if on a horse, his back to the gable stack. He panted and the sweat trickled down him like running mice, but the torches milled and confused voices shouted.

He had foiled them. For now.

For all that, he was only a little closer – he saw the bulk of the Red and White Halls of the foreign wool merchants and knew them. That placed him close to the Maison Dieu, which had its own gate through the ditch and stockade walls, near enough to the ford to chance it when the torches slid away.

The flames bobbed and circled. Dog Boy blessed the silver-smith whose house this was, for his vanity in having a silly wee balcony, so built that you could only access it through windows both shuttered and barred and even then would have to half crouch to enjoy the view from it.

Yet it had permitted him access to the steeply pitched roof, hard slated to foil any wee thieves who might be tempted to dig their way into the smith's home and down to the shop, where the shine would be.

Up here, Dog Boy thought, I am safe until the dawn and the vanished mist. Which gave him some hours yet to let the row die down. Below, he heard the pained calls of his staggering pursuers and smothered an exultant laugh at complaints of injuries and pigs.

Then he heard the horse, slap-clopping up the cobbles from the Briggate, heard the voices hail him – out after *couvre-feu* and mounted, Dog Boy thought, makes him a knight or a man-at-arms, a chiel of worth and on important business.

Not important enough, he saw with a sickening lurch of his belly, that he could not take a torch and join in the search, standing in the stirrups and raising the flame high to search the rooftops. For the reward, no doubt, Dog Boy thought, as well as the glory of being the man who captured the dreaded Black Douglas. The irony of it twisted a wry smile on his sweating face.

He watched the horseman and his trembling flambeau come closer, leaving the men on foot to search the ground-level shadows. Hot and encumbered, he managed to wriggle out of the padded jack, but was reluctant to lose it, so dropped to the cobbles as lightly as he could with it bulked in one arm like a shield, sword in the other; the chill fog cut into his sweat-drenched serk like a knife.

He saw the Silver Street courtyard with its little mercat cross, a squat affair ringed at the top and mounted on a dais of two steps – and the idea struck him with a clarity that made him laugh out loud.

He arranged it swiftly with his jack and his iron hat, frowned a little at the sacrifice of his estoc but rammed it left to right through the jack, the sharp needle of blade pinning the right sleeve up to the chest. He stood back, admired his handiwork briefly and laughed again, before darting out to where the slow, peering horseman could see him.

Then he turned, running back into the courtyard as if he knew he had just been spotted, was gratified to hear the sudden scrape and rasp of iron hooves as the beast was urged on by the horseman.

The rider came in at a trot and heaved up at the sight of the man standing, waiting, a blade winking faint light in a bar across his chest. He had an iron-rimmed hat on and did not look to be running, which made the rider grin; the horseman was mailed and coiffed and armed, and was a skilled fighter, as were all the royal couriers who wore the jupon with the pards of England. Bigod, the others would be envious of what the capture of the notorious outlaw Sir James Douglas would bring him.

'Ho,' he said and slid off the horse, sword out; he did not want to attack on horseback in the slippery, cobbled, confining courtyard and, besides, taking the outlaw on foot would add to the glory of it. God blind me, he thought, he is a big lad all the same.

'Does tha yield?' he demanded and had silence back, which unnerved him a little. He thought of calling to the others, the garrison men, but he wanted none to share this moment, so he shrugged and moved in swiftly, striking out.

The ringing clang of it sent a dreadful shock up his arm so that he recoiled, cursing and barely hanging on to his weapon with numbed fingers. *Nom de Dieu*, did the man have new-fangled plate underneath the padded jack?

The blow took him in the back and flung him face down to the cobbles, where he gasped and spluttered and writhed, all the air driven from him. In that part of his mind not mad with gibber at the thought of having been crippled or killed, he saw the figure he had attacked was a dressed stone cross and that the one who had struck him from behind was vaulting into the saddle of his horse.

Grinning down at him, black beard bright with pearled water, the man reined round and saluted him mockingly.

'I could have killed ye. Remember that and tell them Aleysandir of Douglas has eluded them this day,' the man declared loudly. 'As daring as the Black Sir James – but better looking.'

Then he was gone, in a scrape of iron-shod hooves, a mad laugh and a mist that swirled in where he had been.

Unshaven, snowed with spindrift, hollow-eyed and tired beyond anything they had known, the crew staggered into the merciful wind-dropped morning and called greetings, messages and obscenities.

The bread was sodden and moulded, the cheese so rancid it was thrown over – and Hal realized how bad it had to be for sailors, who would eat almost anything, to contemplate that. They chewed bacon, which was as hard as the peas that went with it, washed it down with water filtered through a linen serk to get rid of the worst in it, while the *Señor Glorioso* pitched and rolled, heavy with cargo and sodden with leak.

Hal, the sweat rolling off him in drops fat as wren's eggs, ate nothing and Sim was too busy boaking to try to put anything down the other way.

'If it holds like this,' Pegy said cheerfully, looking at the sky, 'we will be in Oban in a week, or less.'

Hal, the arm throbbing in time to his every heartbeat, heard the false in Pegy's voice.

'If it holds?'

Pegy shrugged. The truth was that he did not like the iron and milk sky in every direction and thought they had pierced through to the eye of a vicious smack of weather which would be on them in less than half a day. He did not say any of this, but realized he did not need to to the lord of Herdmanston.

'How is yourself bearing up?' he asked instead. 'Have ye had yer wound seen to this morn?'

Hal grunted, the memory of it sharp as the pain Somhairl had inflicted, his great face, braids swinging round it, a study of lip-chewing concentration as he squeezed the pus from it.

'Green it was,' Hal reported, 'as Sim's face. I take it there is slim chance of getting to Oban without worry, at this time of year and without weather?'

Pegy frowned and sucked his moustache ends.

'Weel. . . we have to try, for there is little choice else, other than to put into some wee island and wait for it to blaw away.'

'Which might take hours, or days – or weeks,' Hal replied with a rueful smile, wincing as he adjusted his arm. 'I have little liking to spend weeks in a driftwood shed, living on crabs and herring. Besides that, we will have failed in our endeavour.'

'Aye, right enough,' Pegy answered. 'Ye are poor company for shed-life, but tak' heart, my lord, at least the wind blaws away the midgies.'

'If it blaws us back to where the Bruce waits,' growled a familiar voice, 'it can howl all it pleases. Where are we, Pegy?'

The captain turned to Kirkpatrick, his face a sour smear of disapproving.

'Ye will change that tune when the howling wind makes ye jig to the dance it makes,' he answered. 'Besides, we are in the Firth o' Lorn, coming up to the narrow of it and the last run to Oban. It is no place to be at the mercy of a storm wind.'

'Christ betimes, this is summer,' Kirkpatrick exclaimed bitterly. 'You would think there would be kinder weather.'

Those nearest laughed, none heartier than Somhairl, shaking his head mockingly at Kirkpatrick, who gave him a scarring scowl in return and then turned to Pegy.

'Clap on all sail, or whatever you mariners shout. Sooner we are back in Oban, sooner this cargo is in the keeping of the King.'

'And Sim's innards are back in his belly,' Hal answered, sitting suddenly as the rush of fever-sweat swamped him.

'Oh aye,' Pegy replied, knuckling a forehead dripping as much with spray as sarcasm. 'Clappin' on sail, yer lordship, as ordered. Now if only any of us here had a wee idea of what that might actually do to this baist o' a boat . . .'

171

They plodded on, heavy and sodden as a wet cow in pasture, with the wind full from the east, the men singing as much to raise their spirits as any sail.

Hal stayed on deck and up at the beakhead, until his face was stiff and salted, his eyes bloodshot and his brow ridged; Pegy found him there and had Angus and Donald cart him to the shelter for the storm was rising again. Hal already knew this, since his raggled hair was straight out and whipping either side of his face as he stared ahead and Pegy had to shout above the moan and whine of a rising wind.

The sea greened round the stern, washing over the stepped deck that rose up there – the nearest to a castle it had, since there was none at all in the fore – and the sails flapped and ragged, the men struggling to bring them in.

It became clear to everyone, with each man Pegy put to bailing and pumping, that the ship was taking on too much water, was too loaded to ride this out.

'We are sinking,' Pegy reported to Kirkpatrick and Hal, blunt as a blow to the temple. 'We need to make landfall.'

'Where?'

They were shouting, hanging on to lines, buffeted and shoved by a bulling wind. Pegy bawled out where he thought they were and Kirkpatrick squinted; it had started to rain, squalling and hissing, stippling the wet deck.

'We are closer, then, to Craignish. We could be up that wee loch to Craignish Castle and the Campbells, who are good friends to our king.'

Pegy closed one eye and contemplated, and then spoke, slow and hesitant.

'Aye, we are. If the weather and wind stay as they are we could be in Craignish watter as you say. Run up through the sound at Islay and then hope the wind has changed a wee, to beat back north.'

'I dinna ken much,' Kirkpatrick roared, 'but I ken that is

172

a long way for a short cut. Can we not go on as we are, straight up to Craignish, round Scarba?'

'Shorter, but in this wind . . .' Pegy bawled back, though the truth was that he did not think he or the crew could handle this bitch-boat well enough. He did not want to admit it, but it was clear in his seamed face, pebbled with spray and rain.

'If she is sinking,' Kirkpatrick persisted, with Gordian blade logic, 'we have no time for a wee daunder to gawp at the sights, Pegy. Besides – taking her through the Islay Sound as she is risks being driven ashore and those island rats will strip her bare with nae thought for the ruin that will bring our kingdom. Run her truer than that.'

Pegy's hesitation was underlined by the thrum and moan of wind, the crack of the lateen sails. Hal saw him wipe his mouth with the back of one hand and knew it was not wet he washed away, but exactly the opposite.

'But?' Hal answered, feeling the sudden dry crack of his own mouth.

'Aye, yer lordship is smart as a whip,' Pegy replied, half-ashamed at being so transparent. 'But . . . if we are caught by the wind, on the tack it is on now, we will be hard put not to be driven on to the weather coast of Jura, or Scarba itself. Or through the Corryvreckan.'

Those who heard it stopped what they were doing. An eyeblink of pause only, it held more menace than any shriek of fear and both Hal and Kirkpatrick noted it and looked at each other; here was the real reason for Pegy's concern.

'Bad, is it?'

'They say the Caillaich Bheur washes her great plaid at the bottom of the sea in that place,' Pegy declared, 'and makes the waves whirl.'

The Cally Vaar – even Hal had heard of this old pagan hag, icy goddess of winter, and he crossed himself.

'Coire Bhreacain,' Somhairl declared solemnly, and then

173

added, with a face like an iron cliff. 'The Corryvreckan: cauldron of the speckled sea.'

'Ach, away with the pair o' ye,' Kirkpatrick replied shakily. 'Bigod, sailors are worse auld wummin than my granny. Run round this cauldron and get us safe to Loch Craignish.'

'Aye, aye, lord,' Pegy replied and the crew moved aching muscles, unflaking ragged lateen-rigged sails and cursing the ropes that burst the pus-filled welts on their water-softened palms. Slowly, like a tired carthorse, the *Señor Glorioso* turned towards the unseen shores and wallowed on and Pegy, cursing and praying in equal measure, swore he heard the Devil laugh, though it could have been the wind.

Hours later, with a precision of navigation Pegy could only admire as hellish, the wind rose to a mad shriek, the *Señor Glorioso* balked like the filthy mule he had always considered her to be and started to run with the bit clenched firmly.

Nothing the sweating sailors could do would rein her in, not Somhairl's skill and all the extra muscle on the tiller, not Angus, Donald nor any of the others daringly skipping on wet deck, swinging on wild, windlashed line, dragging in sail until there was practically no more than a bladder's worth.

Slammed by a wind from the south and west, bent on the De'il's course, Pegy thought, the chill of it settling in him like winter haar on his skin.

To the Corryvreckan.

Hal heard it before he saw it, a dull roaring that had him peering out at the outline of islands, hazed through the rain-mist. Then he saw the white swirl of it, the great wheel of the maelstrom; a head appeared alongside his and Sim, white hair flying, face etched with misery, looked on the horror of mad sea they were driving towards.

'Christ be praised.'

'For ever and ever.'

The Corryvreckan was dirty with weather, gleeful with

malice, ringed round with a loom of dark hills and the promised grit of unseen reefs.

'The gullet of Hell,' Pegy roared, almost in defiance, as the *Señor Glorioso* swirled into the throat of it and started on the harvest of the less able. The first vanished, slapped with a wave that came from nowhere, spiralled over in a despairing shriek and a whirl of arms and legs.

The next was his friend, who sprang to try and save him, calling out for them to stop and turn, which would have been a fine jest if it had not been a tragic misery; he half turned accusingly, let go the line he gripped to appeal with both hands and vanished with the next crashing pitch of the carib.

'Hang on, lads,' Pegy yelled. It was all they could do now, Hal realized. Hold on and ride the mad stallion of it, like a charging knight in a mêlée. He thought, suddenly and incongruously, of Isabel in her cage and hoped it was not raining like this where she was . . .

The wheel of dancing, capricious water caught the *Señor Glorioso* and flung the ship sideways – but the weight of the cargo, shifting below decks now, spun it back out of the wheeling water like a released dancer from a whirling jig, into the smack of a tidal race.

It seemed to Hal as if the water exploded beneath the ship; it flung up like a rearing horse, throwing spars and planks and men in the air like chaff from a winnowing and their shrieks were lost in the exultant gale.

Hal clung on, desperate and afraid, his arms shrieking louder than the wind or the doomed; the ship crashed down with a boom like a bell, half spun, rolled crazily. The mast cracked, the white wood of it like bone, and then splintered away to ruin, the rigging and sails falling half in and half out of the vessel, tangled with men. She jerked and lurched and fled out of the whirlpool, dragging the dying trap of her own ruin with her.

Hal heard Kirkpatrick yelling, half turned in time to see

175

something huge and black swing round from his left, grow as large as the world and smack him into blackness and oblivion.

Newminster, Northumberland
Feast of St Erasmus of Formiae, June 1314

There was a drone and stink that John Walwayn had come to realize was the mark of a mustering host. The former was made up of mutter and demand, discontent and greetings, the latter of dung, leather, the rank sweat of too many unwashed and the acrid stench that he liked to imagine was fear but, in truth, was more than likely the great wash of pish that spilled from everything with legs.

The other mark of a muster was the sheer press of people, a smother of them which grew thick as damask the closer you got to the King and Walwayn elbowed and shouldered through them, scornful to his lessers – though there were not many of them – and bobbingly apologetic to his betters.

But he was a *clericus peritus lege* – a man skilled in the law, a scribe to the Earl of Hereford, permitted to attend assizes and given the commission of *oyer* and *terminus* – the right to examine and judge – on behalf of his master, the Constable of England.

Which was why the great and good, knowing whose little secrets-ferreting agent he was, were forced to give way and hem their mouths tight when he was preferred through them towards the presence of the King.

He felt their eyes searing his back. He heard growls and someone spoke in a thick, foreign way which was probably German or Brabant. Hainault's men, he thought, and was mercifully glad he could not understand what had been said and so did not have to react to it.

Inside the sweltering room, he knelt dutifully and waited.

176

It had been the abbot's room, but the simple austerity of that monk had been washed away in the comforts of a royal household which took a score of wagons to transport.

Flames danced in the mantled hearth, which had seldom seen such a luxury of sparks – and did not need it on such a muggy night, Walwayn thought – while the blaze of expensive tallow gilded the oak panelling and a long table festooned with parchments and dangling seals. A dish of diced spiced meat covered with breadcrumbs was half-buried under the scrolls, the debris of it trailing here and there where careless fingers had spilled it.

The King was sitting at one side of the table, dressed in a simple wool robe of green, his hair curled and gilded, a habit he had begun years before in order to emulate the golden cap of the now-dead Gaveston. Surreptitious as any mouse, Walwayn glanced up from under lowered lashes and bowed head, thinking the King looked liverish, though that might have been the green robe.

The chamber jigged with mad shadows from the disturbed candles; another mark of muster, Walwayn thought to himself, is the way no one seems to sleep if the King does not – and he, for certes, is too feverish to sleep. Feverish, bordering on panic, to get his army gathered and on the move.

'My lord John of Argyll is with the fleet?' the King demanded and Walwayn heard the deferential, almost soothing affirmative from one of the cluster around the table; Mauley, he recognized, seneschal and commander of the King's Royal Household troops.

'The Red Earl is muttering about visiting his daughter,' a voice interrupted – Beaumont, the one who wanted to be Earl of Buchan. Walwayn knew that his own master, the Earl of Hereford, had a grudging respect for Henry de Beaumont, if only because he was a fighting man with a long pedigree and a reputation for adventurous daring.

'The Red Earl may ride where he pleases,' the King answered

177

waspishly. 'It is not him I need, but the Irishers he brought with him. And his daughter remains safe in Rochester – tell him so.'

Walwayn knew the Red Earl of Ulster would be dealt with politely, since his support was vital and his situation awkward – the daughter safely shut in Rochester was Bruce's wife and effectively the Queen of Scotland. Not that anyone there acknowledged there being a king in Scotland; their adversary was always, simply, 'the Bruce', or now and then 'the Ogre'.

'I need foot, my lords,' Edward declared, his voice rising, almost in a whine of panic. 'As fast as it accumulates, it melts. I need foot.'

'We have two thousand horse, my liege,' a voice answered, liquid with balm. 'More than enough to crush the rebellious Scots.'

The King turned his drooping eye on this new face: the Earl of Gloucester, the young de Clare who vied with Despenser for the royal favour and who, despite being the King's nephew, was losing out to the charms of 'the new Gaveston'.

'I have fought the Scotch before, my lord of Gloucester. Foot will be needed, trust me,' Edward said flatly. He said it kindly, all the same, and Despenser scowled, but then saw his chance, leaping like a spring lamb into the silence.

'Besides – we have Sir Giles back with us.'

The name buzzed briefly round the room and made the king smile. Sir Giles d'Argentan was the third-best knight in Christendom, it was said – with the other two being the Holy Roman Emperor himself and, annoyingly, the Bruce. Imprisoned by the Byzantines, Sir Giles had been freed because the King had paid his extortionate ransom and summoned him to fly like a gracing banner above the army sent to crush the Scots.

Walwayn saw the others – Sir Payn Tiptoft, Gloucester, de Verdon – nod and smile at the thought. As young men barely into their twenties they and others – Gaveston and his own lord, Humphrey de Bohun among them – had been in the retinue of the King when he was still a prince. Idolizing the older, brilliant dazzle of d'Argentan, they had all trooped off with him to a tourney in France, leaving the Prince's army hunting out Wallace in the wilds. Twenty-two of them had been put under arrest warrants by a furious Edward I and they all wore that now like some badge of youthful honour binding them together.

That had been eight years ago and the gilded youth of then were tarnished and no wiser, it seemed. Particularly the King himself, who now turned to the patient, kneeling Walwayn.

'You are?' he began, but nodded and answered it himself. 'Hereford's clerk and lawyer – well, take this to your master.'

He paused, rummaged and helpful hands found and gave him the seal-dangling scroll he needed. Walwayn looked up then and, over the King's shoulder, saw two faces. One was the triumphant leer twisting the handsome face of Gilbert de Clare, Earl of Gloucester; the other the long mourn of bad road that belonged to Sir Marmaduke Thweng, his walrus moustache ends silver-winking in the light.

Like angel and Devil on the royal shoulders, Walwayn thought, wildly trying to gather himself as he took the scroll from the King's hand.

'Your master and the Earl of Gloucester are appointed commanders of the Van,' the King declared, more for the benefit of any who did not already know than for Walwayn.

The clerk blanched, hesitated.

'Your Grace?' he quavered and the King's eye drooped. Even as a parody of the fierceness of his father, it was frightening enough to the little Hereford lawyer.

'Are you witless? Deaf?'

Walwayn caught the angel Thweng's warning eye and simply bowed and backed out, sick to his stomach at what he had to carry back to his master.

Sir Marmaduke saw the clerk scuttle off, knew what he felt and why.

Joint commanders. The de Clares and de Bohuns were bitter

rivals and appointing them to jointly command anything was a surety for disaster – yet Thweng knew the King had done it to promote his nephew, young de Clare. The Earl of Hereford, Constable of England, would be furious, but de Clare was the new Favourite. There is always a favourite with Edward, Thweng thought. For all the tragedy of Gaveston, the King has learned nothing – and, behind him, he could feel the flat hating gazes from the Despensers.

'Pembroke,' the King said suddenly. 'Where is the Earl of Pembroke?'

'Sir Aymer is in Berwick,' Thweng replied flatly, and then remembered himself. 'Your Grace sent de Valence to oversee matters in Berwick.'

The King had forgotten and did not like the fact of it, so Thweng moved back into the shadows and out of his eyeline.

He is losing control, he thought. He has even brought that stupid lion in a cage, the one he touted round in '04, when he and the rest of this menagerie were young. He brought it in the last attempt to bring Bruce to battle, four years ago, he recalled, though the lion was toothless and mangy then. Now it was blind and bad-tempered and dying. A fitting banner for this campaign, in fact.

But the beast harks back to the gilded youth the King and all his company had, Thweng thought moodily, and are reluctant to let go. Christ's Wounds, the King even calls it Perrot, the 'loving name' he gave to Gaveston. Stupid name for a favourite, be it dog, horse, bird or lion – and too Malmsey-sweet for a man.

Was he a sodomite? Thweng looked at the King and wondered. Tall and imposing – the picture of a warrior, but that meant little. Priests, Thweng knew, indulged in it and, by God, the Templars were given it as the second-worst accusation that could be levelled at them after spitting on the God they were supposed to protect and uphold. But magnates of the realm? A king?

Thweng remembered himself as a youth, draped round the neck of a loving brother in arms with nothing more in it than the bonds of battle-forged friendship. He shook the thoughts of royal sin away from him.

The King was no boy-lover, but neither was he a good king, or half the warrior he looked, Thweng thought, and then surreptitiously crossed himself for the sin in thinking it.

Mark you, he added to himself, if this army gets anywhere it will be because someone marches off and all the others will follow after, like sheep – but whether it reaches Scotland, Wales or bloody Cathay will be by accident and all are equally likely.

He straightened, as quietly as he could, to ease the stiffness in his back; he was too old for these late-night maunderings and, if proof were needed that matters were spiralling out of control, it was this need for frantic conferences well into the dark.

It was hot in the room, stank of sweated wool and desperation and Sir Marmaduke longed to be outside, questing for a bit of wind in the summer night.

Craignish, Argyll
At the same moment

He breached from the dark, like the ship out of the maelstrom, crashing back to a nightmare of creak and slow rending, a mad, pale light and the flicker of shadows.

'Ah, blissin' o' heaven, yer honour – ye're alive.'

Hal was not so sure of it; he struggled to rise and against the thundering pain of his head. A hand fumbled at the trap he seemed caught in, a voice cursed from the dark and Hal was suddenly free to sit up, listening to groans and pig-squeals; a face thrust itself into the light of the torch, grinning with mad relief, dripping sweat and sea-water.

'Niall Silkie . . .' Hal said and the torch bobbed.

'Good, good – ye have yer wits. Now . . . careful. We are lying on our side here and everythin' is arse to elbow.'

Hal saw he had been trapped by the strap of his baldric, which seemed fastened to the floor by an iron hook – until he realized that it had once been hung up alongside a truckle bed, but now the world was canted and crazy.

The ship . . .

The ship was beached and broken, the timbers snapped and splintered as gnawed bones. Like a rotted whale, it was a cave of dangerous dangle and sudden pits that he and Niall had to struggle through, while all the time the gentle sough and hiss of the merciful, calmly breathing tide set the last of the timbers to creak and moan.

'Nothin' so mournful as a stricken boatie,' Niall said, when they paused the once, to get bearings. His face was sheened and gleaming.

'Others,' Hal managed from the great half-numbed strangeness that was one side of his face; there was a ragged, rasping catch inside his cheek that spoke of one or more teeth knocked out or splintered.

'Kirkpatrick is on the beach. Pegy is gone and gone – Donald, too, unless God is merciful to his brother's wails. Almost all the crew . . .'

Niall stopped, trembling.

'It is after being the Feast of St Erasmus,' he said wonderingly. 'May the wee holy man keep them safe as he should.'

He shook it from him like a wet black dog and fumbled on through the dark, Hal at his heels and still clutching his sword and scabbard, all that he could find of his in this dragon's cave of dark terror. St Erasmus, Hal thought, patron of sailors and known to them as St Elmo. Asleep, with all God's other holiest, he added bitterly to himself.

Niall warned him; he dropped with a splash and Hal followed, the jar sending a great wash of pain up through his

182

head, so that it seemed like a bursting blood orange. Then they sloshed on, out through the ribs of the stricken beast, where great blocks like stone lay scattered in the luminous tide. The cargo, thought Hal desperately. The cargo . . .

'See if we can find any other poor souls,' Niall hissed and Hal started guiltily from his thoughts of the wrapped weapons. Slowly, carefully, the torch flattening and flaring in the still-stiff breeze, they moved along, searching the dark and wet.

It was a desolate harvesting in the dim, by touch alone, of objects that might be waterlogged flesh and wool, or sheets of bladderwrack silting the waves like streaming hair. They might be heads fronded with cropped beards, or weeded rocks, all of them veined by the sea, surging and dragging, hissing over pebbles.

The only two men Hal discovered were dead and he gave up on dragging them out of the loll of surf. Somewhere further up he heard shouting, saw torches dance in the darkness and Niall Silkie plunged his own brand into the surf with a hiss, falling into a half-crouch of terror.

'Wreckers,' he said. 'Come to loot the ship and slit the throats o' any survivors.'

But Hal knew at once that the shouter was Kirkpatrick and rose, sloshing up through the surf to the stumbling pebbles, dragging his sword out. Niall, who did not want to be left alone in the dark, cursed.

Moving towards the sound, Hal felt the tug and treachery of tussocks, saw the torches coalesce and the shadows etched against them. He stumbled out of the dark and saw a man whirl towards him, the gleam of naked steel in his hands.

'Friend,' he yelped. Somhairl, both fists full of knife, gave a delighted grin and called out his name, so that all the shadows turned; there were not many of them, Hal noted.

One of them was Kirkpatrick, who turned once to acknowledge him, then faced front again and yelled out a long stream of Gaelic, patiently learned at the elbow of Bruce.

'Bastard Campbells,' he growled aside to Hal, the sodden dags of his wet hair knifed to his face. 'Caterans and worse, who would try and steal the smell off your shit because it belongs to someone else.'

Hal saw the figures, uncertain under their torches, all wild hair and bare legs and wet, sharp steel.

'I hope you are being polite,' he said and knew the mush of his voice was a shock to them both when Kirkpatrick turned to him and raised his own sizzling torch for a better look; Hal did not want to hear his views on the batter of his face, but had them anyway.

'Christ, ye look as if ye had the worst o' an argument with a skillet,' he declared. 'Ye are more bruise and swell than face.'

'A rope's end will do that,' Somhairl added sombrely, 'whipped by a gale like we had.'

So that was what had hit him. Not the whole world then . . .

Kirkpatrick's warning shout buzzed pain through him and, finally, a voice called out in thick English from a throat not used to it.

'Who is that there then?'

Hal, his head roaring with the pain of doing it, shouted back.

'Sir Henry of Herdmanston, a friend to Neil Campbell and in need of hospitality.'

There was a pause, then a calmer, deeper voice, growing stronger as it moved closer, fought the wind to be heard.

'Indeed? You claim the friendship of Niall mac Cailein, which is no little thing and a double-edged blade if you are proved false to it.'

The speaker was better dressed, surrounded by a clutch of bare-legged snarlers, crouching like dogs round him. He squinted, and then grinned.

'I recall you now: Hal of Herdmanston. I was with you

when Neil, son of Great Colin, brought you to the meeting in the heather we had when King Robert fled to the Isles.'

Hal remembered it, though not this man. It had been a low point.

The shadow-man paused and then bowed his neck slightly towards Kirkpatrick.

'And yourself, who brought the news of our king's escape and survival. The King's wee man, though I have forgot your name entire.'

'Kirkpatrick.'

'That was it, right enough.'

He made a brief move and the caterans shifted back, lowering their weapons. The man stepped forward and bowed a little more.

'Dougald Campbell of Craignish,' he said. 'You have the hospitality of my house.'

'That's a bloody relief,' Kirkpatrick said as the man turned away to shout a liquid stream of Gaelic to his unseen men.

To Somhairl he said: 'Gather up those we have found. When it is light, we will return and search for more.'

'The cargo . . .' Hal said and Kirkpatrick patted his arm.

'Away you and get your face seen to. The cargo will be brought, safe and untouched. You heard the man; we have the hospitality of the Campbell of Craignish.'

'Aye,' Hal said. The pain seemed to ebb and flow with the tide now; a sudden thought lanced through it, sharp with the fire of guilt, and jerked his head up into Kirkpatrick's concerned face.

'Sim . . . where is Sim?'

Kirkpatrick's bloodless lips never moved, his greased face never quavered. Yet Hal felt the leaden blow of it, hard as the rope's end which had smacked his face, and he reeled, felt the great burning light explode in his head and bent over to vomit.

Then the light went out.

ISABEL

He came to gawp, the de Valence who is called Earl of Pembroke, hearing that I was a witch or worse. Even earls are not immune to scratching the scabs of their itching minds, to look on the strange wonders of the caged. Malise, fawning and bobbing his head like a mad chook, brought him to the Hog's Tower, but even this rebounded on him, for Aymer de Valence's distaste for what had been done to me was clear. Dark and scowling he was, so that I was reminded of the name everyone called him behind his back, the one Gaveston gave him: Jacob the Jew. I will resolve this, he said to Malise, after midsummer, when the current tribulations are settled. Malise did not like that and I should have been pleased for an earl's help, like a thirsty wee lapdog for water. Of course I was not. Immediately after the tribulations of those days, I answered like a prophecy and before Malise could speak, the sun shall be darkened and the moon shall not give her light and the stars shall fall from Heaven and the power of the Heavens shall be shaken. Gospel of Matthew, I added as the Earl crossed himself. Chapter twenty-four, verse twenty-nine, I called after him as he fled; I saw the punishments flaming in Malise's eyes.

It is almost midsummer.

CHAPTER EIGHT

The Black Bitch Tavern, Edinburgh
Feast of St Columba, June 1314

The Dog Boy pushed through the throng and wished he was not here at all, nor headed where he was going; the one was altogether too crowded, the other such a trial that the setting for it was aptly named.

Edinburgh stank of old burning and feverish, frantic desperation. The castle bulked up like a hunchback's shoulder, blackened and reeking from where it had been slighted; carts still ground their iron-shod wheels down the King's Way, full of stones filched from the torn-down gate towers and bound for other houses or drystane walls.

Without a garrison, the town itself filled up with wickedness, with men from both sides of the divide and every nook in between, with those fleeing from the south and those filtering in from the north seeking loved ones or an opportunity. It packed itself with whores and hucksters, cutpurses, coney-catchers, cunning-men and counterfeiters, while the beadles and bailiffs struggled to keep order with few men and less enthusiasm.

What Dog Boy and the others had brought, of course, did

189

not help, even though it was a handful of parchment, no more. Delivered to the monks of St Giles with instructions from their king, it was a spark to tinder, as far as Dog Boy was concerned.

Twelve parchments he had delivered, each hastily copied and sent here. Six were being further copied here, shaven-headed scribblers fluttering their ink-stained mittened fingers, while six were taken out by large-voiced prelates and thundered from altar and wynd corner.

The shriving pews would fill, soon. Those seeking absolution would creep from the shadows, heaped high with pride, avarice, lust and murder, to dump it at the rood screen in the hope of God's forgiveness. The sensible sinners would flee.

Dog Boy could not read, but he knew the content of those parchments, the copies flying out to Stirling, Perth and every other 'guid toon' in the Kingdom. He had not known the jewel he had plucked from Berwick, bouncing around in the saddlebags of the courier's stolen horse.

A letter, from the Plantagenet to de Valence:

> . . . to spare Leith for the port, but burn Edinburgh town and so to raze and deface it as a perpetual memory of the Law of Deuteronomy lighted upon it, for their falsity and disloyalty. Also sack as many villages around and burn and subvert them, putting every man, woman and child to fire and sword, without exception, for they are creatures who have defied God and king both.

There was more, all in the same harshness, a great long slather of venom which had been read to Dog Boy when he had been taken in to see the King – as if that had not been shock and horror enough.

Bruce was laid up, propped on pillows in St Ninian's with a face grey and blotched, peeling and unhealthy with sheen. He smiled as Dog Boy was brought to him, the ruin of his cheek gaping like a second mouth and his hand barely able to wave the fingers.

'It looks worse than it is,' he said into the wide-eyed concern of Dog Boy's face, while the caring monks fussed, moving awkwardly round the great pillar of his brother Edward, who grunted like an annoyed boarpig.

'Poison,' he said flatly and the King fluttered weary fingers.

'They would have been better at it,' he wheezed. 'Besides, this is not new, even if no one knows the cause.'

There was a silence where no one looked at anyone else, for the cause was already on everyone's lips: lepry. No one dared admit it, all the same, just as they did not dare admit that this might be the end of the King. True, this had happened before and as bad – yet Edward had been made heir this time, just in case . . .

'The Coontess would ken,' Dog Boy blurted and the King managed another ruined smile.

'She is no longer a countess, but Isabel MacDuff's treatments were an ease, even though she fed me the worst of potions,' he admitted, and then glared at the monks. 'At least she sweetened them.'

He turned to the Dog Boy again.

'You were daring and sprung a prize from Berwick,' he said and indicated that Edward should read it. Even in the hot, fetid sickroom the words were rotted with hate.

'Your reward is twofold,' Bruce went on. 'Take a dozen copies to the monks of St Giles and have them make copies and spread the word of this in Edinburgh. Other copies will be sent to all the good towns of the realm.'

'It will cause panic,' Edward argued, frowning. 'Folk will flee Edinburgh like ants from a boiled nest.'

'And so avoid a death that otherwise would have come on them unawares,' Bruce replied stolidly. 'I would rather have panic and mayhem, brother, than the deaths of those I am elevated to serve. Besides, if folk hear what the Plantagenet

191

has marked down for them, they will grow as angry as they do fearful.'

'The best of the realm's men are already here,' Edward insisted. 'The ones who brought their own arms – men of substance, with a holding in this kingdom and a reason for needing its future.'

'Not enough,' Bruce said wearily. 'I had three earls of the realm at my side – one is run off and two I made myself. The Plantagenet, even without half of his, brings thousands – twenty or more, it is said.'

'God be praised,' muttered Dog Boy and everyone fluttered a swift cross on their breast.

'For ever and ever.'

'On your return,' Bruce went on, turning his head to Dog Boy, 'comes the better part of the reward. I am advised, by Sir James Douglas, that you are a master with hounds, which accounts for your name.'

He smiled, lopsided this time for the cheek-drag was irritating him. Dog Boy saw that the portion of pillow under his neck, exposed by his turning head, was yellowed with old sweat.

'You and I are auld friends,' Bruce added. 'Nivver violet a lady.'

Dog Boy jerked as if stung and then flushed; he had not known the King had recalled that campfire moment all those long years ago.

'So you are now made houndsman to the King,' Bruce declared. 'Before witnesses. When I am well, we will hunt together, you and I, and you will breed the best dogs a king can have.'

Dog Boy had quit the place, stunned by it all. Afterwards, all during the swift ride to Edinburgh, he had been silent and numbed – raised, bigod, to be Royal Houndsman. Dog Boy crowned.

The word went out, of course, so that the others knew – Patrick and Parcy Dodd and the others all chaffed him about it and, finally, declared that they would wet the fortunate head of the Royal Houndsman in Edinburgh.

They chose the Black Bitch, as much for the aptness of name as for it being the worst stew in the town, and now Dog Boy shoved his way towards it, forcing through the frenzy of people; he could scarcely tell the difference between those frantic to leave and those frantic to squeeze the last measure of brittle pleasure from the place – but the fear was the same.

Yet there was a strange unreality. Silversmith apprentices paraded a wooden bier with a fat, ornate *nef*, a gorgeously worked fretwork ship of silver blazoned with Mary and Child and an enticement to customers to visit their shop. Butchers, slipping in their offal, bellowed the prices of pork and capon – originally high, they were falling rapidly because doom galloped at them and everything had to be gobbled. A pair of beadles led a whoremonger to the stocks, shuffling him through the dung close to a horse trough which would provide the dirty water he was to be soaked in.

Normal, as if the sky was not falling; Dog Boy ducked into the sweltering roar of the Bitch and his appearance swelled the bellow of it with a joy of noise from the six men who had ridden into Edinburgh with him and now dominated the tavern. The others in it, even the scarred and hard, kept to the sidelines of them.

Shining with sweat and drink, his men thrust a horn beaker of ale into one hand and hailed him loudly; he was their darling now, was the elevated Dog Boy.

'The Royal Dog Boy he is now,' bellowed Patrick and the others roared their approval once again, while Troubadour Tam Napier struck up his battered old viel in a tune that set everyone jigging.

Buggerback Geordie shoved forward a woman, dark-eyed and dark-haired, half-moon sweat under the arms of her dress and her smile only partly ruined by some missing teeth. She had the finest pair of breasts Dog Boy had seen in a time and, coyly batting her eyes, she pulled them out for him to see.

'This is Dame Trapseed,' said Archie Gower, known to everyone as Sweetmilk, for no reason anyone could fathom. 'We brings her as Yer Honour's gift on this night and hopes she elevates ye higher still.'

'*Ma Dame*,' Dog Boy said with a mocking, courtly bow and the laughter rang into the rafters. He went to a bench in the deeper shadows of the flickering tavern and took her on his knee, felt the heat of her through the dress as she wriggled on his lap and giggled at what she was creating underneath her; her breasts were slick.

'If you do not sit still,' Parcy Dodd yelled at her across the fug and noise, 'you will stop our captain thinking entire, as God ordained.'

'God? Whit has God to do wi' this?' demanded the woman, who had fumbled loose the ties on Dog Boy's braies by feel alone. She adjusted herself, hiked her dress a little and Dog Boy could not believe the skill of her when he felt the heat and wet and knew what she had done.

'God it was who created Man,' Parcy went on, 'and gave him both a pyntle and a keen and cunning mind. In His wisdom though, he ordained that Man could only use one of them at a time.'

The crowd roared and demanded more. Parcy obliged. Dame Trapseed wriggled and bounced a little, so that Dog Boy grunted in the half-dark.

'Once,' Parcy began, while folk shushed their neighbours, 'there was a great rain, a gushing scoosh that some folk thought was the second Flood sent by the Lord.'

Dog Boy, anticpitating a gushing scoosh of his own, tried to concentrate on Parcy.

'They ran to their priest, a good wee man, who went out into the pour of it all, even down to the banks of the burn, which rose in spate as he begged and pleaded with the Lord. The watter rose up roon his ankles and the reeve came up to ask if he would no' be better climbin' oot – the reeve would

194

help. The priest refused, saying that the Lord would save him, and the reeve went on his way.'

The woman was in a rhythm now, a gentle sway, like reeds on a riverbank; Dog Boy gave up with Parcy.

'The watter rose up to his waist and still the priest begged the Lord to save him. His own sire rode up on a fine horse, all drookit but come to save the wee priest from the flood. But the priest refused, allowing that only the Lord would save him, and the sire rode away as the river spouted on.'

Dog Boy bit the back of the woman's shoulder, for the place was silent now save for the rhythmic swish of the woman and the sound of her ragged breathing. No head even bothered turning to them, all the same.

'Finally, the watter was at the priest's neck and up comes the King himself in a boatie, rowin' like a bloody raider frae the isles, demanding that the priest save himself by climbin' in. But the priest refused, claiming that God would save him – and the King swept on doon the river.'

'What happened?' demanded an incredulous voice and Parcy paused for the effect, spoiled by the sudden shrill whine of the woman, who felt Dog Boy's moment arrive.

'He drooned, of coorse,' Parcy scathed and the place roared with laughter, drowning out the final noises from Mistress Trapseed.

'Then he went to Heaven and stood before the Lord God Himself, a wee bit annoyed at not having had his prayers answered, for all he had been a good priest an' Christian his entire life. God be praised.'

'For ever and ever,' the crowd answered in a rushing moth-murmur. Parcy held up one hand to silence them, a master of his art.

'He carps about havin' been abandoned. So the good Lord scowls at the wee priest. "I sent ye a reeve, a sire and the King himself to save ye. What more did ye want?"'

The crowd roared and thumped the tables in approval,

demanded more; Dame Trapseed slithered off Dog Boy's lap and he tried to cover himself as best he could, though he had to stand to lace his braies while the woman, sheened and smiling with triumph, turned out of the shadows to Buggerback Geordie and demanded her money.

Buggerback, grinning round his gap of gums, held out his hand to Patrick and had a scowl and a handful of coin, some of which went to the woman.

'I did not believe she could hump ye in the middle o' the tavern,' Patrick complained bitterly to Dog Boy as Geordie went off, jingling the coin in his palm. 'Ye may be practically *nobile* these days, but ye are worse than Horse Pyntle Johnnie there, who would swive a knothole. Yer foul, lowly lusts have cost me a pretty penny.'

Dog Boy, greasy with the ale and the moment, grinned back at him and then froze as the tavern door crashed open. Like a cold wind, the Black strode in and surveyed the silence, aware that those who did not know who he was knew what he was.

'I am truly sorry to spoil yer doings,' he said, nodding to Dog Boy. 'But the English are at Berwick and on the move north. Shift yourselves.'

Then he closed the door on a boiling panic.

Kilmartin Glen
At the same time

Push. Drive. Plod. Tug, strain at wheels, eat dust and then eat the mud that sweat made of it on your face. Work the sun up and work it down again. Hal laboured at it, heaving into the grind of it so that his head thundered and his shoulder ached.

At the end, though, he could fall into a patch of scrubby heather, wrap himself in a cloak and sleep without dreaming of Sim, whirling down and round in the maelstrom with his white crown wisped like maidenhair.

196

In the days after he had fallen in a dead faint, slowly recovering while Kirkpatrick and Campbell dragged the weapons out of the stricken ship and gathered up every wheeled contrivance and pulling beast, Hal had stumbled down to the water's edge and walked the breathing shingle in hope. Kirkpatrick sent a man with him every time, sometimes Niall, sometimes Somhairl, just to make sure he didn't fall in another dead faint, this time face down in a rock pool. And Campbell sent one of his own, a cateran called, in the English, Duncan; he had been a drover and so spoke the southron enough to be understood.

They found bodies, but none Hal knew and only one Niall recognized, kneeling beside the fish-eaten, crab-gnawed face and squinting.

'They are seldom returned by Carry Vaar,' Duncan lilted, seeing Niall's distress. 'She is in her sleeping with them all.'

Hal was torn between finding Sim with his water-bloated face like curdled cheese and not finding him at all. In the end, it was as if he had simply vanished and, by the time they were ready to leave, Hal had to force himself away from the place.

'It's a sore loss,' Kirkpatrick offered awkwardly on the day the Campbells set out to join the King, already having to lever the laden wagons up stony, rutted tracks. Kirkpatrick did not expect an answer; he had seen the yellow-blue ruin of the face and the haunt in the eyes and thought, with a sudden shift of concern, that Hal of Herdmanston was all but done.

The struggle of the next few days made him wonder at the fevered strength in the Lothian lord and, though he wished he could tell the man to slow himself, the truth was that they needed everyone's strength.

There were not enough carts and beasts – Campbell of Craignish, frowning, said that his men did not make war in that way. Once the blazing cross had been fired from crest to crest and the men gathered, they would pack some oats, ready cooked into a slab with water, add a portion of herring for the salt in it, then make a fast lick across rock and heather.

197

Kirkpatrick could believe it; the Craignish men wore onion-dyed tunics in varying shades, from deep yellow to faded mustard, had bare legs like spurtles and bore burdens an ass would have scorned, forging over tussock and hill with corded muscle and the ease of having been born to it.

They bore the residue of what would not fit in the carts, a man-packed collection of iron hats, maille, spearheads and other items labouring down to meet Campbell galleys at Kilmory, which would sail them on to Largs. There, the angels would take the Lord's share, a tithe that would mysteriously vanish, while every Craignish man would arrive at Stirling better accoutred than any man-at-arms.

Yet the journey down to Kilmory was fraught, a Satan twist of bad road and steepness through places with names like Black Crag and worse. When they entered the defile of Kilmartin Glen, the men fell silent, for this was a place of stone rings and underground kists, a land of the *sidhean*, the sheean, who could spirit you away in the night and not return you for a hundred years. Their great faerie hill of Dunadd dominated the area and the panting chatter and good-natured chaffering fell to silence.

Campbell of Craignish, though he preferred to be thought of as an enlightened Christian *nobile*, was as much worried about the *sidhean* as any of his men.

'Pechs? Bogles?' Kirkpatrick challenged, though gently, and Campbell, half-ashamed, waggled his head from side to side.

'My folk believe it. Myself, though, I am after being more concerned about the time it is taking to get these carts to Kilmory. There are MacDougalls loose.'

Kirkpatrick's head came up at that and he was sharp with Campbell when he spoke.

'You kept that close to you – mark me, I can see why. Having your enemies stravaigin' as they please through your lands is not a matter to trumpet.'

Campbell admitted it with a nod and no sign that he was put out.

198

'They are like lice,' he declared. 'Ye think ye have combed them all out and suddenly they are back, annoying ye with their wee itch.'

He glanced at Kirkpatrick.

'It is because I am taking so many of my own to join Sir Neil. There will be long hundreds of Campbell men standing with the King when he fights and little or none to protect our lands. My castle is safe, but these MacDougalls will plooter about for a while, causing trouble, then go home – bigod, most of them are fled to Ireland as it is but, mind you, if they see a chance at a lumbering great slorach of over-laden men and carts they will take it.'

Kirkpatrick acknowledged the commitment of the Campbells and fell silent, staring at the popping fire and knowing the lord of Craignish was right – if it hadn't been for the arrival of Hal, Kirkpatrick and all this cargo, the Campbell men would already be in their galleys and sailing for the Ayrshire coast to join the army at Stirling.

A little way away, Duncan lay on one side of a fire and contemplated the sight of his lord in conversation with the dwarf-dark man called Kirkpatrick. The other, the brooding and wounded lord from the Lothians, sat apart even from that – even from himself, Duncan thought.

These southrons were different, right enough, and he had been away from the droving roads long enough to feel and see it almost for new. These men could not enjoy life as it moved through them; they wanted to take it and make something, as if they could shape it to their own way.

They did not talk of deer and cattle and hill, or let themselves soak in the weather; they spoke of crops and power and business and did not notice the different greens of leaves, or even the sun until its lack was enough to chill them.

Once, on the drove road, he had been sparking a southron woman at Carlisle and they had walked out beyond the gate, which he knew was a great daring for her in the first place, never mind to be doing it with a strange creature from beyond the Mounth.

He knew then, as now, that he could whisper filth in her ear in the True Tongue and she would wriggle and blush, for it was just a liquid trill to her ear, as seductive as it was strange. He recalled, as he spoke and slid an arm round her soft waist, that his free hand had found a winter-woken toad on the rock next to him.

It was sluggish and still cold, hoping for the sun on the rock to give it new life. It blinked its great gold-coin eyes, iridescently green throat pulsing and as beautiful as anything he had ever seen. So he was surprised when the woman, presented with the sheer jewel of it, screamed and ran away.

No woman of his own people would have done so, but the southrons were strange – even their names. But, then, names were dangerous matters and the knowing of a man's true name gave you power over him, for he lay deep inside his name, underneath his talk and his acts, moving like everyone else, yet living in secret and alone. He wasn't concerned that they knew his name was Duncan, for they did not know the whole of it, nor in the tongue of the True People.

The Lothian lord, he had decided, noticed nothing at all, as if some veil had dropped between him and the world. As if – and Duncan shivered at the thought – he is moving with unseen *sidhean*, who are lifting him quietly out of the midst of us and into their timeless kingdom.

He took comfort from the quiet murmur, the men sitting crosslegged or lolling round the flames, attending to a blackened pot and wiping smoke tears from their eyes. Somewhere, an owl screeched and Duncan lay back, tasting the woodsmoked night and letting his eyes close.

Tomorrow they would be at Kilmory, loading this southron matter on to the galleys and away from this place of faerie shadows.

When it came, the next day, the working of the *sidhean* was harsh and sudden.

Hal was stumbling along in the ruts of a cart which seemed to be his own particular curse, a wheeled imp of Satan which stuck more times than it rolled. He was enjoying the roll of it now, the fresh breeze on the sweated bruise of his face and the piping of peewits, while quietly marvelling at the bulging calf muscles of the bare-legged man ahead, the one called Duncan.

I find it hard enough to walk in serk and braies, burdened only by a baldric and sword, he thought, yet this one carries his own weight on his back.

The man, wearing only a sweat-darkened saffron tunic, belted so that a dirk could be thrust through a ring on it, hefted the waterproofed burden a little higher on his back and strode on. Then he gave a yelp, a stumble and fell over.

Hal moved to him, thinking he had tripped, bending to help him to his feet; the flick of the shaft over his head was like the crack of a whip and he knew the sound well, felt the clench and sickening plunge of his belly as he flung himself to the ground beside Duncan. The arrow that had felled the man was now clearly revealed, buried deep an inch below the man's collarbone.

More arrows flew and men tumbled and yelped.

'Sluggorm. Sluggorm.'

The call echoed, the bundles flew away as the Campbells went for their weapons and Hal, raising his head, saw the arrows had been only the heralds of a leaping mass of shrieking men, wild-haired, wet-mouthed and armed: the MacDougalls.

Kirkpatrick, a few carts down from the fallen Hal, heard the cries of '*sluagh-ghairm*', the gathering cry. Campbell of Craignish hauled out a hand-a-half, waved it in a circle above his head and bellowed 'Cruachan'; men flocked to him like a pack of wolves. He looked right and left to see how many he

201

had, grinned at Kirkpatrick and then plunged exultantly forward. Wearily, cursing, Kirkpatrick was dragged in his wake.

Hal was half-crouched and rising when the wave of MacDougalls fell on him and the snarling Campbells round him, though Hal could not tell one from the other and did not care when faced with an armed man wanting to poke sharp metal in him.

The first one tried to spear him, clumsy and running, so that Hal only had to bat the shaft to one side, dip a shoulder and let the man run on to it; braced, he knocked the man off his feet and drove the wind out of him, so that the sword stroke that took him in the neck barely managed a last squeak from him.

Hal barely heard, half turned for the next rushing man, ducked the flail of a spear slash and cut back so that the man stumbled past, bewildered as to why his stomach was emptying out and tangling his ankles.

They were desperate with fear, Hal realized, too few and relying on speed and rush to overwhelm. They should not have done it at all, he thought wildly, but they were madmen from beyond the Mounth, as strange as two-headed calves. The saving Grace of God in all of this was that he was fighting alongside equally mad men, who had recovered from the shock of attack and flung themselves forward with eldritch screeching and a sheen of ecstasy.

Hal cut and parried and made a space round him – but then there was a sudden flurry and a new rush of men, so that Hal spun and slashed to keep the swordlength of space until, through the bewildering whirligig of faces and bodies, he saw one he knew.

Kirkpatrick held up his hands and Hal, sucking in breath in ragged gasps, let the swordpoint drop; gore slid greasily from it and pooled round the tip.

Christ betimes, Kirkpatrick thought, he can still find a fight in him, can the wee lord from Herdmanston. He said as much and had back a pouch-eyed stare from the yellow-blue side of Hal's face.

'Aye til the fore,' he growled and then stopped, for it was not Sim he spoke to, would never be Sim again.

'If it is like this all the way to Stirling,' Kirkpatrick growled, watching the lamb-leaping, blood-howling Campbells pursue their hated enemies over the bracken and heather, 'we will deserve earldoms at the least.'

Hal did not answer and, when Kirkpatrick turned, he saw the lord bend, then crouch down amid the spilled litter of pack which had burst from dead Duncan's back. He peered and saw, with a sudden shock of poignancy, what Hal had found.

Wrapped and stowed when the stuff was packed, Sim's ruined, scarred arbalest winked back into the light, carefully laid up for the day it could be repaired.

Kirkpatrick politely turned away from the sound of weeping.

St Mungo's Kirk, Polwarth
Feast of Sts Marcus and Marcellianus, June 1314

The Hainaulters were drunk, which they claimed was a pious celebration of the martyrs whose day it was, even though most would not know the first thing about them. Addaf was betting sure that they would embrace the holiness of the next saint's day as piously as this.

They were, as a result, a red-eyed, stumbling uselessness against the kirk, though they formed up raggedly enough, weaving in rough ranks, the spearshafts clacking like tree branches in a high wind.

'Get it done,' the old Berkeley had thundered to his son and Sir Maurice, red and tight-lipped, with his own smirking boys at his back, had snapped the same to Addaf. And all because some *cont gwirion* had shot off a bolt from the kirk;

it had hit a horse in the flank and set it to plunging in the trace, upsetting a two-wheeled cart.

It would have been nothing at all, Addaf thought sourly. The *coc oen* who had done it as the English, still damp from fording the Tweed at Wark and straggling past the chapel door, could have been found, bruised a little and sent back to his monk's cell with a kick up his arse.

Save for the fact that the cart held the royal banners, great folds of rich silk and brocade in the long hundreds. And the King was close enough to witness it, rounding on the Earl of Pembroke to ask, bland as frumenty: 'Has this place not been secured, my lord?'

De Valence had spoken harshly to old Sir Thomas Berkeley, who was still smarting over the return of his own bloodied and torn banner, lost by Addaf and brought back by that gloomy walrus Thweng as a sneering gift from the Bruce. And so the chain of scowls came down to the Welsh and the drunken Hainault spearmen.

Addaf was already exhausted and the maille hung heavy on him. His arms ached and the sun was too hot in a day that stank of leather and sweat, dung and horse piss. His face, to the waiting archers, was haggard, dark shadows drawn round his eyes, his iron-grey hair plastered to his skull.

'Smart yer bows,' he called and there was a flutter of sound as the men nocked arrows. Addaf gripped his sword and wished it was a bow, but he was the captain here and his rank was marked by a sword. His Hainault counterpart, swaying a little, belched.

'My men will cover your advance,' Addaf said. 'Break the bloody door down and be done with the business.'

The Hainaulter nodded and licked dry lips; Addaf was not sure he had been understood, but both men were old hands at this and the Hainault men were seasoned in long battles against the Flemings and knew the way of matters well enough.

'Wait, wait – I beg you, in the name of Heaven.'

The voice brought them round, the big Hainaulter frowning in a slow, blinking way at the unshaven desperation of face looking up at him from the kneeling monk.

'The man who shot the bolt was our reeve, a foolish man. There are only two monks within, old Fathers who could not find it in themselves to leave this place. They have been here thirty years and more.'

'You are?' Addaf demanded.

'Father John,' the man answered. 'I also live here, but fled. Now God has brought me back to plead for the lives of those in His house. I beg the blessing of Heaven on you, your honour – let me go to them. Spare all this blood, I beg you.'

Addaf considered it. The Hainaulter shrugged, belched again and wiped the ale-sweat from his fleshy face; he didn't understand all the English in it, but he knew what the little monk was doing.

'Door vill opened be,' he said and he made a good point; Addaf nodded.

Father John scuttled off. There was a hammering sound and everyone waited in the afternoon heat, filled with the creak and grind and shuffle of the edge of the army, passing up Dere Strete and headed for the pass through the Lammermuirs. Anxious about it, too, because this road was the only practical one for the great long trail of wagons and they expected the Scots to spring some surprise.

God curse it, Addaf thought, the train of wagons must stretch for leagues, filled with all manner of stupidity; he had seen a score of them full of the furnishing for a chamber and hall and eight score, no less, were packed with nothing but poultry. Wine and wax and saddlery, dancing slippers and candle-holders – the English were going not to war but a revel, Addaf thought. There was even a mangy old lion in a cage.

He had 104 archers under his command, with 126 horses and three carts – one for the men's baggage, one for the

205

saddlery, a firebox forge and anvil and one for fodder. And that was three too many as far as Addaf was concerned, for if you could not ride and fight with what you had in, around or under your saddle, you were of little use.

He glanced at them, this rough family, feeling the sweat run down the grooves etched on either side of his nose, filtering itchily into the grey of his beard.

They were relaxed, chaffering each other and the big oxen Hainault spearmen, who broiled in their leather and wool. One or two of the Welsh had dug out strips of dried beef and venison from under their saddles, where they had been marinading to softness with the animal's sweat; they chewed with relish and fell into the old argument of whether gelding, mare or stallion sweat made the meat tastier.

Y Crach, as always, was poised like a trembling gazehound. He will hang these with his own hand, Addaf thought sourly, as his own offering to God; Addaf did not care to be reminded that there were too many who would stand with Y Crach.

Others, Addaf was pleased to see, were squinting at the distant riders on a hill. They were Scots, certes, trailing the army like ticks on sheep, but as long as they kept their distance that was fine. Their own prickers on their fast hobs might chase them off, or simply keep them at a distance – and if the rebels closed in on the debris of sick, halt, lame, campfollowers and plain deserters lurking at the rear, it was no great loss to the English army.

The church door opened and the Father, with a relieved and triumphant look back at Addaf, ushered out the rebels: two tottering priests holding one another up – an edgy defiance in grey wool and hodden hood.

'There,' said Father John, wiping his sweating face. 'No harm done, no blood spilled – God be praised.'

'For ever and ever,' Addaf replied piously and heard the sound of hooves like a knell, turning into the black, hot scowl of Sir Maurice Berkeley, his two sons like pillars on either side.

'Is the work done?' he demanded and Addaf nodded, indicating the little crowd. Berkeley, still scowling, reined his mount round to ride off.

'Not before time, Centenar Addaf,' he bellowed over his shoulder. 'Now hang them all and muster on me – the horse forges ahead.'

There was a pause and then Father John looked wildly from Addaf to the retreating back of Sir Maurice.

'Your honour . . .' he began and Addaf felt the cold stone of it settle in his belly. He had done this from Gascony to here and all points in between, knew there was no arguing with it; he was aware, at the edges of his vision, of Y Crach's fevered grin of triumph.

The big Hainault captain saw the Welshman's mourn of face and foraged his mouth with a grimy finger, found the annoying scrap and examined it before flicking it away.

'Leaf viss us,' he offered, grinning brownly. 'Ve fix.'

Addaf hestitated. The Hainaulters wanted the plunder from the church – well, that was fair enough. Let them do the deed; Addaf turned abruptly away from the disbelief on the face of Father John, swept his gaze over Y Crach and his scowl and bellowed at his men to move out, trying to drown the little priest's screechings.

God serves him badly, Addaf thought sourly, blocking the frantic protests from his ears. Stupid little priest, look you. He should have stayed away when he had the chance.

Up on the hill, Dog Boy and the Black sat at ease, one leg hooked across the saddle, with a *mesnie* of riders on either side. They watched the archers mount up and ride off, while the big red-faced sweaters flung rope over the graveyard elm; some moved into the church and began to splinter wood in their search for loot.

'I am sure those are the Welsh we had stushie with,' the

Black offered. 'The wee flag they carry is the same one we took – the King gave it back as a gift.'

Dog Boy could not deny it, watching as the priest who had been most animated and loud was hauled up in a fury of flailing ankles, two big men in metal-leafed jacks pulling on a leg each until his kicking stopped; one cursed when the priest's dying bowels opened.

The other two monks, white-haired and patient, sat like old stones and waited to die, while the pungent, heady scent of yellow-blazing gorse drew in buzzing life all round them.

It was not right and Dog Boy said so. The Black, who had already hanged his share of priests, said nothing; if he thought of what he had done it was with the deep, banked burn of everything the English had taken from him. Even having the Cliffords scoured from Douglas and the promise of restoration to the slighted fortress was not nearly revenge enough.

The sight of the English was a stun to the senses, all the same, spread out round a backbone of carts that stretched for miles, hazed in a shroud of dust from thousands of hooves. Behind was a snail-trail of dung-churned morass, where the detritus of the army stumbled. Ahead, and forging ever faster, the horse and the mounted infantry – like the archers – shifted further from the foot.

'They are in a hurry,' the Black noted.

'Even so,' Dog Boy pointed out, 'they will be hard put to make Stirling by midsummer – they have at least twenty good Scots miles to reach Edinburgh.'

Closer to twenty-five, James Douglas thought, and capable of making no more than twelve in a day's march. By the time they get to Edinburgh, it will have been burned and scorched of any easy way of landing supplies from ships, and that will cost them dearly.

That would put them close to midsummer, so that they would have to push to reach the vicinity of Stirling's fortress in time to claim the siege as lifted. With luck, they would arrive panting and dragging their arses in the dust and Dog Boy, grinning back as the Black voiced this, agreed with a nod.

Patrick, seeing these twin firedogs, marvelled at how they looked nothing at all, no more than dark, good-looking, pleasant youths who could be planning a night of revelry in Edinburgh instead of mayhem on an invading host.

The two old priests hardly kicked at all when the spearmen hauled them up. Parcy Dodd leaned forward on his horse at the sight and shook his head.

'Ach well,' he said, 'let us hope they find a better welcome than auld Brother Cedric.'

'I am hesitating to ask,' the Black answered laconically. Parcy grinned, a farrago of gums and gap.

'Brother Cedric died old and venerated. Upon entering St Peter's Gate, there was another man in front, waiting to go into Heaven. St Peter asked the man who he was and what he had accomplished in his life and the man revealed that he was Blind Tam, ship's steersman, who had spent his life on a vessel taking pilgrims to the Holy Land. St Peter handed him a silk robe and a golden sceptre, inviting him to walk in the streets of Our Lord.'

There was a sound of distant, frantic hooves which brought heads up. Parcy, unperturbed, shifted his weight on the horse a little.

'St Peter', he went on, 'asked the same question of Brother Cedric, who tells him he has devoted the entire threescore span of his years to the Lord – and he is given a plain wool robe and wooden staff. Certes, he questions this – in a polite, Christianly way of course – and St Peter lets him know the truth. "While you preached, everyone slept," he said. "But while Blind Tam steered, everyone prayed."'

Yabbing Andra arrived in a flurry of foam-flecked horse and dust.

'Prickers,' he said and the Black unhooked his leg from the saddle.

'Bigod, Parcy Dodd,' he said, as they broke into a fast canter away from the threat, 'you tell it better than a priest at a sermon.'

Everyone who had heard such heckled sermons laughed, but Patrick shook a mock-sorrowful head.

'There is an inglenook of Hell's bad fire set aside just for you, Parcy.'

Dog Boy, who had seen the great swooping banners, the sea of men and horses and power moving like a relentless tide towards Stirling, was sure that Parcy and everyone else would find out where they sat in Hell soon enough.

The Pele, Linlithgow
Feast of St Alban, June 1314

He had not stopped for the banners of St Cuthbert and St John of Beverley, nor visited the shrines; he knew he had avoided that campaign ritual simply because his father had done it before him and Edward knew, too, that such avoidance had been a mistake from the mutters and solemn head-shaking of his knights.

They were worse than any wattled beldame, Edward thought moodily as he chewed on the fish and enjoyed the sweet of the sauce. Christ betimes, he had banners aplenty – a whole cartload of them – and holy help from a slew of abbots and bishops. He was even eating fish, as any Christian knight would do in order to show his purity of body and soul. What was one flapping cloth more or less?

Besides, this was *his* army, gathered at vast expense and despite the refusal of the likes of Lancaster and Warwick. When this was concluded, Edward thought with savage glee, I will be able to deal with them as I wish – as a true king would wish – but, for now, there is the rare freedom of being out from under the Ordinances, with my own army at my back. Better still, it had men in it he could trust enough to have at his back.

Like Ebles de Mountz – Edward raised his cup to the Savoyard and saw the man flush with pride at being so singled out by his king. A valuable asset was de Mountz, whom Edward had set to watching his wife for a time and then appointed constable of Edinburgh. Too late, as it turned out, because the place fell to the Scotch before de Mountz could take command – but the man had fourteen years of experience in the Scottish wars and had served as constable of three castles in his time. Including Stirling.

De Mountz was bench-paired with Sir Marmaduke Thweng, that ancient warhorse who had also commanded at Stirling – I am not short of local knowledge, Edward thought, of the ground we will have to fight across.

But the men he felt a glow for, a warmth borne of old comradeship and safety, were roistering and roaring all round him: Sir Payn Tiptoft, d'Argentan, the de Clares and the de Bohuns and the lesser lights of chivalry, such as Lovel and Manse and the Ercedenes, all the gilded youth of yesterday who were now the golden warriors of the royal household.

Edward stood suddenly and saluted them loudly, feeling the exultant moment racing in him; they roared their appreciation back to King Edward, second of that name by the Grace of God, ringing the rafters of the rugged, solid storehouse built by his father as a supply base for the armies.

Endless armies, Edward thought, traipsing ever northwards. This would be the last of them. This would end it once and for all . . .

If Bruce stood to fight.

Thweng watched the King, flushed face singing with wine and the moment. The cheers of his salute to the 'golden warriors' were still echoing when the most golden of them all, the paragon of chivalry and the third-best knight in Christendom slammed his cup on the table, levered away from his bench and unlaced himself. Hitching up his tunic, he pissed into the floor-straw not far from the table and his neighbours scrabbled away from the vinegar-reek splashes of it.

'Christ betimes, d'Argentan,' protested Henry de Bohun, 'can you not use the privy like a *gentilhomme*?'

'Like you, little maid?' d'Argentan replied and grabbed his cock so that the last of the stream arced higher and splashed more. 'I give you a look at what a man is like. Compare with your own and be downhearted.'

Those nearest hooted and banged the table. Henry de Bohun's face went stiff. He was young, not yet twenty, and crested with a curling mass of dark copper hair, which he kept like an arming cap on the top of his head, while shaving it all off round the ears.

It was a deliberate statement to all those who had grown their hair long in their gilded youth and still kept it that way, even if much of it was faded and thinner. It hinted at how Henry de Bohun was a warrior in the old Norman way while they were ageing fops, and it did not help that you could see how his hair, if left to grow, would ringlet magnificently round his ears with no need of the curling tongs.

Everything about Henry de Bohun was a slap to the others, from his youth to his cool efficient mastery of the lists and the avoidance of anything to do with the 'golden warriors'. The biggest smack of all to them was his being the nephew of Humphrey, Earl of Hereford, Constable of England and bitter rival to the de Clare Earl of Gloucester, whose men were doing most of the hooting.

'I think you have had too much wine,' Henry answered flatly, his voice a scourge of distaste.

'Not nearly enough,' d'Argentan answered, and drank more to prove it, wiping the dribble off the five-inch scar on his chin – mêlée wound, tourney proper for the Honour of the Round Table, Brackley, five years ago. He licked the remains of the brew from the fingers of his left hand, all but the missing little one – a bohort, in some French town he could not even remember, eight years ago.

'But already too much for you to match,' he added and grinned raggedly at Henry from a mouth extended on the left by a three-inch scar – tourney proper, in Rhodes, all of a decade ago.

The memory soured him, as did the sight of Henry de Bohun, who was already an acknowledged master of the joust, that one-on-one test of arms altogether too popular for d'Argentan's liking and replacing the mayhem of the mêlée these days.

He saw the splendour of youth in the de Bohun brat and wanted his own back again, so that he did not have to think about the three decades and more of his own life, least son of four and owning nothing but a name and the distinction of being the third-best knight in Christendom. Not even the second, which title belonged to the very Bruce they were going to fight.

The years were falling on him like a charging mass of knights and he did not like the fear it lanced him with.

'You stick to almond milk, child,' he growled, more harshly than he had intended and heard the mocking oohs and aahs from his coterie at this clear challenge. He also saw de Bohun half rise, before a voice cut through the din.

'You provoke my nephew's honour, Sir Giles, so you provoke mine own.'

Sir Giles acknowledged the Constable of England with an apologetic bow.

'If your nephew wishes redress,' he said, 'I am sure we can find time to run a friendly passage at dawn.'

'As you wish and when you wish,' Henry retorted sharply.

A pantler went over suddenly, by accident or tripped by the howl of knights at another table, and the clattering clang of his dropping tray was echoed by the baying laughter. He picked himself up, collected as many of the pastries as he could and served them anyway, straw and all; servants and scullions fought the dogs to snatch those he missed.

It snapped the tension and Hereford went back to his close-head mutterings with his clerk, Walwayn; Thweng saw that little man, aware that he was being watched, turn and stare insolently back at him.

Walwayn sweated with secrets, so that any stare made him twitch, but the one from that droop-moustached cliff of a face made his bowels turn; Sir Marmaduke Thweng, he recalled briefly, a lord from Yorkshire reputed to be a hunter of trailbaston and brigands for the head-reward. The thought made him shiver and Hereford scowled, thinking he was not being paid enough attention.

'Stir yourself. You say Lord Percy sent a man, a Templar heretic, to spy out some plot with that discredited Order and the Scotch?'

'Just so, my lord,' Walwayn answered in a softer hiss, appalled at the lack of discretion in Hereford's voice. The Earl saw it and frowned, but tempered his volume.

'What plot? Is the excommunicate King about to visit us with heretic Templars?'

Walwayn shook his head furiously.

'I do not know, my lord. The Lord Percy understands it is more to do with acquiring weapons. Or treasure.'

Hereford stroked his beard while the noise swirled, thick and hot. The famed Templar treasure was a gleaming lure that would not be banished, but Templar weapons, even the expertise of the Order's former knights, would be formidable – and God forbid that Bruce had enlisted fled Templars to his cause.

And Percy, already firmly in the camp of the King's opponents, had said nothing. A thought hit Hereford.

'Who is Percy's spy?'

Walwayn, who wanted away to drink and women, blinked sweat from his eyes.

'A Knight formerly of the Order is all I understand, lord.'

Hereford nodded, thought for a time longer, and then patted Walwayn on the shoulder.

'Keep track of it and keep me informed.'

Walwayn, released at last, merely nodded and slid away. He did not ask if Hereford would inform the King; he thought it unlikely – all was rumour, though Walwayn could taste the truth of it. Hereford would wait until matters were firmer and there was advantage in it for himself, but Walwayn would have to be the one setting such an advantage. Until then, there was drink and women . . .

There were no women of any worth, Thweng noted, which accounted for the knights' behaviour. There were serving trulls, who would be caught and tupped before the night was over, and a wet nurse sitting by the fire with someone's babe, but no woman of quality to put a curb chain on the revels, for this was war and even if the entire court travelled with the King, the Queen and her women did not.

He dropped the fish and wiped his fingers on his tunic front; he thought the sweet taste was less to do with spices and cooking than incipient rot, which echoed the entire court as far as he was concerned.

He watched the great Sir Giles, scarred paladin of the first rank, his red jupon with its silver grail-cups stained with meat juice and his own piss, glowering at the fiery de Bohun nephew.

Young Henry's uncle, finished with his clerk and his rank established like the big-ruffed wolf in a pack, returned to stabbing a finger at the younger Earl of Gloucester. No doubt pointing out that, as Constable of England and a veteran of the Scots wars, it should have been his right to command the Van alone and not in tandem with an inexperienced sprig of the de Clares. Politely and with due deference to rank, of course.

'What say you, my liege lord?' d'Argentan bellowed at the King. 'A chivalric passage of arms on the morrow, to set the start of a glorious day?'

He spoiled the moment of it by belching and Thweng saw the droop of the royal eyelid. Bad idea to mention time to the King, he thought, since he was running out of it. They would be hard put to make it to within three leagues of Stirling by the Feast of St John the Baptist as it was and even then would have to leave all the foot and baggage behind. Delaying for a 'passage of arms' was not an option.

Sir Giles was too canny a court rat to argue the point, bowing graciously and then leering at Henry de Bohun. A hurrying wench, goosed by one of the Nevilles, clumsily dropped a torch and there was a furious moment of stamping, sparks and soot; a dog took the opportunity to filch Miles de Stapledon's meat from his plate and he chased it round, bellowing and threatening until it gave up and dropped it.

Thweng, sweating in the leprous heat, looked at the mortrews and gristle on his plate, the nightlife fliers which seemed to congregate on it and wished he were somewhere else. Anywhere else.

The whole court was here, squeezed into the great ugly fortification of the Pele at Linlithgow, Longshanks's unsubtle stake in the heart of Scotland. He had built it round a former royal residence and swallowed the church of St Michael as he did so, turning that holy place into a storehouse.

It had never been spacious or comfortable at the best of times, was less so now that the fleeing Scots had wrecked it as they had wrecked every other possible refuge and store, and so Hall struggled with Chamber.

The pantlers, cellarers, scullery and scalding house of Badlesmere's stewardship fought for space with Chamberlain Despenser's staff, who in turn elbowed with Charlton's Office of the Privy Seal and ignored the growls of Brotherton's Marshalsea, responsible for all the horses, carts and carriages that moved everyone. A hundred horses of them alone belonged to the King, forty of which were prime destriers.

I have two, Thweng thought moodily. Both of them cost a small manor apiece and the chances are that one or both will be ruined by the time this affair is over. He wished, again, that he was somewhere else.

For all the excitement and freedom this campaigning threw up, Edward also wanted to be somewhere else and would have been surprised to find that he and Sir Marmaduke Thweng were more alike than either of them imagined – they were both, at heart, country knights who preferred building a wall than coping with the backstabbing, fervid hothouse of intrigues that was the court.

It did not help that the clerics were carping on and on about the missing banners of Beverley and St Cuthbert and the grate of it was thrumming on Edward's nerves; he could hear those two old farts, the Bishops Ely and Winchester, discussing it.

'I am sure the Lord will overlook it,' Bishop Sandale of Winchester said, but the fish-eyed stare he had back from John Hothum, Bishop of Ely, gave lie to it.

'The Lord sees all,' Hothum grunted, worrying at the remains of a bone. The weight of his ornate robes made sweat bead his brow – he did not need to wear them, but liked the trappings of his Treasury office; more than that, he liked people to see his power and none more so than the Chancellor Bishop of Ely.

'It might still be possible to fetch the Beverley,' Sandale offered hesitantly. 'A fast rider . . .'

'The Lord is not fooled.'

The voice was a thin rasp, like a nail on slate, the speaker swathed in black and white. Like a magpie, Edward thought sourly, looking at the Pope's envoy, the Dominican Father Arnaud.

'So the damage is done?' he snapped and saw the Dominican's tonsured head raise up, the fat little currant nose twitch like a coney. It was a plump, friendly, avuncular face and a lie; this was the Pope's best Inquisitor and you had to tread carefully for he had flames in those blackcurrant eyes.

He had come with a party of Clement V's Inquisitors – Dieudonné, Abbot of Lagny, and Sicard de Vaur, Canon of

Narbonne – complete with finger-wag abjuration on how, despite there being no torture permitted under England's Common Law, King Edward had better not interfere with the Church's treatment of heretics. God willed it.

The combination of Pope and French King was too strong for Edward to oppose and he had been forced to relinquish the Templars he held into the grip of the Church. Now matters had changed and Edward was warmed by a secret smile he never allowed to get to his lips: Clement was dead and the cardinals couldn't agree. There was no Pope. *Sede vacante.*

That will teach the Church to preach to me . . .

'Do you preach so, Father Arnaud?' he persisted, fired by the wine and moment. 'As your late master did regarding heretics?'

'The Holy See and the Inquisition have saved the lands of the west from heresies, my lord king,' the Dominican replied. 'I humbly offer that I have had a small part in this great work.'

'You give yourself too little credit,' Edward answered. 'If you mean by "saved" that you have reduced the tax-paying tenants of France, you are correct. Though a little late for some, it seems, if you believe Grand Master de Molay was in league with the Devil.'

'He was,' Arnaud said, his voice rising. 'And your lands are as palsied with such. Must be cleansed. God wills it.'

'God forbid it,' Edward snapped back, thinking what a sadistic child this new Inquisition was, a vicious dangerous toddler, petulant and prideful. Then he twisted his mouth in vicious smile. 'I would concentrate on France, priest, where it seems a heretic's curse can bring down king and Pope both.'

'Of course,' interrupted the smooth blandness of Sandale, sensing the banked fires rising in the Dominican, 'His Grace the King is always cognizant of the decisions of the Pope regarding such matters. Even kings avow the necessity of bringing God's Kingdom to fruition on earth.'

'As your father acknowledged,' Arnaud added to the King, smiling sweet as rot, 'when he oathed himself to another Crusade. The holy places of Outremer must be returned to us.'

The implication of Edward taking on the role was clear and the King's eye was jaundiced when he stared at Sandale; the Bishop wished the Dominican had taken a vow of silence.

'Death absolves all oaths,' the King replied eventually.

'I am sure such matters will be more roundly discussed,' the Bishop of Ely offered, 'once the excommunicate Scotch are brought into the Grace of God and the Holy Father . . . when we have a Holy Father,' he added slyly and Edward barked a mirthless laugh.

'Aye – until then, Father Arnaud,' he said, 'there are only unholy Scotch. That land is full of heretics.'

He leaned forward, hawklike and stooping, it seemed to the Bishop of Ely.

'But that land, pretend king or not, is part of my kingdom, which is not under abjuration and where we have no torture. Be aware of it, Dominican – especially since you have no Holy Father to appeal to.'

Arnaud said nothing, though the hatred hazed off him like sweat from a running horse. No, there was no torture permitted in England, he sneered quietly to himself, not when cold, starvation, chains and the odd over-zealous beating would suffice. You would not find a rack, a thumbscrew or a hot iron anywhere in Edward's realm – yet men died being put to the Question, all the same.

Edward, losing interest in the argument, called for a song and his troubadour, Lutz, appeared from where he had been perched in some clean rushes. There were groans and a few mutters; Edward knew they were sneering at how the King surrounded himself with 'Genoese fiddlers' and even those he favoured said so.

They know nothing, Edward thought, gnawing his discontent

like a bone. They sneer in secret at their king for having the ways of a simple country knight – and again for having the sensibilities to enjoy fine music, well played. None of them, of course, knew an Occitan master of music from a Genoese street performer. Or a lute from a lark's tongue.

Lutz was a lark's tongue with a lute, Edward thought and was pleased with the poetry of that, repeating it in his mind and working out ways to voice it for general approval. Then, like everyone else, he was captured by song.

The troubadour from Carcassone sang a few swift verses of the Fall of Troy, another couple of stanzas of the Quest for the Grail. Then he began the Song of Roland and, gradually, the place fell silent as his voice, sweet and silk-smooth, rose up and coiled round the expert fingering.

'With Durandal I'll lay on thick and stout,
In blood the blade, to its golden hilt, I'll drown.
Felon pagans to th' pass shall not come down;
I pledge you now, to death they all are bound.'

Thweng marvelled, then, at how it changed, how all those knights grew silent, how eyes misted. All in a moment, they were altered to something close to what they strove for and, when it was done, they embraced it with quiet, respectful pats on the table.

Even the lines that spoke of hardship in the service of a lord, of having to endure great heat and great cold.

Even of being parted, flesh from blood . . .

ISABEL

O for your spirit, holy John, to chasten lips sin-polluted, to loosen fettered tongues; so by your children might your deeds of wonder meetly be chanted. In honour of the eve and the day, the nun called Constance brought me St John's wort and sat and combed my hair, a blessing in itself. Better yet was hearing the unseen street player, scaling out the monk's chant on his instrument – Ut Re Mi Fa Sol La – to offer his own prayer to the blessed St John.

> Ut queant laxis
> Resonare fibris
> Mira gestorum
> Famuli tuorum,
> Solve polluti
> Labii reatum
> Sancte Ioannes

I sang the words with him then: So that these your servants may, with all their voice, resound your marvellous exploits, clean the guilt from our stained lips, O St John.

As the blessed St John heralded the coming of Our Lord, so this feast heralds the coming of mine. Keep the hearts of Thy faithful fixed on the way that leads to salvation.

CHAPTER NINE

Bannockburn
Vigil of the Feast of St John the Baptist, June 1314

The sun was tipping past noon, a glaring orb searing grass to gold, the half-dried velvet of the great hill sweltering beyond. It glittered the leaves of trees, darkening the long shadows to a tempting coolness – but no one wanted the balming relief of the Torwald's shade; it was safer out here under the fist of a sun which hammered on their maille and leather, wilted the fine plumes and turned jupon and gambeson and haketon to ovens.

Addaf had ordered his men off their horses, because they were mounted foot when all was said and done and that made sense to the commanders of the Van. Now, while they lolled or squatted in the shade of shelters made from their unstrung bows and the corner of a cloak, the proud knights and men-at-arms stayed mounted, their only saving grace being that they were not on their warhorses.

Sir Marmaduke, the sweat coursing down him, noted that the finer of the *nobiles* were not even fully armoured and so had that curse yet to come – yet, if it came to plunging into the dark greening lurk of the Torwald, they would pile all the new-fangled plate-armour bits they could on and wish for more against the evils they imagined waiting for them there.

Evil was there, certes, Thweng thought, though all they saw of it was a handful of Scots riders led by Sir Robert Keith, who had brought the seneschal of Stirling to King Edward, as was right and proper under the terms of siege and relief. When de Mowbray was done informing the King that, by all the accepted terms – coming within three leagues of the besieged fortress – he had effectively fulfilled the terms of the agreement, he would return under the same escort.

What Mowbray thought it might mean remained a mystery, Thweng thought. Did he seriously imagine everyone – Scot and English – would simply nod, smile, turn round and ride off, writ fulfilled? Yet the ritual dance had to be gone through, step by step. By all means, Thweng thought grimly to himself, let us observe the niceties; later we can rip the gizzard from a man in a chivalric and honourable fashion.

He watched the Welsh enviously, wishing someone had the sense to order the rest of the Van to emulate them, but Hereford and Gloucester were hazed with as much hatred as heat; the de Bohuns and de Clares clustered in clearly defined knots apart from each other and were not about to agree on anything.

Thweng, too, had his knot of riders, not only his own *mesnie* of four men-at-arms but the coterie of young knights who had come, as they always did, to beg to ride with him. They had formed – again as they always did – little ad-hoc groupings of brotherhood, sworn to great deeds or death. This one, Thweng remembered, was called the Knights of the Shadow – from the psalm, the lord of Badenoch had informed Sir Marmaduke; the one about singing in the shadow of His Wings. It was clear he did not know any more than that, nor wanted to.

Sir Marmaduke had studied the Comyn lord for a long moment, taking in the red-gold dust of hair, the sandy lashes and brows, the snub nose. He looked like a lean, truculent piglet, Thweng decided, but the Yorkshireman had some

224

sympathy with the young Scot – seeing your father murdered by the man who went on to be hailed as king would have an effect. Standing with only seventeen years on you and your boots in the tarn of your da's blood, watching the killers argue about whether to murder you, too, would make you swear vengeance as a Knight of the Shadow.

'"You have been my help and in the shadow of Your Wings I rejoice,"' Thweng had quoted to the astonished Badenoch. Sir Marmaduke had left him astonished, but did not tell him it was not the first time the name had been so used.

He had heard every permutation of such names from scripture and psalm; the last time I fought at Stirling, he recalled with a shiver, the bold oathsworn knights had been called the Wise Angels, after the Lord Jesus' admonition to St Peter at the time of His arrest.

Most of those knightly angels had unwisely stayed on the wrong side of the brig, to die under the blades of Wallace's men; most of them were angels for true now, sitting at the Feet of God and wondering how they had got there.

There was a stir and the ranks parted as Mowbray arrived back, red-faced and with a constipated strain about him; he made straight for Hereford while a youth broke from the pack and rode over to Thweng.

He was no more than fifteen, dark hair plastered to his sweating skull and a frantic anxiety about him; Thweng recognized him as a squire to one of Sir Maurice Berkeley's young sons and hestitated a name.

'Alexander de Plant.'

'My lord,' the squire replied, brightening with relief that he was, at least, known. 'My lord the King has sent me with instructions for the commanders of the Van,' the boy went on, spilling it out as fast as the words would tumble. 'My lord of Pembroke told me to bring them to you and that you would know why and what to do.'

Thweng grunted and cursed de Valence. Of course he knew

why – because whomever the squire went to with the King's orders for the Van would incur the wrath of the other earl and it was better that a respected veteran such as Thweng do it. That way the wrath would be tempered and the instructions at least considered.

The orders were simple enough: the Van was to proceed straight on while the trusted Sir Robert Clifford took his Battle round to the right, with the intent of cutting the Scots off from retreat. The left, it seemed, was cut about with traps and pits, which Mowbray knew about.

When Thweng approached, Mowbray had already revealed most of what he had learned in his passionate, sweating plea to Hereford and Gloucester not to proceed through the Torwald.

'They are prepared for it, my lords,' he declared, waving his arms. 'Betimes – there is no need. The castle is relieved . . .'

Gloucester, his darkly handsome young face greasy with joy as much as sweat, gave a sharp bark of laughter.

'Did you think we came all this way for the pleasant ride in it?' he demanded and even Hereford had to agree with him, dismissing Mowbray with an armoured wave.

'Return to Stirling and wait, sir. If the King orders the Van to proceed, proceed it will.'

Thweng delivered the King's orders, and then sat silently as the entire place suddenly erupted into a frantic flurry. As Philip de Mowbray rode back under his white banner to where the Scots waited in the Torwald he nodded curtly to Thweng, who answered it as briefly. If all went the way it should they would toast each other and victory in the great hall of Stirling three days from now, at most.

If all went the way it should . . .

Squires hurried off with palfreys, brought up the powerful destriers, most of them fractious with the heat and the imminence of action. Others fetched pauldron, rerebrace and vambrace for the great who could afford this new fashion;

226

there was a clattering and clanking as they began fitting this extra armour to arms and shoulders.

Thweng found his squire at his elbow, leading Garm by the rein. Garm was solid as a barn and old enough not to be champing froth at the possibility that this was more than his master at practice. He was black and gleaming, the polish of him thrown up by a light sheen of sweat and the white trapper bearing the three green popinjays of the Thwengs.

Sir Marmaduke climbed on and settled himself, took the shield and the lance from young John, who then climbed on to his own horse and tried not to tremble. He was no older than Alexander de Plant, Thweng thought, moodily studying the Torwald's tight nap of trees with a jaundiced eye, and I promised his mother I would keep him from harm.

I brought him because I owed the King four men and he qualifies as one, but barely. It was a carping childish rebellion on my part, for all the other good men I have supplied to the Edwards, father and son. Now my petulance has put this lad in danger . . .

He turned.

'Remain here with the rounceys,' he growled. 'No sense in risking them before we know what lies ahead.'

No one spoke, though John went tight around the lips and reddened even more than he had in the heat, because he knew what his lord had done and why – and was shamed at the relief he felt for it. Thweng returned to looking sourly at the wood. A lance was probably more liability than asset in there, he thought.

He waited, watching with his plain, battered old barrel-helm tucked under his shield arm while the feverish knights had plumes fixed, demanded tippets and banners, both of which hung limply in the breathless air. The younger ones, who had never been in such an event before, called out greetings in high, nervous voices, pretending nonchalance and a boldness they did not entirely feel.

Thweng saw Hereford scowl at his nephew as Henry de Bohun fought the mouth of his huge bay, foam-sweated round the neck already and baiting on the spot with huge hooves. De Bohun, encumbered with shield and lance, had his helm clamped under his lance arm and was trying to see over the ornament of it. The helm was a great domed full-face affair, draped in a fold of blue and gold mantle, surrounded by a coloured blue and gold twist of cloth like a Saracen's turban, surmounted by a padded heraldic lion in gold cloth spouting three great plumes of heron feathers in blue and yellow.

He was as proud of this new-fangled confection as he was of his ruinously expensive horse, which he called Durandal after Roland's sword – but, at this moment, he would cheer-fully have rendered it into several hundredweight of offal.

'Tight rein that mount, boy,' his uncle called out, irritated and hot, trying to argue with Gloucester while mounting his own equally annoyed warhorse, which fretted under the leather barding round its head.

'Look to your *conrois,* my lords – and mount those damned Welsh,' bawled the Earl of Gloucester; the Earl of Hereford, hands full of rein and mouth full of his own egret plumes as he fought with helm and horse, fumed helplessly at this de Clare imposition of command.

Addaf caught Thweng's eye and nodded briefly; once he would have knuckled his forehead, but he was too old to care these days unless it was a lord who mattered. Besides, he remembered the Yorkshire knight as a man unimpressed by such things; he had met him years before – by God, during his first campaign, in fact, against the Wallace.

Thweng's was not a face you could forget, with eyebrows so bushy that they looked stuck on with fish glue for some mummer's performance. Two deep, vertical furrows, like the gills of a porpoise, ploughed from the wings of his nostrils to the bearded angles of his wide mouth and the upper lip hung, ape-long, over the lower, which made his drooping moustache seem more baleful.

Thweng did not recognize Addaf, which made the archer smile wryly. He had been a husky, hump-shouldered youth, dark and sullen, in those days, and was now a grizzled, iron-grey veteran – but, from his cool gaze and quiet nod, it was clear the Yorkshire lord knew the worth of the archers. Clear, too, from his frown that he wished they were on foot, flitting through the trees rather than riding.

Addaf would have fervently agreed if they had spoken on it; he led the Van down from the blazing brass of sunlight into the immediate cooling balm of the Torwald shade, such a relief that men gasped aloud. Addaf filtered his mounted men out as far as he could, like a fan on either side of the narrow trackway, threading their mounts through the trees; he felt the place close on him.

Bigod, thought Thweng, here is as good a spot for an ambush as any Vegetius could come up with. Others thought so, too, for the sighs and cries about being in the shade faded and died. Tight-packed in twos and threes, they rode knee to knee in a deep, dark green gloom with only a creak and jingle that was suddenly too loud.

Five hundred at least, Thweng thought moodily, strung out like wet washing; he felt, in the dappled closeness, as if he was under water.

They burst out of the Torwald like a shout of relief, into a blaze of sun and a new barrier ahead – yet another scar of woodland, though this was the New Park, a mere imp of the Great Satan that was Torwald. Beyond that, no more than six English miles away, lay Stirling Castle.

Hereford, his voice muffled and booming inside his splendid helm, bawled out orders which Gloucester, his own helmet tucked under one arm, took delight in repeating so that they would be understood; his red face was beaming with pleasure and heat.

'Sir Henry', he yelled to de Bohun, 'is to command the foot forward while the horse gathers itself. Scour the enemy ahead, sirrah, with all despatch.'

Addaf looked sourly at the great confection that was Henry de Bohun, brilliant in his bright blue surcote and jupon and horse trappings, all studded with little gold lions. He was, with that great lion-topped helmet clapped on his head, identical to his uncle save for the red slash through his shield. A bowl of frumenty, Addaf thought scornfully, and about as much use to me and mine, look you – but it was the way of things that an English lord oversaw what the Welsh did, even if he was a *cont gwirion* on four legs.

Addaf signalled with a wave of his sword and the Welsh dismounted at last, the horse-holders calming their charges while the rest padded forward like hunting hounds, bows smarted and arrows nocked. They filtered into the trees while de Bohun followed and his squire, Dickon, trailed at his back on his own palfrey, encumbered with spare lance and a host of other weapons his sire might need.

Thweng watched them go while the rest of the Van horse came up and reordered, the bright face of the lord of Badenoch like a child's slapped arse as he arrived at Sir Marmaduke's elbow.

'The rebels will not stand, it seems,' he said in polite French and wrinkled his snub nose. 'A pity. I owe the Bruce a mighty blow.'

Bruce is owed one, true enough, Thweng thought to himself, but you are not the one to give it, little lord. He wondered, though, if the Bruce he had seen was the same one he had known in younger, tourney days. Did he still deserve the title of second-best knight in Christendom?

Addaf dashed sweat from his eyebrows and blew it off the end of his moustache. There were men ahead; he had seen them filtering away ahead of them, keeping out of decent bowshot. Beyond, he heard shouts and a familiar rattle of spears, a sound he remembered well.

'Ware – spearmen,' he bawled out in Welsh, and then repeated it in English, so Henry de Bohun knew of it, though whether that lord understood or heard was a mystery, since he was a faceless metal creature who gave no signs.

Arrows flicked and rattled suddenly, so that the Welsh went into a half-crouch, searching for targets and returning fire. An arrow spanged off Henry's helmet, the ring of it jerking him so that the warhorse's head came up and it blew out heavily in protest.

The Welsh, Henry de Bohun saw, were going to ground, which was sensible when you had no protection and were not bound by the chivalry of knighthood. He curled a sweating lip at them and urged his horse forward.

Addaf saw the splendid lord, the padded gold lion and plumes on his helmet nodding, the trailing blue and red tippets fluttering prettily and thought, well, there's the last we will see of that *uffar gwirion* and good riddance to another English. He saw the muttering-anxious squire kick his own horse up past the Welsh and revised his thoughts to include him, too; a shaft hit a branch near him, clattered off into the trees and he forgot the pair entire, bawling at his men to stop shaming him and kill the Scotch bowmen.

Already, though, he saw the Scots archers slink away, knew their task was done; behind them, no doubt formed and ready, would be a host of close-ranked men bristling with spears and, vaguely through the trees, he saw a helmeted horseman.

A spearwall, archers and knights – there was no way through this without a hard fight which needed foot and spears rather than just his nearly-hundred of archers and a lot of heavy horse. He handed command to Coch Deyo and shouldered back through the wood and into the sunlight, squinting at the great horde of wilting, patient horsemen. He padded across like a stiff wolf to Hereford and Gloucester, careful to report what he had seen to both of them at once.

They took it well enough and the young one, the de Clare, was hot for going on but the older Earl of Hereford was more clever, Addaf saw, seeing at once that he might win with his five hundred heavy horse, but would ruin them doing it. Clever, too, the Welshman saw, not to admit that was why he hesitated; instead, he ordered the walrus-faced lord called Thweng to ride forward with his *mesnie* and see how many men opposed them.

And, as Addaf turned to lope back to his men, anxious about what Coch Deyo had done with them in his absence, the Earl of Hereford suddenly barked out:

'Where is my nephew?'

Henry de Bohun was in an oven with the sweat stinging his eyes, the lance rattling and banging off low branches, so that he had to lean it back on one shoulder. The proud trailing tippets of his helmet seemed to hook on every branch and threatened to tear the whole cumbersome affair from his head.

Which might be a relief, he thought to himself – until the first arrow strikes my nose. Through the blurry slit of his helmet, he saw a rider, a vague figure and no more. Behind, he saw – like a deer moving and revealing itself in the dapple of sunlit wood – a great mass of men and spears. He paused, considering, looked right and left and saw no one at all.

Which is at least a mercy, he thought, blowing frantically upward to try and dislodge the sweat coursing down his face and over his lips, for I would not know Scotch from Welsh in here.

It was idiocy to go on – stupidity to be this close to start with – so he started to turn the head of Durandal, who did not like putting his back to an enemy and resisted, baiting on the spot. Cursing, de Bohun savaged his mouth a little to get his attention – and then froze.

The rider had moved, was shouting and waving a little axe. He was on a palfrey and wore a splendid jupon of gold, blazoned with a red lion, a bloody replica of the gold ones Henry himself wore. On the man's head, clapped atop the open-faced bascinet, was a little domed cap in red leather surrounded by a circlet of spiked gold.

A crown.

The King himself and without a coterie of knights, only spearmen and only one or two in maille and plate to show that they might have been *nobiles* – but afoot. Not another horseman in sight.

The blood shushed in Henry's ears, thundering deafeningly inside the cave of his steel helm and he almost cried out. Then he fumbled the lance round, battering it through the clutch of branches until he could couch it, kicked Durandal so that he squealed and rode out at as fast a trot as he could manage, cursing the tangle of his tippets.

'Ogre!' he yelled, for it was only chivalrous to announce his presence and not ambush like an outlaw. 'Face me in single combat. I am Henry de Bohun, knight. It will be glorious . . .'

Bruce was anxious and fretting; he was sure that the English Van had balked at turning to their left and were pushing straight ahead, which was to the good.

Yet Jamie and his riders, now dismounting to fight on foot, had reported that the Van and the Main were coming up together and the third Battle was further to the right of the English, coming up by another road which would bring it out along the Way, to St Ninian's and the castle itself.

That is fine, he consoled himself while the sweat coursed off him. That is where I want them all, round to my left, in the Carse to the north and east – though I wish I knew where this third Battle was now and if Randolph has them under watch. He glanced at the sky and the great relentless ball, slowly, slowly, swinging down to the horizon.

233

Too late for the English to force matters this day, if we hold firm here – and find out where this other Battle is. Clifford, he said to himself. It will be Clifford. Or Beaumont. Hereford is here in front of me and Gloucester with him; that is an unnatural mating, Bruce thought, which may work to my advantage. Yet he is not short of good commanders, is the Plantagenet . . .

Too many ifs and buts and peering at heraldry, trying to work out who and where and with what. A battle lasts as long as the first steps of a plan, Bruce thought; after that, you may just as well try herding cats.

Bruce shouted at the rearguard, about half of his own Battle, chivvying them into a barrier against the English Van when – if – it debouched from the trees, while the archers flitted back and forward like midgies to buy them time. Behind, the rest of the Scots army reordered itself at right angles, marching along under the great hump of Coxet Hill.

Dangerous, dangerous, Bruce thought to himself, to move in front of an advancing enemy – yet they are not in a position to do me harm and all I need do here is discourage them, make it clear there is no easy passage into the New Park. Buy time for the end of this day and then, having taken the measure of them, decide what to do on the morrow . . .

Which would be run, he decided. I do not have the men or the arms to risk anything else.

The shouting brought his head up and he stared, amazed, at the vision which presented itself. He knew the gold lions on blue at once; for one heart-stopping moment he thought it was the Earl of Hereford himself, but then saw the red diagonal slash on the shield. A sprig from the tree, he thought and frowned, because the man was yelling, incoherent under the muffle of great helm.

'The King. Protect His Grace . . .'

Gilbert de la Haye, commander of the bodyguard and frantic for his king, stumped forward on his thick legs like an armoured toddler, screamed his fear loudly. The mass of foot surged forward as the blue and gold knight spurred on and Bruce, for the first time, felt a spasm of alarm, for he knew the knight would reach him first; the sight of the lance, big as an axle and wickedly pointed, made his belly clench and all his skin try to harden with gooseflesh.

The point was almost at him; he heard his own men yelling in desperation, as if they could throw shouts to deflect the horror of the English knight's descent on their king – and then he nudged the palfrey sideways, more by instinct than conscious thought and watched, almost dispassionately, as the blue and gold figure hurtled harmlessly past him in a snorting thunder, a flap of embroidered trapper.

The German Method, he thought triumphantly. Wins every time. Then he reined round and stood while the blue and gold knight scarred up clods of sere turf, narrowly missed colliding with a tree and spun the horse almost on the spot. Good, well-trained beast, Bruce thought and suddenly recognized the rider. Henry de Bohun – he had met the youth once, though he had clearly grown since. The new breed of Edward's warriors, he thought, young, fierce and hot for tourney, as he had been himself once. He felt a strange, mad exultation welling up in him, so that he laughed.

Henry could not believe he had missed. By the time he had wrenched Durandal round, he could see that the foot were running up and would be on him in another minute, a band of open-mouthed screamers frantic to protect their king.

Yet he would not give in – could not. Here was Bruce – and laughing at him. But if Henry wiped the laughter off his face, the entire affair was done, battle, rebellion, all; he launched himself forward, even as a fourteen-foot pike-spear was flung in desperation, skittering under the warhorse's plunging hooves like a giant snake.

Bruce waited, nudged – and the blue and gold knight sailed past him again; he thought he heard a howl of anguished frustration and he laughed so hard he had to lean on the cantle, little forgotten axe clutched in one maille-mittened fist.

Henry routed the horse round, flung the lance at the nearest of the spearmen, wrenched off the confectionary helm and hurled that in a fury, so that another of them bowled over backwards, taken smack in the face by it.

'Face me like a warrior!' he bawled at Bruce, his face a bag of sweat-streaked wine.

Bruce lost his humour in a moment. He knew Henry de Bohun only slightly, but he knew the family only too well. The de Bohuns had been given the Bruce lands of Annandale and Lochmaben by Longshanks and were smarting at having been flung off them since. He did not like this little lord's insults on his manhood and his chivalry – did the popinjay think this was a tourney? A neat little joust with a friendly clap on the shoulder and commiserations to the loser at the finish?

'Get you gone,' he roared back and de Bohun unhooked a mace from the cantle and flung it in a mad temper, so that Bruce had to duck. The spearmen crabbed towards Henry, their long weapons up and forcing him back. He shrieked and pounded the saddle with one metal fist.

'Coward,' he yelled, the spittle flying. 'Coward for a king.'

The fury rose in Bruce then, a great overweening tidal surge of red rage, swollen and festered with all the worry heaped on his shoulders. It burst like a plague boil and he gave a sharp bellow, like the coughing bark of a boar charging. De Bohun, contemptuous of the spearmen, turned his back on them all and trotted Durandal away.

He heard Bruce at the last, heard the tight drumming of fast, small hooves and half turned into the ruin of a snarling face, the sight of the King almost on tiptoe in the stirrups and his arm raised high. The axe in it winked briefly in a shaft of sunlight.

'Chivalry is it? Here is war, you fool.'

The axe crashed down and Bruce felt it crack like a twig, plunged on with the shaft and fought the maddened palfrey round. When he looked up, he saw the proud blue and gold warhorse cantering on with a swaying Henry briefly upright, the last quarter of shaft and axe buried in his skull, through the bascinet and the maille and down to the brow. He seemed like a strange-crested beast with a face masked in blood.

Henry de Bohun swayed, tilted and then slid from the saddle with a crash; there was a huge roar from the Scots foot and Bruce, sick and bewildered at what he had done, saw them leap forward like crows, stabbing with the beaks of their spears, battering the fallen body with the butts.

The frantic, half-weeping squire who rode up was dragged off his horse and beaten, stabbed and bludgeoned; the tight, coiled heat grew thick and heavy with the iron stink of blood and flies droned in like a host of praying monks.

Then hands grabbed the bridle of the palfrey and forced it away to safety, but Bruce did not know much as they led him back into the blazing sunlight; he came to his senses only when his brother and Randolph were shouting at him for having so exposed himself.

'You are the Kingdom, brother,' Edward was yelling, purple-faced. 'You must take more care, for we all hang from your crowned head – and we will all be hanged with it if it falls.'

'I broke a good axe,' Bruce said dazedly, staring at the splintered shaft. Those nearest laughed aloud, even the furious Edward, and spread the word of it, of how the King had defeated the English champion, a full-panoplied knight, armed only with a little axe and royal courage. The New Park sounded and resounded to the cheers.

The English saw Durandal as he thundered out into the sunlight, the saddle empty save for blood. He veered sideways and plunged and kicked, frantic with bewildered fury and fired with the stink of gore and battle in his nostrils, so that it took long minutes to capture him. By then the distant cheers, like surf on a rocky shore, were surging through the dying heat of the day.

Hereford seemed dazed by it, disbelieving. He peeled his own helmet off and dropped it, sat slumped on his horse and stared at the empty, blood-spattered saddle as if the mount itself had contrived some trick or magic spell to hide the rider. It was Gloucester who shook himself from it, turning to the others and raising one hand.

'De Clare,' he bellowed. 'The Van, to me.'

There was a surge, like a sluice gate opening; Thweng fought to control Garm as the knights surged past him and Buchan, reining in, turned and pirouetted his horse, his entire demeanour a question. Wearily, Thweng let Garm have his head and the joyous horse bounded after the others; he found himself, briefly, alongside Hereford, the Earl helmetless and dazed, jouncing like a half-filled sack and carried along by the plunging madness of his own warhorse into the whip of trees.

Addaf felt them before he heard them, saw the acorn and twigs at his feet tremble and knew, from old, what that meant; the blood rushed up in him and he roared like a bull.

'Scatter – scatter. The *mochyn saesneg* are coming.'

The pig English ploughed through the fleeing Welsh archers like maddened boar; Addaf ducked round a tree, saw another that was thicker and made for it, ran into the shoulder of a yellow-toothed, snapping horse and bounced to the leaf-littered roots.

He rolled and scambled up, saw Crach Thomas vanish with a despairing scream under the great steel hooves of a knot of riders, saw a knight in green and white skewer young Ithel Mawr like a skinned rabbit on a spit, and then he ran, blind with panic.

The Scots heard the screams, felt the tremble and those who knew warned the others to brace, brace.

'Hold to the line,' screamed Gilbert de la Haye and, since he was commander here, the King's bodyguard planted themselves like the trees in front of them and braced, the armoured front rank bent at one knee, the second rank, equally mailled, shouldering their long spears and planting one foot firmly on the spear butt dug into the ground in front of them.

A man ran out of the trees, looking frantically behind him and carrying a bow; he turned to see where he was running, spotted the massed ranks of spears and skidded to a halt, screaming. There was a pause, and then he hurled himself at the feet of the astonished front ranks and started to wriggle between the forest of legs, until one of the lurking knifemen in the dark of that sweating thicket grabbed him by his hair and cut the Welsh shrieks from his throat.

They were still echoing when the first elements of the English horse plunged out of the trees, chasing panicked Welshmen out of the dim and into the sunlight. Blinded by the transition, horses and riders balked and wavered, but the next wave was thundering on after them and horses collided, screaming and snapping.

Forced forwards, eyes scarred by light, the leading horses rode up to the ranks of spearmen at no better than a trot, with half of them trying to veer right and left, banging shoulder to shoulder with others. The ones at the fringes discovered the Scots archers on the flanks of the spearwall and the first to find them was Gloucester.

An arrow hit him on the placket, a reeling clang on his breastbone that drove the wind from him, made him jerk the rein and tear his horse's head back. Half-blind, half-mad and totally confused, the animal veered sideways and ran on to a knot of sharp points and glaive blades, worked by furious-elbowed men with screaming mouths and desperate eyes.

The horse's shriek was even louder and the young Earl felt it go, felt the sickening plunge of dying animal and tried to kick free. He only half succeeded – the horse fell and rolled,

239

kicking and shrieking, tangling itself in the long, golden tippets trailing from its rider's helm.

Gloucester rolled free – was snatched up short, as if grabbed by his hair, and collapsed back choking as the helmet thongs dug under his chin. Frantically, howling with frustration and anguish, he wrenched at the great helm, as if the padded gryphon was a living beast which had seized him in its claws.

He saw the adder-tongue flick of spears kill the horse, saw the horror of how close he was to the spear ranks: the legs like a tangled copse; mailled braies, leather shoes, bare horny feet and filthy calves. Scuttling from the dark, fetid depths of them came the dirk men on all fours, moving like mad-grinning spiders to finish him.

He bellowed and tugged, but the helm stayed on and the treacherous tippets chained him to the dead horse; he fumbled frantically for his sword.

Thweng saw it in the instant he broke from cover, saw the dead horse, the shackle of tippets, the frantic struggles of the man, the dark vengeance scrambling out towards him. He bawled at Badenoch and waved his sword in case he could not be heard and plunged forward into the haze of dust and grass motes chewed up from the dry earth by hundreds of hooves.

The darting little figures scampered back under the protective hedge of spears, which started to stab at this new warhorse. Thweng let Garm rear and strike, the neck stretching like a snake as he snapped and squealed; Sir Marmaduke felt the impact of the spears on the padded barding and saw the straw wisp out from the ruin of it, then he threw his lance into the grimace of faces and hauled out his sword.

He slashed once, twice, and the Earl staggered as the tippets parted and freed him. Then, as Badenoch and others rode forward, pressing and cavorting against the wicked hedge which stabbed and slashed at them, Thweng flung

240

one leg over the front cantle of the saddle and slid to the ground, feeling the jolt on his knees. Too old for this, he thought . . .

He cut backwards and forward with his sword, keeping the spears away from him – though one clattered and skidded off his shield as he grabbed the Earl and flung him towards the plunging Garm who remained, obedient and blowing, near his master.

Dazed, fevered, frantic, the Earl knew what Thweng was doing and clambered up into the saddle, sobbing with relief. Thweng flung him the rein, slapped Garm on the neck and the pair of them were suddenly gone from him.

A figure launched from the undergrowth of the spearwall, naked dirk stabbing for Thweng's helmet slit; he stepped into it, shouldered the man to the ground with the shield and cut the throat from him as easy as parting cheese rind. A hooked bill caught his surcote and tore it, pulling him further forward and off balance, so that he half fell at the feet of the Scots.

Another figure came at him and Thweng had time to see that he was bare-headed and part-bald so that the hair left to him stuck up in tufts like a moulting owl. The man collided with him, trying to wrestle him to the ground and thrust the narrow-bladed dirk inside the great helm, but Thweng got his shield in the way and heaved.

The man flew over Thweng, landing on the Earl's dead horse with a thump that drove the air out of both of them with a great farting groan; before he could recover one of the Shadows stabbed him repeatedly with his lance until it stuck and he had to let it go.

Thweng staggered back from the spearwall just as Badenoch forced himself between them, throwing his lance. He would, Thweng was sure, have hauled off his helm and hurled that, too, save that arrows were flicking at him.

Then he heard a horn blast; Hereford had recovered himself and was ordering the Van to break off the attack. Sir

241

Marmaduke trudged away, seemingly contemptuous of the enemy at his back but, in reality, too staggeringly weary to care. He saw Badenoch canter up, salute with his sword and then remain a little way away as a polite escort; Thweng was grateful and made a vow to thank the little Scots lord personally.

A little way into the forest he saw two knots of sweating knights, half dragging, half carrying the bodies of Henry de Bohun and his squire and he wondered how many lives had been lost to achieve that. Yet he knew it was something rescued from the stunning disaster of a knight's death. It was an almost unheard-of event, even in war, for a knight of such high degree to be slain.

The stun of it was already being felt, Thweng thought, seeing the trembling horses and the sweat-soaked, disbelieving riders trail back through the trees, chased by the flickering shadows and the arrows and the jeers of the men they had failed to best.

Sitting slumped on his expensive horse, streaming with tears and sweat, was the black misery of the Earl of Hereford watching his nephew's corpse bob past him, one bloody hand flapping as if waving a last farewell.

ISABEL

Liberation: from liber, *meaning free. Little Constance told me that, come to comb and dye my hair, enjoying it because she is not allowed to perform such an act on herself. The crowds in Berwick town roll like waves, fleeing the armies of both sides, seeking sanctuary here and finding madness. There is drink and dancing, Constance tells me, half excited, half fearful, but that does not surprise me – half will fall on their knees to worship God, the rest will worship, for as long as they can, their own bodies. Constance tells me that one of her own, a nun who has decided to call herself Giles in honour of the saint, has demanded to be immured. She had first demanded to replace me in my cage on the wall until she discovered that I did not live in it all the while, but had a Hog Tower room with a privy pot, a decent cot and a fire in winter. Too soft, she said.*

I told Constance that Sister Giles was welcome to my cage, as I shall be leaving it soon enough. God wills it.

The sky is thick and umber, heavy with that thunder that brings no rain, only oppressive heat – there has been no rain for weeks.

CHAPTER TEN

Bannockburn
Vigil of the Feast of St John the Baptist, June 1314

There had been no rain for weeks, so six hundred cantering hooves slashed up the sere grass and dirt of the carse into a haze that filtered the sun to a gold coin. The Carse was supposed to be boggy, cut about by vicious little streams and hard going for horses, but Sir Robert Clifford saw only a trickle of water in the bottom of steep-sided, bush-choked ditches.

'Still a barrier, my lord,' William Deyncourt noted, indicating the dark-streaked horses, foamed at the neck where the reins champed the sweat into a lather; they'd had to work hard to cross the dry streams.

'Yet the undergrowth is green enough,' Sir Thomas Gray added, 'which means it is watered regularly.'

Beaumont, grimming along in a world of reeling heat, wished he had the energy to argue, to growl at Deyncourt that it was only a barrier if men defended the opposite side of it, to spit at Gray that none here were bloody churl farmers and who cared where a bush got water? But Clifford nodded as if he understood what Gray had meant, which only flared Beaumont the more.

Too clever by half, he thought hotly. He did not like Deyncourt much, the more so because he was in Gray's retinue. He liked Gray even less and knew he should not harbour the feeling, which made matters worse still. Sir Thomas Gray had almost been killed saving him at the last siege of Stirling – Christ's Bones, a decade ago now.

The memory of that great hook, swinging down to try and grab the siege tower, made him whimper even now. It had missed its target and snagged him like a fish, catching in his surcote – the thought that it might have been his flesh still made his hole pucker.

Like a giant hand it had lifted him up and swung him, arms and legs flailing like a pathetic insect, to batter into the walls – but Gray had leaped forward, risking arrows and showers of stones to grab and hack the hook out of the surcote. Just then a springald bolt had taken Gray in the helmet, straight through it and into his face, so that they'd needed smithing tools to cut him free.

Guiltily, Beaumont glanced at Gray now, seeing the great scar like an accusing beacon that flushed more heat through him, composed of shame and gratitude. Gray should have died, Beaumont thought. He had lain under a pile of dead until Beaumont had come to his senses and gone back with men to look for him, expecting a corpse and finding what he thought was one; it was only when they paraded him back, all solemn and sorrowful for burial, that he had groaned and moved, shocking everyone – especially those who had tugged and heaved at the helm and then given up because it was skewered fast to his head.

He should have died anyway, Beaumont thought, from a horror wound like that – but he had recovered and Beaumont knew he should have been pleased for his saviour, should be sending prayers to God to preserve the life of this man who had preserved his.

Yet that face only reminded Beaumont of his bowel-loosening

246

fear on that day, his utter helplessness and what he had babblingly offered to God for deliverance, which no man nor saint could possibly have fulfilled.

He wanted this business done with, so that he could put Gray behind him and if it meant riding across this strange terrain into the gates of Hell itself, he would spur on.

The Carse was strange, no doubt of it. They had all been told how treacherous it was, a sward that looked firm yet was a soft and sinking bog. Not now. Not after weeks of summer sun. Now it was like fresh bread, slightly spongy and new-toasted so that it crumbled; Clifford voiced this and his *mesnie* laughed dutifully, but they were nervous. They had started out slightly later than the Van, knew nothing of what was happening in the New Park away to their left and Clifford was apprehensive. The distant sound of cheers and shouting did not help; who was celebrating and why?

Yet, if he was to achieve his king's orders and ride round to cut off the retreat of the Scots, he needed speed. That was why he had three hundred mounted knights and men-at-arms, all flogging expensive warhorses in the heat to come up on St Ninian's little chapel; the nearest foot were miles away, slogging desperately up with the baggage.

Clifford eyed the wood to his left, which had some outlandish name, as did the plain they rode across; they were coming up on another steep-sided stream and Clifford slowed to a walk, Gray and Beaumont coming up alongside.

'The Pelstream, my lord,' Gray offered. 'Tidal, like all the rest. We are leaving the Carse of Balqhuiderock and heading out into the Dryfield. As the name suggests, it is firm ground even in bad weather.'

No one could tell the difference; the plain looked exactly the same, though Clifford beamed, the beads forming on his fleshy nose and pouched cheeks.

'Good ground for horse,' he exclaimed cheerfully. 'The King will be pleased – this is where the army wants to be, my lords.'

Gray looked dubiously at the constrictions of wood and stream and mentioned them; he and Clifford fell to arguing the merits of the place as a 'good field'.

'God-cursed place,' Beaumont growled into the middle of their polite debate, wiping his face with a corner of his surcote. 'What's that there?'

He pointed one mittened fist and everyone followed it, some rising in the stirrups to try and see better.

It was a line, a scar on the landscape, seeming to undulate and sparkle. Gray laughed, which made Beaumont's scowl all the darker.

'That, my lord,' Gray said, almost joyously, 'is the enemy.'

Bruce had blinked and shaken himself out of the daze, ruthlessly forcing it away along with the memory of that fury, that great, crunching crack as he brought the axe down – hard enough to snap the shaft, by God's Wounds. His hand and arm hurt, wrenched with the power of the blow.

Like a blown egg, he recalled with a shudder. On the back of the boy's head as he rode away . . . he quelled that, too, stuffing it in the choked chest along with all the other sins.

The irony was not lost on him as he rode into an avenue of cheers and furious joy from those who had heard that the English Van had been repulsed, that a proud English champion lay dead like an offering, slain in single combat by their hero king. A good start, for all the sin in it, Bruce thought, and tried not to concern himself with the Curse of Malachy.

Yet it was lurking there, made itself plain when he rode up to Randolph's thousands and found no Earl of Moray, only Duncan Kirkpatrick of Torthorwald, anxious and stumping up and down in front of the serried ranks. At a glance, Bruce saw that the best of the Battle was gone; only the ill-armed were here, stripped down to a shift that barely covered their decency and leaning carelessly on their tall shafts; some had only shaved and fire-hardened points, some had strange hand-scythes and long shafts with other crude blades lashed to them, but none was a proper spear or bill.

I shall defend myself with the longest stick I have, Bruce thought.

Duncan Kirkpatrick, his face twisted as if in pain, blinked the sweat out of his eyes and knelt dutifully, thinking to himself that he was damned by Hell itself to be the one having to explain to his king what Sir Thomas Randolph, Earl of Moray, was doing.

Bruce felt the rise of panic in him, welling up like shit from a privy as he stared at Duncan. Kirkpatrick's kinsman, he recalled. Where is that auld dug – and Hal of Herdmanston? If we do not get them back, their mission successful, then we are done with this day and possibly this life. And where is Randolph with the best-armed men we have? The thought that he might have deserted like Atholl almost crushed him, but he heard Jamie Douglas give a surprised grunt and then a snort of derision.

'What in the name of Christ's Wounds is he thinking?'

'May the Lord forgive you,' said fat little Gilbert de la Haye piously and Jamie barked out a crow laugh, pointing with one hand down across the Dryfield.

'Not me that needs forgiveness, my lord,,' he answered. 'Him.'

They all looked. Out on the Dryfield, long hundreds of men skeined forward, their spears glinting, the Randolph bedsheet banner fluttering boldly alongside the saltire. It was his own *mesnie*, stripped from this command, all the well-armed and best-armoured men committing the unthinkable – the unforgivable – and marching unsupported out into the open against heavy horse.

Coming at them, hard and fast, Bruce saw, the pennons and streamers and blazing flags, the lances and tippets and heraldry glowing brightly through the golden haze.

Clifford's checky banner he recognized. And Beaumont's.

The black fork-tailed lion of the Stapledons. The Leyburns. Tailleboys. Christ's Bones – three hundred or more heavy horse of Clifford's command, bearing down on a little knot of men, already coalescing into a shield ring, as seeming vulnerable and small as a robin's egg in the middle of a busy stone path. Bruce felt the breath squeeze from him with the vice-crush of it.

'What possessed him?' gasped an incredulous de la Haye.

Carelessness, thought the Dog Boy, panting in the heat-flushed ranks of men behind Jamie; The Earl of Moray was supposed to watch for this and has missed it. Now, too late, he puts himself out like a stopper in a leather bottle to prevent the English going further towards Stirling's fortress.

Glory, Jamie Douglas thought laconically. Randolph has heard what the King did with the rearguard and seeks to outdo it, rub all our noses in his paladin splendour. He did not know what would be worse: that the Earl of Moray be ridden into the dust like a martyr or skewer the English to ruin like a hero. Either way, he thought moodily, we will never hear the end of it.

'He sought to prevent them reaching the castle, Your Grace,' Duncan Kirkpatrick offered miserably.

Bruce had his own answer to the why of it, watching with a sick, stone-heavy lump of fear in him as the English closed like a fist on the schiltron.

The Curse of Malachy.

Clifford could not believe it and said so. Beaumont, shaking sweat from his eyebrows like a dog does water, agreed with him, yet the sight gave him a sudden burst of savage exultant triumph.

'Let them come on further,' he bawled out, red-faced and beaming. 'The more ground we give them, the easier they are cut off and cut up.'

'Give them any more,' Gray answered wryly, 'and they will have it all, my lord.'

He meant nothing by it that anyone else could ascertain, but Beaumont swelled like an angry toad and astonished everyone by his ugly snarl; those who knew the tale of it were doubly shocked, for if anyone deserved Sir Henry de Beaumont's undying respect it was the man who had saved his life.

'If you are so concerned about them,' Beaumont savaged out, his face sweat-greased and dark with suffused blood, 'then feel free to flee.'

Now Gray boiled up, almost standing in the stirrups as he quivered with fury.

'You dare?' he demanded. 'You dare say that to me, sirrah. To me?'

'If it fits, wear it,' Beaumont growled, realizing he had been too harsh, yet unable to retreat from it.

'By God, Beaumont,' Deyncourt burst out, his own face raging. 'That is mean – this is the man you owe for being here at all.'

That did not help. Deyncourt, as Beaumont hissed out, was nothing at all and should mind his station when addressing an earl. That drew a sharp seal-bark of laughter from the furious Deyncourt and his brother, Reginald, came scowling up to make his presence felt.

'Earl? You may style yourself Earl of Buchan, Beaumont,' Deyncourt bawled, 'but when you have more than a wife's portion and a parchment to show for it, then you may have your due from me.'

'*Gentilhommes*,' Clifford shouted. He had three hundred mounted men on plunging horses which – already highly strung – not only sensed action but the nervousness of their riders; it meant that men were cavorting in circles to keep them from bolting; Clifford needed calm and did not get it.

'Be damned to you, Beaumont. I never ran from a fight and none should know that better than yourself.'

Gray spat it out with all the venom he could make, wrenched

251

savagely at the reins, dragging the squealing warhorse round. Before anyone could understand what he was doing, he had turned, couched his lance, set his shield and was trotting out, breaking into a canter. Behind him, like a grim shadow, trailed the Deyncourts, fumbling helms on as they went; young Reginald whooped with mad delight.

Alone, they thundered down on the hundreds of men forming into a bristling circle of spears.

In the circle it was blazing. Hot, Will thought. I hate the heat. I have always hated the heat, the way it prickled the skin and turned it dark as a saddle, as a Moorish heathen. When the rest of the bairns longed for the endless days of summer, when barefoot did not mean cold blisters, when they needed to swim in the river to cool off rather than get the dirt and shite off, I knew what it was doing to Da's stock.

My da would be fretting now, Will thought. Down in the undercroft, wondering if it was cool enough and fretting mad. This was more fiery than any heat Da had known, mark you, made worse because I am pressed fore and aft, shoulder to shoulder with men as boiled as me, sweating fear out in a nose-pinching stink. Smelling rank in ranks, he thought and nearly laughed.

Yet my da is to blame for me being here, squashed and melting like mutton tallow in a roaring ring, waiting for Hell to fall on me.

It's not our fight, I told him. What do we care who wears the crown – would the priory not need candles under an English king? And my da put me right on it, as he always did, as he did when he taught me how to measure to the last drop the tallow needed for a candle clock – a proper one, not the thin streaks of piss stuck in a graded pewter sconce that some folk affect.

'Who do we pay rent to?' my da demanded and there it was, perfect as coloured wax; the priory owned us and the rent, though I had never known this before, included service as a man-at-arms. My da had gone before, back in '07 and again in '10 and was lucky to escape with his life both times.

I was nine when he first went, Will thought, and understood nothing. Now I am sixteen and since Da is too old, it is me chosen – so here I am, dripping as if rained on, in Da's rusting rimmed iron hat, patched old gambeson, rattle-hilted sword and a long pike-spear given me by the King.

Yet the hands that hold that spear are mine, the cunning of bone and joint and broken nails was made to answer my order and no one else's, just as were the sweating, stinking feet in the battered shoes and the legs atop them.

He was Will the chandler's boy and he was sixteen and lived in himself, somewhere under the ribs or inside his skull, thinking thoughts that had never been thought, feeling things that were so big and full no one had ever experienced them.

Will the chandler's boy, melting like wax and waiting to be smeared like old grease. No chance now to make a name as great as Master Overhill, who had invented the candle clock. No chance to find some cleverness to combat the creeping horror of steel cogs and wheels that was the fancy Frenchified horologe, no chance to raise himself from dipping wick in tallow to make nothing better than poor light the rest of his life.

No place for candles this, he thought, hearing the booming roar of the vintenars to keep close – charge your pikes. Behind him, in the thinned centre of the ring, barely enough room for him alone, he knew the lord Randolph stood. How he stayed upright in this heat, with maille and plate and padding all over him, was something approaching magic, part of the mystery of the *nobiles* and what they did.

Yet he was not only upright, but roaring defiance and demands that they hold to the ring; out beyond the shoulders of the man in front, Will saw two riders and tried to dash the sweat out of his eyes with a fist swathed in thick leather

253

gauntlet. It made his spear sway and clatter off the helmet of the man in front, but he only grunted, did not turn round.

The riders came on. Just three – someone laughed in disbelief but the men around Will suddenly seemed to stop breathing and Will saw that the riders were coming straight at his part of the ring; if they kept going they would crash into it.

'Hold to the ring!'

Surely no sane man or beast would plunge straight in a hedge of points . . . Will did not even realize he had said it aloud until the man next to him growled out a reply.

'They are no' sane, beast nor man,' he declared and Will turned to look briefly at the grizzled face. It smiled at him.

'Dinna fash, lad. Hold to the ring, keep your pike charged as you trained and it will be fine enough.'

'You have done this afore?'

Will heard the tremble in his voice and was ashamed of it, but the man did not seem to notice and merely grinned brownly.

'Och, this is auld cloots an' gruel to the likes o' us,' he said and men to his front and side laughed agreement. Will could not understand why anyone would want to do this more than once. Then the grizzled man looked to his front and shifted as if to plant himself.

'Fuck,' he said and Will saw the horsemen, big as giants and growing larger, the huge legs of the beasts pounding the ground to dust as they came on them at a full gallop.

Gray's fury thundered with every hoofbeat, a blood pulse that sent him shrieking at the ring of spears, cursing Bruno's slowness and raking him until he squealed. Even the sight of the spear points, wavering as they drew together to point at him, provided only the briefest spasm of apprehension, no more.

That was driven away by the sight of Sir William Deyncourt spurring past him, sitting forward and almost lunging with his lance – bad posture that, he thought, for you are off

balance when you hit and will go straight through the gatehouse, out between the ears like a slung stone . . .

Deyncourt rode Bruno's stablemate, a big Frisian cross
called Morningstar. The pair of them had been trained together,
at the straw men in ranks, at the weak withy hurdles so that
they believed there was no barrier they were put to which
was stronger than their own muscle and bone. All it took was
a madly determined rider and they would try to punch a hole
in a castle wall – or a deadly shrike's nest of points.

Gray sat back, legs stuck almost up by the arched neck of
Bruno, the last furious gallop into the ring a great roar that
rang inside his helm and deafened the splintering crash.

Will saw the leading horseman as a flicker to the left of him,
heard the grating crash and felt the slam of bodies rippling
away from the impact point. Staggering, frantic, he was peering
to see when the second knight erupted out of the golden haze,
a massive monster with bared yellow teeth topped with a
featureless creature of metal.

There was a brief confusion of red and white, a glimpse of
a silver lion on a shield and then the horse struck the front
rank as if it did not exist; there was the sound like a great tree
falling and Will saw the man in front of him flung into the air
to disappear with a shriek. He ducked instinctively at the great
whirl of splintered wood from broken spears, saw the snapped-
off points lanced into the horse's chest and head – straight
through the flaring nostril and out of the other eye.

Then there was a moment when the world seemed to stop,
when the man on the dying horse's back took his lance to
within a foot of Will and skewered the astonished grizzle of
the veteran through the neck; he seemed to float up in the
air, higher and higher so that Will started to follow him with
a tilt of his gape-mouthed stare.

The dying horse, legs flailing still, screaming a high-pitched
shrill, ploughed on and skittled the ranks of men. Time sucked

back to Will, just as the horse capsized, the last mad shriek and kick arriving into the sunlight of Will's world like a huge black cloud.

He felt the blow, felt himself hurled backward into other men and wanted to apologize. He saw himself as if he stood outside the blackness that had cloaked him, with his fine sprout of red-gold beard like stubble on a sparse field, big-handed, big-footed and awkward. Proved and not a coward, all the same, he thought, even if I am in the dark and afraid of it.

I need a candle.

Gray knew Sir William was already dead when Bruno hit the spearwall and died in an instant. He barely had time for the regret of such a loss before he was shot upward as if launched from a trebuchet, sprung up but not cleanly; one foot was briefly caught in the stirrup and he felt his leg wrench. Then it was free and he was flying in a whirl of arms and legs, like the tumblers he had seen at a fair day once. There was a brief flicker through his helmet slit, an eyeblink vision of a boy with his mouth open.

He crashed down in a great heap, the air driven from him. He thought he had been pinned like a sheep's eye on a crow beak, but felt himself dragged and kicked, felt his mind narrowing to a last small point of light. I am too young, he thought frantically. I have achieved nothing . . . he felt the savage wrenching of his neck, then light flared as his helm was torn off; blind, stunned, he blinked into a growl of shadows.

God preserve my soul . . .

This was chaos and Randolph flailed in the centre of it, bawling for the bodies to be cleared away, the dead spat out like gristle, for the ring to hold, for it to crab away from the dead horses. Someone flung a body at his feet and he stared down into the glassed daze of the knight, his red surcote torn, the silver lion streaked with gore.

'Yield, my lord?' he asked, out of politeness' sake, and Sir Thomas Gray, his senses rushing back into the dubious blessing of a world of pain, could only nod.

A few feet away, Davey the Cooper fought the splintered length of lance from the neck of Bannock and rolled him away – helpful feet kept him going, feeding him out of the ring as it drew back. Peel o' the Bannock, Davey thought, the hero of Linlithgow who had driven the haywain under the cullis and stopped it dropping long enough for men to spring through and take the place. It is a weeping shame to be leaving him in his own blood for the birds to peck, him who had sworn to defend his own birthplace. Him and a dozen others, he saw, torn and savaged to death by only three knights.

He examined the boy at his feet, hearing him softly moaning out of his smashed face.

'Swef, swef,' he soothed, though he knew the lad – Will, he thought the name was – had been sore hurt. Christ's Bones, you could see the half-moon circle where the iron-shod hoof had caught him full in the face, the bloody furrows where the raised shoenails had gouged him.

'Candle,' he heard the boy mush out of his ruined mouth; somewhere, men shouted out a warning and Davey had no more time to think about it, drew his knife and slit the boy's throat, the blood scalding on his hands.

No candle would bring light to the poor boy, he thought, wiping his fingers down the front of his tunic. Not when his eyes have been torn from his head and his face so monstered his own ma would not recognize him. Better this way . . .

He helped the press to roll the boy out and rose up, shouldered into a space and braced for the rest of the English to arrive.

Clifford was near weeping with frustration and had torn his helmet off, flinging it away with a bawled curse so pungent it would strip the gilding off a saint's statue. Beaumont, horrified at what had happened, saw that the entire Battle was in disarray.

There were knights flung to the ground trying to fight their horses for control, others who had failed were streaming away in all directions on mad bolters and a good long hundred or so had compromised with their mounts and were rolling forward against the spear ring but at a steady foam-mouthed canter and all strung out.

'Form. Form,' Clifford roared and those remaining fought their plunging mounts into some semblance of tight knee-to-knee order – but the act of this, familiar and tantalizing, simply fanned the flames as the warhorses fought for their heads, squealing and blowing like whales.

'Advance,' Clifford called in desperation and, like a bolt from a springald, the relax of reins sent the whole pack raggedly forward in a fast canter. Throwing up his iron fists, Clifford gave in and followed, his own mount held in a steel grip that Beaumont could only admire, smiling and nodding his praise.

Clifford scowled back at him.

'This is your fault, my lord,' he said as he swept past and Beaumont, floundering for a reply, could only fume in his wake.

In the end, they could only circle the ring, kept at bay by stabbing spears, reduced to hurling their lances and maces. Beaumont cantered round once, threw his lance, thought about hurling his helmet into the sea of wet, open-mouthed scum, but considered the pointless expense and kept it.

His excellent mount, at a trot, picked a delicate step over the flung bodies, snorting at the dust and blood as Beaumont searched for Sir Thomas.

If God had been just, he thought, he would have discovered Gray alive and bloodied, been able to climb off his expensive warhorse and present it to the man and so expunge his odious obligation. But there was no sign of Gray, only the battered and bloodied remains of his horse, something that might have been Sir William Deyncourt – and, to Beaumont's added horror, young Reginald Deyncourt as well, who had clearly decided to avenge his elder brother and paid the price for it.

He swung round as Clifford, red-faced and hoarse with shouting, galloped up to him, flinging one hand behind him. Lifting the fancy visor of his new bascinet, Beaumont squinted; there were more men coming out of the woods, spears up and hedged.

Bruce sat and watched the three riders crash to ruin; Jamie Douglas gave an admiring shout as they did so, even as he shook his head at the futility of it. He had uncowled himself from maille and bascinet so that his tousled dark hair stood up in sweat-spikes and his face was bright with joy.

He loves all this, Bruce thought as he massaged the ache of his right hand, pulling off gauntlet and maille mitt to study it; he carefully wiggled his fingers and noted the signs of blue bruising, mottled and ugly. Count the blessings of Heaven, he thought wryly, at least you can still feel all your fingers. And toes.

'Do you wish me to go to the Earl of Moray's aid?'

The tone was bland but the question was as loaded as any latchbow; when Bruce turned, Jamie Douglas had a face and smile as innocent as a nun's headscarf.

'Let my nephew bide a wee,' Bruce answered laconically. 'He seems to have matters in hand.'

And if you go to his aid, Jamie Douglas, he thought, it will only be to preen and wave the rescue of it at Randolph for the rest of his life, so that he will not forgive either you or me.

They watched while the horsemen rode up in ragged skeins and then balked and circled. One dashed in and the horse

259

went down – men cheered as the rider was clearly pounced on by the dirkmen and sent, as Patrick announced cheerfully, 'all the way tae his ain Hell'.

Other horses were downed, but the riders weaved and staggered away, half walking, half falling. Eventually, as if tiring of the entertainment, Bruce turned back to Jamie Douglas.

'Move your men to the line of the wood. No farther, Sir James, upon your honour.'

Jamie pouted, but then grinned, for he knew what his king was up to and he turned to the waiting men, winking at Dog Boy.

'Rank up, lads. Make some noise, too, just to let the bloody English ken who we are.'

They marched out, shouting and singing as if it was a parade of apprentices on the spree – but, as Bruce had planned, the English saw reinforcements arriving. There was a flurry among them, the distant faintness of shouting and then a horn blew.

Bruce sat deeper in his saddle, suddenly aware of the tension leaking out of him like grain from a burst bag; his arm and hand pulsed with a vicious heartbeat. He heard horsemen and turned to see his brother ride up, grinning like a shark out of his broad face and waving vaguely at the sky.

'The sun is going down,' he declared as if he had been personally responsible for it. 'They will try no more until the morn.'

Bruce nodded and sucked in a long, deep breath; below, Randolph's schiltron was uncurling like a cautious hedgepig, waving their sharpness and hurling jeers at the backs of the retreating knights.

The day had gone well, Bruce thought. Yet tomorrow it would all have to be done again – or else tonight we will have to be gone. And smartly, too, since it is the shortest night of the year.

He wondered, suddenly, why his brother was here at all and not with his own command, turned to ask and saw the broad grin widen further as Edward nudged his horse aside to reveal the men he had been hiding.

Bruce stared. Kirkpatrick was dappled with sweat and leaning wearily on the cantle of his mount's saddle. Beside him, with a great half-bruised face and a bound arm, swaying with fatigue but grim and steady as ever, sat Hal of Herdmanston. Behind them prowled a slew of Campbells, all bristle-bearded and proud, but scowling to have arrived too late for this day's fighting.

His brace of dogs returned. He blurted it out before he could think and saw Hal's raised eyebrow and Kirkpatrick's lopsided smile.

'Aye, betimes,' Kirkpatrick answered, 'with our jaws stuffed with retrievals.'

'There are cartloads coming,' Edward Bruce declared, unable to keep silent any longer. 'Weapons and armour and more of the same.'

His face was shining with it as he stared at his regal brother.

'Now we can stand and fight.'

ISABEL

They can feel it, the irregular heartbeat of it. The seneschal here, a fat and fussy man, has banned Malise from my side by order of the new warden, John de Luka. It is not pity nor mercy that does it, but Your Hand, my Lord. That and the fact that, if all goes badly, I might be a counter for bargaining a truce of peace for this town, as good as gold to some folk. So here I am, curled in my cage like a cat, prinked and preened and dyed and painted and dressed, with one hand clutching an ivory sieve holding balls of musk and crushed amber, the other carefully hidden because of what Malise has done to the nails and fingers. I have a barbette edged with cloth of gold. Nestling between my breasts is a gift from the warden himself, a fat enamelled pendant which has two lovers kissing on one side and, on the other, a grinning Death; it is a common enough theme, but it reveals more sensibility than I saw in the hard face of that royal squire. I wonder if he chose it himself or had someone do it? Either way, Your Hand is in it, Lord. I am still on display, but more gilded and most of those who still come to gawp think I have a toad hidden somewhere the better to curse them, or suck on an emerald in my sleep to preserve my seeming youth.

Let them. I am Isabel MacDuff, with a dowry portion of Fife. I am a long ways past girlhood, yet I am ready to receive my lover. God wills it that he comes soon.

263

CHAPTER ELEVEN

Bannockburn
Midsummer's Night, June 1314

The dusk was soft and blue like woodsmoke, though there was a haze of that, too, from the small flowers of a thousand flames. Looking out, Dog Boy could see the scatter of English fires, like the tail of a long-haired star.

He ate from a wooden bowl, horn-spooning in oats and barley savouried with a good stock bone which had even had some meat on it. There was bread to sop it up and some small beer, but no ale or wine; Dog Boy thought that was deliberate, to prevent everyone getting drunk with little or no time to sleep it off.

He heard the whine and spang of music from a viel, accompanied by the heartbeat thump of a drum and great growling barks of laughter and raised voices; the Islesmen, or the Campbells, who had their own drink and would not be stopped from it. For all that they looked longingly and thought of the fiery drink, none of the Lowlanders would risk arriving uninvited at such a fire, so they sat and stared morosely at the flames until blinded by the light.

'Good, this,' Yabbing Andra declared, slurping the last and

scraping the bowl noisily. 'This is fine fare, is it no', lads? I mind the time . . .'

People sighed, for the only time Andra was ever silent was when he was eating and, even if he scraped shavings off the inside of his bowl, there would be precious little left in it to occupy his mouth for long.

Then, to everyone's surprise, Troubadour Tam interrupted him. He seldom said anything at all, seemed to speak only through the bowing of his viel, but he seemed to have lost his touch for it this night, for he crossed into Andra's ramble with a slashing few words of his own.

'Mak' the best of it – there will be precious little else this winter. Hunger is coming.'

Those who worked the land knew it and nodded. Patrick, who worked cattle more than he did fields of oats and barley, announced that the saving grace of Our Lord in all this was that the English would be visited by the same bad-crop famine – and they had more fields given to wheat and less to livestock or hardy oats.

'So? What use is that to us?' demanded Horse Pyntle and Patrick explained it to him, shaving little cuts off a splinter and curling them into the fire for amusement.

'They will only have beasts left to them. When we raid, as raid we must for food, then we will have meat and lots o' it.'

There were grim snarls of laughter at this, save for Parcy Dodd, who said that too much meat made you sick. Since none there had ever had enough meat to make them sick, there were growling, jeering questions fired back at him.

'Aye, aye,' he declared defensively. 'I never said I had ever been sick from too much meat. Tainted meat, aye – and it tak's precious little of that to make ye boak. But my ma had experience in curin' folk – rich folk, you ken – whose shitholes and insides were choked up with too much meat.'

'Good, was she?' demanded Sweetmilk, while everyone had that wary look you got round Parcy Dodd, since you could never trust anything he said at all, on any subject.

'In a godly fashion,' Parcy declared, frowning, 'though I have long since hauled myself away from her notion that what galled ye or made ye boak was a blessin'.'

'Every mother is the like,' Geordie offered and there were growls of assent at that; there was a vagrant coil of the wild music of the galloglass warriors from the north and west; and Dog Boy saw Troubadour Tam's head come up, cocked to listen to it like a dog sniffs the wind.

'Aye, mayhap and mayhap no',' Parcy replied. 'I have no experience of Geordie's ma, nor none else but mine own, who brewed physick that would gag a hog. She would clutch my neb until I had to breathe – then pour it down my thrapple.'

Dog Boy heard them, bleared with memories, chuckle at this shared moment, but it was not for him; he could barely remember his ma at all these days and certainly not her face.

'Did it work?' demanded Horse Pyntle and Parcy flapped a loose hand.

'It did what it was aimed at – once swallied, ye had better have a bush to boak in.'

'Aye, well,' Patrick murmured dreamily, 'here you are – so it must have been good.'

'Not to my way o' considering it,' Parcy answered. 'Once, as a wee laddie, I swallied a penny. A whole siller penny, my da's rent-price for our ox. So it was out with the physick – and back came the money, so sick it would not spend.'

'Away, Parcy ye liar!'

Parcy held up his hands.

'May the Lord bliss and keep me, the truth it is I am telling you here. The wee reeve said it was a crockard. Rang hollow, he said. Well, it was fine when I ate it, but it comes as no surprise to me that my ma's physick ruined it. It would strip the shine from anythin', that brew.'

'At least they ne'er burned her as a witch,' Sweetmilk said, 'if her brew was so bad.'

He jerked his head up, realizing what he had said and suddenly worried that he might have stumbled into a mire. Parcy let him dangle for a long moment, and then shook his head; Sweetmilk's obvious relief made everyone laugh.

'Not for the want of folk trying, mark ye,' Parcy went on. 'Cost an Inquisitor dear.'

'You nor your ma never saw such,' scoffed Geordie, which was as good as a waved rag to a bull.

'He came to our vill,' Parcy insisted indignantly, 'a wheen of years back, when such black crows were permitted into the Lowlands to seek out the heresies of the Temple. The folk came out shouting that my ma was a witch and should be burned. Burn her, burn her, they were yellin', and demanded the good Brother Inquisitor put her to the test.'

He paused and the wind flared up sparks, as if it was part of the story.

'The Inquisitor, who was interested only in the foulness of Poor Knights, was weary of a deal of the same. Scotland, he had discovered, was full of kindly, helpful folk who seemed determined to broil and roast their neighbours. "What makes you think she is a witch?" he demanded and they told him she stank of old sulphur when she farted. "Burn her. Burn the witch."

'"So do I," the Inquisitor admitted. "She has a third nipple," they told him and demanded that he burn the witch. He frowned. "I have a wart which might be mistaken for the same," he sighed back at them.

'"She takes the Lord's name in vain," they flung at him. "She must be burned. Burn the witch." The Inquisitor, who had had enough of this, flung down his scrip of blessed relics in disgust. "I have also taken the Lord's name in vain," he announced. "Particularly when faced with the likes of folk such as yourselves."'

Parcy stopped and shook his head in mock sorrow.

'Well, he thought he had brought sense to them, for they stopped and muttered among themselves for a minute or two, then raised their heads and untied my ma. "Forget the auld wummin," they said, looking at him with flames in their eyes. "Burn the witch."'

There were dry chuckles, but mostly silence as folk marvelled at the tale.

'What happened to your ma?' demanded Yabbing Andra into the head-shaking admiration. 'Did her neebors burn her as well as that Inqueesitor?'

'For certes not,' Parcy said without hesitation. 'They let her go and concentrated on the unhappy black priest – so she went back to our house and turned them all into toads, first chance she had. That vill is now empty save for her and some hopping croakers and their gener. None will visit it, not even myself.'

'Bigod,' Patrick declared, 'the Auld Carl himself never told such fibs. I am not surprised your ma made brews to make ye boak, if you kept telling her tales like that.'

'I had a physick once,' Yabbing Andra began and people groaned. Dog Boy got up and moved away, feeling strange, at once part of them and not part of them. Perhaps it was their talk of mothers. Perhaps it was the new livery he wore, a smart jupon that was still fresh enough to be clean, fixed with the badge of a royal houndsman.

He had taken it from the hands of Bernard the Chancellor, whom he'd been advised to see as soon as possible and had found as a dry thin stick of a priest in plain brown wool, worse dressed than the gaggle of clever clerks who served him.

'Aleysandir,' he declared when the name was given to him, consulted the rolls and frowned. He issued orders and, in short order, Dog Boy had his new badged clothes and a chinking bag of money.

'You have a stipend, paid quarterly,' the Chancellor declared. He had a face dominated by pink-rimmed eyes and a knife-cut of a mouth, a manner made haggard by the amount of work he had before him. Yet he managed what passed for a smile.

'The King's hounds are at Turnberry. Or Lochmaben – no

269

one is sure. Once this unpleasantness is dealt with, you may take up your duties proper.'

And that was it. Stipended, by God. A rich man . . .

And severed by it from the others, he realized as he moved off through the fires, drawn back over Coxet to the baggage camp. He hung like a mote between Heaven and earth, too low-born for the company of Jamie Douglas, too raised for the likes of Patrick and Parcy Dodd to feel comfortable with.

Now he was looking for Hal and, if truth be told, it was not simply because he wanted to speak of the loss of Sim Craw, or hear the adventure of how Kirkpatrick and the lord of Herdmanston had brought a great load of weapons and armour all the way from Spain. He knew where Spain was – beyond England and further south through Gascony until folk stopped speaking either English or French – but he could not envisage how far it was, or of ever going there.

The truth was that Dog Boy was happy that Hal had survived it all, while the hurting loss of Sim Craw had sunk in him like a wound and would scab over in time. No, the truth of what irked him was that the lord of Herdmanston had not sought him out.

Why should he? We were parted long before he went into Roxburgh's depths, he thought, and he was seven years in that; he is nothing to me, nor me to him. Yet he recalled that once they had been close and wished for that comfort again.

So here I am, he admitted wryly, looking.

The lord of Herdmanston's banner was not hard to find even in the confusion of the baggage camp, tight huddled like sheep in the lee of Coxet, stuck to the side of it like a bloom of fungus. Dog Boy threaded a way through the skeins of doggedly patient men and harassed clerks of Bernard the Chancellor, working by rush lights and against the swoop of a night too short to properly darken, tallying and issuing the weapons and armour. He reached the panoply of Sir John Airth, commander of the camp, where a bored, half-asleep guard stood hipshot under a limp banner on a pole.

He was friendly and informative, which let Dog Boy marvel at the power of his new station in life; before, he would have been told to shift away but now he had a cote with a royal badge on it and was treated politely.

He learned that 'auld Sir John' was asleep, while Sir Henry of Herdmanston had gone off with another Sientcler lord, the one from Roslin. They had gone to the Sientcler camp – the engrailed cross banner was plain to see, the guard added, since the high and mighty Sientclers raised it on a taller pole than anyone else.

There were fires under the shivering cross and a dull regular clang that spoke of a smith somewhere. Folk moved like drifting shadows and one, sudden as a hunting owl, was facing him and smiling.

'Bigod, Dog Boy, you're as braw as shiny watter still, so you are.'

Dog Boy blinked at the woman, her hair a raggle, wearing only a shift dress in the heat and a shawl with a memory of blue in it shrugged across her shoulders. She carried a knife and a basket, while a bairn stood looking up at him with solemn eyes, thumb in her budded mouth.

The face was blurred with years, but the beauty in it was there yet. Bet's Meggy. The sight of her crashed him back to Herdmanston in the heat of another summer, when he and others had played at the kirn, throwing scythes to cut the last stook of corn. He had won and presented it to Bet's Meggy amid the cheers and jeers, for her to make into the kirn-baby, a sure sign that she was next for a wedding.

'Meg,' he said awkwardly and she cocked her head to one side and then shook it with mocking disbelief.

'Come high in the world, Dog Boy. How do I call you these days?'

He found himself and grinned back at her.

271

'Now we are reacquainted,' he said, 'ye dinna have to call at all – just reach out a hand.'

He beamed at her obvious delight and burst of laughter. She had lost the bloom of youth he remembered, the perfect heart of her face had roughened and coarsened a little, the body was thicker – a wean will do that, he thought. Yet he was older himself and the feral-thin girl he'd known then was no longer such a rampant attraction, while the woman who swayed back to her fire was.

She spooned gruel into a bowl, just as a boy came up, staring at Dog Boy with a watchful, defiant eye; Bet's Meggy looked at him and then at Dog Boy as she lifted bread from the basket.

'Fetch a bowl and spoon,' she said. She indicated the thumb-sucking girl: 'This is Bet,' and Dog Boy smiled; of course it would be, he thought.

'And this is Hob,' she said to the boy. He was dark, Dog Boy thought, and rangy, though there was the promise that good food and care would slide some real muscle on him. He thought the lad was about nine, but his skill in judging age was nearly all to do with dogs, so he could have been mistaken.

'Where have ye been?' Bet's Meggy demanded and Hob blinked away from Dog Boy's face and thrust out his hand, which had a coin in it.

'I took the Sire to the forgeman, as he asked,' he replied. 'He gave me a whole siller penny.'

The wonder in his voice was dreamy as Bet's Meggy took the coin and dropped it into her cleavage; it would not find a way out of the bottom of them, Dog Boy thought admiringly and remembered that Midsummer's Night when she had danced the Horse Dance, naked under a green shift dress fixed with madder ribbons and wearing the straw mummer's horsehead.

Clear across the stubbled fields she had pranced, to no more than a whistle and drum, the chants of others dancing and singing behind her and the faint, sonorous prayers of the

272

priest, determined not to let folk lose sight of God in this whiff of heathenism.

She had danced until her feet bled on the stubble, which was the point of it, blessing the fields with her virgin blood. Then, when the field had been acknowledged as watered, Dog Boy had gathered her up and carried her into the night while folk called good-natured filthy advice after them. He had washed her feet gently in the burn on that Midsummer's Night, the pair of them wearing rue against the threat of Faerie pixie-leading them off to spend a hundred years or longer in their hidden *sidhean* mounds.

Despite the rue, something had touched them that night; perhaps they had truly been transformed into virgin Queen and handsome King of Summer, for they had coupled like writhing snakes and, in between, rubbed fern seed on their eyelids and sat crosslegged and naked with the rue tight in their fists, in the hope of seeing the Faerie but escaping being taken by them.

Towards dawn – too short a night, Dog Boy recalled, same as this one – she had sighed and laughed about how she would never dance the Horse Dance again now, for he had broken her yett gate for ever.

Now here she was, as if sprung from a faerie hill.

'I heard ye married,' he blurted and she paused, frowning at what her attempt at cutting the bread had brought; it had broken to crumbs of shrivelled beans and peas, mixed with rye and a little wheat. Dog Boy, remembering the good bread he had eaten earlier, felt ashamed.

'I did,' she answered, scooping the crumbs into the bowls and handing them out. Dog Boy refused the one she handed to him and she looked relieved, fed more crumbs to it and stirred them in.

'John the Lamb,' she answered and Dog Boy nodded. He had been a score of years older than her.

'A good man,' she answered defiantly, as if he had spoken aloud. Then she smiled softly. 'Perfect, in fact – away for days at a time tending the sheep and always bringing back a peck of wool or a tait of mutton.'

Her eyes clouded.

'Died two – no, I lie, three – years since. Cold and a hard winter and age took him.'

She scowled at Hob, who was eyeing the gruel with distaste.

'Eat that. Learn to like it or go hungry – there is little else.'

She sighed and turned apologetically to Dog Boy.

'He disnae care for the meat in it, which is horse.'

Dog Boy nodded; horse was the one meat they were not short of now and he wondered if the fine English who had donated it knew of the fate of their proud mounts.

'You are chewing on the most expensive meat there is,' Dog Boy said to Hob and explained why. The boy's dark eyes flickered with interest, but the scowl remained.

'The priest says it is a sin to eat the flesh of the horse,' he persisted and Dog Boy shrugged as if it did not matter at all.

'If it is still Father Thomas who is priesting you, then he has knowledge of it, for sure,' he answered, staring idly at the fire. 'He was happy to eat it when Herdmanston was sieged.'

'Away . . .'

The blurt was out and Hob took the scowling censure of his mother and fell silent.

'Besides,' Dog Boy went on, 'Jamie says the French eat it – he was in that land for the learning in it. He says it was the Northmen who so upset the priests, for they used to fight prize stots and sacrifice the winner in their heathen rites, eating the meat. Since wee priests hate the raiding Norsemen, horses got called all kinds of bad cess.'

'I likes it.'

Dog Boy grinned back at the smiling little Bet and then looked at Hob, who was half scathing, half impressed.

'Jamie,' Dog Boy added, 'is Sir James Douglas. Good Sir James. He eats horse when he can get it.'

'The Black,' Hob blurted out admiringly and Dog Boy

274

laughed. Somewhere music struck up and people cheered as flames leaped; they were lighting the balefires for Midsummer's Night and Dog Boy glanced at Bet's Meggy with a look of remembrance that made her flush and shift a little. Then he turned back to the boy.

'Sir James is known as that as well.'

Bet's Meggy, smiling, nudged her son.

'Give thanks for being put right on matters,' she said and Hob, gingerly spooning gruel to his mouth, found the scowl again, though it was uncertain this time.

'I dinna ken who he is, Ma,' he offered and she beamed, looking from him to Dog Boy.

'He's your da, boy.'

Bannockburn, the English Camp
Midsummer's Night, June 1314

Like Mongols, Giles d'Argentan bawled into the retelling of the Clifford charge. Round and round and round – a pity they had no bows.

The other laughed and Ebles de Mountz, daringly drunk, shouted out that d'Argentan had never seen a Mongol; for a moment the sweating night was chilled – but Sir Giles threw back his head and roared out a laugh.

'I have too – the Emperor in Constantinople has some. They look like this.'

He put thumbs to the side of his face, pulling back his eyes and squinting, while another finger shoved his nose up to a pig snout. Folk cheered and beat their thighs.

'Begone,' shouted one of the Berkeleys. 'Nothing looks that ugly.'

'It does if it is sired by Satan,' d'Argentan replied and folk crossed themselves, then went back to wassailing one another with loud shouts and laughter.

275

'Like Mongols,' d'Argentan persisted, louder than ever so that it would carry through the leprous night to where Clifford's *mesnie* huddled, morose and silent, round their own cookfires. 'Round and round . . .'

The laughter shrilled out and then died as d'Argentan held up a stilling hand.

'Of course,' he declared, owlishly drunk but not reckless, 'I offer a salute to the brave fallen, who knew their duty. To the Deyncourt brothers and Sir Thomas – I am glad to know that Sir Thomas Gray is held for ransom and not dead. God preserve him.'

Solemnly, the knights gathered at the food-littered trestle raised their cups. Somewhere beyond, the rest of the knights cursed the dark and the steep-sided streams as they coaxed or forced horses across the hasty bridges made from doors and planks culled out of Bannock vill.

It would take them all night, Thweng thought, and the foot are still straggling up and will have precious little rest – the bulk of the baggage will be lucky to have made it before dawn.

'Mongols,' d'Argentan bawled, which was enough to set the roisterers off on another cackle; Thweng moved off into the dark, seeking his own fire. His baggage was a long way off in the dark, so he had no tent and comforts and had only eaten because he had shared the King's table. He had only done that because Edward was anxious, needing reassurance and all the advice he could get.

'Will they stand?' he asked everyone and it was the very question, the caged corpse swinging in the tree of the affair. Would the Scots stand and fight, or melt away? Everyone at the meal had knowledge of the Scots, had fought them before this – Beaumont, Segrave, de Valence, himself. Even the King was no beginner at the work, having been in the campaign of '04 under his father and ones in '07 and '10 in his own right.

'The Scotch will not stand,' Segrave growled, shaking his head while the black-clad wraith that was his son, Stephen, echoed him like a shadow. 'They have run each time we have sent a host at them.'

Which was not quite true: they had stood at Methven, which de Valence was quick to point out with a pompous flourish, since that had been his battle and he had beaten Bruce soundly. Thweng tried and failed to prevent himself pointing out that Bruce had also stood against de Valence at Loudon Hill only a year later – and repaid that lord in full. He wisely did not then add to the black scowl of the Earl of Pembroke by mentioning that he had only won at Methven because he had unchivalrously broken an arranged truce and attacked by surprise.

But it was true enough that the Scots had avoided battle on the two occasions since then that English armies had rolled north. Not once in seven years had they stood to fight, Thweng thought.

The talk rolled on, with Edward's head swinging from side to side to take in all the good advice he was getting, though the best of it was lost on him, it appeared to Sir Marmaduke. When your veterans of the Scottish wars advise waiting another day so that the army can recover strength and morale, you ought to listen.

Eventually, Thweng lost interest in the King's refusal to see that sense, managed to move off unnoticed, a little way into the dark – then found d'Umfraville and Badenoch at either elbow and became aware of their grim looks.

Mark me, he thought, they have been grim for an age now; they probably only managed to smile when the King announced this campaign – they had forfeited vast estates in Scotland to Bruce's insurrection and were never done carping about the loss to anyone who would listen.

Yet this was a darker brother of what they usually exuded, a chilled sea-haar which made Thweng look from one to the other, raising the white lintel of his eyebrows.

'We are missing one for our feast,' d'Umfraville growled out eventually and, for a moment, Thweng thought this was a strangely couched invitation to join all the lords who called

277

themselves the Dispossessed and wore the title like a tourney favour. The English termed them 'the Scotch lords' but most of them were as English as anyone else here, save that they had huge lands in Scotland that they wanted back.

Badenoch, his sandy lashes blinking furiously as if to hold back tears, put him right on the matter of it.

'Seton is missing.'

'Neither with us nor anywhere else. His *mesnie* has also gone,' d'Umfraville added morosely.

Thweng's insides gave a lurch, even though the news was not such a surprise to him; Alexander Seton had had a father gralloched by the old King Edward. His mother was imprisoned in a convent far to the south because she was sister to the Bruce who sat opposite them with an army. Which made Seton the nephew to King Robert Bruce.

'He swore to serve King Edward,' Badenoch rasped with disgust. 'Now we must tell the King that he is foresworn. It reflects badly on all of us Dispossessed.'

A blind man could have seen this coming, Thweng thought, but the Scotch Lords consider the restoration of their lands take precedent over any ties of blood. It was interesting – and disturbing – that at least one of them thought differently, that he considered he had a better chance of having his lands returned from the hands of a Scotch king than an English one.

'I would not take on so,' Thweng offered laconically. 'Seton has served King Edward for six years – yet he once swore an oath to protect the Bruce. Until his dying day, if I recall it.'

'Aye,' sneered d'Umfraville. 'We will see about his oaths when this matter is done. They say every man ends up like his father.'

'Will you take the news to the King?' Badenoch asked and Thweng realized that that was why they were here. He recalled the young squire earlier, charged with carrying the King's

278

orders to Hereford and Gloucester – he had been told to speak to me first, he thought irritatedly. Why am I the stalking horse of this host?

He stroked his mourn of moustaches and smiled thinly back at them. Let them do it this time and reap the reward all heralds with bad news garner. He said as much and watched them wince and huff.

'It may help to tell His Grace the King that we are still ahead in this game,' Thweng added dryly, moving away. 'Atholl for Seton – an earl for a baron. A fair sacrifice in this game of kings . . .'

They moved off, arguing with each other and leaving Thweng with little option but to return to the King's table. There was argument and counter-argument here, too, as the King and his advising lords tried to make sense of where they were and what to do. Gloucester – sensibly, in Thweng's opinion – continued to speak out against fighting at all in the morning; the army was exhausted and the foot were still straggling in, so it would be better to wait a day.

Hereford curled a lip, but wisely bit it at openly scorning Gloucester. The King, of course, would not be halted.

'If the Scotch are willing to fight in the morning, my lord,' he growled, 'then we must do so. They will not wait upon our leisure.'

Which was also sensible, Thweng thought, for if Bruce actually steeled himself for a fight, a day mulling it over in the presence of a force three times his size would leach the resolve from him and he would vanish. Besides, Edward's own army was powerful and large, but the eagerness and resolve in it was brittle since the events of today. Any new setback might throw it over and a day spent under the noses of the Scots might bring exactly that.

There was a shifting of bread and the harrigles of the meal. A curling wetness of wine became the Pelstream, a crooked series of greased chicken bones became the heavy horse, a line of expensive emperor salt represented archers. Gradually, a plan was formulated, argued, scorned and, finally, adopted.

'The horse will form to the fore, then, *gentilhommes*,' the King declared. 'In full expectation of having to pursue the Scots removing themselves at dawn or before it. I want them pinned to the spot and destroyed, my lords.'

And if they do not withdraw, Thweng thought grimly, then the foot and, above all, that little line of white salt, would have to be reorganized to the front, which could take all day and them still weary from having marched into the night to get here.

Still, he mused, it would be as long a day as this night is short . . .

There were shouts in the dark and men rose up suddenly, overturning makeshift benches.

'An attack?' demanded Segrave, but no one thought that likely – they had contrived to place themselves inside a fortress of streams and woods on three sides for that very reason. Like the Stirling Brig affair, Thweng had thought when this was proudly announced and still felt a chill of fear at the memory of those rolling spearwalls coming down on the constricted, trapped horse.

That would not happen again, surely, he thought. The Scots never stand and Bruce is outnumbered considerably, so that only a fool would attack. He will be gone by morning if he has any sense at all.

It was no night sally, but a flaring light sparked the distance like a beacon; de Valence thought it was the castle itself on fire, but Thweng had a better lay of the land.

'Cambuskenneth,' he declared. 'The priory is burning.'

ISABEL

Inter faeces et urinam nascimur – *between piss and shit are*
we born and the way to God's Grace in Heaven also lies
between the two. I told Malise that when he came slithering
out of the dark, knowing his time of power over me is almost
gone. He has scarce any loins left and the strength of his arm
is held from me by Your Grace, O Lord – and the orders of
John de Luka – but he has venom still to spit. It takes only
a word from me, he said with that twisted grin he has, and
you will burn like the heretic we watched together. He made
it sound as if we had stood, arms linked like spent lovers,
quietly contemplating the moon and the future. All your finery
then will be gone, he went on, slathering it out with spittle
as if the rage in him could not be contained. But I knew, O
Lord – had known for a time – that the rage was against
himself. Once, a wolf-hunter came to Mar and told me how
it was done. You take three inches of thin beech wood and
sharpen either end, then bend it into a ring and fasten it with
linen thread. This you hide inside a dead bird, or a lump of
rotting meat, which a wolf will gobble, as they do, all at once,
deadly ring and all. When the linen thread snaps, as it must,
the sliver pierces the wolf's insides and it bleeds to death,
desperately trying to sick up its own life blood and unable
to do so. That is Malise; speared by his own hate and bile
and unable to boak it up. Yet he tried hard enough. Your

hurdies will be sagging in the breeze long afore the De'il comes for you, he sprayed. He touched me then, a trail of fingers; I let him, though my flesh crawled. When the flames touch you, he hissed, your wee serk will shrivel away and this pretty hair with it. You will be trussed in chains on that fire, naked and hairless as a scalded pig. He will do it, too, if matters do not change. He can claim anything and folk already believe I am a cunning-woman. After he had gone, I split a vein with my eating knife and here is what was shown in the pattern of my blood on the floor – a woman who loves. A woman who dies. A saving grace either way.

CHAPTER TWELVE

Bannockburn
Feast of St John the Baptist, June 1314

He heard the clack-clack through the swirl of mist and saw the heads of his men come up; one rode ahead and, by the time Bruce arrived a seeming instant later, there was the tapestry of it laid out: the rider – who was sometimes his brother, sometimes Jamie Douglas; the wee priest in his brown robes, patient as a nubbed oak; and the hooded figure.

There was never any doubting, even in the dream, what the hooded figure was, standing there with head bowed and a pail at his feet. The white hand which held the clapper flapped like a gull wing and the faint smell of rotten meat rose up, even over the stench from the bucket.

Yet it was a dream and he knew it even in his sleep, a skewed version of the true events – but the essential parts of it were always the same and always as they had happened.

It was Liston in the late autumn two years ago, where he had gone with a select band to try the waters of the place yet again and, though no one spoke it, everyone knew the point of the journey was that Liston's well was noted for its efficacy with lepers.

The dream played out: the rider demanding the hooded leper withdraw from the path, the patient priest agreeing and then kneeling, as he had done, in abject, appalled apology when he saw his king. The leper had tried to kneel, a painful display that Bruce had halted.

He remembered the shock of it, the sight of that white hand and, at one and the same moment, wanted to see the face and did not want ever to set eyes on it.

'Who are you?' he asked and the priest began to reply until Bruce's raised hand cut him off. There was silence from the leper.

'Can he speak?' Bruce asked the priest and then the leper cleared a thickness from his throat, a rot of rheum that turned his voice into the growl of a beast.

'Still,' he said, 'though I do not, for I am considered as dead.'

This was only true and Bruce had forgotten it; lepers were always considered as dead men and had to convey themselves as such. He wondered, trying not to shiver, how old the man was and asked but it was as if the man had used up all his allotment of words for that day; his mouth opened and closed and no sound came.

'He was born in the year the Norse were defeated at Largs, Your Grace,' the priest offered helpfully.

Forty and nine, Bruce had calculated. Eleven years older than me – is this me in eleven years?

'What is his name?'

The priest told the details of it; he was called Gawter, came from Tantallon where he had been a sailor, a skilled man at the navigation. Now he was at Liston for a time, working as a gongfermour for the priory.

From sea to shit, Bruce thought. A skilled man brought down to one fit only to handle other people's leavings. In the dream, sometimes, he gave the leper a coin, sometimes a benefice to keep him for the rest of his life without shovelling dung. He could not remember if he had done that for true – but he always knew the last part, for it had happened and was seared on his mind.

The priest, apologetic, said that because Gawter had encountered someone on the path and not warned them away sufficiently, the leper had to be publicly abjured and reminded of his station. So Bruce had sat in the chilling haar and listened to the priest tell Gawter the leper what he must do. Which seemed to consist of telling him what he must not do.

Forbidden to enter a church or brewery or bakery or butcher or anywhere Christian souls use. Forbidden to wash in a stream or drink unless water has been placed in a vessel. Forbidden to touch food, or clothing, or even the ground barefoot. If you buy food, the payment coin is to be placed in a bowl of vinegar and you must eat or drink in the company of others like yourself, or alone. Forbidden to have intercourse with any woman, or to approach any child, or any person on the road, or pass down a narrow alleyway, lest you encounter a decent Christian soul and brush against them.

You must warn Christian souls away from you with your clapper, wear the garb appointed so that all are in no doubt of what you are and must be buried outside the parish bounds when you die. God grant you grace in endurance.

The words echoed still, more chill than the cold mist. Grace. Grace . . .

He woke to hear Bernard, gentle and soft in his urgent call. It was dim save for the yellow pool of Bernard's fluttering candle.

'Your Grace. Your Grace . . .'

'I am awake. What is it, Chancellor?'

'Your brother is here and Lord Randolph.'

'Is it time?'

'Almost – but it is not that. They have news . . .'

He swung out of the bed, splashed water from a basin, pulled on braies and his underserk; his arm and shoulder hurt still and, in the candlight, the hand was dark and mottled with bruising.

Yet he could feel the fingers and the hand would be blue and yellow in proper daylight, not white. He could feel all his fingers and his toes and flexed them thinking 'one more day'.

The night, which had never been truly dark, was a smoked sapphire sparkled with diamonds when he moved to the panoply entrance and signalled for the fretting, impatient pair to be let in. In the distance, puzzling him, was a dull red glow which he took to be part of the English camp.

They were fully dressed; Edward was in maille and jupon and Bruce thought he had probably never got out of it, nor slept. Randolph was dressed, but uncombed, without a belt round his tunic and barefoot; spilled out of sleep like me, Bruce thought.

'You saw it, brother?' Edward demanded brusquely and Bruce blinked a little, trying to rout the last shreds of the leper from his mind.

'Saw what?'

'The glow. Cambuskenneth burning.'

This was a dash of cold water and Bruce sucked in his breath at it, while a slight figure padded silently in bringing a tray with wine and some slices of cold fish and bread.

'The English have dared to fire the priory?' Bruce demanded, feeling the anger well in him and then die of confusion at Randolph's headshake; Edward splashed wine into a cup and handed it to his brother.

'Atholl, Your Grace,' Randolph said, almost languidly. 'One of our men survived the attack and brought news of it. The Earl of Atholl has burned it. The storehouses are in flames but not the priory itself, though the wee monks are having a sleepless night making sure it does not spread. A right balefire for Midsummer's Night, in truth.'

There was little enough at Cambuskenneth – stuff used in

the siege and lifted when the English army drew close; straw hurdles, picks, shovels, fodder for horses, a few lengths of timber in the hope of building some sort of siege machine in time. Guarded, Bruce recalled, by no more than six men.

'A survivor?' he asked and Edward wiped his moustaches with the back of one hand.

'Sole,' he answered gruffly. 'The Frenchman Guillaume, whose piety saved him – he was holding vigil for St John in the chapel. The other five are slaughtered . . . Christ, Sir William Airth is killed. God's Wounds, Rob, young Strathbogie deserves the worst punishment. Bad enough that he runs off on the eve of battle, but this act is the foulest treason.'

'The Earl of Atholl is young,' Bruce murmured, 'and afraid. And I am your king, brother. Not Rob.'

'Not so young that he cannot tell right from wrong, my lord king,' Randolph answered as Edward scowled. 'Forfeiture is the least he can expect.'

Aye, Bruce thought wryly. Dispossess him of his lands to the Crown, so I can hand them out like sweetmeats to the favoured. With Randolph, Earl of Moray, at the head of the line.

'No great loss,' Edward added. 'If he thought to harm our cause by burning stores, he has missed the mark.'

'Sir William Airth,' Bruce pointed out. 'And four other good men.'

Edward had the grace to flush, a darkening of his skin under the yellow candle glow, while Bruce thought of what he would say to old Sir John, William's father. Your son is slaughtered, not by the English, but by the Earl of Atholl – God's hook swung exceeding slow, but it snagged bitterly, for all that.

'There is other news,' Randolph said into the chill which followed. 'A balance of the pan, as it were.'

Bruce waited and saw Randolph stride from the panoply, while the broad grin of his brother gave nothing away. It was the same grin, Bruce recalled with a sharp pang, when he was toddling on fat little legs, bringing some strange insect or animal to present for inspection.

None had been stranger than the one Randolph brought into the candlelight. Tall, so that he had to stoop underneath the canvas lintel, dark-haired, sallow-skinned, his black eyes alive with a fevered light . . . Bruce knew him well.

'Seton,' he said weakly, for it was the last man he had thought to see. Then he recovered himself as the man flung to one knee, reached out and raised him up gently by the elbow. 'Alexander,' he said. 'Nephew. Welcome.'

The noise of clatter and weans woke him, starting him out of sleep with a jerk; he saw little Bet half crouch with the sudden movement, cautious and wary. Beyond, studying him with dark solemnity, was Hob.

Hob. She would call him that, since that was the name of the King of Summer. He was of age and Bet's Meggy had claimed the boy as his, seeded on that very midsummer night. It was possible . . . he had known it even as he said, accusingly: 'Ye might have let me know.'

'For why?' she had replied, tart as young apples. 'For you to stop skirrievaigin' with Jamie Douglas at the herschip and come to Roslin to provide for me? You have no skill for anythin' but hounds and Roslin did not need that.'

She had looked at the crumbled ruin of maslin and smiled.

'I mak' bread, even from poor leavings like this, so I can provide. I did not need another useless mouth.'

He had gawped at her and she had smiled the bitter out of it in an eyeblink.

'No matter how loving a man you are,' she had added softly, and then tapped his arm lightly. 'Besides, John the Lamb took me, Hob and all, and provided for us until he died. Now you have rose up in the world and mayhap the Lady brought you back to better provide for your imp of a son.'

He had glanced at the sleeping boy and managed a wan smile of his own while his head birled with it all.

'Less imp now that he sleeps,' he said and she laughed.

'Aye – maybe he is not yours at all,' she offered and laughed when he'd rounded on her with a scowl.

'Men,' she scoffed. 'You never knew of him until now and scarce thought of me at all, yet the idea of someone else having laid a cuckoo's egg in your nest crests you up like a dunghill cock.'

Abashed, confused, Dog Boy had no answer, so she had provided one.

'It might have been the Faerie,' she said. 'On that night of nights.'

Midsummer, he remembered. As now, filled with the silent moving folk. Her smile only broadened at his look.

'As any will tell you who knew you as a bairn,' she had offered, 'he is the same as you looked at that age.'

Dog Boy thought of it and the blood washed up into his head. There was no one who remembered him at that age left alive, for Jamie and he and all the others had seen to that when they had struck at Douglas Castle. Palm Sunday, seven years ago. Old Tam, former serjeant-at-arms, had hirpled up to their hiding place with news of the garrison attending the kirk in town and they'd fallen on the English like a dog pack, dragging them back and capturing the castle.

After that had come a sin-slather of revenge led by the grim stone of Jamie. Dog Boy recalled Gutterbluid the falconer, pleading for his life as Jamie ordered him strangled with a bowstring. Dog Boy had stared into the hopeless, silent-screaming eyes of Berner Philippe and then nodded so that big, grinning Red Corbie could start turning the stick that slowly broke the houndsman's neck. Put me in the drawbridge undercroft, he'd thought, exultant with the triumph of it. Near killed me there . . .

They had pitched those two down the well, everyone else

in the underground store, pissed on the lot and fired it. The Douglas Larder folk called it and Dog Boy thought he had forgotten it – all but the glory of discovering, in the hound record books, that he had a name.

Aleysandir.

And a place, not far from Douglas Castle itself.

He went back to it, remembering his da and his prized brace of oxen, an amazement of riches that even the reeve or priest could not match. I was sold for that, he thought bitterly, recalling all the half-dredged clues of it. When I was old enough to run fast as the dugs, my ma walked me up to Douglas as the Sire had told her to do.

He could not remember his mother's face, but it must have been pretty for Sir William the Hardy to have been captivated enough to pump a child into her belly. And his da, who had always seemed a distant giant, must have loved her to have put up with it.

And loved me in his way, Dog Boy thought, remembering the sad wistfulness on the big slab face the day he had shown how he could run. He must have loved me a bittie, even though I was not his and a constant reminder of his wife's faithlessness. Yet he had oxen out of it, he added bitterly to himself, so perhaps that was the love in it.

There were no signs of them when he had gone to the small vill, for time and change had brought new tenants to the half-remembered fields and they had no memory of a couple who owned a brace of oxen. Fire and famine and red war had scoured the area more than once – God save me, Dog Boy thought with a sharp sudden pang, I may have ridden it myself. He offered thanks to God then, on his knees, that he had memory of no old couple slain by him or anyone he knew. The thought that he might well have killed his own parents left him trembling every time he thought of it.

Yet they had vanished, as if they had never been, and were almost certainly dead. The clogged drain of it had shifted over the years under the weight of all he had seen and done, so that such memories came back to him at the oddest and most unlooked-for times, clenching the insides of him until he felt he must scream, or weep, or fist something to ruin.

The shift and yawn and scratch alongside him wrenched him back to the present and he turned his head to her, remembered the warm and sticky of last night. Possibly, there now would be another Hob . . .

He fetched his clothes and dressed as she got up and patted Hob like a dog for his cleverness in blowing life back into the fire. She clattered pots and mixed water and oats; little Bet played quietly with a straw doll and, beyond the confines of the mean withy and cloak shelter, the whole camp stirred like fleas on a dog.

Dog Boy went out into the poor night, which was racing towards lighter hues of blue; it was cool now, but would be a hot day for it, he thought, unlacing himself and making sure where he had picked would offend no one. He grunted with the pleasure of it, becoming aware, slowly, of the boy's eyes.

'Are you my da, truly?'

That cut him off mid-flow and it took a long moment before he managed to renew it; longer moments still, of shaking and lacing, before he turned and looked at the boy. Dark and wary, thin, with a deerlike crouch that spoke of an alertness to run.

It was himself at the same age, he thought with a sudden leap of certainty. I would have looked like this when I was turned into the kennels at Douglas and all that went with it.

'What does your ma say?' he demanded and the boy frowned at that.

'She says you are.'

'Is she to be obeyed and always in the right?'

Hob considered it a while, before nodding uncertainly. Dog Boy grinned.

'Aye, well, there is your answer. I am your da, God help you.'

There was a silence, and then Dog Boy moved back to the fire and the bent figure of Bet's Meggy, stirring the oats and water in her cauldron; mean fare, he thought. I will bring better when I can.

'I must go,' he said and she stood and faced him, hipshot and with her head tilted. The smile was slight, but her eyes were serious.

'Will you die?'

Bet's Meggy wheeshed Hob and threatened him with the spurtle for his cheek, but he never moved, kept staring at Dog Boy.

'I'll come back,' he said awkwardly, turning to Bet's Meggy. 'When I can. I'll bring vittles and . . .'

'I make no claim on you, Dog Boy,' she said softly. 'Neither for him, nor last night.'

Dog Boy knew that Hob did, though he would not voice it, but he nodded, and then grew more firm.

'I will be back, God willing, when this is done with.'

She dragged him close then, held him hard for a moment or two, and released him so quickly that the pair of them staggered. He blinked, frantic not to unman himself with tears, and bent to little Bet, who put a thumb in her mouth and stared.

'Have you a buss for me, wee yin?' he asked and she looked uncertainly at her mother, who nodded. She took out the thumb, grinned and kissed his cheek, a sparrow peck that left snotters on his beard.

Hob stood, eyes large and bright, so that Dog Boy was lost, had no words. Then, suddenly, he dipped in his boot top and came out with his long dagger, thrust the hilt at the boy and watched his eyes widen further.

'Take it. Defend your ma until I come back.'

Hob looked at the hilt, up at Dog Boy, then across to his

292

ma, who smiled. He reached out a hand and took the dagger, dragging it close to his chest and cradling it like a new pup.

'Dinna cut yerself,' Dog Boy said with a grin, 'or we will both of us suffer an even sharper edge – your ma's tongue.'

There was a shared moment, the pair of them against the women, before Dog Boy nodded to Bet's Meggy and turned away, aware of all their eyes on his back and anxious to put distance between them, yet feeling every step drag.

He was still bleared with it when he came to the forge, red-glowed and shifting with silhouettes, eldritch against the rising sun behind him. He stood, peering and shifting to try and see better, until a voice growled out of the last shadows of the night.

'Dog Boy, stop jigging there and come closer.'

He knew it, even before he saw the shock of the battered face, the filthy wrappings round one arm and a body gone past lean and saluting scrawny. Yet the eyes were bright enough and laughing at him.

'Sir Hal,' he said. 'God's Wounds, it is good to set an eye on you.'

'Set the pair – I do not charge.'

Dog Boy was still grinning when the loss of Sim Craw fell on him; Hal saw the eyes cloud with misery and knew at once what it was.

'Sore,' said Dog Boy, bowing his head. 'He will be much missed.'

Hal had no words to say to Dog Boy, for all of them had been taken out by him in the past days, examined and thrown away as not adequate. Sim was gone and the hole he left in the world was filled only with black sadness.

Instead, he gripped Dog Boy by the arms – Gods, there was iron in them – and drew him close. For a moment Dog Boy stood limp, then his own arms came up and wrapped Hal and they stood for a moment, sucking the comfort of it into one another, before breaking apart.

'You have grown a tait,' Hal said, noting the height and width of him. He flicked the badge on the mostly unstained jupon. 'Come up a station or two, betimes.'

Dog Boy nodded, and then blurted out the wonder of the last night before he could stop himself.

'I have a son,' he ended.

Hal listened to the tale of it, spilled out in fits and starts as if Dog Boy could scarce believe it himself. If my Johnnie had not died, Hal thought, he would be of ages with Dog Boy. Maybe sired his own son. The realization hit him hard and he blinked. I could be a grandda. I am now the Auld Sire of Herdmanston, as my father was.

'They are here,' Dog Boy went on, as if he had read Hal's mind. 'All the Herdmanston folk who could come to support the Kingdom and our king.'

There was marvel in his voice, but Hal already knew, had been told by his kin from Roslin about how the Herdmanston fields were being tended. Chirnside Rowan, grizzled and grinning, had come up with Sore Davey, pox-marks unfaded. One by one, old familiar faces had come up to him out of the midsummer night, bending a knee and anxious to give him news, to offer balm and solace for the loss of Sim Craw.

Fingerless Will, Dirleton Will, Mouse – they were all here, older and leaner and with wives and bairns and even grandweans. Full of news and hope.

Alehouse Maggie had died the previous month, they told him, so it was a blessing that Sim had not lived to learn of that, for it would have broken his heart. Cruck houses had been rebuilt around Herdmanston's broken tower, the garth wall had been drystaned anew, but neither brewhouse nor forge nor bakery had been rebuilt – the first because they had no brewer with the death of Maggie, the second because they had no smith since Leckie the Faber had run off to spend a year and a day in a town and so escape his bondage. And the third because Bet's Meggy had no one in the keep to bake for.

It was probably burned out anew, he thought, by the English foragers, or the deserters and outlaws from both sides – but the hopeful eyes lashed him to silence on this.

He had thought only of Isabel, yet he was still the lord of Herdmanston – the Auld Sire, no less. He told them he would be back once matters were settled here. He told them Herdmanston would be rebuilt – which got him a look from Sir Henry of Roslin, worried that he would be asked to help foot the bill. Hal put Henry at ease by telling him he would not call on his liege-lord aid and, because of what he had done to help the King, Henry relaxed, thinking Hal had been promised royal largesse.

The truth Hal kept to himself; underneath the stone cross, nestling with the remains of his son and his wife, were six Apostles, buried long ago by himself and Isabel; those wren's-egg rubies which had once graced the reliquary of the Black Rood would more than pay for Herdmanston.

Given by Wallace to Isabel as a gift, he recalled.

Isabel. He stared at the dawn until the light started to blind him; somewhere beyond the glare of it, she waited for him. Or so he hoped.

A horn blared and Dog Boy shifted.

'Muster,' he said simply and Hal nodded. Dog Boy waited expectantly, but Hal made no move and, when he spoke, the bitterness tainted it.

'On your way, Dog Boy,' he said. 'I remain here, by order of the King. I have, it seems, done enough service.'

He managed a wry twist of smile up into Dog Boy's obvious confusion.

'What he means is that I am auld and wounded and long removed from the practice of arms. He means it well, but I am left with the women and bairns.'

Dog Boy felt a rush of anger at that treatment of this man, but let it slide away – even from just looking, it was clear that Hal of Herdmanston would be a danger to himself if he put on harness and stood in a wall of men in such an affair as this.

Unlike Kirkpatrick, who stumped up, cowled and braied in maille and wreathed in smiles. He thrust a shield at Hal.

'Fresh done by the limner here. I took your advice.'

Hal stared at the upraised iron fist, clutching a dagger which dripped blood. It was exactly as he had described it to Kirkpatrick in a fit of venomous pique.

'Aye,' he said, seeing the glint of laughter in Kirkpatrick's eyes. 'You will put the fear in them with this, certes.'

'They will ken me, which is to the point,' Kirkpatrick declared vehemently. 'They know me as the royal wolfhound, a wee sleekit backstabber. Now they will see that I am a knight of this realm as well.'

Hal did not know whether Kirkpatrick meant the English or all the Scots lords who fought them. Both, he decided as Kirkpatrick frowned down at him.

'I am sorry you have to remain here, but Sir John will be happy to have some expert help. See what came out of those tun barrels . . .'

He turned away to follow Dog Boy, laughing as he did so, then paused.

'The smith says your sword is ready.'

Hal went into the forge lean-to, wondering what Kirkpatrick meant about the tun barrels. The smith was a dark, unsmiling man, his leather apron pitted with old spark-burns, and he handed Hal the sword wordlessly; it had been cleaned and sharpened and polished lovingly.

Behind the smith was a clatter and rattle, a curse and then the limner came into view, spotted with paints from where he had been touching up lordly shields all night. Red-eyed and weary, he was a small, mouse-haired ferret of a man, indignant and angry at what he had been given to do.

Hal craned to see: iron hats, rimmed and tumbled like scree, every one of them black, with a white crown and a red cross.

Templar war hats. Of course, Hal thought, this is the stuff out of the tun barrels, the stuff that had not been issued because of the old ghosts that haunted it.

'Blue,' the limner raged. 'With St Andrew's white cross on it. By the time I have pented them all anew and they are dry enough to wear, the battle will be ower – and a dozen more like it. What is so wrang with clappin' them on needful skulls and being done with it?'

'There is no Order of Poor Knights,' the smith answered sonorously, 'and our king will not wish it back to life.'

Hal heard the pain in it, knew at once that the man had been a Templar. He and the smith looked briefly at each other; the other nodded.

'At Liston, until the St John Knights took it,' he said. 'I was only a lay brother, skilled at smithing, so I broke no oath to man or God to leave that which was cast down by the Pope himself.'

Hal nodded, then thought.

'It is the Feast of St John,' he said, smiling lopsidedly because his face still hurt. 'A quarter day – a hiring day. Are you serviced?'

'I'm Davey of Crauford, your honour,' the smith replied. 'Serviced to none but the King by my own desire and God by my birth into this world.'

'I need a smith at Herdmanston.'

Hal saw the hesitation, and then the smith jerked his chin at the naked blade in Hal's hand.

'If you tell me where you had the sword and the answer suits me I will service to you.'

It was proud, but he was a smith and knew his worth – as did Hal, so he took no offence, simply studied the sword more closely.

'You know this blade?' he countered, lifting it slightly and the smith nodded. Somewhere, a horn blew, stirring Hal to a half-movement, until he realized with an avalanche of loss

297

that it was not for him. No longer for him, for he was done
. . . he felt like that white and red fighting cock, hauling itself
on to the corpse of its opponent, crowing bloody victory and
half-dead because of it.

That brought a reminder of Sim, a sharp pang that sucked
breath from him for a moment.

'I may do,' the smith replied. 'There are many like it, but
they are crockards – the inscription is hammered into a made
blade and hilt, whereas this was forged with the letters in it.
Only one is like that and it belonged to the de Bissot, who
was one of the founders of the Order of Poor Knights long
ago.'

'I had it from a de Bissot,' Hal answered. 'Rossal de Bissot,
who is dead in Castile and did not want this blade in the
hands of his enemies.'

'Blessed be,' the smith said. 'I am sorrowed to hear it, for
he was the last o' his line if he handed it to you for keeping.
So that is the true sword – I never thought to see it in life.'

'Has it a name, then?' Hal said wonderingly, handling it
as if it had suddenly warmed. The smith smiled and shook
his head.

'No name, your honour. Only fame. It was made, they say,
from the heathen crescent ripped off the roof of the Temple
when Crusaders took the Holy City. Gold, they thought it
was and were mightily disappointed to find gilded iron. Yet
they put the iron to good use – the letters were put in it
during the forging.'

'What do they mean?' Hal asked and the smith reached
out one cracked thumb, running it in a caress across the fat
round pommel inset with the Templar cross, then traced the
letters of the hilt: N+D+S+M+L.

'It is in the Latin,' Davey of Crauford said. 'I have no great
skill with it, but I know this – every decent smith does. "*Non
Draco Sit Mihi Dux*", which means "let not the dragon be
my guide" if I have been told true.'

298

Hal nodded confirmation and touched the blade's letters: C+S+S+M+L.

'Then that says "*Crux Sacra Sit Mihi Lux*",' the smith went on.

'"The Holy Cross be my light",' Hal translated and the smith smiled.

'So it is said. A good, blessed weapon, fit for St Michael himself. Or a Sientcler of the shivered cross.'

He went down on one knee so suddenly that Hal took a pace back, alarmed, as he felt hands round his foot. But the smith, head bowed, simply swore fealty to the lord of Herdmanston and, as the words rolled out of the man, Hal felt something shift and fill him.

He was a knight and a landed lord. He was the Sire of Herdmanston, auld or not, and folk depended on him. Neither he nor the Kingdom was done yet . . .

The horn blasts racked him, flared his nostrils, brought his head up like a warhorse.

They crowded into the sweating tent while the horns farted and blared. They stank of staleness and leather and oiled maille, clanked when they moved and were stiff-ruffed like strange hounds, trying to sniff another's arse to take the measure of the meeting.

The Scots lords gathered, the high and wee and as many as could be brought together, fretting to be away and attending to their *mesnie* as the men gathered for muster. Hot and anxious, hungry some of them and weighted with fear, Bruce thought – but not as bad as the ones opposite, if Seton was to be believed.

His brother Edward, broad face already framed by a maille coif, grinned from one side to the other as he chatted to Jamie Douglas and young – God in heaven, painful young – Walter Steward; both of them would be raised by the King, as was the custom before a battle. Young Walter would become a knight and the Black, lisping when he spoke and gentle as any woman now, would be elevated to banneret.

Edward Bruce did not trust Seton, even when he had sworn on his life, on being drawn and quartered, that what he said was true; the English were exhausted and demoralized by the marches and defeats of the day before, the capture of Thomas Gray and the death of Hereford's nephew. Their foot was still straggling in and they believed the Scots would flee, not fight.

'A trap,' Edward had growled and Seton, bristling like a routed hog, had sworn he spoke the truth.

Drawn and quartered, Bruce thought. Does Alexander Seton know what it means? He remembered Wallace, remembered watching the bloody horror of it, the moment when he hung there, with the blood pouring down his thighs and pooling underneath him because the executioners had already emasculated him, slit his belly open and let his entrails out.

Alive still, he made only one protest, when the pair of muscled men grabbed his arms, forcing his chest out so that the executioner could reach in the belly and up to grab the heart.

'You are gripping my arms too hard.'

Bruce bowed his head. A stranger's hand is fumbling at the very core of you and you can say that. God keep you at His right Hand, Will Wallace.

The other thought rattled the lid of the black chest, burst briefly out – until he was gone, I could not set my foot on the way to the throne. Then it was wrestled back into the dark and the lid slammed on it, leaving it to coil and writhe with all the other sins he had committed to get to here.

Here, to this tent, with these lords, he thought wryly. In a month I will be forty years old. In an hour or two I might be dead, if these men do not fight and we fail. Dead. Not captured . . . the thought of capture brought a lurch of terror that almost doubled him; by God, he thought, I will not suffer like Will. Not that. They can stick my head on a London

300

spike, but I will not be paraded like an entertainment of offal.

Nor fled . . . victory or death. Yet there was the nag of that, like his tunic catching on a nail as he went through a door, hauling him up short. The thought of returning to flight and harrowing if he failed, ducking back to heather and hill and outlawry, was a crushing weight – but if he stood and died rather than flee, then everything was for nothing. The deaths of his brothers, all those who had loyally served him and paid for it with lives and livelihoods . . . all the sins which bulged that chest in his head and, though he tried hard not to believe it, breathed out their foulness so that each one showed in the wreck of his face for all to see. All suffering made worthless if he gave in to noble death at the point of sure defeat.

And Elizabeth, his wife, lost to him for ever. Not that there was love in it – Christ's Wounds, her father's Irishmen stood opposite with the English – but the flower of the de Burghs held the chalice of Scotland's future.

If his disease permitted such matters as an heir by then, of course. He wondered about the others, the soft night bodies that consoled him, the Christinas and Christians and ones with no name that he could recall. They were not repelled by the rumours, he noted. More to the point, none of those women had been felled by his very breath, poison to all if he was truly a leper. And one at least had conceived him a son, a fine boy – but that had been a time ago and the lad was now old enough to be a squire. A king, he thought wryly, if I die and brother Edward with me.

The *nobiles* would never permit it, of course; young squire Robert Bruce was too bastard to be a king and if the worst happened here – as it might – then the Kingdom would be plunged into more chaos.

He felt the sour weight of it all, crushing him into the shape of a throne.

The crowded tent waited, shifting impatiently and wondering

301

why they were here. They were here, Bruce thought, because I need them to fight and need to have them believe it is their own idea and not mine. I have led them to this ring, but they must dance to my tune, so that I know they will follow the steps and not jig off in entirely the wrong direction.

'We have lost brothers, friends, relatives,' he began and the murmuring died. 'Others of your kin and friends are prisoners. Prelates and clergy of this kingdom are closeted in stone.'

He saw that he had their attention and told them what Seton had reported.

'If their English hearts are cast down, the body is not worth a jot. Their glory is in heavy horse and heavier carts,' he went on, while the air grew thick and still; outside, he heard the great, slow drone of men moving and talking.

'Our glory is in the name of God and victory.'

He had them, could sense it swell like a fat prick. He told them he would fight and watched that chase itself across their faces. He told them they did not have to agree with him and that if they all believed it was right for them to withdraw, then he would do it, with a heavy heart.

'If you stay to fight with me, my good lords,' he added, 'know that this is a just cause and so a divine favour is with us, that you will garner all the great riches the English have brought with them, while your wives and children will bless you for defending them.'

There were shouts, now. 'God wills it.' 'St Andrew.' Even a growled-out 'Cruachan' from Neil Campbell.

'The enemy fight only for power,' Bruce added. 'Take no prisoners or spoils until all is won, my lords. Know also that all previous offences against me and mine are pricked out for those who stand with me this day and that the heirs of all those who fall will freely receive their just inheritances.'

It was, he knew, a jewel of plaint, pitched perfectly between honour and greed.

'Are you with me?' he demanded and knew the answer

before the roar flapped the sides of the panoply with a dragon's breath.

Addaf watched them butcher the horse in the stream, so that it ran red with blood all the way back to the sea. It had been worth a year's wages, he thought bitterly, and had foundered trying to cross the tidal-swollen, steep-sided curse of a stream the night before; there were half a dozen more, slipped off the makeshift bridges of boards and tumbled to expensive ruin, unveiled as bloated, stiff-legged feasts for flies when the tide sucked the water back.

Men moved stiffly, red-eyed from lack of sleep. Most of the men-at-arms and knights had lain fully armoured by their bridled horses, starting fitfully at every noise, for everyone thought the Scotch imps of Satan would use the night for some foul, unchivalrous attack.

Now they levered themselves up, all the fine surcotes and plumes and trappers streaked with dust and dung, snatching bread or a mouthful of wine if they were lucky or had clever squires.

Addaf had not slept, nor many of his archers other than the eight who had been sent to eternal rest, ploughed under by the Van horse the day before. Now the remainder stretched, gathered their gear and moved like a black scowl into the day, smouldering still at what had been done to them.

They would not fight, Addaf thought. Not after being ridden over by the pig English, but it probably did not matter, since it seemed only the disarray of heavy horse would take to the field. He hoped that was so, for he did not want to put his men to the test.

Ironically, it would be Y Crach who fired them up, with his demands to do God's work. I will have to deal with him, Addaf thought, sooner rather than later. But the thought crushed him with weariness.

Sir Maurice Berkeley would have been surprised to find

that he was in agreement, at least with the latter part of Addaf's reckoning. The foot, exhausted from a long march – and still struggling to the field – were littered like fallen trees, Hainaulters, Genoese crossbowmen, Cheshire archers and all.

Only my Welsh dogs, Sir Maurice thought, are fit to get to their feet and draw a bow, and he did not much like the lowered brows of them; he was angered at what had been done to them by Gloucester and Hereford, but kept that choked.

He was glad to be quit of the Van, back with the King's Battle and assigned to the Earl of Pembroke's retinue: the further his Welsh were from the *mesnies* of Hereford and Gloucester the better. He wished he could keep his son and two grandsons out of it as easily.

Just as well the Scotch won't stand, he thought.

Addaf glanced at Sir Maurice, seeing the blackness on the man. The Berkeleys should have that chevron on their fancy shields turned up the other way, he thought, as a better representation of the scowl between their brows.

Mounted men worked the stiffness out of horses and their own muscles, calling out the bright, shrill '*Je vous salue*' one to another. These were the ones who had risen early and found a priest who could take their confession and shrive them – now the priests were too busy taking Mass as the sun filtered up, for this was the Feast of St John.

Sir Marmaduke had mounted Garm, feeling half-dead and chilled; enjoy it, he growled to himself, for it is the best part of the day, which promises to be hotter than Hades – and better half-dead than entirely so.

He turned as a ragged wave of shouting spread from head to head; Sir Giles d'Argentan, splendid in scarlet and silver, cantered through the throng, heading for the mass of horse out to the front. He smiled and waved right to left, the perfect paladin leading the King to battle.

Edward followed, even more splendid in scarlet, the three gold pards glowing in the rising light. To his left, de Valence kept pace with him and, trailing behind, came the royal *mesnie*, a little bedraggled but still grinning.

Thweng fell in beside Sir Payn Tiptoft, who raised a gauntleted hand in greeting.

'*Dieu vous garde.*'

Thweng returned the compliment, but he had hands full of reins and shield and lance, so it was an awkward fumbled affair; Tiptoft's squire, he saw, rode unarmoured at his master's back, carrying lance and shield both, but Thweng liked his own squire, young John, too much to place him at such risk.

'Will he speak, d'ye think?' Tiptoft demanded and Thweng knew Sir Payn referred to the King. He did not think so and saw the headshake and frown when he said as much. No holy banners from Beverley and no rousing royal speech. No knightings either – every custom and usage of battle, it seemed, was being ignored.

He saw the King rein in suddenly, forcing everyone to hastily follow; horses veered and swerved and there were muted curses and a clatter of arms and armour. Perhaps he realizes he should have done more, Thweng thought as the King screwed round in his saddle and flung one triumphant hand to the east.

'The sun, my lords,' he yelled out, his coroneted helmet flashing with the first rays of it. 'Come to look on our glorious victory.'

There were cheers, soon fading, and they rode on with their shadows stretched thin and leading them on.

Addaf watched them go; it was clear that the foot were being left to their own for now and he was not sorry for it. He saw his own shadow, turned and stared, narrow-eyed into the first rays of dawn.

Right in the Scots' eyes, look you, with them lit up plain as day for any one-eyed squinter to hit – well, once the horse had pinned them, the bowmen would finish them. Not those silly little slow-firing Genoese crossbows either, nor the plunking Cheshire men, but the steady volleyed mass shafts of his veteran Welshmen – and if hatred of the pig English made his men tardy, then the thought of plundering Scotch would put wings on their heels.

He felt the sun soak warm glory into his stiffness and almost smiled.

Nyd hyder ond bwa – there is no dependence but on the bow.

ISABEL

There were fires all last night beyond the walls of the castle and town, the old way of celebrating Midsummer's Eve. Even in the town they lit wakefires and danced and drank – I could hear them and smell the stink of the bones they threw in to ward off evil spirits. All it did for me was bring a harsh memory of the poor girl they burned. The night never got truly dark and early in the morning Constance brought boughs of greenery, for every house and shopfront is decorated with garlands and birch branches. Tonight, she told me with hugging delight, there will be a parade of men, with weapons and torches and mummers – and naked boys painted black to look like Saracens. And services and Mass, she added, remembering God just in time. If you wish to be shriven, she told me, I can fetch a priest.

I do not need to be shriven. I need freedom, O Lord. Your Son, blessed Jesus Christ, restored Lazarus to life after four days. You Yourself preserved Jonah in the belly of a whale, drew out Daniel from the lion's den. Why then, O Lord, can You not liberate me, a miserable wretch, from this prison?

CHAPTER THIRTEEN

Bannockburn
Feast of St John the Baptist, June 1314

They formed up at the edge of the woods, a great, fat line muted but not silent, a soft noise like a stirring beast, composed of the muttered drone of prayer and orders, the jingle and clatter of arms and armour, the creak of leather, the crack and rustle of branch and undergrowth.

Dog Boy, cloistered in the deep ranks of Jamie's command, itself part of the massive block commanded by the King himself, saw only the rust and filth-streaked gambesons of the men in front. He squinted between their shoulders, into the sun, seeing a forest of silhouetted spearshafts and a sparkle of firefly lights in the distance.

It took him a long time to realize, with a cold-water shock, that the sparkling was the sun bouncing from gleaming spear point and helmet to burnished armour. The Enemy.

There were a lot of them, a great glowing sea that curdled his bowels, made him look right and left to find Parcy Dodd, Troubadour, Sweetmilk, Horse Pyntle and the others, a cage of shoulders and tight grins, grimed calloused hands flexing on the sweat-polished shafts of their weapons.

A great block of such men was no accidental mob, Dog Boy knew. It started with a Grip of five men, called so because it was likened to five fingers curled like a fist on a spearshaft. Two such, lined up one behind the other, was called a Charge, because when you charged your spear, you gripped with both fists. Two Charges made a Vinten, twenty men ordered about by a vintenar, who was Sweetmilk in that part where Dog Boy stood. Vintens were ordered into ten times ten, called Centans, though the reality was the 'long hundred', which actually came to 120 or thereabouts – and were commanded by centenars. Dog Boy was centenar for this part and all the men under him were from Jamie Douglas's own *mesnie*.

After that, the Centans were grouped in tens, so that a Battle could have 1,200 men or any number up to twice that – rarely more, since it grew unwieldy. The one Dog Boy stood in was the King's Battle, with 2,000 men. Since the King would be busy commanding the whole army, half of his Battle was ordered by Jamie and the other half by Gilbert de la Haye, Scotland's Constable.

To the right and slightly ahead was another Battle of similar size, commanded by Edward Bruce, to the left yet another with Randolph's arrogant banner waving about it.

Flitting in and out, as if wandering lost, were Selkirk and Gallowegian bowmen and the tribal caterans from north of the Mounth: MacDonalds of Angus Og, Camerons, Campbells, Frasers, MacLeans, a wildness of men who did not fight in a great square of pike and glaive and bill but preferred leaping about with little round spike-bossed shields, long knives and axes. Scowling in with them came the strangest of all, the Irish of the O'Neill, O'Hagan and others, more interested in finding their English-supporting counterparts and settling old scores. The best of them had great jingling coats of mail to their ankles and fearsome long-handled axes.

Nearby, squeezed tight together, was the small – ludicrously small, Dog Boy thought – huddle of Keith's horsemen.

It was all small, Dog Boy knew, seeing the golden horde ahead of him. It had been better in the days when he had not been cursed with knowing that he stood with a third or less men than the enemy opposite, that good men who might have made the difference had been turned away and left to mutter their displeasure in the baggage camp, because they could not be fed, or equipped, or trained in time.

Then he heard, above the rasp and mutter, clatter and creak, the incongruous plaint of birdsong, a fluted throating furious at being disturbed from praising the dawn. A moment later the sudden blare of horns drowned them out, sending them flurrying skywards like swirls of black smoke signalling the advance.

He saw the two Battles ahead of him shift and roll forward ponderously, thought of his son and laughed for the sheer, birdlike joy of the moment.

Hereford, a pillar of dull iron clanking towards his splendidly trappered warhorse, paused briefly as the figure wriggled through the throng like a pup through a fence. John Walwayn, he thought sourly, come a little late. Everyone was a little late – Gloucester, he had heard, had even ridden off without his surcote. Rather than permit me to get to the Van first and start ordering it about, he thought moodily.

Walwayn was breathless with rush and self-importance, ignoring as best he could the sneers from the squires, scornful of this ink-finger with his dagged tunic and dun-coloured hose.

'Well?' Hereford demanded and Walwayn knew his lord was eager to be up and away, though he was pouch-eyed from lack of sleep and had spent the night in prayer beside the body of his nephew Henry; somewhere nearby they were boiling him down to the bones, which would be carried home. Walwayn knew that his news had arrived late – but not too late, as he pointed out.

311

'My lord Percy's man has failed,' he said in a low, hoarse whisper. 'I have word from Alnwick that the Templar Knight he sent is dead in Spain and Bruce has succeeded in gaining a cargo of weapons. If they encountered no other trouble on the way, my lord, then the Scotch have Templar arms and armour aplenty. That message was at Alnwick a ten-day ago.'

Hereford blinked and pursed his lip, the scowl of his face framed in metal links. If that was true . . . He glanced briefly at Walwayn and knew it to be; the man had never failed him before with intelligence. It also meant that Percy had not bothered to inform the King of his failure and the possible delivery of arms and armour to the Scots. It would make all the difference, Hereford knew. Well, there would be a reckoning with Percy after this was all done with.

'The Scotch will stand, then,' he mused and waved for a squire to leg him up on to the tall horse – the new leg armour made it awkward to mount unaided. Settling himself, he looked down at Walwayn.

'You have done well. When this is done, come to me for reward.'

Walwayn wondered if Hereford had understood and almost said as much, but broke into a sweat at the near error and forced a smile. It was not for him to question whether his lord and master had fully grasped the import of the news he had brought.

The Scotch would stand and fight, was no ragged army of trailbaston, but one which had had weeks to train and was now armed and armoured with former Templar weapons – perhaps even captained by former Templar Knights, the most formidable fighters of the day and now raised to righteous fury at what had been done to them.

He moved away, jostled to a stagger by squires and men-at-arms mounting and trailing after their earl; after a moment, he realized he was alone, with the sickly sweet smell of Henry de Bohun's boiling seeping into the air like the worst of omens.

Somewhere, Walwayn heard shouting, drifting on an errant wisp of morning breeze and, for all it was a faint ghost of sound, it made him shiver, so that his long shadow trembled.

Tailed dogs, he heard, like the Devil whispering.

Jamie Douglas took the staff from the hand of the King and raised it high, so that it caught the morning sun and the welcome breeze blowing out of the wood. Freshly, ritually, shorn of its pennant streamers into the square of a banner proper, the flag rippled with the arms of Douglas and, even if there had been no breeze at all, the roar of thousands of voices would have been breath enough.

Bare-headed, Jamie vaulted into the saddle of his little rouncey, while Bruce watched and envied the man his youth and his moment. There was no other way for a knight to be created banneret, a step only slightly lower than an earl, than to have it done on the field of battle by the sovereign himself. Such moments were hen's teeth, but part of the ritual of committing to battle and important, Bruce knew, because it let the army see the King raise folk to greatness in the panoply of the court; you did not do that if you worried about losing.

Now he saluted the darling of the host: the dreaded Black Douglas if you were on the opposing side, the Good Sir James if he stood with you. The great stained horde roared their pleasure, for all that half of them were shivering with fear and fevers. Bare-legged and bare-arsed because disease poured their insides down their thighs, they still flung their arms in the air and cheered back at him – and the King they were prepared to die for.

A Douglas, Jamie yelled, and they screamed it back at him. Tailed dogs, he bellowed with delight, riding the length of them with his banner in one fist and flung into the air – and they howled that back at him, too.

Tailed dogs, popularly believed as God's just punishment on the English for their part in the murder of St Thomas Becket: the Scots taunt never failed to arouse their enemy to

313

red-necked rage and Bruce, cantering on in the wake of Jamie Douglas, nodded and smiled even as he felt his ruined skin tighten at that coming anger.

The mummery was almost done and everyone saw the final act of it: Maurice, Abbot of Inchaffray, stumbled unsteadily across the tussocks with his coterie of priests, bearing the Mayne, St Fillan's own arm bone in a silver reliquary; one cassocked boy trembled so much that his swinging censer almost brained the brindle-haired abbot and the prelate had to duck. Those nearest laughed, brittle and harsh, as the abbot raised his long-staffed crozier – the Coygerach, holy icon of St Fillan Himself, no less – as if to strike the boy, then thought better of it and passed along the line.

They knelt, the thousands crammed into three large blocks of bristling nails, Edward Bruce and Randolph, Douglas and de la Haye and the Bruce himself, while the vintenars and centenars took the opportunity, as the old abbot moved down the line blessing them with sonorous mumbles, to dress the ranks for the last time.

Dog Boy wondered if that bone inside the reliquary really was the famed left arm of St Fillan, said to glow in the dark so the wee holy man could read the Scriptures at night. Bigod, he would like to see that marvel one time! He crossed himself for the impiety of the thought.

When the priests had gone, this great forest of spikes would rise up and roll down on their enemy and, if the priests had done their job true, then God would hand them victory in the name of St Fillan.

Patron saint of the mad.

Thweng arrived into the jingling splendour that surrounded the King in time to have Badenoch thrust his beaming face forward, a manic grin fixed on it. Behind him, equally toothy, was another sprig of the seemingly endless forest of Comyns – Edmund, Thweng recalled suddenly. From Kylbryde.

314

'My lord,' Badenoch called out, 'splendid news.'

Thweng eyed the Scot sourly; what the man considered 'splendid news' boded ill, he was sure. The next words confirmed it.

'I have permission for the Knights of the Shadow to join the Van.'

Every fool was petitioning to join the Van, Thweng thought, because the Van was where the first glory and best of the ransom plunder was to be had. It was also the most dangerous place to be and sucked far too many into it, making it huge and impossible to order as well as impoverishing the other Battles.

And he has dragged me into it. The thought made Thweng's scowl so venomous that Badenoch's eyebrows went up in the coif-framed face.

Gloucester's arrival broke apart any twisting tension and all heads turned to him. The King, splendid in his blood-crimson royal surcote with the three golden *lions leopardes,* sat tall in the saddle of an ice-white horse and knew exactly how he looked. Surrounded by the royal standards and the sinister, jewel-eyed, flickering-tongued Dragon Banner, he stared haughtily at Gloucester, who did not wear his spendidly blazoned surcote.

'You are ill-dressed and late, my lord earl.'

Gloucester, his coif hooded down his back, flushed to the roots of his unruly hair.

'Not too late, Your Grace, to plead that you honour the saint whose feast day this is and refrain from fighting. The army needs rest . . .'

The chorus of protest that went up from the eager young throats round the King was loud and scornful enough for Gloucester to bristle. D'Argentan, Thweng noted, stayed silent.

'It seems no one agrees with you, my lord earl,' Edward growled, and nodded out towards the serried ranks of horse. 'My lord Hereford is already with the Van.'

Which was a dismissal Gloucester should not have ignored,

315

Thweng thought afterwards. But the Earl, almost desperately, repeated his plea for the army not to fight and everyone saw the drooping royal eye flicker dangerously.

'You would have better employed your time fetching your cote than inventing reasons not to fight,' Edward rasped out venomously. 'But vacillating was ever your way – you allowed my Gaveston to die because of it.'

The only noise was a deep grunt of assent from behind the King – Aymer de Valence, of course, Thweng realized, who had pleaded with Gloucester to come to his aid when Lancaster threatened to sieze Gaveston. Gloucester had refused, Lancaster had succeeded and Gaveston had died.

All the raw wounds reopened and everyone saw it. Gloucester, his face purple, wrenched at the reins of his protesting destrier, the words flinging back over his shoulder as he went.

'There is no treachery in me, my lord king, and the field will prove it.'

Badenoch, after a moment's surprise, waved half-apology, half-farewell to the King and spurred after him; with a swallowed curse, Thweng kicked Garm into his wake.

Edward, blinking and uncertain at what he had created, tried a harsh laugh which came out too squeaked to be reassuring. The noise of voices and rasping last-minute whetstones on blades seemed suddenly deafening.

'If the Scotch are standing,' d'Umfraville offered into the awkwardness, 'then we should reorder, Your Grace.'

Attentions were all sucked back into the moment; heads turned to the dark line of enemy and Edward frowned, stood up a little in his stirrups and pointed one mailled fist.

'They are not standing, they are kneeling,' he declared and then beamed. 'Are they asking for my mercy?'

D'Umfraville, who had clearly had enough, almost spat and nearly choked on swallowing it.

'No, lord King,' he managed to rasp out politely. 'They beg

forgiveness, certes, but not from you. From God. They will win or die this day, it seems.'

The King scowled blackly at the admiration he heard in that voice, but the sudden great blare of horns made them all jerk; a few horses were taken aback, bounced and baited. Horrified, everyone saw the dark line seem to swell.

'We should beg our own forgiveness,' d'Umfraville added, 'for they are not standing nor kneeling, my lords, but coming down on us.'

'God's Blood,' de Valence bellowed. 'Too late. Too late.'

Too late, Addaf thought with belly-clenching terror, to get the horse out of the way and the foot forward. Too late, as it was at this place's bridge seventeen years ago, when the Scots of Wallace and Moray came down on the English, trapped in the coils of the river.

Now they were trapped again, and again by their own making, the reassurance against night attack of the streams and ditches on three sides now a deadly bag. Addaf remembered the last time, the frantic rabbit-running, throwing away everything he had save the bowstave itself, the desperate plunge into the river, the floundering like a wet cat to drag himself out, panting and half-drowned.

He turned, stunned as if by a blow to the temple, and Sir Maurice Berkeley saw it, saw the same look on other lordly faces around him and the bewilderment of those they led, waiting for orders that did not come.

'Ware archers,' he bawled, throwing one iron fist to his right. Heads turned and men fell into the unconscious movements that braced the stave and felt for the bowstring, though they would not string the bows until ordered by Addaf.

'Addaf Hen,' Maurice roared and that jerked the man as if stung, so that he seemed to shake himself like a dog, looked at his lord, then to where he pointed; enemy flitted like starlings, working their way to the flanks of the army and

317

protected from horse by the steep-sided ditch of a tidal run Addaf had heard called the Pelstream.

'Smart your sticks,' Addaf bawled, starting to feel the reassurance that came with familiar things. 'Pick your targets, look you. Shoot only when I say.'

Even as he had them nock and draw, he could feel the sick, leprous presence of that great mass rolling down on them, like a fever heat down the side of his body. He did not want to turn and look.

In the camp under Coxet Hill, they had lit a glare of fires and danced round them all night – the young, single girls had to circle and prance round seven of them if they wanted to marry the next year and they were diligent in it. They had eaten the destiny cakes, though there was more pea and straw in them than good barley or wheat. They'd made wishes on wisps of straw, which were burned and sent as dangerously flaming embers into the hot night sky.

It had ended with Threading the Needle, a skein of folk moving in a seemingly endless dreamy dancing procession to the sound of drum and viel and fipple flute.

Now in a rising-hot St John's Day of ash and bad heads, Hal saw a mood of resentment move towards where he sat with Sir John Airth, enjoying the brief cool of the morning. Sir John, red-faced, big-bellied and with a beard like a great burst of dirty wool, had not slept well for the loss of his son sat heavy, while the noise and his gouty leg was no balm; he was scowling at the shuffling group even before they spoke.

Hal was no better, for he could hear the horns and had seen men clattering off, late to muster and clutching their gear, hopping with one shoe on. He wanted so badly to be with them that it was a bone ache, though not as deep as the one which had replaced Sim in his heart. Added to that was the dull fire in his wounded arm, while his face, still splendidly blue and yellow, thumped like a bad tooth.

318

The guard stopped the men coming closer, but they stood in a nervous huddle, with one thrust out in front and clearly expected to speak for them all; Sir John waved them forward.

'Well?'

The spokesman was an average man in all but forearms, which came from working the handquern. Hal had seen him endlessly turning it to grind what poor grain folk brought to him to be milled, taking a tithe of it for himself as payment.

'Beggin' the blessings of your lordship,' the man began, twisting his felted cap in his hands and then indicating the men behind him with a nervous flap of one hand. 'I have been asked to speak to your lordship on a matter.'

'Name?' demanded Sir John. 'Who are you, man?'

'Begging yer blessing, sir, John of Noddsdale, sir. Miller to Sir Robert Boyd, God bless and keep him.'

Hal saw Sir John close his eyes briefly and sympathized, for John the Miller of Noddsdale had a voice like the whine of a stonemason's saw and was, for all his nervousness, clearly impressed at having been picked from the pack to speak for them. It was not, Hal thought wryly, because he had the finest voice, nor because he was most respected, but the opposite; he would not be sadly missed if Sir John decided to hang him out of hand.

The gist of it was clear enough. The pack behind whining John were all in this camp at the behest of some lord now setting himself to battle. They had been left out of matters and did not care for it much.

'We wish tae fight, Sir John,' the miller finished. 'Yet we are held here by yer wish.'

'The King's wish,' Sir John answered flatly. 'If you were proper called-out men you would come with an iron hat, a coat of plates or a gambeson, a long spear and another blade. Have you such?'

The men shifted and shuffled. They had seen others of their rank and station handed iron hats and spears, but there had not been enough for everyone and they had been given to ones who had been here for some time and seen at least a measure of training in their use. These were the come-lately men and they knew it. Someone called out that they had made spears and waved a shaft with a lashed-on hand-scythe. Hal smothered a smile.

'There you have yer answer,' Sir John growled dismissively. 'A heuch on a pole, carried by an unarmoured, bareheaded chiel of no training and less account is of no use to the King.'

It was harshly said, from the lips of a man crushed under the loss of his son that very morning, killed at Cambuskenneth by a petulant swipe from the Earl of Atholl. These folk did not know that, Hal saw, or care. Faces darkened.

'Others are going, slipping away,' John of Noddsdale blurted out daringly. 'Chiels from beyond the Mounth. Women amang them.'

Now Hal grasped it; the women and older bairns, men too old to fight and those who had contrived to avoid it, were sneaking out, hunkering down at the fringes to wait and watch for a chance to plunder the dead, and these men wanted a share of it. Fighting was not in it at all and they saw the sneer on Hal's face when he stood up; there were some brief, defiant glances, but all of them lowered their heads in the end and shuffled, shamed.

Yet Hal could see the beast of it almost unleashed. The camp was full of men and women like this, anxious for their loved ones already fighting, struggling with hunger and thirst and fearful of the outcome. They would want something plucked from it, no matter who won, and if thwarted would cause more trouble than could be controlled.

If they could not be prevented, then they must be led.

The idea soared in him and he turned to Sir John Airth, who saw something of it in Hal's eyes. Truthfully, Sir John was glad the Herdmanston lord was here, for the loss of his son had stripped the last fire from him. He had known he was too old for this even before arriving, but had come, bolstered by the determined joy of William to be here, on this momentous day. Now William was laid out, cold and stiff, in the dead room of Cambuskenneth Priory and all the determined joy in the world had dissipated for Sir John Airth.

'With your lordship's permission,' Hal began and Sir John waved one hand. So Hal turned to the men and laid it out for them, all the glory and riches of it, so that their eyes gleamed and they were his men before he had stopped speaking.

At the end of it, when they were scattering eagerly through the camp to fire others to the work, Sir John eyed Hal with a jaundiced look.

'You can borrow William's big stot,' he said. 'His name is Cornix, a good, well-trained beast. And my boy's armour will fit you better than me and you can carry the weight at least.'

Hal began stammering his thanks, but Sir John waved them away, frowning.

'It is a dangerous stratagem you have began,' he growled. 'For even if the enemy are fooled by it, your own king may not thank you.'

'Victory forgives all sins,' Hal answered and turned away, hoping it was true. Victory was essential, not just for king, not only for kingdom.

For Isabel.

ISABEL

Constance came to me and we sewed, sitting like peaceful sisters together in the cage. It was a defiance for her, placing herself in full view of the sweating gawpers and hecklers in the bailey and, because she was a nun, placing God with us both. I was grateful, but aware of feverishness in the air that had nothing to do with the heat, a tremble that made me slip and stick the needle in my finger. Constance saw it and gave a little cry, her hand to her mouth, but moved to draw it out, slow and careful as she could so that the bone needle would not break. I have enough bone in my finger, I said when it came free, and we laughed. Then she took some stale bread and wrapped it round the dark welling of blood. Perhaps you will fall asleep, like the princess in the tale, she whispered daringly, to be woken by a lover's kiss in your imprisoning tower. I told her the truth of that story – it was not a princess, but the daughter of a merchant, whose maid slipped and stabbed her with the pin of a golden brooch, so that she fell in a faint. The furious father had the maid put to death and her blood used to water his garden – whereupon the roses grew fast and equally furious, pulling down the merchant's house in only three days and killing everyone in it save the sleeping daughter. She woke on the fourth day and her lover found her wandering the wilding garden, her wits vanished entire. When I had finished, Constance sat, stunned and silent,

323

and I was sorry for having torn the happy child's tale away from her. I tried to go back to sewing but the blood had seeped through the bread and, when I peeled it off, a drop still welled, bright as a berry, dark as an omen.

Somewhere men were dying.

CHAPTER FOURTEEN

Bannockburn
Feast of St John the Baptist, June 1314

He knew battles, did Marmaduke Thweng, knew them as a shepherd understands sheep or a wee priest how to handle hecklers in a sermon. This one, he saw as he rode up in the furious wake of Gloucester, was already spoiled and rotting.

'The enemy, my lord,' Gloucester bawled out to a blinking, confused Hereford. 'We must attack at once.'

Hereford glanced to where the dark line scarred ever closer, resolving in the glare of a full sun into a wicked wink of sharp points and glowing men, moving steadily under a flutter of bright banners. The St Andrew's cross on blue, the chevrons of Carrick. The brother Bruce, Hereford thought, with a deal of men . . .

'We must attack.'

Hereford turned into the full of Gloucester's face. No helm, he saw – nor surcote either. Fool comes charging up, half-dressed and bawling like some green squab of a squire . . .

'We must withdraw, sirrah,' he bawled back. 'Make way for the foot . . . the archers.'

'God's Bones, it is too late for that,' Gloucester yelled, and then turned to the milling confusion of knights. 'Form, *gentil-hommes*, form on me.'

Hereford's roar was incoherent and loud enough to make everyone pause. Red-faced and driven long past the politic, he slammed a mailed fist on the front of his saddle, so that his mount shifted and protested.

'Bigod, de Clare, I am Constable of England. I command here, not you. Do as you are bid, sirrah.'

Thweng arrived in time to see Gloucester rise up in his stirrups, the fewtered lance squivering like a tree in a gale and his face dark and flushed.

'Be damned to you. I command here, by order of the King, and while you argue, de Bohun, the enemy laugh their way to a slaughter and king's carp of treachery. Well, I will not wait for defeat and dishonour.'

He savaged the horse's head round so that it squealed and thundered off, trailed by Badlesmere and others of his *mesnie*. Payn Tiptoft looked at Hereford and then at the disappearing back of Gloucester; when he had no guidance from the former, he flung up his shielded hand in exasperation and spurred away. With a sharp bark from under his full helm, de Maulay, the King's steward, announced that he had joined the Van to fight, not run, and thundered after, trailing more men with him.

Badenoch and his kinsman, the Comyn of Kylbryde, looked pointedly at Thweng, who gave Hereford a pouch-eyed mourn of stare, and then put his helm over his head, as clear a signal as any shout. With a whoop, Badenoch and his kinsman thundered off, hauling all the other Knights of the Shadow after them and, a reluctant last, Sir Marmaduke.

Hereford, his temples thundering, watched them ribbon their way obliquely across to the dark line of Edward Bruce's Battle and felt the tic kick under his eye as he saw another line, this one to the left of the Bruce brother and more distant. It had the blazing banner of the lion rampant marking where

Bruce himself marched. Beyond that, further to the left of it, was another growing line, the banners in it proclaiming a third command.

The Earl of Moray, Hereford thought, coming up on his master's left. The Scots were in an echelon of Battles, as steady ranked as any Macedonians of Alexander, and Hereford, with a sickening lurch, knew that Gloucester was right – there was no time left. No time at all.

Hew stumbled and fell to his knees, had curses and kicks for it as the ranked men baulked and tried to get round or walk over him. A hand took him by the collar and hauled him up as he struggled like a beetle in the forest of legs and feet.

He tried to mutter thanks, but the sweating mass was an animal that did not care, simply hammered him in the back with a curse and a call to keep moving.

He kept moving, spearless, the axe in one hand, the dirk in his belt and in his free hand a fist of the dirt and grass he had grabbed when he fell. Bad soil for digging, Hew thought. Not stable. Looks fine now, but it will be as dangerous as scree when it rains here; the ground will seep water. If you came here after rain, he thought, and thumb-tested the ground as was proper, you would lose most of the digit up to the first joint.

Cannot dig a ditch in such, he thought, half falling again, the motes and dust swirling with the grunt and clack and clatter of the sweating press. You need no more wet in the ground than a thumbnail-length entry for a good ditch. Incline the walls away, to prevent fall-ins. Most folk did not know that a square ell of soil weighs as much as a full-armoured knight on his big stot and if that falls on you, you are in the grave, certes.

He heard the men next to him shout out and grunt, saw hands flex and heard the great bawling roar that was Edward Bruce, the King's brother himself, standing in their sweating, stinking midst and bellowing for them to keep going, that it was only a wee man on a big horse.

A square ell of soil, Hew thought, moving fast on four legs and about to fall on someone . . .

There was a noise like a clatter of cauldrons on a stone path and the great block Hew was in trembled like a fly-bitten horse's haunch; men rippled away from the front. Someone shrieked, high and loud, and voices called out, but they kept moving, forcing Hew onward.

You should properly shore up steep sides – wood if it is no more than a ditch, but good stone cladding if it is a decent, perjink moat . . .

He stepped on something that moved and groaned, fell forward with an apology as he tried to skip round it, appalled that he had put his foot on a wounded man.

'Kill him, man,' someone growled, forcing past him and Hew saw the groaning figure was a knight, helmed and mailled and lying on his shield. There was blood on his metal links and he had no surcote. Hew started to try and turn him, to see the device on the shield – there was a lot of expensive war gear on this one for him to be a simple man-at-arms – but feet trampled and baulked and cursed him.

'He has no mark, is of no account. Kill him and be done with it,' the voice savaged at him and Hew looked up, blinking into the great, broad, red face, sweat-gleamed and truculent as a thwarted boar. He saw the surcote beneath it, stained and torn but blazing with the device of Edward Bruce.

With a last, annoyed snort, the great lord moved on and Hew, swallowing, took his dirk and began to prise open the downed man's fancy new visor. It took some time and he gave a sharp cry when it finally popped up to reveal the half-dazed, rolling-eyed face beneath. A young face, grimaced with pain and with blood on his teeth.

'Yield . . .' said the man, but Hew the Delver had been given his orders by the Earl of Carrick, who was James to

Jesus as far as the ditcher was concerned. He hauled out his axe and blessed the man with the blade of it – the sign of the cross, writ bloody in a blinding stroke across the eyes and then one which split the face from brow to nose.

He looked up, wiping the sweat and a splash of blood from himself, saw the retreating backs of the block he had lately been in, saw it stop. More men came trotting up, a loose leaping of axe and dirk men, like a fringed hem to Edward Bruce's battle.

'What are you after having there, wee man?' demanded a voice and Hew stood up into the gaze of a mailled and well-armed man with a proper shield and the air of a lord. One of the Gaelic spitters from north of the Mounth, Hew thought, and was clever enough to be polite.

'I dinna ken, lord, He has no device. I was told to slay him.'

The north lord called out and men came running up, obedient as dogs, and bent to roll the dead knight off his face-down shield so he could turn it to see who he was; Hew glanced at the solid line of backs down the slope and licked his lips, wondering when he could get back to the dark, sweating forest of it. Wondering if he wanted to, while the sun shone here, on this sandy loam of hill.

'Christ's Bones.'

The curse jerked him from his reverie and he saw the Gaelic lord staring at the dead knight's revealed shield. Then he turned to Hew.

'Run to the King – that way. Look for the great lion banner and the man with a crown on his helm,' the lord spat out in his sibilant, singsong way. 'None of mine can speak your tongue well enough, so it has to be you. Tell him that Neil Campbell of that ilk begs to inform His Grace that the Earl of Gloucester has been slain.'

He paused.

'What is your name?'

'Hew. Hew the Delver.'

329

'Tell him you did it.'

Neil Campbell watched the man trot off and shook his head. A great shout from his front made him look up and set his shield, feeling the heat beat on him like a fist.

A great lord is dead of a ditch-digger, he thought. There will be more of that this day.

Garm did not like the scattered bodies, the horses that were down, screaming and kicking in a frantic fury to get back on all fours, the slicked skid of entrails and slimed fluids. He had been trained to ride into anything if his master insisted, but was cat cautious and prancing over the bodies.

Thweng was grateful. He saw no sign of Gloucester, but caught the flash of blood-smeared jupons and dead eyes all around him, saw Badlesmere and others circling and bellowing, stabbing and throwing and as ineffectual as a breeze on a stone wall.

They suffered for it. As he rode up to the bristling, snarling dyke of spears, which had stopped and braced, Thweng saw the stained, crumpled heap that had once been Sir Payn Tiptoft, crushed and bloody underneath his still-kicking horse.

Thweng, moving no faster than a trot, turned sideways and rode the length of the hedge, stabbing with the lance, hearing the clack of it on the long spearshafts, felt the tremble of it up his arm. At the end of the line, he threw it like a javelin, wheeled left as he drew his sword, circled and came in again, avoiding the mad rush of Badenoch and a fat knot of the Shadows, forcing forward to impale themselves on the shrike's hedge.

Then, suddenly, in the gilded haze of raised dust, he saw the bright flash of a familiar shield, raised aloft by some saffroned warrior at the rear of the wall of spears – the de Clare arms. Gloucester was there, on that slope of hillside behind the Scots, and Thweng spurred Garm mercilessly so that the horse chested into the ranks, then reared on command, striking out with his great iron-shod hooves.

330

Points lanced, clattering off his shield. A hook snagged in the horse barding and Garm crashed down on all fours with more force than intended, screamed aloud as he landed on a bloody hoof, speared through when he struck out.

Stabs and slashes spilled expensive cotton padding from the horse-armour, drove the breath from Thweng with a few well-aimed blows which did not penetrate, but reeled him in the saddle. Then he saw sense and turned Garm away, rode him hard for a few steps and reined in.

Sweating, trembling, Garm stood, the injured leg raised so that only the point of one hoof touched the ground. Cursing, Thweng levered himself out of the saddle, feeling his legs buckle as he hit the hard earth and the full weight of his harness fell on him. Too old, he thought. Too God-cursed old for this. And the Earl of Gloucester was down – taken, he hoped, but recalling the triumphantly waved shield he felt a sick horror at what that might mean.

He was examining Garm's wound when he felt the sightless open eyes of a dead man staring at him. He turned to the gore-spattered ruin of a face. The arms on the tabard and shield belonged to the Comyn of Kylbryde, but Thweng would not have known the man after what spear and a tearing hook had done to his face.

'Should not have thrown away his helm.'

The bleak voice spun Thweng round into the grim stare of Badenoch, his own face sheened with sweat and the loss of yet another of his kin. Yet his concern was all for Sir Marmaduke.

'Are you injured, my lord?'

Thweng shook his head.

'Need a new mount. I will lead this one off and find my squire.'

He paused, feeling the madness of the moment as he sought to find words of consolation while shrieks and bellows and dying whirled round them; the ground was now a churned red mud.

'I am sorry for your loss.'

Badenoch nodded, as if he had expected no more. Then he took a breath, as if about to plunge underwater, slid the domed helm over his head and reined back into the fray.

Wearily, trying to avoid the mad, plunging arrivals of the rest of the horse, Thweng led the limping Garm back across the blood-red mud to where the ground firmed and the dust billowed like cloth of gold.

Deep in the clacking forest of spears, surrounded by the grunts and pants and squealed curses, Tam Shaws thought this the worst moment of his life. He had thought this before, from the moment the heidman of Shaws had picked him for the wool path.

It was bewildering then. Tam, who had never been away from Shaws, had travelled down to Coldingham Shore with six others and the staple, that year's wool from Shaws. That had been a mazed journey, almost a dream to Tam and gilded with the knowledge that fifty pounds of the fleece-wrapped wool on those three pack ponies was his.

He remembered his old life as part of that same dream, now. At the height of that summer he had, with the others of the vill, driven the sheep in fours to the pool, ducked them, rubbed them with ashes, doused them with fresh water and then let the herders shoo them, complaining loudly, to a prepared fold in the hay meadow.

All that day the sun had smoked the water off them and the next Tam had joined in the back-aching work of shearing, trying not to scab them with careless clip and having to dab the wounds with hot tar when he failed. Then, their shaved arses daubed with a varying swirl of ochre shapes, the beasts were sent bounding and kicking back to pasture and men grinned wearily, backs aching but glowing with the knowledge that the job was done.

'Up beyond the Mounth,' Davey's Pait announced, 'they

332

pluck the wool aff their sheep, like taking feathers from a chook.'

'Away!'

But Davey's Pait swore he'd had the truth from his auld grandsire and they went off, marvelling at the work involved in plucking sheep.

When the wool was delivered safe to Coldingham Shore, where packmen would take it on to Berwick and beyond, the heidman had come to Tam and told him he was chosen again – this time to go as a sojer. Lord had picked Tam as the Shaws obligation to their liege, Earl Patrick, because Tam had no wummin or bairns dependent on him.

So Tam, done up like a kipper in a padded jacket and iron hat, a big, awkward spear in one hand and a dirk bouncing strangely at his hip, had endured the jeers of the others and knew it had been more out of relief that it was him and not them.

He had been handed two silver pennies for the journey, told to report to the steward at Dunbar's castle and announce that he was 'the obligation from Shaws'.

Four years ago. Tam Shaws had thought, then, that the worst moment of his life was being sent as garrison, first to Edinburgh, then to Roxburgh, clearly never to be returned to Shaws after his forty days were up. He thought, often, of simply leaving but did not trust in the Law that much.

After a while, bitter as aloes, he realized he had been forgotten by the lord of Shaws and by God Himself; he had grown accustomed to the life, settled to it. Not long after that, the rebels had come to Roxburgh and Tam thought that had been the worst moment of his life, for he had come face to face with the dreaded Black Douglas and had actually surrendered the castle to him, because his commander was dying and unable to even speak.

He had, in fact, surrendered to a wee lord from Lothian, a man who had been prisoner in Roxburgh for seven years.

Tam had been sure this Lothian lord would be vengeful but, to his surprise, the garrison survivors had all been spared. Sure of what would happen if he stayed in his old 'oblige-ment', he had switched and joined the rebels, which moment he had been sure was truly the worst of his life.

He had been wrong all along, he realized, looking round him at the blood and the shrieking. Nearby was Davey the Cooper, the man who had mourned the loss of his friend, the man who had cut the throat out of the blinded boy yesterday. Davey had three arrows in him, buried to the fletchings, and even as he knelt by him Tam heard the whirring hiss of more arriving. Like clippers and us the fleece, he thought, and then they hit, like stones thrown against a wet daub wall.

Someone behind Tam grunted as if slapped; the man in front seemed to have been hit by a forge hammer, lifted off his feet and flung past Tam like a loose-packed grain bag.

'Up, lad.'

The voice dragged up Tam's head until the iron rim of the helmet dug into his shoulders. He saw the maille and the jupon and then the great, frowning, bearded face of the Earl of Moray himself.

'No hiding place there, lad,' Randolph declared, as careless of the arrows as if they were spots of rain. 'Besides, you are needed.'

An earl needs me. The thought made Tam get up, wobbling on shaky legs; he glanced out to where the enemy archers stood, on the far side of the steep-banked stream and with a clear shot. Randolph, with a satisfied grunt, turned away and shouldered into the struggling, howling mass of the schiltron as if he was only trying to get to a friend across a crowded courtyard.

The men in front of Tam suddenly seemed to tremble and stir, then braced with a great stream of sibilant curses – the English horse, spiked like shrike offerings, were being rammed into the wall of spears by the blind eagerness of those behind.

This, Tam thought, leaning his shoulder against the man in front and bracing, his head down at the man's waist, seeing shit-streaks down the naked legs and sucking in the stench of it, really *is* the worst moment of my life.

Kirkpatrick felt the pressure of his bladder and tried to ease the crush of maille and gambeson on it by shifting himself slightly in the saddle. That made the warhorse think movement and action was imminent, so it dragged the bit and jerked him forward. Cursing, he reined it savagely back, clattering lance against shield; the visor of his fancy new bascinet dropped with a clang and blinded him.

'You need to pinch that.'

Kirkpatrick, fumbling with four things and only two hands, raised the visor into the sardonic grin of the Earl of Ross, sitting easily on his own mount. He made a gesture with one gauntleted hand, the lance locked upright in the crook of his arm and firmed into the stirrup fewter.

'Smithing nips,' he elaborated, beaming. 'Get your man to pinch the hinges a little, so that it stiffens and remains up until you want it down. That's what I did with mine.'

Kirkpatrick hated him and his good advice, hated the bloody warhorse which had cost an entire season's wool tolts and hated the beast's name – Cerberus – which he was starting to realize was because it had clearly been spawned in Hell.

Above all, he hated being here in the metal huddle of Sir Robert Keith's horse, nervous and awkward on a baiting destrier, being clumsy with shield and lance. Aware that his skills with weapons and horse were not only inadequate, but marked him as a rank beginner to the armoured men around him, he knew they watched and sneered, enjoying the sight of Bruce's loathsome 'auld dug' trying to be a true knight of the realm.

'Thank you, my lord,' he managed to grit out and Ross nodded politely, but then frowned.

'Would you not be better with the baggage, Sir Roger?' he asked innocently. 'For certes you seem a little out of place. Should you be here?'

Kirkpatrick, rocked back and forth by the head-tossing Cerberus, felt the rush of blood through him at this casual viciousness, washing away the cold sweat on his spine.

'No,' he answered thickly. 'For certes I should not. Nor any of us. Nor would I be if it had not been for those less than loyal.'

Which made the Earl of Ross jerk so hard with shock and anger that his own horse threw its head up and squealed. Kirkpatrick's smile was a twisted ugliness, for he thought Ross more than deserved the lick of a viperish tongue; here was the man who had been on the English side until recently, who had broken the sanctuary of a holy place to capture Bruce's queen and sisters seven years ago, sending them to captivity and Bruce's brothers to death.

And Isabel MacDuff, Kirkpatrick recalled suddenly. As well Hal is not here, since he would care even less than myself for Ross's rank. As the King should have done, instead of gathering this earl into his peace with a forgiving kiss . . . the things you do when you want to wriggle your arse to fit on a throne.

'Bigod,' Ross spat out eventually. 'When this matter is done . . .'

'I will be back to my old tasks,' Kirkpatrick finished and Ross clicked his teeth shut in his sweating face, remembering the fearsome reputation of the King's right-hand man. He tried to pull his own visor down to cover his confusion, but it had stuck and Kirkpatrick grinned.

'You need to loose the hinges on that,' he offered in a voice like poisoned silk. 'I have a wee sharp dirk that will do it.'

There might have been more, save that a knot of riders flogged up and, with a shock, Kirkpatrick saw the blazing lion and the gold-circleted helmet. Bruce . . .

He watched, feeling sick, as Keith, Marischal of Scotland, kneed his mount close to the King, who spoke quickly and gestured once behind him with an axe – he has a new one, Kirkpatrick thought wildly. To replace the one he broke yesterday . . .

Then, with a rush of spit to his dry mouth, he realized the Marischal was detailing men – and one of them was himself. Sixty or so, he reckoned, with that part of his mind not numbed. He fumbled Cerberus after the trail of them, finding himself next to a knight bright with gold circles on flaming red. Vipond, he recalled. Sir William . . .

'What are we to do?' he asked, feeling his voice strange. He was aware that, somehow, his lips seemed to have gone numb.

'Chase away that wee wheen of bowmen,' Vipond replied gruffly, 'who are annoying the Earl of Moray.'

The bugger with the Earl of Moray, Kirkpatrick wanted to say. Let him look to himself . . .

'Dinna fash,' Vipond said and Kirkpatrick realized he had been muttering to himself and felt immediately shamed, another great rush of heat that made him dizzy.

'Stay by me, my lord,' the knight said, smiling a sweat-greased sickle on to his face. 'You will be as fine as the sun on shiny watter.'

'Form.'

Kirkpatrick found his hands shaking so hard that he could not make them do anything, but the loose visor of his bascinet clanged shut as if he had ordered it; the world closed to a barred view, as if he was in prison.

He heard the command to move at the trot and did not seem to do much, but Cerberus knew the business and followed the others; he heard his own ragged breathing, echoing inside the metal case of the helm, turned his head a little and saw Vipond sliding his great barrel heaume on, becoming a faceless metal ogre.

337

'On – *paulatim*,' he heard and Cerberus surged forward so that the cantle banged Kirkpatrick hard in the back. He felt the warm, sudden, shaming flush as his bladder gave way.

Nyd hyder ond bwa.

They roared it out as they nocked, savaged strength into their draw with it and shrieked it out on the release of the coveys of whirring death they sent into the men struggling in their ragged square of spears.

There is no dependence but on the bow.

Addaf, striding up and down behind his men, streamed with sweat and his clothes stuck to him as if he had plunged into the stream they had just crossed. All the men were dark with stains, but there was no water in that stream, only a slush of bog at the bottom, ochre pools that stank.

Yet the sides were steep enough that men had had to haul themselves up by the choke of weeds – but it had been worth it, for they were now given a clear shot straight into the left of the rebel ranks.

The ripping silk sound of the arrows fletched away into the great roar of the battle and Addaf clapped a shoulder here, patted another there and bawled out for them to be steady, aware that there were not enough of them.

He looked across, trying to pick out one of the Berkeley lords; he needed more bowmen – even the Gascons with their silly, slow latchbows would do.

He turned and put a hand on the shoulder of Rhys, planning to bawl the message in his ear and have him repeat it before sending him away; it took him half a sentence to realize that Rhys was neither listening, not shooting, but staring, his mouth slightly open.

Addaf followed his gaze and felt as if he had been struck by lightning. Horses. Riders were coming at them, fast, and the banners they flew were all blue and white, red and gold.

'Away,' he roared and was astonished to hear a scream of

outrage – and another voice, raised in shrill counter to his command.

'Stand. Shoot. Kill the heathens.'

Y Crach, shaking with fervour, glared at Addaf and pointed his bowstave at him.

'You run if you wish, old man.'

Addaf felt the rage in him, so rushed that it seemed the top of his head would explode and shower them all with the foul thoughts surging in it. Hywel, Y Crach, the whole sorry mess . . . he was, in the one small part of him still calm and sane, astonished to see the vale of Cilybebyll there in his head, the patch of land he had once owned and had not been back to see for decades. The ache was like a sudden blow.

Y Crach had not realized the old man had it in him. He knew he had badly miscalculated when the hand reached out and gripped the front of his tunic. The shoulder muscles, honed to a hump by years of pull and not yet completely ravaged by age, twitched like a horse's rump and Y Crach felt himself fly.

Men gawped as the scabby archer whirled to the edge of the steep-sided stream, then vanished over it with a despairing yelp.

'*A fo ben, bid bont,*' Addaf roared, his red face scattering sweat drops and spit.

If you want to be a leader, be a bridge.

The old proverb, so aptly delivered, made the others laugh, but Addaf was done with it and turned from the hole Y Crach had left in the air when he vanished over the lip of the stream. He found the horsemen rolling relentlessly towards them. Too close, God blind me, he thought . . .

'Run,' he bawled, 'if you want to live.'

This was the dark heart of the matter and Dog Boy knew it with every man he dragged out, with every man he grabbed by a handful of cloth and flung in. Most of those dragged out were not even bloody, just felled by heat.

Yet they are thinning us, Dog Boy thought. Down to four

deep and growing less. He helped Parcy Dodd pull out a man, turned and took the first gambesoned shoulder he could find in a grimy fist.

'There,' he ordered. 'Get ye there.'

There was little sound now, from men too weary to roar, but the eldritch shriek from beyond the line of backs ruched the skin on Dog Boy even as it leaked sweat. Horses never made such a sound, he thought. Not ever, save now, when they are dying in pain.

A knot of men surged past him, saffron cloth flashed and he realized that the moment had come for the madmen from north of the Mounth to go in, filtering through the spearmen ranks, baring their long axes and feral snarls. He saw shields with the black galley of Angus Og of the Isles and felt a brief moment of pity for the English.

Out in front, horsemen were stuck fast, some of them unable to move forward or back; there was a dead horse, belly to belly with its neighbours and held upright by the press as the man still struck wearily from its back. Two down from him, Dog Boy knew, was a knight either dead or heatstruck on his still living horse and sitting there like a wilted metal flower, again jammed in with his neighbours and unable even to fall.

'Ah, Christ betimes.'

Parcy's bitter voice turned Dog Boy into his face, then down his gaze to the body at his feet. Parcy had just dragged him out and the bloody waste of what had been Buggerback Geordie lolled like a discarded straw man.

He remembered Geordie in the Black Bitch Tavern in Edinburgh, thrusting the gift-whore at him and grinning the remains of his bad teeth. Sweetmilk had been part of that, too, Dog Boy recalled, and glanced at the straining forest of legs; he is somewhere in that.

'I hope he did not owe you money, lads,' said a resonant voice and they looked up into the maille-framed face of Jamie Douglas, greasy with sweat and joy. Parcy, with a bitter grunt, flung himself away and back into the fray, while Dog Boy looked into Jamie's grin, marvelling at how the gentle, lisping courtier vanished to be replaced by this, a hellish version written in hate.

'Ye're a hard man, Sir James,' he offered and had back a wolfish grin.

'Hard times. Besides, have you not heard that I am called the Black?'

Then he was gone, axe in one hand, shield in the other and roaring out his name so that folk glanced over their shoulders and tried to make way for him.

In case he cuts them down to get to the English, Dog Boy thought savagely. Which he may well do.

He became aware then, sitting by Buggerback Geordie's shattered remains, with the great haze of dust sifting like gold down into a ground made slurry by blood and shit, that he wanted no more of this. He thought of Bet's Meggy and the bairns.

My son, he said aloud. All that needs be done to get back to him and Bet's Meggy is to kill Englishmen until they give up and go away . . . or are all dead.

Then, as if in a slow-motion dream, the ranks ahead seemed to part for a moment, opening like the Red Sea to Moses. Beyond, across a rampart of dead men and horses, he saw a knot of riders surrounding a single man, blazing with colours unstained, the gold pards gleaming, his helm proud with a padded silk lion on it and a clear crown embracing it with gold.

King Edward, by the Grace of God.

An Englishman.

The squire flogged up on a failing palfrey, wet mouth open and the sweat almost trailing behind him in the wind. Before he had reached two lance-lengths from the King, d'Argentan had spurred forward and raised a halting hand.

De Valence saw the squire's livery, with the lions of Clifford smeared and spattered; he grew cold as the squire and d'Argentan exchanged words, the former panting, mouth open like a dog. The wheyed shock of his face made de Valence grow colder still, but he was turned from the sight by the King's uncertain voice.

'My lord Earl of Pembroke, have we sent for the foot?'

De Valence nodded politely.

'We have, sire. They will be along presently.'

'It seems to me', Edward said querulously, 'that our horse is being sore hurt. Get archers here, de Valence, and with all speed.'

D'Argentan arrived back, his sweating face twisted with concern.

'Clifford is down. Dead,' he said. Then he blinked a little and added harshly: 'Sir Miles de Stapleton also. And both his sons.'

'God blind me,' de Valence spat. 'They are carving us like a joint.'

The King turned, his grim face puzzled beneath the lappets and ermine and padded lion confection of his visored helm.

'Who orders there now?'

'Huddleston, according to that squire,' d'Argentan answered, pleased that he had remembered to ask. The King shook his heavy head.

'No, no, no – that will not hold. Huddleston does not have the rank for that. Tailleboys, or Leyburn – de Valence, send word that Leyburn is to order poor Clifford's host.'

God curse it, de Valence thought bitterly as he screwed round in the saddle to where his retinue sat expectantly, what does it matter who orders? In that heaving mass no order given could be obeyed anyway . . . he caught the glow of a shield with a barred cross and waved to the man. A moment later, Sir William Vescy cantered away in search of the dead Clifford's command.

'Well, my lords,' the King said, lowering his visor until his voice grew to a metal muffle. 'It is time for the King to strike a blow. Give them heart.'

'Certes, Your Grace. We will scatter them like chaff,' boomed d'Argentan, grinning.

Christ's Wounds, de Valence thought. Is he seriously contemplating riding his royal person into this? God save us all . . .

He followed, all the same, urging his mount to the King's left side while men, caught out by the quickness of it, fumbled with shield and lance on the backs of their fractious, eager mounts.

Even as they picked a way over the scattered dead, the screaming, kicking horses slick with fluid, the groaning men, de Valence saw the thickening carpet of it, then the mound, piled with horse and man – some were still alive and pinned, limbs waving like weary beetle feelers.

And over it, sliding out from the bristling ranks and through a gap in the jammed wall of horse, he saw figures, creeping horrors winking with naked blades.

Dog Boy knew the knight, knew him from old and, it seemed to him in that moment, had been fighting him all his life. Blue and white stripes and a rondel of little red birds – an important knight, for sure, and there was a name for him somewhere in Dog Boy's head, but he could not recall it. He went for him, all the same, half-crouched and snarling, aware of Patrick and Parcy and others at his back.

De Valence saw the figures, the leading one with a feral scuttle, axe and long dirk in his hands, his rimmed iron hat dented and his black-bearded face twisted; he was slavering, de Valence saw with wonder, like a rabid wolf . . .

The curving overhand blow of the axe made him cry out and the destrier reared – too late, de Valence saw that had been the intent, for the dirk flashed out and the warhorse shrieked and lashed out front and back; de Valence felt the shock that told him someone close behind had received the brunt of it.

Trying to cut the saddle girths, he thought wildly – and then his men surged forward and he lost sight of the slavering man. There were others, all the same, and de Valence knew they had recognized the King.

'The King,' he bawled. 'Ware the King.'

De Valence, Dog Boy thought suddenly. His name is de Valence and he is an earl, no less – then he was whirled away by the sudden arrival of more horsemen, found himself next to a prancing power of a horse, a white beast draped in red and glowing with gold pards. He looked up into the metal face and the surmounting lion. King Edward, by the Grace of God – an Englishman . . .

Dog Boy struck and the King, unable to lower his shield enough, felt the shock of the axe blow on the padded armour of his warhorse, which squealed and snaked out a vicious bite. Dog Boy jerked away from it, slashing with the dirk; he saw, out of the corner of his eye, the screaming figure of Patrick launch himself forward.

The sword that snicked the iron hat from Patrick's head, and most of his skull with it, came from a knight in red and silver, who hurled his shield at Dog Boy and then used the free hand to grab the king's rein.

'Away, sire . . .'

Dog Boy, staggering under the battering of the shield, blinded by the vision of Patrick's iron hat flying bloodily into the air, gave a last, despairing lunge and a mad swipe of the axe – but the King of England was gone.

De Valence battered his way through his own men to the side of the King, who had shoved up his visor and now stared from a sweat-coursed daze of a face.

'Get the King away,' de Valence said to d'Argentan, shouting above the howling din.

'You get him away,' d'Argentan replied tersely. 'I am unaccustomed to fleeing.'

He reined round and de Valence, at once heart-leaped with admiration and cursing him for dereliction, took the King's bridle in one metalled fist and started to force a way through the press to safety.

D'Argentan was all fire. As he had been in his youth, he

344

thought, exultant and roaring with the moment. Third-best knight in Christendom – he would raise that ranking by seeking out and slaying the Bruce himself, if he had to carve through the entire Scotch army to do it.

Beginning with that weeping little scut in the iron hat . . .

Dog Boy saw the knight ride at him. It was the same one who had killed Patrick, a red figure with little silver goblets on his jupon, shieldless but with his sword drawn back ready to sweep down. Dog Boy was blinded by snot and tears and could not be sure if it was for Patrick, or all the others, or simply rage.

Or for himself, who was surely about to die. He flung the axe, almost wearily, in a last futile gesture.

D'Argentan saw it coming and raised his shield to block it. The shield I do not have, he remembered at the last. The axe whirled over his forearm and struck him on the chest, bouncing off. He had time to bless the padding and maille before he lost his balance, like a tyro, and fell with a clatter as the warhorse crow-hopped delicately over the dead.

There was a moment of disbelief, of sheer incredulity. Third-best knight in Christendom. It came to him then how that had been when he was younger, for a rank beginner would not have fallen so easily. Then d'Argentan realized he was flat on his back, half-draped over a dead horse, and began to struggle upright.

The figure landed on him with both feet, driving all the air out of him, so that he whooped and gasped and knew, with all the experience of his tourney years, that something had snapped in his chest.

'Bastard,' the man snarled and d'Argentan, struggling weakly, felt the visor wrenched up, stared into the black-bearded hate of the Scot; slaver dripped on his cheek.

He had time to feel unutterably weary, to wonder if God would forgive him his many sins.

Then Dog Boy drove the dagger into his eye and roared out revenge for Patrick.

'On them,' he bawled out, looking right and left. 'They fail.'

ISABEL

*I woke striped with light. I do not often sleep in the cage,
save when the heat is oppressive as now; it does not happen
often in Scotland. It annoys the gawpers, who come to see
a scowl of witch, not a wee auld wummin snoring. Constance
stirred me, then begged me to come into the chamber to
eat the meal she had brought and was so flustered and
secretive that I did, wondering. She presented her daring
gift – mother's milk. Brought from a wet nurse whose wee
charge died, she told me, greatly daring. I did not want it,
especially from a wet nurse whose charge had died – who
was to say it was not the milk? I did not say this, for I knew
why Constance had brought it. She would say it was because
it was the perfect food for the old and invalid and begging
my pardon as she did so, for insinuations – but it was all
because of Sister Petra of Cologne, whose story had just
reached Constance's ears. That nun, so the story went, had
eaten nothing else, nor moved much. She closeted herself in
a tower and drank the mother's milk through a reed in the
door, waiting – so it was said – for her lover to come for her
and she would have the face of the girl of fourteen he knew
when they parted and she was forced to the veil. I did not
ruin it for Constance by telling her the rest of the tale – how
the other nuns grew tired of milking the village women, who
were tired themselves of being heifers. So they simply stopped*

347

and Sister Petra, too weak to move after years of lying around, could not get out and died when her exertions at the door snapped her heartstring. When the nuns found Christian charity and courage enough to break down the door of the tower they found her, emaciated, wizened, dead and with the face of a 70-year-old, which matched her age to perfection.

I will not need mother's milk to preserve my face for Hal – he will come before I age out another year. I read it in the pattern of the mother's milk I threw in the bailey when Constance had gone. If Malise wants a witch to burn I can give him one, for God is dead and Heaven is ugly.

CHAPTER FIFTEEN

Bannockburn
Feast of St John the Baptist, June 1314

Thweng stood patiently as John, his arming squire, fought to relace the skewed ailettes, and another squire, William, took the saddle and clothing off Garm and put it on Goliath. Garm stood, his pained hoof up, snuffling now and then as another squire soothed him.

There was a strange, summer-singing quiet here, dusted with drifting motes and only faint squeals and screams and the clash of metal, where the murmur of the surrounding voices was no louder than bees. It was as if there was no battle at all, Thweng thought, for all that it looks as if one had already taken place.

The whole of the toasted-bread carse around them was littered with bodies, slumped or sitting in the hazing of heat and dust, some of them dangle-headed with weariness. They were not dead, but most of them wished they were, felled by a crippling march in a heat that sucked the strength away. Others gathered in knots, leaning on spears or tall shields to talk earnestly and all of them wondered what was happening.

What was happening, Thweng thought grimly, is that the

foot have been marching all night and are arriving in dribbles, like wine from a drunk's slack mouth. The folk who should be ordering them have all charged off.

This whole affair was beyond rotted now, he knew. John finished with the ailettes and stood back to review his lord; he nodded and smiled, his face sheened and eager to please. Thweng felt a sharp stab, as if someone had driven a dagger under his heart, at the thought of this one going under the dirk-wielding horrors. John de Stirchley was the least of a neighbour's brood, not yet fifteen, not yet knighted and bursting with having been brought here by the great Sir Marmaduke while his elder brother had to stay behind.

Thweng recalled the boy's father and his mother, a spring bride for a winter groom. A late fruit is John, Thweng thought, and favoured because of it. I promised both his parents I would not get him bruised.

'Listen carefully,' he said to the squire and then laid it out: saddle palfreys, gather up as many as you can of the men who came with us, take food, and make sure every man has a weapon. Leave the carts and the panoply – it is sticks and canvas, no more – and plate and furniture. Kilton can afford to lose a little carved oak and some pewter, but do not forget the Rolls, those vellum lists of who is owed what. Be ready to ride – you will know when, even if I am not here to tell you.

He saw John's throat bob as he swallowed the dry stick in it, but the nod was firm with understanding. Thweng wanted to reassure the lad, but he was leaving him with the burden of it all, for his duty lay with the King and he was not so sure there would be an afterwards.

He was spared the awkward moment of it by a voice, thick with the south in it, talking to William as he fought with the girth of the saddle and Goliath's attempts to be mischievous and blow out his belly.

'How bist?'

The man was red-faced and sweltering in a padded jack, the iron helmet dangling from his belt, the spear dark with hand-sweat and old use.

Thweng saw William, flustered and damp, spare the man a sour glance and then shoulder Goliath's big belly until the animal grunted and let out air.

'Does tha ken what?' the man persisted and Thweng, finally freed from his armouring, stepped forward so that the man was forced to look at him instead. The expression changed, the hand came up and knuckled his furrowed, dripping forehead.

'Beg pardon, yer honour. Lookin' to find what is.'

'Who are you?' Thweng asked and the man drew himself up a little, permitting a small shine of pride.

'Henry, my lord. I orders ten from Wyndhome for the Sire there, good Sir John.'

'Where is good Sir John?' Thweng asked patiently and had back the look someone gave a dog who would not fetch.

'Why, ee be with old Sir Maurice, baint ee?'

Berkeley, Thweng thought. They are Gloucester men, spearmen of Sir Maurice Berkeley brought by some fealtied lord called Sir John; Thweng had no idea who he was or where Wyndhome lay – but he knew where good Sir John would be.

'He is there,' Thweng said, shooting one metalled arm to where the dust was a thick cloud laced with shouts and clangs and screaming horses, faint as birdsong. 'You should go.'

'Without us havin' ordern?'

Henry shook his head vehemently, and then turned as someone shouted his name.

'Oi, 'Enry, lookee there. Be that not our king?'

A man pointed, squinting and shading his eyes with his entire iron-rimmed hat.

The knot of riders cantered out of the pall of dust and the sun flared off the gold on the centre rider's fancy war hat.

Behind, the coterie of armoured men rode under the streaming pennant, the Dragon and the huge royal banner that marked them for all to see. The King, Thweng thought, feeling the stone settle in his bowels.

'It be our king. Be ee leavin', then?'

'No,' Thweng lied and signalled for John to leg him up on to Goliath's back. When the squire came close, he whispered harshly in his ear, aware of the Gloucester men turning one to the other, frowning and gabbling like chickens.

'Now is the time. Go, boy, and do not look back.'

He reined round, seeing Henry and the other Gloucester men craning for a better look; others were climbing to their feet to watch the gilded passage of the King, riding to the rear. Thweng felt the whole day shudder, like a sweated horse in a chill wind.

He cantered after them, caught up and forced himself alongside a flustered, bewildered de Valence.

'Turn about,' he yelled, scorning protocol for an earl. The Earl of Pembroke turned his streaming, boiled-beet face, the scowl on it like a scar; he reined in a little so that the pair of them fell behind the cavalcade.

'They think the King is leaving, that the day is lost,' Thweng roared out. De Valence's scowl grew deeper, his eyes black caves of misery in the blood of his face.

'What makes you think it is not?' he answered.

Thweng, astounded, jerked Goliath to a halt and let the Earl surge away to join his king. What now, he thought, that the truth is out?

He looked left and right, at first disbelieving that the great host of men he saw, uncommitted and waiting, were defeated. Even as he stood, bewildered, he saw the resting foot surge to their feet as someone shouted and pointed off to the right, up to the wooded heights.

Thweng followed the gesture . . . there, fey as Faerie, figures moved on the distant hill beyond the Scots. A rider with a banner – he squinted to make it out, saw other banners floating above thick clumps of black shapes. The sun – God, it was not even noon yet – flung itself back and forth like fire from sharp metal tips.

More men? Thweng could not believe it. More Scots, coming down on the flank of the army? And that banner – black and white. The one the rider carried had a huge cross on it, he was sure even at this distance and with his old eyes.

It could not be, was impossible . . . yet the thrilling terror that the banner might be Beauseant, that the God-rotted proscribed Templars had launched their perfect vengeance on all Christendom's chosen warriors, shot through Thweng like a fire.

Unbelievable . . .

Others believed it and even those who did not saw an armed host, for certes. They shouted it, one to another, sucked up the memory of their king riding to safety and drew their own conclusion. Men began trotting, aimlessly at first and then, like a covey of starlings, all in the one direction.

Away.

In a second, Thweng saw the brittle might of Edward's host shatter like poor pottery.

The big banner seemed to have a life of its own, a bedsheet straight off the Earl of Hell's canopy, as far as Hal was concerned. It did look right, he admitted as he glanced up at it, for the limner's blue paint had smeared from the arms of the cross and produced, almost perfectly and by divine accident, the shivering blue cross of the Sientclers on the spread of linen.

That, at least, was an acceptable device to ride under, he thought, and then looked to where Davey the Smith strode, forge hammer in one massive fist, Beauseant in another and the black and white Templar hat just one among the many.

Last wave of that banner, Hal thought. I hope it works,

for the Bruce's wrath will be mighty and only victory will turn it to smiles. If we fail, then I am a lost man for bringing the spectre of the Order to his army and his great battle; he will think it the final curse of St Malachy on his head. It will not matter, for if we fail then Isabel is lost and it does not matter about the world after that . . .

The idea had been daring, but the camp on Coxet Hill had embraced it like a fervent lover, since it let them loose with little or no danger to plunder the fallen. So they took up the Templar gear uncovered in the unpacking and put it on, laughing, and Sir John Airth, glowing like an ember and puffing in the heat, had been carried up in a litter to present the Beauseant, unwrapped from the bottom of the Templar armoury like the sick horror of a bad dream.

'You mun be hung for the whole sheep as the half lamb,' he growled and then shook his head, scattering drips from his jowls, his face like a raspberry mould and his fat legs bandaged against the gout.

'I will pray for you, Sir Hal, as I pray for the soul of my son,' he added and watched as the silk Beauseant was tacked crudely to a tall pole and handed to the smith, who could carry it one-handed.

I hope Sir John is praying now, Hal thought, and that I have timed it right.

He looked right and left at the straggling mass, loping like wolves down the hill and into the fringe of the fighting and the scattering of bodies. If it came to a fight, of course, they would run like leaping lambs, but all they had to do was look fierce and magnificent for a glorious eyeblink.

The figure loomed up at his stirrup and he glanced down to see the impish grin of Bet's Meggy, an iron hat tilted sideways on her head and a pole clutched in one fist. It had a sharp kitchen knife tied to the end of it.

'Sir Hal,' she shouted. 'Is your army ordered to your lordship's satisfaction?'

Full of cheek, that one, Hal thought, yet he found himself grinning. Then he saw the boy, serious as plague and gripping a dirk as long as his arm in one hand and the hand of a wee girl in the other.

'Christ's Wounds,' he bellowed. 'Did you need to bring the bairns to this?'

'Who would look after wee Bet, lord?' she yelled back at him, her grin wild as a cat snarl. 'And you could not hope to keep Dog Boy's son out of such an affair.'

Dog Boy's son. Hal looked at the boy and laughed at the fierce look of the lad, drowning in a borrowed – stolen – maille coif, with his too-big Templar warhat and his long dirk. Hob, he remembered Dog Boy saying the boy was called. Hob. He was younger than the Dog Boy Hal had first met all those years ago in Douglas, but he had the same look. The look that had reminded Hal of his own son, John, dead and dead these many years.

Dog Boy had balmed the loss of John, and now here was another. He wondered if the new Royal Houndsman would countenance his son coming to Herdmanston. If Bet's Meggy was going off with her new man, we will need a new baker, he thought. Or a new dog boy.

Hal saw a succession of them, all the way into the future of Herdmanston and laughed with the sheer joy of it; Bet's Meggy joined in and, after a moment, Hob cackled out a laugh as well, shrill with the moment if not the complete understanding. Even wee Bet, finger up her nose, smiled beatifically.

Then, sudden as a cold wind, the loss of Sim scoured his joy away and his sudden blackness soured its way to the others, so that they stopped laughing, all at once. After a moment, they all put their heads down and plodded, as if through a rain squall, down to the war.

He had been sitting for some time, had lost any idea of how long, so that it came as a cold-water shock to snap back to reality. He blinked at the bloody teeth of the man he sat next to and realized he had the man's hand in his own.

Vipond. Kirkpatrick remembered bobbing along in the knight's wake, trying to control reins, shield and lance until, with a curse, he had thrown the latter away and then tried to screw his head round to see out of the narrow slit of the helm.

He hated it, the sweating cave of the helm, the jostle and bounce and desperate straining of the warhorse, which wanted to be moving faster after the others; in the end, Kirkpatrick had let it and hung on. He heard his breath rasp in and out in the furnace of his helmet, heard dull clangs, felt a blow on his shield and panicked, thinking they had contacted enemy.

Unable to see, he had dragged out his sword and swung it wildly left and right, cursing his own foolishness in ever having thought to ride as a knight, at ever having thought he was one, for all his dubbing.

Suddenly, through the slit, he had seen Vipond, half turning towards him and reeling in the saddle. The knight seemed to slip sideways, put out one arm and grasping hand, as if to clutch Kirkpatrick, and then fell and disappeared from view.

Kirkpatrick had hauled the warhorse to a halt, cursing it. He had been told that it was beautifully trained and biddable, worth every penny of thirty marks, but Kirkpatrick would have fed the beast to the pigs he kept on the manor which this warhorse represented in price.

He climbed off it, half sliding, half falling, threw down the shield and unlaced the helm and hauled it off, whooping in air as if he had breached from water. Then he tore off the bascinet, forced the maille hood back and ripped off his arming cap, glorying in the feel of air on his sweat-tousled bare head.

When he managed to focus, he found himself looking at his own shield; two broken shafts were in it, neatly puncturing the fist with the upraised dagger. Those were the blows I felt,

Kirkpatrick thought with a sudden lurch. If they had not hit the shield . . .

Then they would have hit me, he thought when he found the body of the fallen Vipond. As they had hit him – the knight lay on his back, metal face pointed to the sky, a shaft so deep in the bicep of his right arm that Kirkpatrick knew it had gone through and then snapped off in the fall. A second arrow was buried almost to the fletch in his right side.

Kirkpatrick's legs were buckling as the weight of maille fell on them. He lumbered up to Vipond, not knowing what he was about to do with a dead man – and then he heard the metal rasp of breathing from the faceless creature and dropped his sword. He grunted his way down to one knee, fumbling with the knight's helmet lacings; when he drew it off, Vipond's sweat and gore-streaked face stared up at him, the smile on it crimson; he had vomited blood, Kirkpatrick saw.

'Thank . . . you,' Vipond wheezed and Kirkpatrick looked him up and down, went to touch the arrow in his side, thought better of it and grasped the one in the knight's bicep; the man groaned and Kirkpatrick let it go as if it had been on fire.

He sat down with a hiss of maille links and the clank of pauldron and ailette, aware that he was as useless at phys-icking this man as he was at knightly combat, that he was flapping his arms like a hopeless chicken and no help to anyone.

'I will get help,' he muttered. 'Water . . .'

He found Vipond's fierce clutch on his wrist.

'Stay.'

The knight's eyes had become hot and afraid.

'Do not . . . let . . . me die . . . alone.'

You are not alone, Kirkpatrick wanted to say. God is watching. But it sounded trite and hollow, so he said nothing at all and sat there holding Vipond's hand while his destrier cropped contentedly, picking delicately at the grass not tram-pled or soaked to muddy gore.

Vipond's own mount had vanished, but three others moved across the sprawled bodies, their trappings torn and streaked. A fourth limped back and forth, every now and then making a plaintive screaming whinny from a snaked-out neck, as if shouting for help.

Somewhere, time slipped away. Kirkpatrick was half aware of the sudden increase in the noise of battle to his right but it did not seem important enough to turn and look. He was fixed, frozen, staring at nothing at all, yet aware of surge, like a flood tide, as the fighting moved away from him. The heat beat on him, melted him to dull lethargy.

When he snapped out of his daze, it took him a moment to realize that movement had done it; a horseman was coming, wavering through the heat haze, all faerie and stretched.

'A rider – help is coming,' he said, turning to Vipond. He had intended to remove his hand from the knight's clutch and pat it soothingly, reassuringly – but the death grip was fierce and Kirkpatrick had to prise it free, shocked at the fact that the knight had died and he had not known when it had happened. He might as well have died alone, Kirkpatrick thought bitterly, for all the help I have been; he smelled the rankness of himself, remembered what he had done and felt sick shame.

The rider stopped. Kirkpatrick was suddenly aware that there was only himself and the man on the horse in this part of the world; to the left was the great hump of Coxet Hill where, incongruously, birds sang and insects whined and hummed, headed for the feast. To his right, the battle was a carpet of dead and the moaning dying, with a great mass of heat and dust haze beyond where figures flitted and roared sullenly.

The English have been forced back . . . We have won, Kirkpatrick realized with a sudden heartleap of exultation. We have actually won . . .

The rider was closer and now Kirkpatrick saw that the

warhorse was plodding, head bowed with weariness, the trapper on it stained and torn so that dags and tippets of material trailed on the ground. The rider had lost all head coverings – torn them off, Kirkpatrick thought, as I have done, to get some relief from the heat – and his surcote was streaked and splashed with fluids. He had no shield, but held a sword in what appeared to be a tired fist, dangling dangerously close to the horse's unsteady feet. He looked as if he had ridden out of some ancient barrow mound.

Kirkpatrick watched the rider pick a careful way round the litter of dead here – mainly archers, he realized. So we did as we were bid, he thought bitterly, even though I had no good part in it. He stood up, levering himself to his feet and feeling the dragging weight of maille chausse and hauberk; the horse stopped a moment later, the rider straightening in the saddle and bringing the sword up.

He thinks I am a danger, Kirkpatrick thought to himself and laughed with the irony of that. He opened his mouth to call out – but froze, gaping as the sword came up and pointed at him.

He knows me, Kirkpatrick thought, and felt the blood in him stop, had a surge of mad panic as he saw, through the blood-spatters and stains, the man's device; three gold wheat-sheafs on red. No cadet marking of any lesser branch of the Comyn, so this was the lord of Badenoch himself.

Red John, he thought wildly. I killed you. At least I slid a wee dagger into your heart, though the Bruce had already done the work. I watched your vain wee raised bootheels spatter up the tarn of your own heart's blood in Greyfriars, years since . . .

He caught himself. No ghost, he told himself firmly and looked round for his shield and sword. Worse than that.

The son, delivered by the Devil to the one part of the field of struggling men where he would find Kirkpatrick, the man he hated above all others.

The man who had murdered his father. Aye, Kirkpatrick added bitterly, and would have done for the boy, too – the boy now grown to stand opposite me – if Hal had not intervened.

Badenoch sat for a moment and Kirkpatrick, glancing wildly left and right to see if any help was close, saw his sword sticking in the sere turf like a grave cross. He eyed it, but did not move; like a mouse to the cat, the act of going for it might spring the puss forward and Kirkpatrick did not want that. Not a man on a warhorse, he thought desperately, with blood in his eye . . .

Then Badenoch, slowly – painfully, Kirkpatrick thought with a sudden thrill – clambered off the beast, which stood, legs splayed and head bowed. The man patted it fondly before he turned, straightened, twirled the sword lightly in one hand and started forward.

Not wounded then, Kirkpatrick thought, just weary, though not as done up as his mount. He sprang then, tore out his sword and turned. Badenoch stopped, close enough for Kirkpatrick to see his face, which was straw-coloured and sheened slick with sweat so that the beard seemed darker and was pearled with droplets. Perhaps he is injured after all, Kirkpatrick thought. Or heat-struck. Not that he was in any better state himself, stiff with sitting and crushed by the unfamiliar weight of maille and pieces of plate steel.

'You,' Badenoch declared curtly. Kirkpatrick managed a grin.

'It was when I rose this morning,' he replied, and could not resist the vicious stab, for all that prudence told him to toggle his lip: 'You will be the new Badenoch. I knew your father. I knew you, too, when you were a stripling and would have known you better if someone had not got in the way of it.'

The whey face flushed and then drained to an almost unnatural white; Kirkpatrick saw his knuckles tighten on the hilt of the sword.

Clever Kirkpatrick, he cursed silently, who never could keep his tongue still . . . the man's savage rush drove whimpering panic into him and a thrill of shock like a bolt of lightning that seemed to spear through his groin to the soles of his feet.

He barely managed to block the first cut, almost lost the sword parrying the second and slashed wildly right and left even as the echoes of the steel faded and Badenoch drew away.

He knew then, in that first exchange, that a sword was no dirk and that Badenoch, trained knight that he was, younger as he was, would kill him.

Badenoch knew it too, and smiled.

The King wanted to turn and fight. Which was laudable and courageous, but no bloody help at all, de Valence thought bitterly.

'Your Grace is best kept from the grip of the rebels,' he explained, though it was hard to seem reasonable and pragmatic when you had to bawl to be heard above the din of an army gone to a baying horde of runners.

Around them, kept away by the hard-faced *mesnie*, the fleeing mass surged and jostled, battering up to the walls of Stirling, clambering – and falling – from the rock it hunched on, already clotted thick with the peasantry who had run there long before. Perched like gulls on a cliff, they defied the roaring soldiery, who begged and shrieked for entrance at the stubbornly closed gates.

'My lord de Mowbray,' the King said and de Valence heard the mix of astonishment, anger and bitterness. There was no point in replying that Mowbray was right to shut the gates of Stirling Castle to everyone, King included – the battle was lost and now he would have to hand Stirling over to the Scots, as agreed. To do other risked slaughter of everyone in it, as per the accepted rules of war, so refusing to let the King into a cage where he was sure to be taken was only sense.

King Edward had none of that left, de Valence saw, only stubborn courage and the surety that they had been, somehow, betrayed. We have been, de Valence thought. Betrayed by our own arrogance, which has been enough to irritate God.

They beat a path through the maggot-boil of infantry, cursing and flailing at them until they parted. They breasted through them, down from the castle, into the coiled loops of the Forth, which forced them back across the littered dead and the howling vengeance of Scots who ruled there now, hunting in wolf packs. De Valence, looking round him, saw a handful of knights and the last remnants of mounted Welsh archers.

'My lord earl . . .'

De Valence turned to where old Thomas Berkeley pointed one mailled fist; riders were picking a determined way over the dead and dying, coming at them fast. Like magpies, de Valence thought, attracted to the glitter of that bloody crown.

'Get His Grace the King away,' he growled to Vescy, and then detailed off the knights he needed and lowered his helmet visor.

'*Bonne chance*, Pembroke.'

De Valence acknowledged the King's fading cry even as he spurred the weary warhorse, followed by a tippet of riders. He felt rather than saw the men on either side of him as he cantered up to a low bush and popped a jump, cruel spurs raking his tired horse up to a gallop; he had the surge of exultation, familiar and strangely comforting as old shoes, as the enemy came closer.

Someone streaked ahead – de Valence saw the labelled lion device and noted it for later censure at this outrageous breach of protocol. A Kingston, he registered. Sir John or Sir Nicholas . . . I shall have words with them later.

They clattered into the riders and swept halfway through them with a series of shrieks and bell-clangs. De Valence took a sweeping blow on his shield, answered it with a pointless one of his own, and then was wheeling round and round in a mad pirouetting dance, striking blows and being struck in turn. Little shaggy men on little hairy horses, like all the Scots, de Valence thought. Knights who ride deer-hounds to a battle . . .

Suddenly, the beating stopped and de Valence, blinking through the sweat-blurred slit of his helm, stopped flailing with his sword, turning his head this way and that to see.

The Scots had all been downed or were running – but more were coming and, worse than that, de Valence saw the mad scramble of axe-wielding foot, with their wild northern cries and bare legs. Rats, lice and Scots, he thought savagely, you can keep killing all three, but no matter where you turn, there they are again . . .

'Back,' he cried, waving his sword in a circle and reining round.

They cantered off, leaving the pursuing Scots floundering and yelling insults. A long way away, riding hard on blowing horses to catch up with the King, de Valence stopped and tore off his helm, whooping in air while the rest of the *mesnie* cantered up. Some were laughing, mad with excitement still. One – young Hastang – was hauling off his helm and pouring the puke out of it, trying to wipe his face with the decorative mantle dangling from the crest.

It took a moment to find out who was missing: Sir Thomas Ercedene, the Lovel of Northants and the Lovel of Norfolk both – and the brace of Kingstons. Well, de Valence thought dully, no need to find out which of them dared to ride in front of me then.

And old Thomas Berkeley. No one had seen him fall. Back with the King's party, de Valence broke the news to Maurice, Thomas's son, and offered up the slim hope that he was captured and not killed – though the memory of those leaping axemen welled in his mind and almost robbed his mouth of the words.

Maurice said nothing, though Addaf saw the tight-lipped tension in the man and hoped he would not do anything mad-brained, like try and avenge his old father. If he did, Addaf thought, he will do it alone – all me and mine want now is to be gone from this place.

'Protect the King.'

The cry went up and the armoured riders closed round Edward to force another great surge of milling foot to part like the Red Sea.

Protect the King. Addaf hawked and spat.

Let God protect the King of the English, he added to himself, though it was clear to everyone that He had removed His Hand from them this day.

And the Welsh. Addaf found out how poorly the Welsh stood in God's Grace less than an hour later.

That was when they turned at bay to face the pursuing Scots riders, who had been closing in for some time, held up by knots of scattering foot. Those running spearmen contributed less than nothing to the day, Addaf thought bitterly, and now they are getting in everyone's way, us as much as the Scots.

'Dismount.'

Addaf heard the shout and cursed; Maurice was speaking earnestly to de Valence, who trotted after the knights huddled round the hunched figure of King Edward. Addaf watched the blue and white striped trapping of the de Valence's horse flap heavily, sodden with blood, streaked and torn. None of the knights left to the King looked any better, he realized, which is why the work is now given to us. Welshmen protecting the King of the English – the savage irony of it was not lost on anyone, as Addaf saw from the sullen embered looks.

'*Nyd hyder ond bwa*,' he shouted and the Welsh laughed, though it was bitter, as the horse-holders took the mounts and the others sorted themselves out.

There is no dependence but on the bow – Addaf had always

held that to be a fundamental truth, but he did not think there were enough bows now. He looked at the line of them, counting: twenty shooters, perhaps, no more. Ahead he saw running men and recognized them as Hainaulters, trying to scatter from the path of the oncoming riders.

He raised his bow so that he could judge the wind from the trail of ribbon – there was one, by God's hook, a blessed breeze suddenly blowing cool in the sweating dragon's breath day. Addaf turned to where Sir Maurice sat like a sullen sack on his big horse.

'*Dduw bod 'n foliannus,*' he grunted – God be praised. Maurice, who had been around the Welsh long enough, stared unpityingly from eyes miserable with loss and gave him the rote response in Welsh.

'*In ois oisou.*' For ever and ever.

The last Hainaulters staggered out of the path of the riders – sixty, Addaf thought with a sudden bowel-curdling chill. Or more. He saw the banner flying above the sweat-foamed garrons they were riding and anger burned up in him – stars on blue, the mark of the Black Douglas himself. He remembered his men, dead and dying in puddles of their own blood, spilled from the stumps of the right wrists Douglas had chopped off with an axe.

'Draw.'

There was the familiar sound of drawn strings, that creaking-door rasp.

'Shoot.'

The air quivered and thrummed. Addaf saw horses and men fall, saw the others veer left and right, reining round and flogging their mounts out of range. He looked up at Sir Maurice and had nothing back but a poached-egg stare and knew they would stay here for a time, letting the King put some distance between himself and his enemies.

He looked at the sky, saw clouds building up like bulls herding in a paddock, felt the breeze, a freshening balm on his face. It was a good day, he thought, to stand peaceful and cool . . .

The Hainaulters staggered away. More men followed, a few riders, a handful of horses – all fleeing from the Scots, who stayed out of range, waiting. More of them came up.

'Mount.'

The sigh was audible.

'*Dduw bod 'n foliannus*,' Addaf grunted, but did not turn around or move, deliberately waiting until everyone else was in the saddle and already moving off. Last to leave the field of battle, he thought to himself proudly. Does no harm to let folk see that . . .

'*In ois oisou*,' said a crow-harsh voice and, surprised, Addaf turned.

He had time to see the twisted knot of savage vengeance that was the bruised face of Y Crach before the scything arc of blade whirled into his ribs, driving air, sense and light out of him, all at once.

Hal was left only with the smith, stolid and determinedly stumping along in the wake of Cornix; all the others had dropped off, one by one, half-apologetic, half-ashamed. Chirnside, Sore Davey, Mouse – all lured by the glint of gold spurs, or the sight of a ring on a dead finger.

Hal shifted in the saddle and looked at Davey of Crauford, holding up the great silken Beauseant banner, so fine it rippled like maiden hair in the sudden breeze. Lay brother though he might only have been, the smith was proud as any deadly sin at being chosen to carry this, the famed Order banner, in what was its last flutter on a field of battle.

'Tear that aff its pole,' Hal said, more harshly than he had intended, but saw the sad regret in Davey's eyes and felt a flicker of sympathy.

'Fold it up,' he added more gently. 'I ken where to take it when this is done with.'

Aye, and Rossal de Bissot's sword as well. The anonymous black brothers of Glaissery could keep their venerated relics in secret, for they had no part left in the world of men.

He heard the clang and spang of metal even as he rode on, leaving Davey to his task, the horse threading its own path through the groaning, slathered mass of spilled bodies, the blood making a sucking mud that stained the feathering on its hooves.

Two men fought still – well, one did, while the other, white hair whisping in the breeze, seemed to be at his last, down on one knee and weakly fending off the wild blows. If his opponent ever gathers himself of sense and strength, Hal thought, yon wee auld man will be carved like a joint at table.

He was filled with the useless waste of it; the battle was done and he was sure Bruce had won it, so this was a pointless exercise and he was about to shout that when he saw the horse draped in its trapping and bright still with heraldry.

A blue shield with the cross of St Andrew – Hal knew that mark and that Kirkpatrick had not had time to change it on the horse trapping or his surcote, though his actual shield wore that arrogant hand holding a bloody dagger.

'Ho,' he bawled and the pair sprang apart, the old man – Kirkpatrick, Hal now realized – falling backwards and lying outstretched on the bloody grass like Christ crucified.

The other was Badenoch. Hal saw it at once and the shock of it was a sickening thrill at this, the clearest indication of the Hand of God. Badenoch, who had watched Kirkpatrick kill his da, who had stood there as a gawky 17-year-old youth while Kirkpatrick was restrained from killing him, too. By me, Hal thought. By me.

Now he is grown to prime and has killed Black Roger. A great surge of feeling swamped Hal, a wave crested with the knowledge that he had let the youth live then, to visit his vengeance on Kirkpatrick. The Christ-crucified vision of the man lying there roared luridly into his head and he hissed the Templar sword out of its scabbard.

Badenoch saw Hal, saw the smith behind him and the scatter of men, coming up hard from their plunder and trying to make up for their shameful greed by being first back to Sir Hal's side. He sprang for Kirkpatrick's horse like a hare, was in the saddle and reining round in a fluid movement.

It was all the spur needed; before he had thought, Hal was after him.

He raked Cornix into a jagged canter, weaving as best he could between the scatter of bodies; once or twice the big horse swerved and hare-hopped before struggling on after the fleeing Badenoch.

Headed the wrong way, Hal thought triumphantly. Keep going and you will run into the Forth . . .

There was a great growling roar and a sudden flash which jerked Hal's head up and made the horse falter and stumble. Thunder and lightning, he registered, and then they were bursting through some low bushes, into the kicked-up haze still swelling from Badenoch's mad gallop, the motes dancing in it. The light had gone strange and yellowed.

Badenoch realized his mistake, turned sharply and lost his balance, reeling a little in the saddle; Hal turned more sharply still, gained a stride or two, leaped a bush and thumped down with a jar that banged his belly into the pommel and rattled his teeth.

They burst from the bushes to where the bodies started to clot again, horses among them this time. Hal saw Badenoch veer to avoid a still-kicking one, guided his own to the left of it and heard the beast's iron hoofs clatter off something – skull or helmet he did not know.

They were coming to a crease in the ground: the Pelstream, by God, Hal thought. Now he will have to come at bay . . .

It took him a moment to realize that Badenoch was not coming to a halt, but checking to a canter, turning and riding parallel to the steep-sided stream – looking for a narrow part, Hal realized. By God's Hook, he plans to leap it.

Badenoch suddenly spurred; Hal heard the horse squeal in pain, saw it surge and knew Badenoch had chosen his leaping point. He watched as the beast flung itself in an ungainly four-legged sprawl of jump, hit the far side, stumbled forward to safety and collapsed like a burst bag, spilling itself and the rider.

He cantered up and checked; the point was narrow, right enough, which was why all the fleeing Welsh archers had tried to use it. Hal had no idea how deep the narrow wedge of the Pelstream was – at least the height of a tall man – but it was choked to a bridge by bodies.

Hal saw Badenoch struggling on the ground, trying to free himself from a tangle of reins and realized what he had to do if he wanted to get to the man. Did he want it that badly? Kirkpatrick was dead . . . the thought burned him. *Mea culpa*, he voiced, savage with the loss and the horror at being the cause of it.

The horse could not leap the stream and would not step on the bodies, so Hal slithered off and put out one foot, only to draw it hastily back when he heard the farting gasp from the body. Dead air, he said savagely to himself. Only dead air . . .

He walked the bridge, three, four ungainly steps, no more, feeling the sickening roil of soft death, hearing the groans which might only have been the last gasp of the dead or men still dying.

Badenoch was up, weaving, sword at the guard and his eyes rat-desperate.

'Different,' Hal said coldly to him, 'when you face a knight who actually knows the ways of sword and lance, my wee lord.'

'You saved me,' Badenoch blurted out, his voice harsh and rasping in breath. 'The day my father was slain in Greyfriars.'

'I did,' Hal replied and then moved forward, de Bissot's sword arcing round. 'No good deed goes unpunished.'

Badenoch's sword stopped the blow, glissaded away and the echoes were lost in another growling roar of thunder. Hal realized the world had darkened, wondered if the battle had lasted so long that it was now night.

Doggedly, Badenoch gathered himself and came back, lashing right and left, sweeping blows that thrummed the air; Hal countered, hitting nothing. They circled like wary dogs.

'You could yield,' Badenoch offered suddenly. 'No shame in it. You are ower old for this, after all, and I will kill you if you do not, for all I owe you my life.'

'I own your life since that day – now I have come for my due,' Hal answered flatly and moved in as the wind hissed down on them, whirling up the tired, torn grass. Badenoch crouched, half turned and struck, the sword whicking the last flat of itself on to Hal's mittened fist; even through the maille he felt the blow of it, the numbing that spilled the sword from his grasp.

With a howl of triumph, Badenoch went for the killing strokes, but caught his gilded spurs and stumbled a little; Hal scuttled away, staggered over a body and made for a nearby spear, stuck point down in the hard ground.

He had no feeling in his right hand; he gripped with his left and wrenched, but the spear was buried deep and would not come loose. Behind him, he heard Badenoch closing in like a panting hound.

Hal lurched forward, still gripping the spear, so that it bent – but it still stuck fast. He let it go just as Badenoch rushed in, snarling – and the shaft sprang back and took the man in the chest and face, a smack like a hammer; he went flying backwards, his own sword spilling free.

Ahead, Hal saw a shield and made for it; a man with a shield had a weapon yet. He fumbled it up – and cursed, for the straps had been sheared and it was useless. Badenoch, back on his feet and his face a twisted mask of blood, sprang forward and wrenched the spear free.

Now it comes free, Hal thought bitterly. He lurched to one side as the point of the spear stabbed at him. He kicked out, hearing himself squeal like a horse.

The blow took Badenoch in the thigh, made him cry out and reel away. Then he hurled himself back into the fight, the spear flicking out like a snake's tongue; Hal spun, found the shaft under his right armpit and himself with his back to Badenoch; in a panic he gripped with his arm and heaved sideways, hoping to tear the spear from the knight's grasp, or spill him to the ground if he held on to it.

The shaft snapped, which came as a shock to them both. It cracked like an old marrow bone, so that Hal found himself with the last foot of wood and the wicked tip couched under his armpit like a silly lance.

Badenoch, left with four feet of splinted shaft, flung it down in disgust and hurled himself at Hal, all mailled fists and vengeance.

Hal whipped the shattered spearshaft from under his arm with his left hand and drove it into Badenoch's face. The man ran on to it like a charging bull, impaled himself through his open, snarling mouth and staggered on past for a few reeling steps before falling forward; Hal saw the bloody point burst from the back of the skull.

He stood for a long moment, and then something inside seemed to give up and he fell on to his knees, rolled to one side and, finally, on to his back, staring at the sky and listening to Badenoch's mailled feet kick wetly in his own blood.

Like his da, Hal remembered. He wanted to get up but could not move, only stare at the sky, which had turned bruised and ugly. It is all over, he thought dully. Badenoch is dead. Kirkpatrick . . . bigod, the world is slain this day.

The thunder rolled, sonorous as a bell.

He lay like that for what seemed an age, until the spatter of water made him blink. It grew and started to hiss like a nest of adders: rain, sheeting in a curtain which suddenly parted to reveal a limping grey figure who reached out a sodden hand to haul Hal to his feet.

'Bigod,' said Kirkpatrick. 'That was well done – but you should have let me end him in Greyfriars and saved the pair o' us all this bother.'

Goliath was dead. Thweng had not known when the horse had been hit, only the moment it had checked, coughed and started to sink, slowly, like a deflating bladder. He had time to kick free of it and drop with a jar to the ground, watched it fall to its knees and finally on to one side, blowing blood out of its nose; the arrow that had killed it was buried so deep, just to the rear of the girth, that only the span of peacock fletchings could be seen. A great spreading stain of blood soaked the trapper.

Welsh archers, Thweng thought bitterly, God curse them. That horse was worth more than fifty of those dark mountain dwarves put together . . .

Men flooded round him, splitting right and left, away from the sword-armed, mailled figure and his dying horse. Our foot, Thweng thought moodily, running like chooks; he hoped John and the others had managed to get away – and, with a surprising detachment, wondered if he would manage that himself.

He walked away from the horse, stepping over bodies. Archers had let loose here and felled a deal of Scots horse; there were little shaggy ponies down, kicking and squealing among the ragdoll shapes of men. Arrows littered all around, in beast and man and turf, broken, splintered and trampled – and one hit Goliath, he added bitterly, though there was no telling if it had been an accident or some vicious last Welsh swipe at the English.

A man rose up suddenly with a whoop of sucked-in air and Thweng took a grip of his sword as the man felt himself, as if in wonder at finding no injuries. Thweng saw the stained gambeson and the two roughly tacked strips of cloth in the shape of the St Andrew's cross on one breast. A Scot . . .

Dog Boy hauled himself up from the ruin of his horse, could not help but run his hands over his body, amazed that he had escaped the sleet of arrows.

He had thought he had done enough for this day when he had stopped chasing fleeing Englishmen – but then Jamie Douglas had come up, mounted and grinning, streaked and stained and joyous.

'Get yerself legged up on this, Aleysandir,' he ordered and Dog Boy, weary and sick of it all, saw the others and the extra garrons they had.

So he had hauled himself up and followed after them – chasing the King, he had been told – until the horse had squealed and veered and pitched him off. He did not know whether it had been hit or just so tired it had collapsed; he was only vaguely aware of the archers, but he was so exhausted himself that he did not struggle much when he fell.

Until now, when a tait of sense had come back to him and he'd heard someone coming. He did not want to lie there while some harridan with a dirk gralloched him, uncaring what side he belonged to.

Now he eyed the knight warily. He knew the markings of the man, though he could not recall the name – and then he saw a pile of nearby dead heave like a rise of marsh gas; a body rolled slackly away and a figure crawled out from the heap.

Thweng saw the man lever out from under bodies, rolling them to one side and climbing painfully to his knees. He raised a blood-spattered face and Thweng, with a shock, realized suddenly that he knew the man. An old Welsh archer . . .

Addaf stared from one to the other. He recognized Thweng by his heraldry and, with a shock, saw the dark, slim shape he was sure was Black Sir James Douglas.

373

'Kill him,' he croaked to Thweng, pointing at Dog Boy, who fumbled in his boot with a curse, only to realize he had given his spare dagger to Hob. Weaponless, he trembled and waited, wild-eyed and watching.

'It is the Black,' Addaf persisted and Thweng, knowing it was not, waved his sword wearily.

'We are all done with killing here,' he replied and sank down on one knee, feeling the weight of his armour suddenly drag at his sixty years. Addaf, confused and bewildered, angry at having been so careless of Y Crach as to have imagined him dead if not cowed, suddenly felt the sharp, stabbing lance of pain in his ribs and sat down in a squelch of bloody puddle, aware that he was probably dying and that nothing mattered, not even Y Crach's betrayal. We were all betrayed here, he thought.

They stayed that way for some time, it seemed to the three, surrounded by dead and dying, groans and cries for God and mothers, while the wind rose and the light turned sickly in the brightness of the day. Then the first thunder growled and brought heads up.

'Well,' said Thweng. 'It seems you have won this day, Scotchman. Have you a name?'

Dog Boy eyed the English knight, sure he knew the man and desperate to remember him.

'Aleysandir,' he said, and cocked a jaundiced eye at the wheezing Welsh archer lying in a tarn of his own blood. 'As daring as the Black Sir James, but better looking.'

Addaf flapped a weary hand in acknowledgement of his mistake, but it was a pallid gesture and Dog Boy saw the Welshman was nearly gone from the world. Addaf lay back, looking at the great slow wheel of the sky and thinking dreamily of his ma. There was a point when he passed out of the world but no one recognized it, not even himself.

Dog Boy eyed Thweng and then straightened a little, haughty as any earl.

'Do you yield, then?'

Sir Marmaduke barked out a short, harsh laugh.

'Not to you,' he replied and Dog Boy shrugged and pointed behind Sir Marmaduke.

'Is he more of a rank for you, then?'

Bruce had picked his way slowly through the great maggot carpet of dead and dying, riding in the wake of his leaping, howling, vengeful army, the huddle of horsemen with him so stunned by it, so overwhelmed by victory that they could not speak more than low, awed murmurs.

'We have won,' Keith kept saying.

We have won, Bruce thought and felt the divine glow of it. God made me to a Plan and I have made the Kingdom, out of the stones of these bodies and the mortar of their blood. Christ's Bones, what a slaughter . . .

The sheer scale of it was numbing, yet Bruce already felt it crushing him, felt the black chest of sins in his head creak at the seams with what it had to contain now. It would get worse, he knew, when the price for this victory became clear.

Ahead, he saw two figures, turning to face him. To his astonishment, he knew both – the Lothian man he had made his houndsman, the one called Dog Boy.

And Sir Marmaduke Thweng.

He levered himself off the horse, ignoring the warnings from Keith, and stumped across to face the knight.

'Sir M,' he said weakly.

'Sirrah,' Thweng replied. There was a pause and then they were wrapped in each other's arms before stumbling apart.

'I yield. You have won a great victory,' Thweng said, managing a wry twist of grin. 'I should now call you Your Grace the King, for it has been hard-earned.'

The King. Bruce nodded. He had taken the Crown and, at long last, made a Kingdom for it . . . yet, even now, he knew that it was not the end of anything, certainly not the English.

375

They might be skulking south, bewildered and beaten, but they would be back – unless Edward could be persuaded to give up his claims and end this war, it would rumble on . . .

Thunder rolled out and he looked up, half hoping, half afraid to see some holy sign. It was there, but it was clear that Malachy, as ever, had a cursed saintly hand in it.

Heaven parted and God and all His angels wept into the Bannock burn and the sightless eyes of the dead.

ISABEL

The town drones like a smacked byke; there has been a great
battle at Stirling and King Edward is fled. He came to Berwick,
having sailed to Bamburgh from Dunbar and ridden back up
to the town, to meet his escort lords who took the coast road.
I saw him, clattering into the bailey with no more than four
riders, but I could not say which one had been him, for they
all looked pinched and afraid, arriving drookit as gutter rats
in the lightning-split dark so no one would see them. Save
me, crept into my cage to peer down through the rain and
feeling, suddenly, more liberated than whichever of the dark,
wet shadows was the King. That was a fortnight since . . .
Constance came this day to say that now King Edward is
leaving, fleeing back to London before Berwick is proper
besieged. She was frightened and pale; Malise slithered in not
long after like a mottled spider and snarled at her to be gone;
poor wee nun, she had no courage for it and fled, weeping.
Then he fell on his knees and raised his face to me as if I
was Heaven itself, his mouth like a wet opening in a bog.
Christ Jesus, he moaned, who was conceived by the Holy
Spirit, born of the Virgin Mary, suffered, was crucified, died
and was buried – I know You. You touched Heaven and came
to Hell and cast out that which offended You. What You
loved, O Lord, You destroyed. I understand that.
There was more, so that it was clear that Badenoch was

377

dead and Malise had no more liege lord, nor living to be had, either from him or me. Now he has thrown me to the Hounds of God, who will need some witch to blame, to sacrifice as in darker times to older gods, to make sense of such a loss to the English.

O Lord, I am shamed and sorry to have so vexed You with myself. Give me leave to repent, for You shall know me well, soon enough.

CHAPTER SIXTEEN

Berwick
Octave of the Visitation, July 1314

He was in there, the King of England. Jamie said it twice so
that Hal would hear, though he was not sure if it had worked,
for the man gave no sign. Just kept staring across the mirk
of a sodden day at the faint grey streaks and worms of pallid
light that marked Berwick.

'Are we going for him then?' demanded Yabbing Andra,
and Horse Pyntle snotted rain and worse from his nose, which
was expressive enough.

'We are bliddy not,' Sweetmilk replied vehemently, and
turned uncertainly to the Black Sir James Douglas. 'That's the
right of it, is it not, yer honour?'

'That's the right of it,' agreed Jamie Douglas, clapping
Sweetmilk on his rain-sodden shoulder, hard enough to spurt
water. 'We are not here for the glory of snatching the son of
Longshanks at all.'

He paused for effect and lowered his voice to a mockingly
husked whisper.

'We are here, lads, for . . . love.'

We should not be here at all, Kirkpatrick told himself, on

a mad-headed fool's errand like this. But he kept it to himself, for there was no way of avoiding it and he owed the Herdmanston lord this much and more.

He eyed the man who stared unflinchingly into the grey mirk; if the Devil was here to give him it, Kirkpatrick thought, Hal Sientcler of Herdmanston would sell his immortal soul for the power to drag Isabel MacDuff out of her cage and to his side with his eyes alone.

He crossed himself for the thought and waited, sitting with the others in the dubious shelter of a copse of trees while the twilight drained the land of colour and the rain filled it with misery.

It had been raining since the evening of the battle, Kirkpatrick thought, a downpour that drowned what was left of the fields and ruined the last chance of a harvest. Livestock plootered in mud, promising hoof rot and murrains – famine was coming with the winter and it would be hard.

He muttered as much aloud, so that Jamie Douglas turned to him. Expecting the uncaring rasp of the Black's hatred of all things English, Kirkpatrick was surprised.

'Sair,' agreed James Douglas. 'The price of bread will be crippling. The poor always suffer worst.'

Hal, face pebbled and eyes burning, turned at last from trying to see her through the miles and mist. Kirkpatrick nodded and smiled, aware – as he had been since he had hauled Hal to his feet beside the body of Badenoch – that he had been responsible for the Lothian knight's crazed pursuit of that lord.

He had it that I was killed and that it had been his fault, Kirkpatrick thought. I was not and cannot – will never – reveal that I had just given up and lay there, waiting for Badenoch to kill me like a done-up heifer. Now I have the guilt of having driven Sir Hal to slaughter Badenoch, the man he stopped me killing once before – Christ's Blood, here's a tangle of sin and redemption that even God would have trouble unravelling.

It had been the last act of a bloody day, the stunning glory of it numbing yet. Such a victory, such a tumbling of great English lords to dust and ruin – aye, and death. The tallymen had been busy as fiddlers' elbows noting the names: the Earl of Gloucester, slain. Sir Robert Clifford, slain. Sir William Marshal, slain. Sir Giles d'Argentan, slain. Tiptoft, Vescy, Deyncourt, Beauchamp, Comyn – great names whose holders were all slain, brothers and cousins and nephews all.

Fifty of the great and good of England were no more than a nick in a hazel stick now, a notch the thickness of a palm for an earl, the breadth of a finger for a banneret, the width of a swollen barleycorn for a lesser knight.

Hundreds of hazel sticks – and not one sliver for any of the great slather of corpses, blanching in the wet, stripped naked so that their wounds showed red and puckered as hag's holes on the blue-white of their marbled skin. Thousands of them, Scots and English, Gascon, Hainaulter, Welsh, all left unrecorded so that, on the Scots side, folk could exult that only three had died: Sir William Airth, Sir William Vipond and, like justice from God, Sir Walter Ross, third son of the Earl of Ross.

Others had been more fortunate and survived to be ransomed, the greatest of them being Robert d'Umfraville, the Earl of Angus, and Humphrey de Bohun, Earl of Hereford, taken prisoner at Bothwell just when they thought themselves safe.

The de Bohuns particularly, Kirkpatrick knew, had been so dragged in the dust of Bruce's glory that you had to wonder how that family had so angered God: the Earl's nephew, Henry, killed like a battle sacrifice by Bruce himself; the Earl and his kinsman, Gilbert, taken prisoner to be used as a ransom bargain for the return of all the imprisoned Bruce women – sister, wife and daughter.

And Isabel MacDuff.

All we have to do is wait, Kirkpatrick thought, in the safe

and the dry while wee advocates arrange the business of it. By year's end, Isabel could be back at Hal's side and no risk in it at all. He had dared to argue that when he and Sir James and the King had considered the matter, with Hal waiting to be told whether he would be assisted to such a daring rescue.

Hal had not said a word – but the look Kirkpatrick had from the King would have stripped the gilt from a stone saint, so that he had given in with a wave of the hand.

'Sir Hal has waited long enough,' the King had declared.

'Isabel has waited long enough,' Hal corrected tersely. Which was a truth Kirkpatrick had not considered at all, so that it fell on him like a dropped brick; seven years, he had realized, in a cage on a wall, waiting for rescue. Aye – overdue indeed.

In the end, of course, Bruce had officially forbidden it. No one, especially Sir James Douglas, was to set as much as a toe on a Berwick wall. Truces had been arranged. There was his own sister and wife, the Queen, waiting to be released; matters were delicate and not to be plootered across with heavy feet.

Kirkpatrick had agreed while shooting Hal warning glances to stay quiet; he knew the Lothian lord would go anyway. He was sure Bruce knew that, too.

So, while Edward Bruce and Randolph stumbled down the muddy roads to Wark and out to Carlisle as the mailled fist, the King returned the bodies of Gloucester and Clifford – and the boiled bones of Humphrey de Bohun – with all due care and mercy, as the lambskin gauntlet. And turned a blind eye to Sir James Douglas, Kirkpatrick and Sir Hal of Herdmanston, riding off on their own towards Berwick with a knot of hard-eyed men.

The day dripped on, and then a rider flogged a sodden garron through the grey and skidded to a halt in a shower of clots.

'He is left,' Dog Boy declared, wiping his streaming face

while the steam came off him like haze. 'Headed out to Bamburgh and then York with a great escort against capture.'

Jamie's face brightened with the possibilities at once, but caught sight of Hal's own and shrugged, shamefaced, abandoning the glory that might have been.

'Well,' he said, 'Love it is then, though you can scarce blame me for thinking of scooping up such a prize as Edward of England.'

'Less risk in that,' Kirkpatrick growled morosely, but Dog Boy, shaking water from him, grinned into his damp-smoke mood.

'Would ye not risk the same for your own wummin, then?' he demanded. 'For love?'

Kirkpatrick gave him a jaundiced eye. He had a woman he would marry before too long and the bounty of that and the lands she brought was a glow in the core of him. He would risk much for that – but love? He had never considered love in the matter of getting wed and said so.

Dog Boy, bright with the joy of Bet's Meggy, little Bet and Hob, laughed at how the *nobiles* arranged such matters. Yet he had to agree with Kirkpatrick regarding the risk: he had watched the cavalcade quit Berwick, the hunched and smouldering King Edward in the centre of it, so there was a better chance of sneaking up the walls than if he had been there. A slight shift in risk, but welcome all the same and he said as much, to give heart to everyone.

'King Edward has been given the advice the Holy Father gave to the beggar,' Parcy Dodd answered and folk shifted expectantly, for a story was as warming as the fire they dared not light.

'I am half afraid to enquire,' Jamie Douglas said laconically and Parcy grinned his wide grin, the rain pearling on his nose.

'The Pope is visiting town,' he began, 'and all the people are turned out and dressed up in their best cloots, all lining the way from the gate, hoping for a personal blessing from the Holy Father. One stout burgher, a man of stature and local note, has put on his best fur-trimmed cloak and gold chain for the moment, for he is sure that sight will pause the Pope and that the Holy Father will bless him.'

'A bad plan,' Horse Pyntle grunted, 'for your clerical is a magpie for the shine and yon burgher will not, I suspect, own it long if he flaunts it at such a high heidyin.'

'Ah,' Parcy declared, as if he had been expecting that very point, 'but he is standing next to a beggar, a man with more stain and rag than cote and who smells like a privy on a hot day. The stout burgher thinks to impress His Holiness by handing such a man a coin at the crucial moment. Certes, as the Holy Father comes walking by, the burgher ostentatiously offers the coin, the beggar takes it, bites it with the one black tooth he has left and vanishes it into his rags. The Pope leans out of his litter then – and speaks softly to the beggar. The burgher is stunned; the Holy Father ignores him and passes on, having spoken only to the beggar.'

'Aye, well,' muttered Yabbing Andra, uneasy at Parcy's constant blasphemies, 'the Holy Father is more interested in the poor and feeble ones.'

'Just what the burgher thinks,' Parcy declared cheerfully, 'so he thrusts the rest of his bag of coin at the beggar and trades cloots with him. Then he sprints down the street – for certes, the crowd parts before a man who smells so badly – and flings himself almost into the path of the Pope's processing litter. Sure enough, the litter stops, the ringed hand beckons and the burgher proudly walks up to get the blessing he has worked and paid so dearly for.'

Parcy paused and grinned.

'Then he hears, hissed in his now flea-bitten ear: "I thought I told you to get yourself to Hell away from my path, you beggarly misbegotten pile of shite."'

There were a few loud barks of laughter, a lot of head-shaking and admiration for Parcy risking his soul with such a tale. But they were cheered by it, all the same, Jamie saw – and they would need such heart for what they intended.

'When it is darker, then,' Hal declared, capping the laughter like a candle snuffing flame.

They went back to sitting, dripping in the rain, and the Dog Boy thought of what he had learned: Berwick had been put in the charge of Sir Aymer de Valence, Earl of Pembroke. The knight with stripes and little red birds, Dog Boy recalled, whom I almost tumbled off his fancy horse.

He is like snot on your fingers, de Valence said to himself. You think you have got rid of it and then, the Lord alone knows how, it appears again, on the other hand. He looked at the Dominican and wished him as gone as the Italian abbot and the King, both ridden off to the safety of the south.

Leaving me, he added bitterly to himself, with the ruin of it.

And it was a ruin. What was left of the army straggled south by a dozen different routes, too fearful of what snarled at their heels even to find time for loot and rape, too sodden to burn anything. The lords who were left would be of no help in bringing them to order; those who were mounted had long since vanished and those unhorsed were either already dead or taken.

The vellum rolls lay like white mourning candles on the table in front of him, a litany of lost lives and shattered hopes painstakingly scraped out by the clericals. Even now they were not complete; new revelations of the fate of the barons who had fought at Stirling were still being discovered.

One at least was accounted for and de Valence was soured to his belly at what he would have to tell his sister, Joan. Your son, the young lord of Badenoch, is not coming home – slain by the same God-damned Scotch rebels who murdered your husband.

Faced with that, the canting cadaver that was Jean de

385

Beaune, piously name-changed to Brother Jacobus, was a misery de Valence could have done without, but the matter the Dominican had thrown at him would not be lightly dismissed. Yet de Valence vowed he would scourge the Cathar-hunting little prelate back to Carcassonne if he had to wield the whip himself.

'The lady Isabel,' he persisted, 'is within the King's Peace.'

More so now than ever, he said to himself, for she could easily become a counter in the game of ransom.

'She has been accused,' Jacobus growled. 'You shall not suffer a witch to live.'

'The accuser is more of a Devil's spawn than the lady in question,' de Valence spat back. 'Malise Bellejambe has been the creature of the Comyn for as long as I can remember, God forgive my kin for it. I know him well enough for he came to me only recently, hoping to slither his way into my patronage, and I sent him away as I would the serpent in Eden.'

'God be praised,' Brother Jacobus intoned at this last, crossing himself piously.

'For ever and ever,' de Valence answered by rote. 'Now this Malise seeks your patronage – is there not a reward for exposing a witch? Apart from the love of Christ and Mother Church?'

'You stand in the path of the Inquisition,' the Dominican persisted.

'I obey my king,' de Valence replied savagely, weary of the whole business. He saw his clerks hovering, arms full of rolls that almost certainly continued the litany of ruin for his king's cause.

'She is a heretic.'

'You have proof? Other than the word of a disenfranchised, dismayed worm like Bellejambe?'

'I . . . that is . . .'

'You mean no,' de Valence interrupted roughly, and waved

a hand so that the candles guttered in the wind of its passage. 'Get you gone, Brother.'

'I will investigate further . . .'

De Valence glared at the Dominican.

'You will not go against the King's Peace. Three miles, three furlongs and three acre-breadths, nine feet, nine palms and three barleycorns – within that, Brother, Lady Isabel MacDuff is inviolate until the King himself decides her fate.'

'Or God,' Brother Jacobus persisted. 'You may find that the good folk of this town consider the Lord's Will takes precedence over suffering a witch to live in the King's Peace.'

De Valence's ravaged hawk of a face made Jacobus recoil a little.

'Should the good folk of this town voice this opinion,' de Valence said, soft as a blade slice on skin, 'I will know where to look for the cause. Fomenting discord and riot in a town under my command is treason, Dominican, and I have been given the writ of Law here.'

He leaned forward a little, the candlelight turning his face to a twisted mask of shadows.

'Break it, Brother, and you will discover that, for all there is no torture permitted in England, your Inquisition is a squalling baby compared with what I can inflict on those who thwart the King's writ. Pleading a knowledge of Latin will not help you.'

For a moment, they were locked in stares, and then Brother Jacobus turned on his heel and swung away. De Valence waited until he was almost at the door, the trailing wind of his fury making the sconces dance madly, before calling out.

'Jacobus.'

The Dominican whirled, his face a scowl.

'You forget your station.'

The prelate's face flushed so that the veins stood out, proud as corded rope. Then he bowed.

'My lord earl.'

'You may leave.'

The Dominican's face was a beautiful thing and de Valence took some vicious comfort from it before he turned from the closed door into the bustle of the clerks. For all that, he knew that Isabel MacDuff was in danger. If the game of kings being played out above their heads did not include her as a vital piece, then she would fall to the flames.

The clerks moved in with their blizzard of bad news in vellum and the room seemed suddenly stifling, every candle flame a sear. De Valence moved to the shuttered slit of window and pulled them open, so that the night breeze, sodden with damp, snaked in to shiver the sconces.

He stood for a moment, hearing the muffled noises of the castle settling for another night, saw the red eye of brazier coals flaring in the breeze and the figures moving past it, no more than shadows. A wall guard shifted into the lee of a merlon and left his dog to trot the walkway; de Valence felt a spasm of irritation at this slackness, just because the King had quit the place.

Then, however, he heard the dog bark and was reassured: a good dog more than made up for a bad guard.

Out in the cloaking dark, Jamie Douglas gave a muffled curse at the sound. No one needed reminding of the last time the Scots had attempted to stealth their way up the walls of Berwick's fortress – foiled by a barking dog.

'It will be the same one,' Parcy Dodd muttered miserably. 'Aulder by a bit and wiser than ever.'

'Given Fair Days and petted,' Dog Boy agreed softly, his grin white in the dark. 'Fat with the finest for having saved an entire wee town.'

'I dinna see any cheer in this revelation,' muttered Sweetmilk.

'Never fash,' Dog Boy answered. 'Just make sure you move gentle as spider silk and get Sim Craw's marvel up under the wall without discovery. Leave the wee beastie to me – tonight I am more Dog Boy than Aleysandir.'

Hal heard the mention of Sim Craw and watched Sweetmilk scuttle into the dark, half-crouched and hunchbacked under the rolled-up ladder. As much as the arbalest, that ladder was Sim's legacy, he thought to himself, as the ache of loss settled in him again, bone-deep. He thought of Sim then, turning slowly in the bladderwrack and weed, his face wrapped in the wisps of his own white hair . . .

The slap of a hand on his shoulder wrenched him from the sorrow into the face of Jamie Douglas, the expression on it a large, silent question. Hal shrugged it off and went ahead, following Kirkpatrick, Dog Boy and Sweetmilk; somewhere, Parcy Dodd and Horse Pyntle held the horses.

'We were kine the last time we did this,' Jamie muttered, 'which let us get close to the walls.'

Not now, Hal thought. A cow this close to Berwick and still uneaten would excite more interest than not, while stumbling people, seeming starved and shut out from safety by *couvre-feu* and caution, were all too common in these times.

It took them a long time in the dark and wet, all the same, as they crept slowly to the foot of the mound, slipping into the wet ditch and up out the far side, shivering and cold. They carried no swords, only long dirks, and wore no armour other than jacks – though Jamie's had metal plates sewn into the padding, rather than just straw stuffing.

The only ones burdened were Sweetmilk with the ladder and Dog Boy with the long pike-spear – though Kirkpatrick eyed Hal's slung latchbow with a jaundiced stare. It had been Sim's and he had brought it more for remembrance than use, Kirkpatrick thought. Unnecessary and risky, he added sourly to himself as he climbed painfully up the castle mound. Above them the White Wall loomed ghostly in the dark.

Sweetmilk, panting like a mating bull, scrambled up the mound almost on his hands and knees with the Dog Boy close behind and everyone else trying to avoid the twenty-foot spear he carried low to the ground.

389

At the foot of the wall, Sweetmilk shed his load as silently as he could and then leaned his back to the ashlar, his face gleaming sweatily in the dark. He cupped his hands and Dog Boy, the spear notched into the neat socket at the top of the rolled ladder, stepped into the stirrup of them, then up on to Sweetmilk's shoulders. The man grunted and buckled a little, so that the others held their breath; then he straightened and braced, grinning.

Dog Boy, perched on Sweetmilk, raised the spear high, straining against the tipping weight of the ladder, until the padded prongs slid softly over the crenellation. Slowly he withdrew the spear and passed it back down to the hands of Hal, who disposed of it in the grass. Wiping his lips with the back of one hand, Dog Boy tugged gently on the length of cord, heard the soft click of release and then the ladder pattered down the wall like a cat after mice.

Almost before it had cascaded on to the muffled curses of Sweetmilk, Dog Boy had tugged a test on it and then was up it like a rat up a spital drain.

He was almost at the top when he heard the growl and froze. Now came the hardest task. . .

He reached into the dangle of his scrip, broke off a piece of what was there and tossed it up over the merlon to the walkway. The growl stopped; Dog Boy climbed until his head was up above the level and dog and man stared at each other in the dripping mirk. It growled.

Dog Boy threw more, mumuring gently. The dog snapped it up and whined uneasily; the tail flickered. Dog Boy climbed up to waist height and held out his hand, so that the animal had to creep close for the prize – which it did.

'Swef, swef,' Dog Boy soothed and the dog whined and let him come over to feed another delicious morsel. Dog Boy sat in the dark-shadowed lee of the merlon and fed the last to the dog, fondling its ears while it ate, tail wagging.

Is a dog bound by a blood pudding? It is, Dog Boy thought

sadly, caressing the animal and drawing it close while it licked his fingers and whined, tail working furiously. Bound and tied by it, especially if it had tasted such before, when it was fêted.

But folk are fickle and forgetful, he thought, slowly, gently, drawing his knife. That was then and this is now and the wee beastie craves what once it enjoyed.

It does not deserve this, he added sorrowfully, feeling the blade of the knife cold as poor charity. The animal gave a choke, no more, as voice and life were cut from it, and before it could take its last wheeze of breath, Dog Boy had it by the scruff of the neck while its heart pumped thickly out of the gaping throat, trailing like ribbons as he threw it over the wall.

Below, the rush and thump of it falling made everyone jump and Sweetmilk, spattered with blood, had Jamie's hand clamped on his mouth to muffle the curses.

'Gardyloo,' Jamie growled. 'That will be our signal.'

'Not yours,' Hal replied flatly. 'You are forbidden to set foot on the wall . . .'

'Away with you,' Jamie said, releasing Sweetmilk so suddenly that the man stumbled. 'I did not come to this jig to stand at one side and admire you lassies.'

Hal looked from him to Kirkpatrick, but any help he sought from there was stillborn with the man's weary shrug.

They started up the ladder.

Hal led the way, panting and sweated by the time he reached the top. Wet inside and out, he thought laconically as he heaved himself as quietly as he could over the crenellation. The misery of Dog Boy's face brought him up short and he stared as the man looked bitterly at his bloody palms and then wiped them on his tunic.

'I am ill named,' he growled to Hal. 'I am the curse of dogs. Every one I meet dies.'

Never mind the men – aye, and women, too – that have regretted bumping into you, Hal thought, but he held his tongue in his teeth and merely patted Dog Boy on his sodden shoulder, glancing up and down the length of gleaming, empty walkway as he did so.

A distant brazier glowed to his left; to the other side was the bulk of a tower, one of the nine Berwick's fortress possessed and the one they wanted: the Hog Tower. Below, the bailey courtyard flickered in the dancing shadows from stray lights, pale as corpses in the sea-haar – forge, brewhouse, bakehouse, Hal recognized. The dark mass would be the stables, where no light was permitted. No one moved.

Jamie Douglas slithered to his side and grinned, before wiping his streaming face.

'Bigod,' he hissed. 'I should have brought more men. We could capture it easy.'

'We could not,' Hal flung back at him. 'We could try and capture it and it would be hard and bloody. It would also ruin any rescue. Mind that, Sir James, when your heid is bursting with glory.'

'In and out,' added a panting voice as Kirkpatrick came up alongside them, 'quiet and quick.'

He beamed mirthlessly at Jamie Douglas.

'Like you were taking the favour of someone else's wife,' he added.

'You might have thought of another way to put that,' Hal glowered back at him and Kirkpatrick acknowledged his lack of tact with an apologetic wave.

'Aye, weel – the husband is long deid, Devil take him . . .'

'Whisht, the lot of you.'

Dog Boy's glare froze them all and they obeyed him, regardless of station and suddenly, shockingly, aware of where they were perched. Like eggs on a high ledge, Hal thought, and cackling like gannets.

'Bide here,' he declared to Jamie, who scowled and looked about to protest.

'We need to protect the way out,' Hal pointed out. Besides,

he added to himself, you should not be here at all and your lust for glory and your bloody-handed temper will carry you away when we least need it.

Jamie, unused to taking orders from the likes of Hal, looked about to protest and Dog Boy thrust himself into the path of it.

'I will also stay,' he announced, 'to guard our way to safety.'

Jamie, suddenly realizing that this was not his quest and given a suitable task of bravery and honour, nodded and grinned. With a brief look of raised-eyebrow relief, Kirkpatrick passed Hal and led the way towards the Hog Tower, skulking along the walkway, pressed to the crenellations.

There was a door and he imagined it would be shut and barred, which was the way if the castle was guarded, all perjink and proper. He tested it, heard the bar behind it clunk softly in the pins and did not know how they would get it open. He turned to say so to Hal, found that man's face turned up and pebbling with moonlit rain.

Hal stared up at the cage, clamped like a barnacle to the outside of the tower. She was there, the thickness of a wall, a few long strides away . . .

Kirkpatrick saw it, too, and blinked the rainmist off his eyebrows.

'A quick and strong young man', he hissed, 'could be up on that and inside in no time.'

It took a moment for Sweetmilk to realize Kirkpatrick was staring at him and he blenched when he did so.

'Aye, right,' he whispered back scornfully. 'In through the door it does not have, for what would be the point of that on the outside of a cage hung a long drop from the ground?'

'It has a wee slanty half-roof,' Kirkpatrick pointed out, 'to shed the rain. With wooden shingles, easily removed. The bars, too, are wooden – ye might snap yer way in.'

Sweetmilk eyed the half-roof, no more than a ledge to shoot rain into the courtyard below, and then the wrist-thick timber grill of the cage. He looked at Hal and saw the misery there, the rain like tears; he does not want to tell me to do something so foolish, Sweetmilk thought. But he wants his woman free.

All folk's plans for the best seem to involve me putting myself in the hardest places, he thought, moving to the wet rock of the tower and looking for handholds. Well, I came through the bloody horror at Stirling, so I will come through this also. He fumbled the dirk into his belt, ignoring Kirkpatrick's advice to take it in his teeth. An idiot would suggest that, he wanted to say, for all it does is make you look like a red murderer and put cuts on your tongue and lips.

He felt between the weathered mortar of the stones for crevices and nicks and little ledges. Christ's Wounds, this would not be easy.

Hal watched him swing up and out; he held his breath, seeing that Sweetmilk had removed his shoes and tied them round his neck. Clever – slick-smooth leather soles were no help at all and Sweetmilk's shoes were more status than necessity for a man with such horned and calloused bare feet.

As if to mock them, the rain started in earnest, a hissing curtain that shrouded everything to a few feet and sent rivulets and streams coursing down between the stones of the tower. Sweetmilk, arms and feet screaming in strained agony, reached up one wobbling hand and grasped the underside supports of the cage.

For a moment he swung free, dangling by one hand like a limp banner while everyone held their breath. Then he swung up the other hand and slapped it on to the timber. Slowly, laboriously, he drew himself up and then hung on the outside of the cage, a grey figure in the misting rain.

'Bigod,' Kirkpatrick declared admiringly, 'he climbs like a babery ape.'

'He will fall like a bliddy stone,' Hal muttered.

Then the bar clunked out of the pins and and the door started to open outwards. Kirkpatrick, swift as shadow, moved into the swinging lee of it while Hal, caught like a thief in a larder, could only crouch and freeze, the rain dropping in his dry, open mouth, looking up into the shrouded, murderous stare of Sweetmilk, who clung to the outside of the cage, not daring to move.

A man shouldered through the open doorway, cloak shrouding his head and shoulders, unlacing his braies and hunched up against the rain so that he saw only the tops of his own shoes.

'Dinna loit on anyone,' a voice called out from behind him and the man, head down and drawn in, cursed and stood between the merlons, fumbling out his prick.

'No sensible soul is abroad on a night like this,' he growled back, and grunted as his stream joined the rain. There was a moment, a long moment, when he stood and emptied himself, enjoying the feel and wishing it would hurry – he would have gone into the Witch's cell and used her pot if it had not been for the sleeper across her door. That and the fact that she was called the Witch, of course.

He shivered at the thought. Fine-looking woman, mark ye, for all her age . . . He turned sideways and stared into the face of a rainsoaked man, crouching like a hare on the walkway where he should not have been. The man grinned a sickly grin, his hair plastered wetly down his face in pewter daggers.

'Who the f—'

He was cut off, mid-flow, from speech, piss and life as Kirkpatrick took a step from the shadows and shoved.

'Gardyloo,' he muttered as the man fell off the wall, his last curse trailing behind him as he whirled his arms and legs in a futile dance in the air. There was a distant thud.

Hal was already past them both, into the dark of the tower. Stairs, circling up and down; Hal went up, to where a light flickered.

'Hurry up and close the door, else the candle will go out.'

The voice was booming loud in the enclosed space and Hal froze; then he edged up and round until he could peer over the last edge of the floor level above. The man sitting at the table, idly working at a leather strap, stared straight back at him, astonished.

They sprang for one another at the same time and Hal's wet soles slipped, so that he fell on the last part of the stair. Should have hung my shoes round my neck, like Sweetmilk, he thought wildly, and had to fall back a few steps as the man came down at him, sword out.

Disadvantaged in every way, Hal thought, armed only with a knife, below a man with a longer weapon on a spiralling stair designed to suit him and not me. Sparks flew as the man struck and missed; Hal saw him glance wildly over his shoulder, saw the iron rod dangling from a hook, waiting to be struck like a ringing bell.

The man slashed once more and sprang back, heading for the alarm iron; Hal was after him, stumbling, stabbing wildly. He felt the blow up his arm, the grate of it on bone and the man gave a sharp cry and fell, slamming face-first on to the table even as he groped for a soothing grasp on his pinked heel. Hal leaped on him, heard the air drive out with a choking gasp and battered his own head on the table so that it whirled with bright light and stars.

Dazed, he rolled free, blood in his mouth, and felt the man scrabble up – and a dark shape moved past him like a wind from a grave; the man yelped as Kirkpatrick's arm snaked round his neck and drew it back. The dagger gleamed in the guttering candle flame like a basilisk eye before the man's throat smothered the wink of it.

'Mak' siccar,' Kirkpatrick muttered and held the kicking man until the breath left him; there was blood everywhere, spattering in pats as the man struggled his last.

Hal rolled on to all fours, spitting, to see Kirkpatrick wiping his bloody hand on the man's tunic, following it up with the dagger; his entire sleeve was sodden with gore.

'Aye til the fore,' he growled and Hal, blinking the last of his daze away, climbed wearily to his feet and started up the stairs, Kirkpatrick behind.

The shape was wraithed and black, hidden in the shadows and would have clattered the pair of them back down the stairs if a sharp warning voice had not called out.

'Look out for her.'

Hal saw the black shroud of nun rush from the shadows and had time to stick out a fist so that the woman, already starting to shriek, ran her face on to the ram of it. Her scream choked off into a grunt, her legs flew out from under her and she clattered limply to the flags at the foot of the door.

That voice, Hal thought. It is her.

The door was barred from the outside and he lifted it easily and wrenched it open.

She saw the dark shape and felt her heart catch in her throat. There was so little light that he was all planes and shadows, might have been anyone – but she knew it was him. Hal. At last . . .

She was not ready for it, had always seen this moment in her mind as something much different, with her in barbette and sewn-sleeved gown, her face immaculate, her hair glowing like autumn bracken. Sitting in her little room with her hands in her lap, all composed beauty.

Not rousted from her bed, with straw in the greying raggle of her hair and barely dressed at all . . .

'Lamb.'

The old term flung all that away like shredding mist and he took a step to where a shard of flitting moonlight sliced across his face. Lined, grey-bearded, even in a moonlight never kind to colour, but with the eyes she remembered, focused like flames on her.

'Am I so changed?' he asked and she heard the uncertainty,

397

the tremble, and the inside of her melted with knowing that he felt exactly the same as she.

'I would know my heart's delight anywhere,' she managed and then they clung, fierce as tigers. She tasted iron and salt on his lips – blood, she realized.

'*Estat ai en greu cossirier, per un cavallier q'ai agut,*' he said, husky and muffled into the top of her head and she smiled. 'I was plunged into deep distress, by a knight who wooed me' . . . the words, in *langue d'oc*, belonged to the famed troubairitz the Countess of Dia and Hal and Isabel had played this game of line and line about before, when they and the world were younger and each moment almost as precious as this.

'*Eu l'autrei mon cor e m'amor, mon sen, mos huoills e ma vida,*' she replied and looked up at him, a smile blurred by tears. 'To him I give my heart and love, my reason, eyes and life.'

'Bigod, be done with sucking kisses aff her and find a way to get me in . . .'

Isabel whirled, startled at a voice where none should be and saw the black shape clinging to the outside of her cage, outlined in rain.

'Sweetmilk,' Hal growled, and called out to the man, his voice hoarse and low: 'Break the roof tiles, man, and keep yer voice down.'

Cursing, Sweetmilk clung with one hand and worried the slick, stiff wooden tiles with the other; one came free with a crack and he forced it between the grilled bars of the cage, not wanting to clatter it like an alarm iron into the bailey. Then he stopped, craned his head to see and then back to where Hal and Isabel held each other.

'Jamie and Dog Boy are discovered.'

He came along the walkway through the rainmist, making kissing sounds and cursing between wheedles, wrenched from the comfort and warmth of his distantly glowing brazier and makeshift shelter. Dog Boy knew it was the owner of the

398

hound he had throat-cut, wondering where his wee guard pet had got to. He shook his head, more at the bad cess of the dog's revenge than to get the water out of his eyes.

Beside him, Jamie crouched, balanced on the balls of his feet; in three more steps they would be seen.

Jamie darted forward, lunging out of the shrouding water in the hope that surprise would conquer all – but the guard was a good man and trained well enough that the spear he was holding in one fist came down and level before he had even registered who or what was coming at him.

Jamie, armed only with a long dirk, skidded to a halt, fell backwards and scrabbled upright; for a long moment they stared at each other, the guard with water dripping off the rim of his iron hat, studded jack soaked black, the spear pearling water from shaft and tip.

Then Dog Boy came up and the man blinked out of the numbing shock, opened his dry mouth and bellowed.

'Ware afore. Ware afore.'

'Christ and His bliddy saints . . .' Jamie hissed and threw the dirk. It whirled, struck the man in the face haft first and sent him staggering. Dog Boy, with a grim grunt, hurled forward and rammed the man to the wet walkway; the spear flew free, rolled off the edge and clattered noisily on to the cobbles below.

The guard struggled and spat and cursed, but Jamie was on him now too and helped pin one arm and a leg, leaving Dog Boy, fighting the mad, fluttering panic of the man, to free up his dagger hand and drive the weapon into the man's ear, the most vulnerable spot.

For a moment he was years back, leaping on the back of a man fighting the Bruce – and winning – in a dark corridor of a leper house. He had knifed into an ear then, too, felt the same gush of blood over his hand, so hot he was amazed it did not scald him . . .

Panting, slick with blood and rain, the three of them wrestled and grunted and gasped until, at last, one kicked frantically and then was still. Jamie, dashing rain from his eyes, grinned and got to his hands and knees, was about to say how Dame Fortune was smiling when the bitch betrayed them with the iron clang of an alarm.

Dog Boy looked at the cage, where Sweetmilk clung like a barnacle, then to where men were spilling out of butter-yellow doorways below and up the stone stairs, more coming along the ramparts so that they would pass through the Hog Tower and along to where the ladder snaked to safety. There was no way he or Jamie could stop them.

'Away,' Jamie declared, clapping Dog Boy on the shoulder and half dragging him to his feet. 'Or we are taken.'

'We cannot leave them,' Dog Boy spat and Jamie whirled him until they were face to face.

'Too late, Aleysandir. All we can do is give them the best chance of escaping on their own.'

Dog Boy did not see it. If the guards already spilling up to the Hog Tower passed through it they would send some up one level, to check on the prisoner. When they did, all would be lost for the trapped Hal and Isabel, Kirkpatrick and Sweetmilk.

Jamie saw all that in the Dog Boy's face. He grinned and sprang along the walkway towards the guards, spreading his arms wide and bawling like a rutting stag.

'A Douglas. A Douglas. The Black is here. Come ahead if you think yourselves warriors.'

Even as he sprinted for the ladder, two steps behind Jamie, Dog Boy knew that the guards were elbowing each other to get through the door of the Hog Tower, desperate to close with the legendary Black Douglas, to capture or kill him, for ransom or reward. All of them, Dog Boy thought with a savage moment of exultation as he slid down the ladder, his palms and fingers scorching.

Hal and Isabel clung to each other, breath pinched off. Kirkpatrick, half-crouched and with his knife out, looked from their gleaming faces to the dark shape of Sweetmilk, hanging on to the outside bars of the cage. It was so quiet Kirkpatrick could hear the hiss of the rain – and the loud shouts of 'A Douglas'.

Clever Sir Jamie, he thought as the thunderous clatter of men below spilled through from one walkway to the next, too eager to think; the throat-cut body of the guard below only spurred them on to more vengeance.

There were loud shouts – but no one came up. Everyone clattered on through, bawling loudly about the castle in danger from the Black Douglas. They would be balked at pursuit, all the same, for the White Wall had a postern gate at the foot of a set of steps known as the Breakneck Stairs, with good reason. The only other way was to follow the Black down his own ladder in the dark.

'We must go,' he hissed and Hal looked, agonized, at Sweetmilk. He is doomed, Kirkpatrick wanted to say, but the nun groaned and focused all attention on her.

'Strip her.'

Isabel moved swiftly on her own advice, while the others gawped for a moment, before helping her. It took hardly a moment to pull off the nun's outer habit and scapular, then Isabel had Hal and Kirkpatrick drag the woman into the cell. She came round as Isabel's face came out of the scapular and they looked at each other, the nun round-eyed with astonishment; her mouth opened as if to scream.

'I would not do that, Sister Alise,' Isabel said and looked to where Kirkpatrick stood with the dagger in his fist. The nun's eyes went huge and round with fear, and then Isabel spoke to Kirkpatrick.

'I would not like to hear that she had died,' she said coldly. 'A wad in her mouth, tied with a bit of her habit cord, will suffice. Her wrists and ankles too, I think.'

Kirkpatrick obeyed her and Alise was trussed and staring, snoring through her damaged nose.

'How the world turns, Sister,' Isabel said, her gentle voice no less of a scathe than a hot iron. 'If you had not contrived to have Constance kept from me, out of spite, it would be her across my door and not you. Malise will not be pleased – his power may have been removed, but his hate is not and he will visit it on you. It seems that you may burn in Hell before I do.'

'Time we were away,' Kirkpatrick interrupted and Hal stared miserably out at Sweetmilk, who pressed his face close to the bars and grinned a wet, wan farewell.

'On yer way, lords. I will scrauchle free of this, dinna fret.'

'Down to the bailey and out the gate,' Isabel declared, shoving Hal out of the tower cell. 'A nun and her braw escorts, headed back to her convent and away from all this Godless trouble.'

'Bigod,' Kirkpatrick declared admiringly, 'you can strop your wits when you walk with your ladyship and no mistake.'

They slithered like dancing shadows down to the level where the guard lay, down the spiral of stairs further still; somewhere beyond they heard men cursing and picking their way carefully down the worn-smooth, steeply pitched Breakneck Stairs.

At the foot of the tower, Hal led the way out into the bailey, walking smartly, but more casually than his thundering heart; behind came Isabel, hands folded piously in the sleeves, scapular hood drawn up against the rain and to hide her face. Kirkpatrick, at the tail end, saw the great gates of the castle start to close, and Isabel called out sharply to let her and her escort through. The gate commander, a long-time garrison resident, looked at the black-shadowed Bride of Christ and shook his head.

'Sorry, Sister, while the alarum is up, the yett is shut and the bridge raised as well in a meenit. You mun wait.'

The tile clattered at his feet and made them all leap away.

from it, looking round wildly. Above, Sweetmilk swung and capered and launched another so that the guards scattered. Someone yelled to fetch a latchbow and the gate commander, squinting up through the rain with a face like bad whey, crossed himself. It was an imp of Satan, for sure – Christ's Wounds, this was a night when Hell had unlatched its door . . .

A man ran up with a crossbow spanned, slid in a leather-fletched bolt, aimed and shot. Just as he did so, the gate commander remembered the nun and turned to warn her to get to safety – but she was gone.

Then the body fell, a whirl of arms and legs crashing to the cobbles with a sickening wet thud; the gate commander was disappointed to see that it was no imp at all, just a man with his face twisted in agony and his head leaking into the gutter like a broken egg.

Hal knew Sweetmilk was dead and the sour sick of it dogged his heels as he wraithed through the last crack of the gate and across the bridge, which trembled and creaked under the raising windlass even as they scurried.

'He saw we were shut in and contrived to help,' he muttered. 'God forgive us, he could never have survived the fall.'

Kirkpatrick, feral eyes flicking this way and that as they moved along the lee of buildings, growled back that the bolt would have killed him before that; it was meant as a soothe but did not balm the loss much. Isabel snapped the glare between them.

'Best we do not stand here like a set mill, for I am resolved never to go back in that cage.'

Hal blinked the rain from his face, felt it scamper, erratic as running mice, down through his collar and back. She never would, he vowed, for he would die before he let it happen and, when he said it, had back the glow of a smile and a kiss on his wet cheek.

The streets were dark – they had called *couvre-feu* hours before – but not empty; the place was stuffed with the debris of war, the sour wash of those flung out of their old lives and forced to run for the dubious shelter of Berwick, with nothing more than hope to cling to.

Huddled in doorways and up covered wynds, soaked and starving, they made a mockery of the orders that were supposed to keep folk indoors, by law of the Governor. Too miserable even for the oblivion of sleep, they stretched pale hands out of the shadows: 'Alms, for the love of Christ.'

'Here is aid for us,' Kirkpatrick voiced. 'A nun, delivering succour to the poor, with two braw lads to keep her from harm . . .'

'Until the cry is raised and Alise found like a goose trussed for a Yule table,' Isabel answered. 'Then two men and a nun will be all they look for.' She looked pointedly at Hal and added: 'One with a bloody great crossbow slung on his back.'

'It was Sim Craw's,' he answered and she heard the bleak in his voice, knew it for what it was and brought one hand to her mouth as if to choke the misery that wanted to spill from it. Sim. Gone. There was no time for the tale of it, but she knew the truth and simply nodded silence on the matter of the crossbow.

They moved as swiftly as they dared, away from the brooding bulk of the castle, pausing now and then like mice on a dark larder floor when they saw the lambent sputter of torches that marked the Watch on their rounds.

'Dog Boy did this,' Isabel said suddenly, sinking into the lee of a rough wall. 'I saw him when he came here and heard the alarm raised later – yet he escaped.'

'Well minded,' Hal said admiringly. 'He did and was raised in station for his daring. The way he told the tale involved rooftops and running.'

He was half our ages, Kirkpatrick wanted to add but did not.

'How did he get out?' Isabel persisted patiently and Hal, nodding, frowned and thought.

404

'The Briggate.'

The distant clanging of the alarm iron brought their heads up, like stags hearing a baying. There was shouting.

'Shut fast now,' Kirkpatrick mourned bitterly.

They went on all the same, walked round a corner and into four men of the Watch. They knew nothing yet and Isabel was on the point of saying so when Kirkpatrick, panicked, gave a sharp yelp like a dog. Hal saw the hackles of the Watch come up, already bristled by the alarm.

'Run,' he said.

They ran, she gathering up her wet habit and looping it through her belt as she went, making a pair of fat breeches to the knee so her legs moved more freely. They went down streets and up alleys like gimlets through butter, half stumbling over the cursing sleepers seeking the shelter of the narrowest of places, where the houses almost came together like an arch against the rain.

Up steps, over courts, and Kirkpatrick, turning to tumble a water-sodden butt in the path of their pursuers, was stunned to hear her laugh and Hal's answering wild cry of 'gardyloo'. Like bliddy weans, he thought bitterly, with no idea of the dangers here.

Panting, drenched, they paused to gasp in air and Hal clung to Isabel, who grinned back at him from her pearled face. The warp has found the weft, he thought, the song the throat. No matter what happens now I am as happy as when the sun first found shiny water and I know it is the same for her.

They moved on, at a gentler trot now, burst into a wynd and shrank back from fresh rush lights, mounted on a cart. Behind, the Watch flames bobbed – one less, Hal noted with grim satisfaction – and circled in confusion.

There was a smell here, a stink they all knew well, and Isabel covered her nose, while Hal and Kirkpatrick fell into the old trick of it, breathing through their open mouth.

The dead were here.

There were a heap of them. Brought and dumped, they were the ones too weak from hunger or disease to stay in this world any longer. Two men in rough sack overtunics worked with grunts under the poor light of damp torches to load them on the cart.

Kirkpatrick looked at Hal.

'They will not be taking them to anywhere inside Berwick,' he said pointedly and Hal, after a pause, nodded and drew out his dagger. Isabel laid a hand on his arm and strolled forward, folding her hands into her nun's tunic, hearing Hal and Kirkpatrick slide sideways into the dark.

The two men paused and looked up, saw what it was and waited deferentially. One even hauled his rough hood from his head.

'Sister,' the taller of the pair said. 'Ye are ower late to bring succour to these.'

There was bitterness there, but whether at convent charity or his own condition at having to manhandle the nuns' failure was a mystery; his comrade nudged him sharply for his cheek.

'I am sorry for it,' Isabel said piously. 'Right sorry for this and everything else that will happen.'

The first man shuffled, made ashamed by the vehemence of her words.

'Ye cannot tak' the weight of God's judgement all on yerself, Sister,' he said.

'I am glad you feel so,' Isabel answered. 'And so doubly sorry for this.'

They were puzzled as long as it took for the tall man to feel the savage wrench that took his head back, baring his throat for Hal's dagger. The other, bewildered, half turned and took Kirkpatrick's thin, fluted dagger through the eye.

There was silence for a moment or two, broken only by ragged breathing, the whisper of rain and the choke of dying men; blood washed down the cobbles into the open gurgling trench of the drain. Isabel looked at the two men and tried to feel some pity for innocents, but failed. The world was full of innocents, all as dead as these, she thought. A wheen of them are scattered nearby – and more are on the cart. They, at least, would serve the living one last time.

Then, in a flurry of movement, they stripped the rough tunics from the men and put them on. Isabel flung off the nun's habit and stood soaking in her undershift while Kirkpatrick tried not to stare at the cling of it. She shot him a warning glance as she climbed up on the cart and silenced Hal with another, so that he saw the inevitability of it.

'If you make a single comment on what has been exposed here, Black Roger of Closeburn, I will blind you, so I will.'

Kirkpatrick, with a wan grin, held up his hands in mock surrender and watched, admiringly, as Isabel laid herself down amid the loaded corpses, as if settling for the night in a feather bed.

'Roll on your side, lady,' Hal advised, 'lest the rain get in your eyes and make you blink.The right side, mind.'

So you do not have to look into the blue-tinged wither of an old woman with her own marbled stare, Hal thought. Christ's Wounds, I have missed the courage of this woman among all else.

They each took a shaft and heaved; the cart ground reluctantly away, the torches bobbing and trailing sparks into the night.

Malise hurried through the slick streets, wrapped in a dark cloak and a hot fury. He might be a great lord, he ranted to himself, but de Valence had no right to speak to him the way he did. Jacob the Jew, indeed.

He wished he'd had the courage to spit Gaveston's old nickname for de Valence right in the Earl's face when Pembroke had looked down his long, hooked nose at him. It had been hard enough getting entry to the castle at all and his anger and fury at that had been fuelled by the fact that he had been sent from it in the first place by the same Earl.

But the guard knew him and let him in – eventually – growling that the 'enemy was at the gate'. Malise suspected differently, saw the Earl himself in the bailey, naked sword in hand but unarmoured and sending men right and left with barely concealed irritation.

He had elbowed through them and demanded to know what had happened to Isabel MacDuff. Then he had had the Look.

'Gone, though the matter is nothing to do with you,' the Earl had spat coldly and rounded on a luckless passing serjeant.

'You – Hobman, is it? Yes. Go to the gate, find out who let this man in and arrest him. Then take the gate yourself and let no one in. You hear? No one. We are under attack here.'

He turned back to Malise.

'You will go with him and leave. If I see you again I will make you suffer for the irritation in my eye.'

'There is no attack. They came to free her,' blustered Malise. 'You must send men to the town gates or she will escape . . .'

A look brought Hobman's hand on his shoulder and his firm voice in Malise's ear.

'Come along now, there is a good sir.'

The soaking rain trickled down Malise's neck and brought him back to the moment, the night and the wet. He recoiled away from the dark mouths of alleys, fearing the feral eyes and worse that he imagined lurking there, and tried to work out what the bitch would do.

Not alone, he thought and the savage exultation of it drove into him like a spike: the Lothian lord, Hal of Herdmanston. It had to be him, silly old fool, come to rescue his light o' love as if he was Sir Gawain plucking the Grail from a high tower.

There was no way for her to escape, he thought. But if it were me, I would head for the gate nearest the Tweed where

408

the old bridge, destroyed so often that Berwick had given up rebuilding it, was no more than a staggering line of black stumps like rotting old teeth.

Now folk had to ford the Tweed instead, but the postern that led to it kept its old name.

The Briggate.

He came down through the surging streets, worried at first by the knots of flame-lit men with grim faces and iron hats but realizing they were stumbling burghers, called out to the half-done walls and trembling at the idea of the Scots breaking in. Even if many of them were Scots themselves, Malise thought as he hurried through the trail of their torch embers, they had families and livelihoods here that Bruce's army would not treat kindly.

At the Briggate, he paused uncertainly; the area around the gate was thick with armed men now, at least twenty and perhaps more, all bristling with spears and crossbows, rain dripping from the rims of their helmets and soaking padded jacks.

Malise spotted the serjeant in charge by his maille and his attitude, bawling orders left and right, his bucket helm under one arm and his surcote dark with rain and bright with the badge of de Valence.

'Have some men and a woman gone out the gate?'

The serjeant turned at the sound of the voice, saw the dark, dripping figure and thought at once of a wet weasel in a dark wood.

'Who are you?' he demanded, only half interested. The men he had were all call-outs, barely of use even when placed behind merlons. God help us if the Scotch come at us out of the dark, he thought . . .

'Sir Malise Bellejambe.'

That snapped the serjeant's head round and he stared more closely at the wet weasel. It was possible this man was a *nobile*. Just possible enough to allow caution in dealing with him.

'Well,' the serjeant said and added, with a hint of scathe,

'my lord. Nothing has gone through this gate. Nor will it, coming or going.'

'The deid kert.'

They both turned to the voice and the owner of it blinked from under his soaking hood, looking from one to the other uncertainly and wishing now that he had never spoken.

'The what?'

Gib heard the tone of the serjeant and wished even more fervently that he had kept his lips snecked on the matter. But it was out now, so he stammered out the truth of it: the dead cart had been manhandled out through the open gate just before everyone had arrived.

'You opened the gate?' the serjeant demanded and now Gib heard the growling thunder, so that he started to sweat, despite the rain.

'Aye, for a brace of auld chiels. I telt them the gate could not be opened, for the alarm was sounded. So they said they would leave the bliddy thing, for they were not inclined to roll it back the way they had come.'

He looked imploringly at the serjeant, willing him to see the shock of it.

'I didnae want a pile o' corpses blocking up the way and stinking my door all night.'

'Ye opened the gate,' the serjeant replied in a disbelieving knell of a voice.

'I said they would not be allowed back,' whined Gib, 'but they laughed and answered that it was a fine excuse for their wives and they would spend the night at the Forge.'

Malise knew the Forge, a smithy just across the ford set to capture the passing trade. It provided a howf for travellers too late to gain entry to the town and was a notorious stew, providing drink and food and whores, even in times like these. More so, he added to himself, for folk trapped beyond Berwick's walls needed to lose their fears in drink and lust. Even the women.

'They were rebels,' he explained to the frowning serjeant, 'who have freed a prisoner from the castle and are now headed for escape. If you provide some men, we can overtake them . . .'

'Open the gate?' thundered the serjeant. 'Again?'

'In pursuit . . .' Malise began and the serjeant closed one eye and scowled.

'Aye, you would like that, I am sure, if you were a rebel spy. Get me to open the gate and spill in a lot of your friends.'

'I am Sir Malise Bellejambe . . .'

'So you say.'

'He is, though,' Gib interrupted helpfully and withered under the glare. 'The Witch-keeper.'

Now the serjeant knew who the man was: the jailor of the witch in the cage; an idea struck him.

'Is she the one sprung, then?'

Malise, all nervous impatience, nodded furiously and the serjeant, wiping the rain from his face, thought with agonizing slowness and then nodded.

'You can go alone,' he said, 'out the postern. If there are only two old men and a woman, you should have little trouble. Mind – you will not be allowed back in this night.'

No one will, he added to himself, watching Malise scuttle to the small door set in one of the large ones. He gave a nod and the man unlocked it with a huge key while Malise fretted at his slowness; it was barely open before he wraithed through it.

'Fair riddance to you,' the serjeant declared and spat, listening to the comfort of the lock clunking shut.

She rolled, stiff and shivering, off the cart and accepted the rough sodden sacking which Hal stripped off and gave to her.

'Time we were not here,' Kirkpatrick muttered, looking back towards the distant gate; Isabel nodded, and then looked dubiously at the huge steel-pronged arbalest Hal handed her.

'It is spanned. All ye need do is slot a bolt in it,' he said and handed her one with a look as sharp as its point; she nodded again, feeling the dragging weight.

'Move yerselves,' Kirkpatrick hissed and Isabel paused once more and signed the cross over the tipped-forward cart of lolling dead.

'God be praised,' she said.

'For ever and ever,' they muttered and turned into the river. It only came up to their shins, but had spated with the rain and the force of it was enough, with the stone-littered gravel bed, to stumble them. They moved like sleepwalkers towards the distant flickering lights of the Forge, Kirkpatrick in the rear and concentrating on his footing, cursing the dark and the wet and bad cess of the whole business.

Lucky to get away with it, he thought to himself, just as he heard the scatter of pebbles sliding under an unsteady foot. He turned, saw a dark shape and started to duck – and then the world exploded the side of his head into a bright light.

Hal and Isabel turned as Kirkpatrick reeled backwards and hit the water with a great spray; Isabel screamed and part of the rain-soaked dark seemed to tear itself away and lunge at Hal. He had time to see the winking flash that sliced the explosion of water, had time to realize that the wild, flailing hilt of that dagger had felled Kirkpatrick. Had time for the crazed eyes to sear a name into his head . . .

Malise.

Then the black shape was on him and all was mayhem.

Isabel saw the shadow and screamed again, knowing who it was even as Hal took the rush of it and Kirkpatrick toppled into the water like a felled tree. She saw him, arms out and loose, launched away on the shallow water and turning like a log, so that she knew he was unconscious and would drown unless she helped.

She floundered to him, underkirtle and sacking and the

412

slung arbalest conspiring to suck her to a stop, levered him face up, hearing the splash and grunt of the two men fighting.

'Wake,' she roared at him, slapping his whey cheeks, aware of the great bloody bruise on one side of his face, but his head rolled back and forth and she shrieked her frustration at him, and then began hauling him to the nearby bank in a fury of panic that she would not get back to help Hal in time.

Hal thought Malise was the ugliest thing in creation, his greasy pewter hair plastered to his skull, his face a braided knot of hate, studded and pitted and marked down one side with nicks and glassy pocks and a nose bent sideways like a ruined spoon.

They held each other like fumbling bad lovers, Hal's fist clamped on Malise's wrist as he tried to bring the dagger down, Malise's other arm flailing wildly and blocked, time and again, by Hal's forearm. Hal felt the dull pain there and, in desperation, struck out between Malise's blows, felt the man stagger; for a moment they lurched and lumbered in the fountaining water, before Malise recovered and they strained, almost still.

'I will finish you, Lothian.'

His breath was fetid as a dragon's; Hal remembered watching Bruce in a fight long ago and spat his own sourness into Malise's face, which made the man roar and tug. Malise tried to bite and gouge.

A mistake, Hal thought, clinging on with a panicked sense of his failing strength, the sear of the old wound along his ribs, the trembling ache of his wrist – he has turned rabid . . .

Malise, in a maddened, careless fury, tried to butt Hal; then he swung round, tumbling them both into the water in a spray fine as diamonds. Spitting and growling like soaked dogs, they rolled apart and came up looking for one another.

Hal turned an eyeblink too late and took a blow meant for his throat on his wildly flung hand, so that Malise's forearm smashed into the wrist Badenoch had damaged at the Pelstream fight. The shock and pain made him cry out; Malise gave a bellow of triumph and kicked, but the water hampered him enough to cushion the blow. Yet Hal, off balance, stumbled and fell, floundering.

Malise gave an exultant howl and started forward – only for something to drop round his neck and haul him up short, so that he almost fell backwards. Furious, puzzled, he twisted round in the grip of what felt like a noose – into the wet, grim face of Isabel, her hair a Medusa of wild wet snakes over her face and the arbalest held in both hands.

She had struck with it, but it was spanned and she had missed, dropping the loop of a prong and the taut braided cord over Malise's shoulders like a noose; there was no quarrel in it, for she had dropped that. He saw the lack, looked at her and snarled. He started forward and she pushed back, keeping him away as he came hard up against the braided cord. He reached up his dagger-free hand and started to lever it over his head.

'You will burn in Hell,' he screeched and she heard the wild, strange cry, almost like a plea – and all that he had done to her, all the foul things he had poured on her body and in her ears, washed up like old sick. He saw it in her eyes.

'Then I will meet you there,' she said and pressed the sneck.

The arbalest bucked and thrummed. The string took Malise in the throat like a ram, crushing apple and pipe and forging such a searing pain that he shrieked away from it and tore free, ripping the weapon from her grasp. He fell in the water, floundering free of the tangle of the arbalest and rolling over.

She picked up Sim's legacy, planning to club Malise with it, but instead she stood and watched him gasp. Like a fish, she thought. Drowning in air. Hal climbed to his feet, staggering a little, and she moved to him, supporting him, aware that riders were approaching.

So near to escape . . . She wondered if she could find

Malise's dagger in the spate and stones of the Tweed, for she would not go back to the cage. Not with breath in her . . .

The riders came up and a great grin split the face of the leader, the black hair plastered to the diamond-netted beard.

'Bigod, ye made it then. Who is that chiel?'

The Black Douglas. Isabel sagged, so that now Hal had to hold her up.

'Malise Bellejambe,' he answered numbly and now he saw Dog Boy and Parcy and the others. He thought of Sweetmilk and felt the souring loss of him.

'Is it, bigod?' Jamie Douglas said, looking down at the man making gug-gug sounds as he tried to suck breath into a throat long past caring, floundering in the rush of river. 'I thought he would be bigger.'

Kirkpatrick came up, half staggering and with blood all down his face.

'Time,' he began and could not finish it.

'Past time,' Jamie Douglas agreed, 'for we have fired the Forge. Mount up and let him drown here.'

But Dog Boy was off his horse and wading to the side of the gasping Malise. He looked down at him, looked down into the desperate rat eyes of him and, when he had recognition, nodded slowly.

'Aye,' he said, strangely gentle. 'Ye mind me, I can see. The wee boy from Douglas. You poisoned the dogs and red-murdered Tod's Wattie.'

Those old sins washed back into the fevered brain of Malise and he tried to explain that he had not meant to kill the dogs nor Tod's Wattie, which was a lie. But all that came out was a horrible rasping gurgle that appalled him – as did the blade appearing in the man's hand. The lurch of harsh realization sucked the final strength from him and he knew he had no future to speak in.

He saw flames flare and the Witch, outlined stark and eldritch as she turned on the back of the horse, her wet hair blown by a rain wind into a halo of snakes. The sudden sharp fear that he had lost her, his only love, was swamped by a sharper, disbelieving sorrow that everything would go on as before, save that now he would not be part of it.

Dog Boy slit the ruined throat, one hand over the man's eyes to still him, as you did with a dog that was too old or done up to live; the blood skeined away in the spate like an offering.

Then he rose up and went silently to his horse, swung up into the saddle and splashed back across the ford to safety without a backward glance.

EPILOGUE

It had started snowing on St Andrew's Feast and had scarcely stopped since, so that the world was all rime and white drape. Birds fell from under the eaves, killed by cold and leaving no more than a brief hole in the snow piled up round Herdmanston.

Folk moved slowly, less to do with the difficulty of forcing through the sifted banks than with the lack of energy. They were living now on nettle roots and burdock, which helped fill the belly and tease out the largesse of Herdmanston's lord, who still had oats and barley to give in a world where gold was easier to come by.

God's world starved and froze and those who knew the truth of it blessed the fact that they huddled round Herdmanston, where there was still food and warmth to be had.

Hal was in the undercroft looking at stores and calculating what he could keep as seed for next year, for he was sure that every villein and cottar on his land was eating their own stocks. They kept the weans in the dark as much as possible, to fool them into staying under poor covers and sleeping, but when they woke and wailed, bellies griping, Hal could not condemn parents for feeding them with next year's hope.

The calling summoned him up into a welcome heat; the undercroft was colder still than anywhere else, even the yett hall which needed a constant charcoal brazier to keep Parcy Dodd's teeth from rattling out of his head.

Swathed in wool, his face mottled like spoiled mutton, Parcy was out on the short stretch of walkway, manhandling the wooden bridge between it and the stairs. Below, sitting like a pile of washing on a rouncey, a familiar face squinted up into a clear, cold sky with enough blue to make a robe for every Virgin. A blood-sun sparkled diamonds from an endless world of white.

'Kirkpatrick,' Hal said and the man acknowledged it, before waving to the even more shapeless bundle on an ass.

'It would be good for myself and young Rauf here to sample some of your warm hospitality.'

Hal waved them up, sent Horse Pyntle to see to the mounts and brought the pair into the hall where the fire was banked. Folk, contriving to find work close to it, parted to let Hal and his visitors come up.

Hal waited while the pot of wine that stood near enough the flame to keep it warm was emptied into cups and seared with a hot iron, Mintie grinning at the trembling youngster called Rauf as she stirred in spices.

'This'll thaw your cods,' she said, handing it to him, and he nodded, speaking in bursts between the chitter of his teeth.

'Cauld. Ride. Long way frae Roslin.'

'Why suffer it?' Hal asked pointedly and Kirkpatrick, unwrapping himself, waved an insouciant hand.

'I was passing.'

It was a lie so blatant that the cold Hal felt on him was more chilled than anything God had handed the world so far. He waved Mintie away, waved all of them away, so that they moved off, reluctant and sullen at leaving the fire. In the end there was himself, Kirkpatrick and Rauf, who became aware of the eyes on him, looked from one to the other and grunted his way upright, clutching the precious warmth of the cup; melting droplets sparkled in the slight of his beard as he turned and lumbered off, trailing woollens.

'A good lad,' Kirkpatrick noted. 'Nephew to my wife and raised to squire, a station he could hardly have realized afore.'

'I heard you got wed,' Hal replied easily, taking the sting out of the reminder that neither he nor Isabel had been invited to the September affair. Kirkpatrick had the grace to look embarrassed.

'It was hastily arranged,' he said, but did not elaborate on why. 'I hear your own is due in the spring,' he added by way of balm and Hal nodded. He and Isabel had planned it for May and he added, for the politeness of it, that Kirkpatrick was welcome.

'Aye, it will be a rare event, I am sure,' Kirkpatrick added. 'The King was pleased to sanction it. You will be equally pleased to know that he will not attend it and so save you a deal of expense.'

Hal raised his cup to that; the arrival of the King meant the arrival of the court, newly freed Queen, sister and all: a host of mouths eating like baby birds in a land of famine. They had been in Edinburgh for the Christ's Mass feast, which Hal had attended with Isabel because it was expected of him; he had, to his surprise, been given the gift of a sword, fancy-hilted and engraved on the blade with the words '*Le Roi me donne, St. Cler me porte*'.

'To replace the one you delivered to Glaissery with the Beauseant banner,' the King had said and Hal had acknowledged it with a bow of thanks and a concern that his visit there had been so noted. His own gift – a silver medallion of St Anthony, said to have been worn by his namesake, the blessed Anthony of Padua – seemed less than worthy after

419

that, particularly in the light of St Anthony being the patron saint of lepers and the scabby peel of the royal face.

'The court now moves to Perth,' Kirkpatrick went on, 'afore it eats Edinburgh down to the nub. Yet we fair better than the English, since oats and barley are a hardy crop and wheat is not. They are starving beyond the Tweed.'

'They are starving because Randolph and Jamie and the King's brother scourge them of all they have left,' Hal pointed out. Kirkpatrick waved a placating palm.

'The winter has done for all that stravaigin',' he reported. 'They have gone to their own homes. Jamie is back in Douglas, putting it in order.'

Hal had seen Douglas and Randolph at the Christ's Mass feast, red-faced and greasy with joy and victory, reeling to their feet every so often to throw toasts at Bruce, the hero king. Isabel, as ever, had been quietly scathing.

'You would think they had fought the Philistines,' she muttered. 'Instead, they took a kingdom from the son when, in all his life, they never managed to take as much as an ell of good Scots dirt from the father.'

It had been a harsh judgement on a victory which had cost so much blood; Hal mentioned it now for the enjoyment of seeing Kirkpatrick wince at the memory of his attempts to hush her as politely as could be managed.

In the end, only Dog Boy had soothed Isabel. He had moved up from below the salt, seeing her distress from down the length of the table, and brought his new wife, the smiling Bet's Meggy, to be reminded to her. They had fallen at once to talk of Bet's Meggy's mother, whom Isabel had known; Hal had nodded his thanks and relief to Dog Boy, marvelling at what the years had created: a tall, dark copy of Sir James Douglas in the livery of a royal houndsman, with his round-eyed son taking care of his wee sister down at the end of the feast table and trying to miss nothing of this glorious night.

Hal had been sorry to leave them, if nothing else at court.

'How is your lady?' Kirkpatrick asked with a lopsided smile, breaking Hal's reverie. He was leaning back, at ease and with one foot carelessly thrown over the arm of his seat, dangling and bobbing to some unheard music; his boots smoked gently from the heat of the fire.

'Fine as the sun on shiny water,' Hal answered and Kirkpatrick heard the uncertainty, cocking an eyebrow.

'She talks to God a wee bit more than she did,' Hal added, almost defiantly, and Kirkpatrick nodded as if he had known that all along. He had not and the knowledge of it made him need to hide his frown; there was nothing worse, in his opinion, than a good woman gone to piety. A cage would do that, all the same, and he said as much.

'These surroundings are safer and more of a comfort,' he added, waving his cup to encompass Herdmanston and all in it. 'You have restored a deal of it.'

The smell of cut wood and stone dust permeated the air and every time he breathed it in Hal was reminded of Sim, who had worked so hard before to restore a burned-out Herdmanston. The absence of that great soul was still an unbalmed sore.

'There is a roof over us,' he said, to chase away the memory, 'but the floor above that is unfinished, while the top still opens to the sky. And the outbuildings are being redone in stone – harder to tear them down.'

Kirkpatrick nodded soberly at this pointed reminder that war still lurked, an unseen beast just beyond the hill, capable, he knew, of sweeping back and destroying all this and his own place at Closeburn, for all the victory at Bannock's burn.

'Must have cost a fair sum,' he added, innocent as a nun's headsquare. 'The King is convinced that you achieved it with the rents from his gift of Cessford.'

Hal stuck his nose in his cup and said nothing. The barony of Cessford was the Bruce reward to Herdmanston for his service, a poisoned chalice of burned-out manor and ruined fields whose folk needed as much help as Herdmanston or they, too, would starve.

'Or using rents from Lady Isabel's wee holding at Balmullo, which is hers by right,' Kirkpatrick added gently, swinging his foot still and seeming to take great interest in it. 'Of course, that is also long burned out by a wrathful Buchan when he lived. So both it and Cessford needs money more than sends it.'

'God provides,' Hal replied carefully and Kirkpatrick laughed softly.

'He does, I am sure of it.'

'Your point, Kirkpatrick?'

Hal's voice was sharp as the spice in the lees of Kirkpatrick's cup and, before he could reply, another voice cut across.

'His point concerns God's provision.'

Isabel came the last few steps up to the fire, having entered the hall unheard and unseen. She wore soft wool in a colour of green which perfectly set off her autumn bracken hair, left daringly loose under a simple white kertch. Kirkpatrick started to his feet for a polite bow and she graciously waived the honour.

'The King himself sends his good wishes,' Kirkpatrick said, resuming his old position. 'He asks if you would attend the court and himself with your expertise and grace, though he does not insist on it.'

'Nicely put, Kirkpatrick,' Isabel answered. 'And well delivered. I will not, of course, attend the King but I will give you an ointment he can physick his face with. There is no balm I can offer for him and his Queen – he will have to find that cure for himself. You may tell him that.'

Kirkpatrick managed a wan smile. The Queen, newly returned with the Bruce sister and his daughter, Marjorie, had swept into a court unused to her and a king who had never known what to do with the luscious young Elizabeth de Burgh.

Obsessed with the imperative for a legitimate heir, he had

422

thought to put her at her ease regarding what he considered the most important trouble to their marriage – the rumour of his leprosy, whose very breath could kill. So he had brought out the women he had sought comfort from in the Queen's years of captivity, adding a dash of wee bastards like a sprinkle of bile to it.

It was designed to put the newly arrived Queen at ease, since it showed that the women the King had been ploughing – and the offspring circulating, all self-aware and defiant – were fine and healthy and that rumours of leprosy were just that.

Of course the women, younger by far and sweeter and more proud, had rotted the moment with their own display and Isabel, there at Hal's side for the Christ's Mass feast, had shaken her head in sorrow and muttered: *'Fenêtre d enfer.'*

Window of Hell was apt enough, Hal thought, to describe the sewn-into dresses, slit daringly up to the thigh, fox tails hanging underneath at the back so that the strained fabric did not fold into the crack of their buttocks, front cut to the navel, so tight on the hips and groin, to show off their little fecund round bellies, that folk called them mumble-cut because 'you can see their coney-lips move, but you cannot hear what they say'.

Isabel knew then, from the purse-mouthed, fake-gracious smile on the Queen's face, that the court was no place to be from now on; Elizabeth would scourge the mistresses from it, for she was no longer the naïve girl Bruce had known and her English captivity had robbed her of what sweetness she'd had and replaced it with intrigue.

Kirkpatrick watched Isabel fold into composure on a stool brought by Mintie, hands arranged neatly in her lap, fur-trimmed gown draped round her shoulders against the draught. No *fenêtre d enfer* here, Kirkpatrick thought, and a wheen of years on her – but still a woman to take your breath away.

'So,' she declared eventually, sweet as new honey. 'You did not come here with the King's wishes or requests, for he made the same at Edinburgh and had the same answer. So why are you here?'

Kirkpatrick nodded slowly and took a deep breath, as if about to plunge under cold water.

'God's provision,' he answered, echoing Hal's earlier answer and seeing the Lothian lord's bewildered frown.

'A provision,' Isabel added, lowering her voice, 'made possible by His Apostles. Is that not why you are here, Black Roger?'

That name, so redolent of the dark nature of the man, coupled to the conjuration of the Apostles, chilled the air and made the wine lees even more bitter. Kirkpatrick's foot stopped swinging and Hal lost the frown as the realization washed him.

'The King', Kirkpatrick said slowly, 'was curious as to why Hal went to Glaissery with twenty armed men. He thought it overly solicitous of some wee Order relics, but was not unduly worried when I told him the history of de Bissot's sword. Which is why you had that blade gift from him. He values loyalty and friendship these days, does King Robert.'

'You ken different, of course,' Isabel answered flatly.

'The Kingdom is not yet cleared of trailbaston and worse,' Kirkpatrick answered. 'They would have use for some expensive wee gems on the way up to Glaissery, more so for the money those baubles fetched and which was brought back to pay for all this reordering.'

Hal was silent. He had hoped that the last remnants of the Templars, now simply Benedictines in the wilds of the north, would have kept a close mouth on the matter. He had hoped that bringing two of the fat rubies known as the Apostles to them, under the guise of returning Rossal de Bissot's Templar blade – and the Beauseant banner – to its final rest, would be a shrewd move, since they had contacts still who could get a good price for them, even allowing for a donation to

424

their wee church. He had not liked the secrecy, but bowed to Isabel's sense when she pointed out that the gems had once graced a holy relic and a king need not be reminded of it.

The two Apostles were from six Isabel had acquired, from Wallace himself no less. Originally, they had formed part of the cross on the reliquary that held the Holy Rood, taken south by Longshanks and subsequently stolen from his Minster treasury. Twelve gems had formed the reliquary cross, pigeon-egg rubies so perfectly matched and red it was said each bore the blood of a different Disciple.

'I had six,' Isabel said suddenly. 'A gift from Wallace, who had them from his kin, Jop. In turn, he had them as his share of the loot for helping in robbing the Minster. He thought to sell them to Will Wallace, not being able to rid himself of them and thinking of all the loot Wallace must have accumulated.'

'And Will simply took them, for the Cause,' Kirkpatrick added and chuckled, shaking his head admiringly. 'I was there when Jop said this.'

'I recall it well – you knifed him,' Hal reminded him and Kirkpatrick heaved a sigh and shrugged.

'Aye, well,' Kirkpatrick said slowly. 'If you need to sell more, you would be best to do it through me. I want nothing from it – but as long as I remain in the King's service, your secret is safe.'

'Why would you do this?' Hal demanded and Kirkpatrick shifted a little in his seat and waved a dismissive hand.

'For the same reason I helped free your lady. I owed both you and she thanks and service.'

For seven years of my life, Hal thought viciously, but let the bad air of it hiss away, so that he sagged with relief and a strange kind of freedom.

'With this I am quit of it,' Kirkpatrick added and Hal saw that the thing mattered to him, too.

'Is the King so fashed about the Rood jewels?'

Isabel's question slashed Kirkpatrick's eyes away from Hal; he swung round to sit properly in the chair, as if to concentrate on the answer.

'It is long since the relic was lost and the Rood itself is returned, kisted up in a new reliquary – if you believe that it is the true one.'

'It has been longer still since that Minster theft,' Isabel went on into Kirkpatrick's stone stare. 'Wee baubles of the Plantagenet treasure pop up over all the lands abroad and few bother about it – not least the present Edward. If he does not share the wrath his father had for having been so robbed, why would King Robert?'

Kirkpatrick stayed silent and Isabel, bland as old porage, studied her hands for a moment, and then stared Kirkpatrick in the face.

'Their worth, perhaps? It is an expensive business, raising a new army for what he expects will come in the spring. And the famine bites. There are wee merchants stirring from Flanders and elsewhere thanks to the victory at Stirling, but mayhap trade is too slow for our king's liking.

'Besides,' she added with a wry twist of smile, 'Robert was never good with siller – liked getting it, certes, but could never keep it long.'

Hal, blinking, looked at Isabel, who was locked in a stare with Kirkpatrick so intense he swore he could see blue sparks.

'The King', Kirkpatrick answered softly, 'knows nothing. He will remain in that state of bliss if I have my way – but wee monks in Glaissery tell me matters because they wish it to reach the ears of the King, for his safety and concern.'

Of course they would, Hal thought miserably. The wee monks of Glaissery, trying hard to pretend they never belonged to the Poor Knights, owe the Bruce everything they have in this kingdom. So they would tell him, through Kirkpatrick, his ferret of secrets, his doer of black deeds in the Royal Cause.

'Let me guess why Robert would care if he knew,' Isabel went on softly. 'Not because those gemstones are from the lost relic of the Holy Rood, nor because they are worth siller. There are four Apostles remaining with me now that two are sold. There were six. Wallace's six, which he had from Jop. The other six went to Lamprecht. Folk think they were taken by the Order when they killed him and then recovered by the English later . . .

'But not all six,' she added, gently vicious as the kiss of a razor on a cheek. 'Five only came from Lamprecht, for the sixth had been given away . . .'

'To Bruce.'

Hal's almost-shout snapped the stares. He remembered the day, the ruby thumbed into a cheap loaf by Lamprecht as his provenance for inveigling his way into Bruce's confidence. It had been a plot, of course, only discovered later and at risk of their lives.

'Bruce had the sixth. He kept it.'

Kirkpatrick seemed to tip a little, like a bag of grain with a leaking hole. He looked at Hal and smiled wanly.

'You remember it. Of course you would.'

'That Apostle is the only one whose name I know,' Isabel said, almost in a whisper. 'It is the only one Longshanks ever got back – delivered to him when it was plucked from Wallace's scrip, together with his safe conduct from the King of France. The latter ignored as the former never could be.'

Judas.

That ruby made sure Wallace would never be forgiven at the last after he had been betrayed to the English and put on trial – Longshanks might have been persuaded to clemency for a repentant rebel, but never for a Minster thief. And it had to have been put there by Kirkpatrick, given to him by Bruce. A rich, unfortunate gift or a cynical betrayal?

Hal stared at Kirkpatrick, the sick horror of it swamping him as he looked from the man to Isabel and realized that

427

she had known of it for a longer time. Kirkpatrick, too, saw it all stripped bare, breathed in deeply enough to raise his shoulders, set the cup down gently and got stiffly to his feet.

'Well, there you have it,' he said. 'If you wish my help, you need only ask. I had better take these old bones back to Roslin. Then on to Edinburgh – or Perth if I am unlucky and have missed the court entire.'

'Did he know what he did when he ordered the gem into Will's scrip?'

Hal's hoarse question flapped in like a red kite on a corpse and Kirkpatrick paused briefly in wrapping himself back in his woollens, not even looking at Hal.

'Not what you should ask,' he replied in a voice rasped as a hidden reef. 'Ever.'

Hal and Isabel looked at each other and felt the old fear close on them like a claw. If it was true and the King suspected someone knew of it . . . Out of one cauldron into the fire, it seemed a great weariness engulfed Hal and he almost staggered under the weight of it. He did not want to believe it of the Bruce, but neither could he discount the possibility – the man had it in him to commit any sin for the furtherance of his destiny.

Kirkpatrick saw Hal's horror and felt it, a deep pang as if it had just happened to himself.

'As long as you deal the stones through me, you are safe,' he said. 'After that, let them sink into legend and oblivion. The King does not know anything of the Apostle stones now and need not ever be remembered of them, to his undoubted troubling. Besides, he has enough to concern him in the getting of an heir and mending at least part of the life between himself and his queen.'

He turned and smiled at them both.

'He would give crown, Kingdom and all for a lick of what you pair possess,' he added and that stunned them both to silence until he had reached the yett, the miserable Rauf trailing coldly in his wake.

'Stay well,' Kirkpatrick said at the door, pulling on his gauntlets as Horse Pyntle led their mounts to the foot of the stairs. 'I will dance at your wedding.'

Hal watched him go, even gave the lie of a cheerful wave. There never was an end to it, he thought, never a happy after. For all their loving life together, he and Isabel had lived in the shadow of a vengeful Earl of Buchan and Badenoch and red war.

Now, just as it seemed they could walk to a wedding in a sunlit meadow with no shadows at all, there was the old thundercloud, black and fresh with menace, rimmed with uneasy crowns and bloated with a war that did not seem sated with slaughter and dubious victory at Stirling.

Under it was a king, whose every act to preserve the Kingdom could be no sin, and the faithful dark-hearted hound he sent to commit it was the dog Hal now had to trust to keep them safe in a world where only the sword and the tower could be truly relied on.

'O Lord, Heavenly Father,' Isabel murmured into the seeping cold from the open door, 'let Your angels watch over Your servants that they may reach their destination in safety, that no enemy may attack them on the road, nor evil overcome them. Protect them from fast rivers, thieves, wild beasts – and troubled kings.'

'Amen,' Hal answered vehemently, sure that her prayer was not simply one for Kirkpatrick and Rauf's safe journey.

The cold swept in the yett; Hal put his arm round Isabel like a fortress and led her into the thickness of Herdmanston's walls.

'Parcy,' he called out over his shoulder. 'Double bar the door.'

AUTHOR'S NOTE

The problems of Scotland in 1297 are not strangers to most of the Scots of the twenty-first century, not to the ones who voted in the SNP for five more years in 2011, nor those who may well vote us out of the Union some time within that span.

Certainly not to all those with an enormous chip on their shoulder, born out of a strong sense of grievance and a casual, institutionalized racism on both sides.

But that has always been the problem with Scots – dominated by England, Scotland has resented, struggled, died, bristled impotently at being so treated and retained a legacy of striving for freedom, however nebulous the chance or the reality.

The memories run deep. On one glorious day in the year this book is set, the Scots won a great victory against all the odds, cocked two fingers at English ambitions – and, of course, only managed to annoy its more powerful neighbour, who recovered sufficiently to make the Kingdom suffer for it for the next several hundred years.

For all that Scots love to believe it, Bannockburn was not the end of matters. It achieved everything – and nothing. It consolidated Bruce on the throne, sent Edward II's relationship with his rebellious barons into a downward spiral from

431

which, ultimately, it never recovered, but it did not end the cycle of invasion, slaughter and harrying.

It did not even keep a Balliol from the throne; supported by Edward III in 1332, Toom Tabard's son, Edward Balliol – and there is wealth of revelation in that first name – took the throne from Bruce's young son, David. Ousted almost at once, he was promptly reinstated by English might, only to be ousted once more. Returned to power a third time by the English, he was finally thrown out in 1336 and this time he took the hint.

From this, you can see that war between Scotland and England rasped along, right through the Rough Wooing of Henry VIII (another abortive attempt to force the Scots to bow the knee), and only ended most of the brutal bloodshed with the Union of the Crowns in 1603. It finally grumbled to a grudging halt with the Acts of Union in 1707, flared briefly in 1715 and '45 and then died forever at Culloden.

Bannockburn, resplendent in the panoply of great battles, was simply one more in the bloody tapestry of Scotland's history. Together with Culloden, they mark both the highest and lowest point of the Scottish martial bid for freedom.

For all that, Edward II was not his father, against whom Bruce never took a yard of ground. Edward I, in his turn, was never so bloody or brutal as his grandson, 'the perfect king' Edward III. From an English perspective, Edward I and his grandson are golden monuments to chivalry; the Scots, of course, have a different view.

Bannockburn, for all its impact on history, is one more battle of which we actually know very little. Numbers, actual site and progression are all best guesses and I have used numerous sources, taking the bits I think fit best as a historical novelist creating one more fiction around the event. In an age of military shock and awe, it is worth remembering that the entire of Edward II's army, a monstrous host for the time, could have fitted into Edinburgh's Meadowbank Stadium, capacity 16,000. Bruce's spearmen could have crammed in, shoulder to shoulder, on a football pitch.

Bannockburn itself, on the day, is also best guess, though the idea has perpetuated that the boggy ground hampered the English heavy horse, an idea no doubt culled from all the later historians who bothered even to walk that ground in a typical wet summer.

But the summer of 1314 was not typical, just as the battle was not typical. There are hints, in other extant accounts, that May and June of 1314 had been rainlessly hot – and Bannockburn's carse, given weeks of beating sunshine, is firm and perfect for cavalry, even if the steep-sided streams, tidal washed twice a day at one end, retain a measure of damp.

That year, 1314, marked the start of a climate change which saw long, harsh winters, arid summers and wet autumns, all of which conspired, for the next few years, to ruin harvests. The year after Bannockburn saw famine in Britain, worst of all for the people of northern England, whose wheat crops were ruined by weather and the ravages of victorious, raiding Scots. Scotland also suffered, though the despised oat, staple of the Scots diet, was a hardier plant for wet weather and the Scots were not being burned out of what little they had.

Another persistent idea concerns the Templars and the debate about their presence continues to rage on. Did Bruce give them shelter? Did he, as is claimed, become head of the Order, or form a new Order out of their ruins? Are the Masons of today the direct inheritors? Is the Scottish Rite handed down from the Templars? Did they lead an army of 'sma' folk' down Coxet Hill at the crucial turning point of the battle and so bring Bruce victory?

If you want proof that a writer has gone mad, see if he has become involved with the history of Templars in Scotland. For my own part, I dismiss all of it. Bruce was not foolish enough to shackle himself to a discredited, disbanded Order simply because he had been excommunicated. The whole thrust of his life in the aftermath of Bannockburn was to undo that and gain papal approval of his kingship, so he was hardly likely to be flaunting heretic Templars in the Vatican's face.

The Templars ended in Scotland, just as they did everywhere else, but there is no doubt that disinherited Templars were treated with more leniency in Scotland, as they were in Ireland. There is some evidence that both those countries were back-waters for Templar commanderies, a sort of retirement home for aged servitors of the Order. No one was too concerned to punish old men in a care home.

Was there a Templar treasure, taken from France to the north of Scotland? Possibly – define treasure. If the Templars thought they possessed the Grail, the Shroud of Christ and other such holy artefacts, which was their speciality after all, it may be that kings and popes spent a long time looking for the wrong fortune.

There may not, however, have been a fabled Treasury at all; most accounts of commanderies taken over reveal very little in the way of loot. If there was a Templar treasure for Bruce it would be in the weapons and harness he needed – constant war, raids and English domination is not conducive to garnering the money needed to trade or create the amount of weapons and armour, simple though it was, with which the Scots army was equipped.

So where did he get them? Probably not as I have stated, using Templar money to buy Templar weapons from the beneficiaries of the fallen Order in northern Spain, the new Order of Alcántara. But it gave an adventure for Hal and Kirkpatrick while the events leading up to Bannockburn warped and wove themselves into a bloody tapestry of Midsummer's Day, 1314.

Incidentally, the Glaissery Castle I have Bruce handing to the 'simple Benedictine monks' in exchange for their help is now known as Fincharn Castle, a former MacDougall stronghold on Loch Awe and not more than a prayer away from Kilneuair Church, a sadly neglected ruin with Templar symbols on gravestones. Loch Awe is the place where the Templars from France brought their fabled treasure, if you believe the many theories.

All of it is too good for a novelist to pass up. Historians would be wiser to treat tales of the secret continuation of the Templars in Scotland with a huge saline pinch.

The salient points of the battle at Bannockburn are fairly well confirmed, source to source: the arrival of the English, weary and exhausted; their hasty and ill-conceived assault; the death of Sir Henry de Bohun at the hands of Bruce personally; the belief that the Scots would not stand for a second day and the shock of them not only still being *in situ* but actually attacking.

The victory was the culmination of Bruce's struggle to ensure that Scotland recognized him as king. It would take fifteen more years before the rest of the world recognized it as well.

The start of this book is purportedly written by an unknown monk in February of 1329, three months before Robert the Bruce is finally acknowledged as King of Scots by the Pope – and four months before his death, ravaged and ruined by 'an unspecified illness'.

Think of this as stumbling across a cache of hidden monkish scribblings which, when read by a flickering tallow candle, reveal fragments of lives lost both in time and legend.

If any interpretations or omissions jar, blow out the light and accept my apologies.

LIST OF CHARACTERS

ADDAF the Welshman

Typical soldier of the period, raised from the lands only recently conquered by Edward I. By this time, however, Addaf is a contract captain – leader of a band of mercenary Welsh archers, well armed, mounted and time served in the wars in France. The Welsh prowess with the bow and spear was already noted, but the true power of the former, the Crécy and Agincourt massed ranks, was a strategy still forming during the early Scottish Wars. Like all of the Welsh, Addaf's loyalty to the English is tenuous and, as a captain of mercenaries, he is aware that some of his own men have a loyalty to him which is just as threadbare.

ARGENTAN, Sir Giles d'

Shadowy character save for his appearances, like a bright flame, beside the pale light of Edward II. He was one of the many knights present at the famous Feast of the Swans, when Edward I knighted his son and many other gilded youth in an attempt

437

to bind them to the young prince. D'Argentan chased Bruce at the Battle of Methven and, if his horse had not foundered, history might well have seen an epic struggle: he was considered the third-best knight in Christendom, the second being Robert the Bruce and the first being Heinrich, Holy Roman Emperor. Not long after, d'Argentan is mentioned as one of the knights a furious Edward I ordered arrested for leaving his son's army during campaign in Scotland to attend a tourney in France. In 1314 Edward II, in the middle of his acute financial constraints, found time and money to ransom d'Argentan from prison in Salonika – he had gone to Rhodes to join the Knights Hospitaller and fight the Saracens. Knights of his calibre and chivalric fame were clearly needed by Edward II, if only for the morale value – certainly d'Argentan's heroic, if typically rash, death at Bannockburn brought him considerable renown.

BADENOCH, Lord of

Here, it is the son of the Red Comyn murdered in Greyfriars. John IV, lord of Badenoch, was a youth when his father met his death and thereafter was firmly in the English camp – his mother was Joan de Valence, sister of Aymer de Valence (see below). He was killed at Bannockburn, though the actual circumstances of it are unknown.

BALGOWNIE, Pegy

Fictional character, commander of the cog which takes Hal and Kirkpatrick to Spain on behalf of the King. Pegy is a nickname; it is the small, topmost portion of the mast used to fly a pennant from. I have made him an ex-privateer, one of the captains of the very real Red Rover, a French pirate called de Longueville who assisted Wallace back and forth to France. Also real is Jack Crabbe and when de Longueville gave up piracy in favour of a privileged life ashore, his captains made their own way. Pegy Balgownie, the fictional one, joined Bruce. Jack Crabbe continued on his own and, captured by the English in later life, became a firm adherent of Edward III for whom he used his expertise with the new-fangled 'gonne' to direct the ordnance in the 1333 siege of Berwick – which eventually fell.

BEAUMONT, Henry de

One of the most experienced warriors in Edward II's retinue, he was also Earl of Buchan by his marriage to Alice Comyn, niece of the Earl married to Isabel MacDuff. The title of Countess of Buchan, clearly removed from Isabel, passed to Alice – though de Beaumont had the title 'in parchment only'. He campaigned in Flanders, and then fought against Wallace at Falkirk, where he had a horse killed under him and was lucky to escape with his life. He returned to Scotland in 1302 and 1304, where he was at the English siege of the Scots-held Stirling Castle. His near-death experience and rescue by Sir Thomas Gray (see below) happened as described here, as did his quarrel with Gray at Bannockburn. De Beaumont accompanied Edward from the field and thereafter became an implacable supporter of the Disinherited, those English-supporting lords whose lands and titles in Scotland were confiscated by Robert the Bruce. From 1314 until his death in 1340, de Beaumont led assault after assault, both military and political, on Scotland – to no avail. He died never having achieved the Buchan lands and, when his wife, Alice Comyn, died in 1349, the title finally reverted to the Crown until bestowed on Alexander Stewart in 1382. He was known as the Wolf of Badenoch for his rapacity and cruelty.

BELLEJAMBE, Malise

Fictional character, the Earl of Buchan's sinister henchman and arch-rival of Kirkpatrick. For years he has been the official gaoler of Isabel MacDuff in her tower cage in Berwick, first for the Earl of Buchan and then for the lord of Badenoch. His relationship with her is becoming increasingly psychotic, violent and sinister.

BERKELEY, Sir Maurice

Known as the Magnanimous, he was at the Siege of Caerlavrock with his father (see below), was made Warden of Gloucester (1312) and Captain of Berwick (1315). He was Chief Justiciar of South Wales in 1316, then became Seneschal of Aquitaine in 1320. Shortly after his father's death he joined the Earl of Lancaster's rebellion against Edward II, was captured and sent to Wallingford Castle (1322) where he died four years later.

BERKELEY, Sir Thomas

Known as Thomas the Wise, he was appointed Vice Constable of England in 1297, fought at Falkirk against Wallace and was at the Siege of Caerlavrock in 1300. At Bannockburn he brought a *mesnie* (a personal following) of serjeants and mounted archers – I have placed Addaf and his men among them. Sir Thomas was unhorsed and captured; the subsequent ransom was crippling. He died at Berkeley, peacefully, in 1321.

BISSOT, Rossal de

Fictional character, descendant of Geoffrey de Bissot, one of the nine founding knights of the Templar Order. He is trying to rescue what remains of the disbanded Order while, at the same time, aware that the power and arrogance of the Poor Knights of the Temple are what has brought them to the brink. He and de Villers, Widikind von Esbeck and de Grafton are the last of the Templar Knights in Scotland, attempting to barter money and weapons with Bruce for a peaceful resting place for fleeing members who wish to remain as simple Benedictine monks.

BOHUN, Henry de

The Earl of Hereford's nephew, probably no more than twenty-two in 1314 and one of the new breed of knights excelling in *tournoi*, the new one-on-one style of knightly combat gaining ascendancy over the old-fashioned mass combat of *grande mêlée*. Famously, he charged against the lightly mounted and armoured King Robert, only to be killed. The style of fighting described as favoured by Bruce is accurate – the German Method involved avoiding heavily armoured opponents trying to bowl you over and attacking them on a faster, more manoeuvrable mount. In the *grande mêlée*, when capturing a knight meant a deal of prize, it was a sensible if unchivalric way of fighting, but such combats frequently degenerated into brutal riots with scarcely a trace of chivalry. Here, I use it as it was almost certainly designed: to hit your bigger, stronger, better-armoured opponent from behind.

BOHUN, Humphrey de

The Earl of Hereford in 1314 and Constable of England. As such, he should have been given command of the army, but was out of favour with Edward II over the murder of Piers Gaveston. Command instead went to Gilbert de Clare, Earl of Gloucester (see below). At Bannockburn, therefore, Hereford argued with Gloucester constantly over the conduct of the army, making coherence virtually impossible. Following the defeat, Hereford was forced north, taking refuge in the only English-held castle left, Bothwell. However, the commander of Bothwell promptly changed sides and imprisoned him and all the other lords who had escaped with him. Hereford was eventually ransomed for Bruce's sister and daughter – pointedly, Isabel MacDuff was not included. Historically, this is a good clue that she was probably dead by this time.

A firm opponent of the Despensers, Hereford eventually rebelled against Edward II. At the Battle of Boroughbridge, Hereford led a desperate assault to try and force the said bridge and so avoid being trapped between two armies. In the affray, he was stabbed from below the bridge, up under his armour and into his anus, the soldier allegedly twisting the pike into his intestines; his dying screams helped to panic the army into fleeing.

BRUCE, Edward

King Robert's sole surviving brother and, in lieu of any other relevant offspring, heir to the throne. History has it that his ill-conceived truce with de Mowbray, English commander of Stirling, enraged Bruce, who then had to fight a pitched battle. While I am sure it did enrage his royal brother, I am also certain Edward knew exactly what he was doing and for the reasons I mention. Rash and ambitious, Edward was given men and means to invade Ireland in 1315, ostensibly to carry the war to England's supporters. He made himself High King in Ireland but was defeated and captured in the Battle of Faughart (also known as the Battle of Dundalk) on 14 October 1318. He was hanged, drawn and quartered and his head sent to Edward II. Ironically, among the many other Scots lords who died fighting with him that day was a certain Sir

Philip de Mowbray, former commander of the garrison at Stirling and reconciled to King Robert's peace upon the surrender of the fortress following Bannockburn.

BRUCE, Robert

King Robert I, now known as Robert the Bruce. His father, also Robert, was Earl of Annandale. His grandfather, also Robert, was known as the Competitor from the way he assiduously pursued the Bruce rights to the throne of Scotland, passing the torch on to his grandson. While Edward II vacillated and wilted under setbacks, the harried Bruce shouldered on; the story of the spider, though apocryphal, shows that the spirit of the man served as an uplifting moral message for later generations. The Curse of Malachy was a very real threat to the Bruces, silly though it may seem to our twenty-first-century irreligious sophistication, while the illness Bruce suffered was a continual worry. It may well have been leprosy – there are many forms of it – or a simple skin complaint, but investigations of his skull reveal extensive damage to the right cheek and a considerable wound injury above and below the left eye, though he was not blinded. The Pilkington statue at the Bannockburn Heritage Centre may well show the glory of the king, but the reality seems to have been painful, ugly and, towards the end of his life (in his mid-fifties), his face may well have been blurred and coarsened by illness as well. Myth and legend have similarly blurred the Hero King, bathing him in a golden glow that masks the reality of both appearance and character.

CAMPBELL, Dougald, Laird of Craignish

The 6th Laird of Craignish, the lands on the wild Argyll peninsula, is in his early forties at the time of Bannockburn and heading off to support his chief, Neil Campbell. The Campbell of Craignish shields are defiantly recognizable and much copied by re-enactors, even over the famous black galley on gold of the MacDonalds of Angus Og. Described as *gyronny of eight or and sable, the shield hanging from the mast of a lymphad sable*, it simply means a series of eight triangles, alternated yellow and black, on a shield seemingly hung from a horizontal black bar. It is, in fact, an even older runic symbol which gives more than a hint at the Craignish Campbells' Viking ancestry.

CAMPBELL, Sir Neil

Known as Niall mac Cailein (Neil, Colin's son), he was a firm adherent of Edward I, having sworn fealty to him on the Ragman Roll of 1296. A decade later, however, with Edward handing Campbell lands to English knights, Neil Campbell was ripe for rebellion and finally joined Robert the Bruce in 1306. He was one of the few men who stuck with the ill-fated King Robert following defeats at Methven and Dalrigh. Eventually, as a reward, Neil Campbell received Bruce's sister, Mary, as a wife and the lands confiscated from the turncoat David Strathbogie, Earl of Atholl (see below). His son, Iain, eventually became earl.

CLARE, Sir Gilbert de

Earl of Gloucester, whose mother was Joan of Acre, Edward I's sister. Being so closely related to Edward II, he was yet another of those favourites who replaced Gaveston. Aged only twenty-three, he was given command of the army over the head of Humphrey de Bohun, Earl of Hereford (see above), who was Constable of England. In fact, Edward fudged the issue by declaring them joint commanders, which was a recipe for disaster since they disliked one another. Unhorsed and barely rescued on the first day of Bannockburn, Gloucester was killed the next day, though the actual circumstances remain unclear.

CLIFFORD, Sir Robert

One of Edward I's trusted commanders and a member of the original gilded youth of the Feast of the Swans in 1306 – but, eight years on, the youth and gilt are wearing thin on all that band. Clifford and Sir Henry Percy were given the task of subduing the initial Scottish revolt and negotiated Bruce and other rebel Scots nobles back into the 'King's Peace' in 1297, but could not overcome Wallace. Clifford also brought a retinue to fight at Falkirk which included knights from Cumbria and Scotland, one of the latter being a certain Sir Roger Kirkpatrick of Auchen Castle, Annandale, and the 'real' Kirkpatrick who murdered the Red Comyn. Clifford was at the Siege of Caerlavrock Castle in 1300, according to the Caerlavrock Roll – the list of knights present – and at Bannockburn in 1314, where he was killed.

CRAW, Sim

A semi-fictional character. Sim of Leadhouse is mentioned only once in history, as the inventor of the cunning scaling ladders with which James Douglas took Roxburgh by stealth in 1314. Here, he is Hal of Herdmanston's right-hand man, older than Hal – who is himself old – powerfully built and favouring a big arbalest, a steel-constructed crossbow spanned (cocked) using a winding mechanism and usually used in sieges.

DALTOUN, Thomas

Technically, a real character. A Thomas was Abbot of Inchaffray in 1296 and I have found references to Thomas Daltoun as Bruce's chaplain. Since the Bruce chaplain in 1314 was supposedly Maurice, the abbot who came after Thomas, I fancy there has been a confusion somewhere and that

Thomas, resigning as abbot in favour of Maurice, then became the Bruce chaplain. Consequently, I have arbitrarily decided that it was he who famously blessed the army at Bannockburn with the arm of St Fillan.

DOG BOY

Fictional character, the lowest of the low, a houndsman in Douglas and of age with the young James Douglas. By 1314, the skinny youth has grown into a formidable warrior and the very image of the equally fierce Sir James. It is clear to most folk that they are sprung from the same sire. However, while the long years of brutal warfare have simply honed the hate of Sir James, the Black Douglas, they are beginning to tell on Dog Boy.

DOUGLAS, Sir James

Lord of Douglas Castle in south-west Scotland, son of Sir William the Hardy, he was known both as the Black Douglas (if you were his enemy and demonizing him with foul deeds) and the Good Sir James (if you were a Scot lauding the Kingdom's darling hero). In the years between his return to Scotland – just as Bruce became king – and 1314 he has become a byword for vicious cruelty. Particularly memorable is the Douglas Larder, where he famously slaughtered the garrison and collaborators of his own castle, then held by the Cliffords, put them in the storehouse and burned the place. His implacable hatred of the English is matched only by his daring and, save for one slight hiccup, his loyalty. Following Bannockburn, Sir James Douglas made the Border area uniquely his own, and the form of warfare – fast raiders on light horses – a lasting legacy for that region. In 1327, he surprised and destroyed an army led by yet a third Edward, almost capturing the young King. In 1329, following the death of Bruce, he famously took the royal heart on Crusade, to Spain to fight the Saracens. At Teba in Granada the following year, he took part in a battle where the Scots pursuit of the broken enemy led them too far and some were surrounded. Attempting a rescue, Douglas himself was surrounded and, taking the casket with Bruce's heart, flung it forward into the enemy, yelling that, as always, he would follow Bruce. He and all the men with him were killed. Ironically, the knight Douglas originally went to rescue was a certain Sir William Sientcler of Roslin.

EDWARD II

King of England. At the time of this novel he has spent seven years being frustrated in his attempts to secure Scotland – each campaign he has led there has resulted only in an increase of Robert the Bruce's power. Finally, facing the constrictions of the Ordainers, his own rebellious barons, he seizes the chance to finally bring the Scots to a decisive battle in 1314. The result was, arguably, the worst defeat for the English since Hastings in 1066. It plunged Edward into a vicious struggle with the Ordainer barons and, eventually, with his own queen (see below) and her lover, Roger Mortimer. Deposed and imprisoned, he was subsequently murdered, according to some accounts, by having a red-hot poker shoved into his anus. Historian Ian Mortimer argues a decent case for Edward II actually having survived, the death being faked by Mortimer and Isabella – but other historians disagree with his methodology.

GRAFTON, Sir William de

Real character whose life I have stolen and fictionalized. He is listed as one of the Preceptors of Templar commanderies in Yorkshire, arrested in 1308 and then released to the care of Henry, Baron Percy of Alnwick, in 1313, who was at odds with Edward II over the murder of Piers Gaveston. Here I have shamelessly used de Grafton as a recusant Templar sent to spy on Bruce's Spanish adventure by Henry Percy – who then does not inform his king of the vital findings. De Grafton, of course, then decides to make his own profit on the affair with ruthless murder and villainy. I chose Henry Percy as the baron betraying the English at Bannockburn with his omissions simply because he died at age forty-one of unknown cause – and rumoured poison – in October 1314 . . .

GRAY, Sir Thomas

Real character, whose quarrel with Henry de Beaumont led him to a rash charge at Bannockburn and his unhorsing and imprisonment. Ransomed and freed, he returned to the family lands at Heaton, where he died circa 1344. Ironically, his son, also called Sir Thomas, was captured by the Scots in 1355 and also held for ransom, whiling away the hours in Edinburgh Castle by writing the *Scalacronica*, a history of Britain from the Creation. The portion concerning Edward I and onwards is based on what he learned from his father and so is an interesting and near-contemporary record – allowing for a son's bias regarding his father's exploits, of course.

ISABELLA, Queen of England

Seen here briefly on an actual and vital mission to her father on behalf of her husband, one of the many she undertook. Still a teenager, her son – the future Edward III – is already two years old. I almost certainly malign the woman with the 'She Wolf' image she was handed by history. Despite her later betrayal of her husband and her desposing him to rule with her lover, Mortimer, I don't actually think she was as vicious or calculatingly clever as that makes her appear.

448

KILWINNING, Bernard of

Bruce's Chancellor in 1314, former Abbot of Kilwinning and later Abbot of Arbroath from 1310 to 1328, he served as Chancellor until 1328 and died two years after his king, in 1331. More importantly, he is generally considered to be one of the chief authors of the Declaration of Arbroath, the stirring document asserting independence in general and Scotland's in particular, which includes the famous and much-quoted lines:

> . . . for, as long as but a hundred of us remain alive, never will we on any conditions be brought under English rule. It is in truth not for glory, nor riches, nor honours that we are fighting, but for freedom – for that alone, which no honest man gives up but with life itself.

KIRKPATRICK, Roger

Fictional character, but based on the real Sir Roger Kirkpatrick of Closeburn, whom I have as kin to the fictional one. This is because my Kirkpatrick is a staunch Bruce supporter from the outset and the real Sir Roger was not – he even fought for Clifford in the English retinue at Falkirk. My Kirkpatrick assumes the mantle of Bruce's henchman, prepared for any dirty work on behalf of his master's advancement, including murder. By 1314, Kirkpatrick has been elevated to Closeburn's barony and knighted, but he owes Hal of Herdmanston a great debt and feels bound to repay it. The Greyfriars murder both elevated and haunted the Kirkpatricks: in 1357, another Sir Roger Kirkpatrick of Closeburn was murdered by Sir James Lindsay in 'a private quarrel'. Sir James was the son of the man I have with Kirkpatrick and Hal and Dog Boy in Greyfriars the day Red Comyn was murdered.

MACDUFF, Isabel

She is a real character whose life I have shamelessly stolen, investing her with a love affair with Bruce, which was almost certainly scurrilous propaganda of the time, and another with the fictional Hal of Herdmanston, which forms the cornerstone of this and the other books of the series. Their love affair, hagged by the vengeful husband, the Earl of Buchan, is also dogged by war and great events. A member of the powerful, though fragmented, ruling house of Fife, she acted as the official 'crowner' of Robert Bruce in 1306, a role always undertaken by a MacDuff of Fife – but the only other one was her younger brother, held captive in England. In performing this, she not only defied her husband but the entire Comyn and Balliol families. Captured later, she was imprisoned, with the agreement of her husband, in a cage hung on the walls of Berwick Castle. Her husband died in 1308, harried and broken by Bruce's ethnic cleansing of the Buchan lands and the Buchan title passed to another, which means that, in between, the Earl had divorced his wife, or she had died. In my version, Isabel has hung in a cage from the Hog Tower of Berwick Castle, under the watchful eye of Malise Bellejambe, for seven years, waiting for the day of rescue . . .

PIMENTAL, Doña Beatriz Ruiz de Castor y

Fictional character, sister of a Knight of Alcántara, the Order which took over Templar commanderies in Castile and Leon and which was, at this time, commanded by the shrewd Ruy Vaz. Treacherous and beautiful, she is based – with absolutely no foundation other than the splendid name – on Doña Leonor Ruiz de Castro y Pimental, wife of Prince Felipe, who was the younger brother of King Alfonso the Wise of Castile and Leon – and a Knight Templar (clearly celibacy was not part of the Spanish Knights' tradition).

RANDOLPH, Sir Thomas

A Bruce supporter, he was captured at Methven and changed sides. Captured by the Scots later, he promptly changed sides again and, in 1314, he has just been raised to Earl of Moray. He is always described as a 'nephew' of Robert the Bruce, though the exact relationship is uncertain. By this point, he and Sir James Douglas are great rivals, a fact Bruce promoted to his great advantage: no sooner has Douglas taken Roxburgh Castle by daring and stealth than Randolph takes Edinburgh Castle by subterfuge. He commanded one of the great spear blocks – Battles – at Bannockburn and, on the death of Bruce, became Regent for his young son, David II. He died three years later, ostensibly of poisoning, though this is now thought unlikely.

SETON, Sir Alexander

In 1306 there was a mutual indenture – one of those frequent chivalric oaths – made between Sir Gilbert Hay of Erroll, Sir Neil Campbell of Lochawe and Sir Alexander Seton of Seton at the Abbey of Lindores, to 'defend King Robert Bruce and his crown to the last of their blood and fortune'. Alexander was the brother of Christopher Seton, who had not only helped save Bruce at the Battle of Methven, but paid the price for supporting the King when he was captured defending Loch Doon Castle, a Carrick stronghold, and hanged, drawn and quartered. Another kinsman, John de Seton, was captured while defending Tibbers Castle and was also hanged, drawn and quartered. It may have been that which drove Alexander to ignore his oath and join the ranks of the Disinherited, the lords with vested interest in an English victory. But, the night before the Battle of Bannockburn, Alexander Seton had had enough of the English. He defected and brought news to Bruce of the disarray in the English ranks, helping to persuade Bruce to stay and fight.

SIENTCLER of Herdmanston, Sir Henry

Known as Hal, he is the son and heir to Herdmanston, a lowly tower owing fealty to kin, the Sientclers of Roslin. He is typical of the many poor nobles of Lothian who became embroiled in the wars on both sides of the divide – except Hal has fallen in love with Isabel MacDuff (see above) and their ill-fated affair is shredded by war and her husband's hatred, culminating in the capture of them both. Isabel is condemned to life in a cage hung from the walls of Berwick; Hal is condemned to die – but Edward I's death in 1307 leaves him imprisoned and forgotten in Roxburgh Castle. In 1314, seven years later, he is freed when the castle falls to James Douglas. Despite age – he is around forty-seven in an era when fifty is the average for a man and thirty-five the life expectancy of a woman – and weakness, he is determined to free Isabel and, at last, find a measure of happiness, even if he has to fight his way through all the English at Bannockburn. The Sientclers of Herdmanston are a little-known branch of the Sientcler family, in actuality appearing prominently only for one brief moment in fifteenth-century history. Herdmanston is now an anonymous pile of stones in a corner of a ploughed field and any descriptions of it are pure conjecture on my part.

STRATHBOGIE, Sir David

The Earl of Atholl, son of the man hanged, drawn and quartered for supporting the Scots rebellion in 1306, he had been held by the English as a boy. Restored to the earldom by the English, he initially supported Bruce and then deserted him in 1307, only to return shortly before Bannockburn. Famously, on the very eve of Bannockburn, he turned coat again, almost certainly because of Edward Bruce's careless dalliance with his sister, Isabel. At the time he had been appointed Constable by Bruce, to keep him sweet, but it was clearly a title devoid of command, because the only thing Strathbogie controlled were the siege stores – which he sacked on the way out. This fatal decision eventually cost him his lands and title, appointed to the firmly loyal Neil Campbell.

THWENG, Sir Marmaduke

Lord of Kilton in Yorkshire, a noted knight and married to a Lucia de Brus, distant kin to Bruce himself, Sir Marmaduke is the chivalric, sensible face of English knighthood. A noted thief-taker – bounty hunter – in his own realm, he was also part of the tourney circuit with the young Robert Bruce. He fought at Stirling Bridge and was one of few to battle his way back to Stirling Castle, where he was eventually taken prisoner. He took part in subsequent campaigns against the Scots, including Bannockburn, where, in his sixties, he fought until he could surrender personally to Bruce and was subsequently released without ransom.

VALENCE, Sir Aymer de

Appointed the King's Lieutenant in Scotland and, in 1314, Earl of Pembroke, he was one of the leading supporters of Edward II against the Earl of Lancaster, mainly because of Piers Gaveston. Originally one of the Ordainers, de Valence had assisted in the capture and arrest of Gaveston but considered his dignity and honour outraged when Lancaster high-handedly seized Gaveston from de Valence's prison and summarily executed him. At Bannockburn, de Valence was one of the voices of reason and, when that failed, helped get the King to safety from the debacle of defeat. Subsequently, he supported Edward II against the rebel barons and, when Lancaster was eventually captured and put on trial following the Battle of Boroughbridge, de Valence had his revenge and assisted in the conviction and execution. In 1324, on an embassy to France, he collapsed and died in Picardy and was returned to be buried in Westminster Abbey. In the eighteenth century, looking for a place to install the hero of the moment, General Wolfe of Quebec fame, the Dean of Westminster wanted the de Valence monument removed; he mistakenly thought Aymer was one of the Knights Templars, whom he considered to be 'a very wicked set of people'. When he found out that Aymer was not one of these he allowed the tomb to remain. The tomb was restored in the early nineteenth century.

VILLERS, Gerald de

Actually named after Gerard de Villiers, a named Templar Knight in the Crusades. One of the last of the dying Order.

VON ESBECK, Widikind

Fictional character, though a real von Esbeck was a Master of the Templars in Germany. With de Bissot, de Villers and de Grafton, Widikind is one of the last Templar Knights in Scotland.

ACKNOWLEDGEMENTS

As ever, the list of people who made this book possible is enough to form both sides at Bannockburn – but special mention must be made to:

Katie Espiner, who edited me to within an inch of my life.

Jim Gill, my agent, who spotted the potential and to whom I raise yet another glass.

My wife, Kate, who handles all the stuff I bodyswerve in order to selfishly write.

And the folk at the Bannockburn Heritage Centre. I am glad they are pulling it down – in order to build a spiffy new one in time for the 700th anniversary in 2014.

Hard on the heels of these has to come Nigel Tranter, whose books on Scotland's history, particularly the trilogy on Bruce, are hard acts to follow. I hope he is not birling in his grave too much.

I am also continually indebted to the members of The HWA (http://www.thehwa.co.uk), Glasgow Vikings (www.glasgowvikings.co.uk) and the rest of the Vikings, national and international (www.vikingsonline.org.uk) who have all contributed to shaping this trilogy one way and another.

The process of writing this has been encouraged by a firm band of fans, who have followed the Oathsworn and now want to carry on reading – so thanks to all the honest reviewers from all over the world with whom I have exchanged views.

Slainte mhath!
Rowallan House, Malvern, 2012